I Take Thee, Serenity

The Kendal Trilogy

Diligence in Love
The Autumn's Brightness
I Take Thee, Serenity

Other Books

Now That April's There
Mount Joy
A Procession of Friends,
Quakers in America

I Take Thee,
Serenity

DAISY NEWMAN

HOUGHTON MIFFLIN COMPANY BOSTON

1975

Library of Congress Cataloging in Publication Data

Newman, Daisy.
    I take thee, Serenity.

    Third volume in The Kendal trilogy, the 1st
of which is Diligence in love; the 2d, Dilly.
    I. Title.
PZ3.N46417Iag   [PS3527.E877]   813'.5'2   75-8984
ISBN 0-395-20551-4

Printed in the United States of America

W 10 9 8 7 6 5 4 3 2 1

for Ellen

Only that day dawns to which we are awake.

HENRY DAVID THOREAU, *Walden*

Part One

*T*hey were already late, but he stopped at the news-stand in the air terminal to buy two Chocomarshes, dropping one into her book bag. That was nice of him, except that all Rennie really wanted to take with her was Peter himself. She kept begging him to come, telling him again how she hated going to a strange place to see a strange, old man.

"Please, Peter, won't you?"

Instead of answering, he gravely unwrapped the second Chocomarsh. Then, grinning wickedly, he stuffed the whole candy bar in Rennie's mouth. That shut her up. She didn't dare laugh; she'd choke.

"Come on." Peter grabbed her hand. "Run!"

Rennie gasped. If she fished the gooey thing out, her fingers would get disgusting, just when she wanted to look cool. It didn't go down till they reached the security place.

"This wasn't my idea," Peter murmured.

Rennie was hunting in her purse for the ticket. "What wasn't? Me going to see Oliver?"

"No. Getting married."

That made Rennie mad. "As a matter of fact," she retorted, "it wasn't my idea, either."

But Peter was cocking his bright yellow head on one side, grinning again, and Rennie saw he was only teasing. She should have known. He kissed her, licking the chocolate off her lips. When he

3

handed over the book bag, the mischief had left his eyes. They were full of anxiety.

"I hope the guy'll be nice to you."

The possibility that Oliver might not be nice alarmed Rennie. Nervously crumpling the ticket, she would have begged Peter again, only it was too late. A loud-speaker urged the passengers for Providence and Boston to board their plane.

In that last minute, Peter's eyes told Rennie how he loved her. He had such a nice face — more finished, she always thought, than most of the men's at college.

She wanted to tell him something, too — something she'd never said. She wanted to —— No, not tell; give — a keepsake, something for him to hold while she was gone. But she had nothing and there wasn't time to explain. She had to go.

"See you Sunday night," he called after her. "Come up to my room, soon as you get back to college."

A couple of women snatched the book bag and Rennie's purse. They went through everything, even peeking into her sneakers. Before they'd admit that she wasn't concealing any weapons, a cop made her walk under a guillotine.

I'm not a hijacker, she wanted to assure him. I'm only going to Rhode Island to ask my first cousin once removed —— Wouldn't her saying that just make the cop suspicious? Besides, Rennie was already out from under, retrieving her belongings, looking back at Peter.

This was it — the moment when she'd have to get on that plane without him.

"It's your wedding, too," she reminded him through the guillotine.

"I know," he called across to her. "Just get the address of the church. I'll be there."

The passengers around them burst out laughing. *Very* funny!

Rennie made a rush for the door, tagging after a stream of people. Outside, the sun was blinding. If it was this hot already, beginning of May, what would summer be like?

4

The last thing Rennie saw before her feet left earth was Peter waving from a window in the terminal. Then a stewardess in a magenta uniform welcomed her on board. Half the seats were already taken by a noisy crowd from Syracuse or some other college. Nobody from Tilbury. The cabin smelled. Canned music made the scene unreal.

Strapped in by the window, Rennie smoothed the pleats she'd worked so hard to press into her skirt. Peter hadn't noticed what she was wearing — at least, he hadn't said anything about it. He never did. So Rennie still wondered whether he liked how she looked on those rare occasions when she dressed up.

Even more, she wondered whether he liked her face. Not many redheads have really blue eyes, clear skin and high coloring. Other people were always commenting on how unusual she was. A guy in her art history class told her once that the short hair, curling in a soft fuzz around her head, was cadmium red with a touch of burnt sienna, like autumn leaves. But Peter didn't talk like that. Was it her looks he went for? Her personality? Or was it simply that she had fallen into his arms?

The plane taxied down the runway, then rose sharply. Rennie's stomach preferred to stay on earth. Thankful that no one was sitting beside her, she leaned back, feeling more and more uncertain. If she upchucked, all those kids from Syracuse would laugh at her.

Directly across the aisle, a big blonde was reading. She didn't seem to be bothered by the motion.

Why me? Rennie wondered miserably, closing her eyes and gulping. Then she thought, Maybe that's why Mother ——

Her mother was so afraid of planes, she wouldn't fly unless it was unavoidable, like when Rennie's grandfather died. Then she clutched Rennie's hand all the way to Florida, keeping the window shade down for fear of getting dizzy. Rennie wasn't supposed to fly. The plane might crash, be hijacked. If her mother knew where she was right now, airborne, feeling queasy, she'd say — or, if she didn't say, she'd think — I told you so. But she didn't know.

Rennie's stomach was calming down. Daring to open her eyes,

she glanced across the aisle again. *War and Peace* — that's what the girl was reading.

I ought to be studying, too.

Though she was way behind in those ed courses, Rennie turned to the window. Tiny houses and highways were faintly visible below. Clouds floated over the wing, looking almost near enough to touch, piled on one another like those dollops of whipped cream Rennie's mother used to shake off the beater before her father went on his diet and they stopped having desserts. Rennie still remembered how the dollops plopped into the bowl and how uptight her mother got that day, years and years ago, when she returned to the kitchen after answering the doorbell. Rennie's hands were in the bowl. Whipped cream covered her wrists and oozed delectably down her short arms.

Was Mother uptight!

These clouds gave Rennie the same baby desire to plunge in. It seemed completely possible because she was free up here, as dazzlingly free as she'd been that day when her mother left the kitchen.

Cushioned on a cloud, Rennie sailed gently into the unknown. On the ground, it had been threatening, but across the sky, the unknown beckoned to her with a promise of something she must have felt homesick for all along, though she hadn't been aware of it — a reality she'd never experienced. Could one be homesick for something one never knew? Was this what birds felt when they migrated, seeking a congenial climate, not sure where they'd land?

No walls. For the first time since Rennie came into this world, she was seeing it without walls. Neither in the foreground nor in the farthest distance did anything block her vision. Her eyes could travel across the horizon, taking in a universe more vast, more splendid than anything she'd ever encountered, even in looking at her favorite pictures, even with Peter.

He was thousands of feet below, now, and miles behind. Was he still standing at the window in his blue work shirt and chinos, his bright yellow head thrown back, watching her soar through the sky?

6

I'm sorry, she told him, hoping he'd somehow hear. I'm sorry I was mad. I know teasing's just your way of saying you love me.

When he cocked his head on one side endearingly like that, the fun and gentleness of his eyes didn't quite match the modeling of the mouth, which seemed to be saying firmly that Peter Holland knew who he was and where he was going.

Rennie still wished that she'd had something to give him, a keepsake to hold while she was gone. What? Sadly she saw that it wasn't a *thing*, just serenity. That's what Peter wanted most from her. But, like her father'd said, she didn't have it. No one in her family did.

I'm sorry, she kept repeating. I should have been glad you were light-hearted, for once — your old, happy-go-lucky self.

Since this marriage business came up, he'd been so serious. Those life insurance premiums —— Before that, for almost three whole months, the two of them lived in a carefree world. It had always made Rennie think of primitive paintings of the Garden of Eden, where food hangs from trees for the picking, one doesn't need clothes and never has to do a lick of work. Rennie hadn't dreamed such a world existed in real life till she happened on it in Peter's room.

Well, it wasn't quite like those primitives. For meals, they had to go to the cafeteria. There they picked food off counters instead of off trees. They had to work — study and attend classes. All the rest of the time, though, they were blissful in their secret world, which was really a drab dormitory room. Their love made it sunny, safe, a place of completeness, where nobody got hurt. The outside world never touched their secret one. They had the best of both.

Suddenly, everything became complicated. The outside world butted in, demanding decisions, commitment, celebration. It threatened to saddle them with household linens, place settings, appliances. In a garden, who needs these?

"Rite of passage," Priscilla called a wedding, now that she was majoring in anthropology. "One of those vestigial tribal customs," she would add, turning up her nose.

Rennie's parents had always maintained that a girl ought not to

7

marry till she finished college. Yet it was her parents' idea that she and Peter get married at the end of her junior year. They sprang it on her in January, when she was home for intersession.

The day before she was going back to college, just casually at breakfast, Rennie'd mentioned that she and Peter were thinking of spending the summer camping in the Rockies.

"Who with?" her mother asked in that placid tone she always used when she meant to assure her children that, while she mightn't understand their intentions, she believed they'd do the proper thing. But her right hand was working nervously. The thumb kept rubbing the tips of the fingers, back and forth, back and forth. "Who with?"

Hadn't Rennie just said? "Peter — Peter Holland. He's very responsible." He'd take good care of her, protect her from those bears.

"Just you and Peter and the bears?" her father expostulated. "That won't do. Unless you're going with a group — no."

"But I thought you liked Peter."

Neither parent responded to this. And Rennie, experienced in avoiding trouble at home, dropped the subject.

Then, after supper that night, in the den, her father switched off the news abruptly and turned to Rennie. He had removed his jacket and loosened the knot of his tie. Otherwise, he was still dressed the way he'd been when he came home from the office. The beam of the reading lamp, hitting his white shirt, highlighted the bulge of his stomach.

"Why don't you marry him?" he asked, almost fiercely.

Rennie jumped. "Peter?" No one had spoken about him since breakfast.

"You love him, don't you?"

"Oh, I do!"

"And you're certain he loves you?"

"Y-yes."

"Mother and I've been thinking about you a great deal lately and we've come to the conclusion that it would be best for you to

8

get married in June. Then you two can go camping or anything else you decide to do together."

"Married?" Rennie repeated, appalled. "Me? Don't you think I'm too young?"

"Much too young! At nineteen, few people know their own minds. But if you're going to run around with this man, it would be preferable. I'm putting you through college," Rennie's father promised, looking, she thought, defeated. "I'll support you, single or married, as long as you're getting your education."

Rennie's parents had been very nice to Peter when she brought him home. Yet, now, even while they were suggesting that she marry him, they disclosed a certain reserve, a coldness, that seemed inconsistent. Could it be that they suspected ——? Was that why they wanted her to get married — before something happened? But, nowadays, who need worry?

There was a worn place on the knee of her jeans and Rennie concentrated on it, scratching the frayed threads until she made a hole. Marriage, she said to herself. Is *that* what we want? What will Peter say when I get back and tell him? Why can't we go on the way we are?

Rennie's father came across the room and stood by her chair, patting her downcast head. Then he tipped her chin up so she had to look straight into his eyes. "You're still our little girl," he said. "Mother and I love you very much. We think marriage will give you the security you need. It troubles us that we don't seem able to give you that security ourselves."

But I have Peter, Rennie thought. Peter's my security.

"We just want you to be happy," Rennie's mother was saying, sounding anything but happy herself.

"I am!"

Didn't Rennie and Peter have the best of both worlds? True, lately she'd felt this strange homesickness. They seemed to be missing something. But she wasn't about to tell her parents that.

She simply said, as her father went back to his chair, "Quit worrying about me. Everything's okay." Getting up, she turned the television on, real loud, spinning the channels till she found some stupid comedy.

"Of course," her father shouted above the din, "it's up to you. Don't think your parents are in any hurry to get rid of you. Far from it."

2.

When Rennie got back to college, she rushed to Peter's room and described the whole scene.

"For a second," she confided, recalling her father's face as he lifted her chin and looked into her eyes, "I thought I was going to break down and tell them everything."

Rennie was glad she'd kept the situation under control. Her parents wouldn't understand. Or did they really suspect? No, she couldn't believe it. They were so naive. They trusted Rennie completely and they were right. She wouldn't do anything she felt was wrong. It was simply that none of her friends, with the exception of one or two squares, believed, as her parents still seemed to, that what she was doing was wrong. How could it be, as long as nobody got hurt?

"Would you want to get married?" she asked Peter. She was really asking herself. "So many couples break up after a while. If we broke up, there'd be no fuss, no lawyers, no hard feelings, just good-by, nice knowing you. But if we got married —— Would you want to?" She could hear her voice waver.

Peter didn't answer and Rennie fought the fear that gripped her throat. Then Peter said something that stunned her. "I guess if I were your father, I'd feel the same way. We couldn't go on like this forever, Rennie. One of us would be bound to get hurt, sooner or later. I just never dreamed your parents would let you marry for ages — marry a guy like me. Trouble is, you haven't developed the nesting impulse yet. Maybe later ——"

Was he accusing her of not being enough woman? He knew very well —— As for timing — maybe he was right. Later, after she graduated, when she'd had an interesting job for a few years, she'd like to marry then — settle down, cook, have kids — the bit. Now ——

"Would you want to?" she repeated.

"I don't know. But let's quit what we're doing."

"*Why?*" After playing it so cool with her parents, Rennie surprised herself by starting to cry. She couldn't stop. She wished she hadn't told Peter what her parents said. How could she guess he'd be on their side?

He wiped the tears away, spreading them over her cheeks with the palm of his hand. Then he ran his fingers through her curls. "We're lucky, Rennie," he said softly. "Your father's being very decent. He might have made a stink."

"Of course he's being decent! Daddy's sweet. He does try to run things, but he can't help that. He's an executive."

Peter was suddenly quiet.

"What's the matter?"

"I need time. Think things over."

"Daddy'll support me as long as I'm getting my education," Rennie assured him, "even if I'm married."

"If you're married to me, *I'll* support you. But money isn't all we have to worry about, Rennie. Marriage — it's a big step."

How big, she only just realized, seeing the look on Peter's face.

He clammed up again, frowning the way he did on study dates, when he was trying to do a math problem. "Give me a week," he said finally. "I'll tell you definitely next Thursday."

"Thursday!" How could she wait till Thursday?

He had to be by himself, he explained, go off on long walks. Rennie couldn't figure out why he didn't want her to come along. But she stayed away.

Now she was thrown back on the company of the girls in her

dorm. They were a friendly crowd, especially on Rennie's floor. Until she started going steady, she had loved the socializing. Then, suddenly, she lost interest in everyone but Peter. If a girl came to her room, she hinted that she had a lot of work.

But now, banished from the men's dorm, terribly lonely, Rennie started looking for her friends again. All of them, she discovered — even those who were wrapped up in their courses or politics or the woman's movement — were thinking about marriage. As far as Rennie knew, neither Priscilla nor Audrey nor Harriet had a man — not a steady one, anyhow. But they were already dreaming about their weddings. Rennie, who just possibly might be getting married very soon, hadn't considered hers. Listening to those girls — two of them were seniors — she thought, They sound like children.

Wasn't a wedding simply a formality, required by law and parents? The only reason Rennie saw for having one was if the couple wanted a family. And that was certainly the last thing she and Peter wanted right now. So why get married? Judging by statistics, those vows were whistles in the dark. *For better, for worse, in sickness and health* — what people meant when they said *"I do"* was *"maybe."*

Still, Rennie could see that her parents were right. She did need the security of belonging to Peter and he wasn't willing to straddle both worlds any longer. She felt the muscles of her stomach tighten and twist as she thought, Suppose he decides we've had it? He wouldn't do that to me, would he?

.The week was endless. Those term papers on Child Development and Classroom Management were due. Rennie couldn't concentrate, what with the best of both worlds about to collapse. All her fault — she never should have told Peter what her parents said.

If she pretty nearly died without him in just one week, how was she going to get through the rest of her life? It wasn't only that she missed him. Her being depended on his loving her. If he stopped, her life would stop, even if she went on breathing.

Wednesday afternoon, when Rennie came back to the dorm from her French class, she found a florist's box lying on the mail desk. *Serenity Millburn Ross,* the label read. How strange! Nobody ever used Rennie's real name, except the bursar or the dean's office, and even they didn't know her middle one. She'd never told anybody but Peter. Why would *he* be so official? With frozen fingers, she picked at the knot on the box. Red roses! The whole time they were going together, Peter had never sent Rennie flowers. Now —— This was his way of saying all was over. He couldn't bear to come and tell her.

He didn't even wait till Thursday, she wailed to herself, opening the little envelope. Inside was a card.

I'm willing, if you are,

PETER

He was going to marry her! He really was.

Rennie's eyes filled up. It wasn't a romantic proposal, but she knew how much the words conveyed. She'd phone right home and tell her parents, the minute she got to her room. They'd be so glad! "We just want you to be happy," her mother had said that night, back in Neville.

Luckily, it was Wednesday. Rennie's father always left the office early on Wednesdays. Spring and fall, he played golf. This time of year, he'd be home, sitting in the den, reading the paper. Rennie's mother would be fixing supper. When her father picked up the phone and heard Rennie's voice, he'd call to her mother and she'd listen in on the kitchen extension.

Rushing upstairs, happily swinging the long, narrow box, Rennie already imagined her parents' joy when they heard what she was about to tell them. It was all their idea, her getting married. She must remember to thank them.

So brilliant of you! she would say. Thanks for thinking of it.

In the housekeeping closet on her floor, Rennie found a vase. She went to the bathroom and filled it with water. Then she carried the vase carefully down the corridor to her room.

They were the most beautiful roses she'd ever seen — dewy red, like the ones in that painting, *Moss Roses*. By Monet? Renoir? Would it be Cézanne?

No, not Monet, not Cézanne. I don't think so. That luminous scarlet lake, flowing into vermilion — wasn't Renoir the one who used this color so much? Must be Renoir.

But Rennie wasn't quite sure.

As she pushed each stem down into the vase, she noticed how much more lively the flower became the instant it was out of the box and light glowed through the unfolding petals.

In her excitement, she pricked her finger. Sucking on it, she told herself she must call home right away. But when she had stuck the last rose in water, she couldn't wait to see Peter. She flew to his room.

He looked years older. Only a week — how could he have changed so in a week?

"Reason I want to marry you," he whispered, holding her close, "is: I want to spend my whole life telling you how I love you — not just how much, but *how*. I know it'll be hard making you believe I mean it for keeps. That's because I started in wrong. But I mean it." He moved back a step so he could take Rennie's face between his palms and look into her eyes. "I wish we could be married some morning at dawn in blue jeans on a hilltop, just you and me, no minister." He squeezed the breath out of Rennie. Then he let her go.

Just the two of them, no minister. Was that possible? What about their parents?

She remembered something. "Quakers don't have ministers, at least I don't think so."

"Oh?"

"My Great-grandmother Serenity, the one I'm named for, was a Quaker. But her daughter married my grandfather, who wasn't anything, so the family stopped being interested in stuff like that and I don't know much about it, only that we have this old-fashioned picture on the third floor landing at home. It's called *A Quaker Marriage*. The girl is wearing the most beautiful, plain dress and one of those bonnets. The man has on knee breeches and a courtly sort of coat. They're standing, holding hands, looking serious and yet happy. There isn't any minister in the picture, just people sitting around the couple on benches. I always loved that picture. When I was small," Rennie confided, hoping Peter wouldn't laugh at her, "I used to stop and talk to the girl every time I went to the third floor." She'd never told this to anyone.

Peter didn't laugh at Rennie's childhood fantasy, but he failed to see that the picture still meant something to her. "Probably an illustration for one of those nineteenth century romances," he murmured.

"Oh, no," Rennie cried, hurt. She'd always believed in the reality of that picture. To have Peter reduce it to just a story —— "It can't be," she said firmly. "I'll ask Daddy."

She hadn't called her parents yet. How could she have waited all this time to tell them the wonderful news? That pay phone in the basement of the men's dorm —— She fished in the pockets of her jeans, hoping to find a couple of nickels or a dime for calling collect. There was nothing in them but lint.

"Peter, have you got —— Oh!" His alarm clock had caught Rennie's eye. "The cafeteria! It'll close in five minutes. If we don't rush, we'll miss supper."

He paid no attention to her warning. Then, Rennie saw that he was throwing clothes into a suitcase.

"What are you doing?" she cried, panicking. Was he leaving her already, just when ——?

"Going home. Phoning's no way to break news like this to one's family. Besides, my father has a heart condition. I mustn't surprise him, though I know he and Mom'll be pleased. They like you."

He was skipping supper. There was a night bus he could catch if he left right now. That way, he'd miss only one day of school.

Rennie didn't go to the cafeteria, either. Alone —— All of a sudden, she wasn't hungry. She wanted to be in her room with the roses, the proof of Peter's love.

Ought she to go home, too? Peter'd said that phoning was no way to break news like this to one's parents. But hers were expecting it — hoping. Her father had nothing the matter with him, apart from his weight. It would take forever to get to Neville. She had to tell her parents right away. This was going to make them so happy!

She put in the call, chewing her nail, counting the long rings. One, two, three, four ——

"Daddy, guess what! Are you on the phone, Mother? I've got the most wonderful news. I want to tell you both together. We're getting married, Peter and I!"

Instead of the joyful exclamations Rennie expected, there was a freezing pause. Her father, who was always the leader, said nothing. Her mother managed, after a bit, to murmur, "That's nice."

"*Nice*? It's terrific."

Had they changed their minds?

"It's what you wanted me to do, isn't it? I mean, it was your idea."

"Yes," Rennie's father answered, finally taking matters into his hands. "Mother and I did think it would be best for you to get married. We're just — well, you're our baby, you know, and awfully young. It's hard, having you leave us already. We hope the advice we gave you will turn out to be right."

"Oh, it is! How could it be anything but? Don't worry — we aren't going to break up after a while."

There was another pause.

"Peter's gone home to tell his folks. You haven't changed your minds, have you?"

"No," Rennie's father declared without conviction. Then he repeated, sounding less sure of himself than she'd ever known him to be, "It would be best for you to get married."

Hadn't they meant it the other day? Were they simply playing with the idea of her marrying because they suspected that she and Peter —— *Did they suspect?* Had they hoped, by bringing up the subject, that she'd see how they felt about what she was doing and quit? Probably they never believed Peter would marry her. Now that the fact was staring them in the face, they were drawing back.

I should have gone home, Rennie reproached herself. Peter's right. Phoning's no way ——

But her father was fast rising to the occasion. "Well," he said, sounding as if he were determined to put a good face on the matter, "we'll make it a bang-up wedding. Our only daughter ——"

Rennie heaved a sigh of relief — or was it sadness, the one feeling she'd never expected to have at this moment?

"Yes," her mother broke in, perking up, too. "We'll make it the most beautiful wedding that ever was, a wedding to remember."

3.

After that conversation with her parents, Rennie felt depressed. She'd done just what they'd wanted her to do and they weren't even pleased.

All through her childhood, they'd been so proud of her. She'd been the most satisfactory little girl any parents ever had. It was when she suddenly refused to put on those smocked dresses her mother was always making — other girls were wearing jeans — that this tug of wills developed. Now, Rennie either pleased her parents or herself. Impossible to do both.

They're so unreasonable! Do they want me to stay a child all my life?

Yet, how surprised Rennie's parents would be if they knew how she really felt. Even at nineteen, when she was leading a completely adult life, part of her still longed to be that good little girl in the smocked dresses.

She was glad when Priscilla and Audrey dropped in to rap. Making them promise to keep it a secret, she confided that she was getting married in June.

These same girls, who, a few days ago, had been dreaming about their weddings, jumped on Rennie. "Are you crazy?" Priscilla cried. "Getting married before you've had a chance to live!"

"And your career," Audrey added. "Do you just want to be an

unpaid houseworker all your life? Unless you get launched in something first, unless you can earn as much as your husband, you'll just be his property, a sex object."

Rennie sighed. "Trouble with us," she observed, "is: we haven't developed the nesting impulse yet."

Priscilla hooted. "The nesting impulse! That's for the birds."

Rennie knew how desperately the other girls wanted to get married. Yet, it seemed, the more they hankered for it, the more marriage scared them.

As a matter of fact, I'm scared, too, Rennie admitted to herself. Then, seeing the glowing roses, she thought, That's how I am with Peter's love shining through me. Before, I was simply shut up in a box. "But I love him," she said aloud.

"That's okay. Move in with him. Get an apartment off campus. Just don't do anything drastic," Priscilla implored. "If you knew how my father pushes my mother around —— It's degrading. Keep your independence. As long as nobody gets hurt ——"

With her parents urging her to marry, when they didn't really want her to, and her friends urging her not to marry, when they really wanted to, Rennie was totally confused. I love him, she repeated to herself. Isn't that what counts?

When Peter returned, everything would be all right.

But the moment Rennie spied him on the breakfast line in the cafeteria, sleepy from spending two nights on buses, she knew everything was all wrong. To his surprise, his parents had put up tremendous resistance. It wasn't, he explained to Rennie, that they had anything against her, just that they couldn't see how he was going to support the two of them so soon. And didn't he want to go to grad school?

"We should have thought about all this before the whole thing started," he told Rennie sadly.

The following week, Peter flunked his math exam.

Rennie couldn't keep her mind on her work. Sitting in her room, trying to absorb *Teaching Creative Writing in the Primary Grades*, she stared mournfully at the roses. Most of the petals had fallen.

Those that still clung were droopy, dark and brittle. But Rennie couldn't bring herself to throw the roses out.

In the end, Peter's parents backed down. It would have been better, Mr. Holland wrote, if Peter were established. Nevertheless, his parents didn't wish to stand in their son's way. Peter and Rennie's love for each other should be the determining factor. "Love beareth all things," he concluded.

Peter explained to Rennie that those words were from the Bible. That was in February.

The middle of March, Peter went home with Rennie and spoke to her father, who suddenly began calling him "Pete." This annoyed Rennie. She'd always felt that "Pete" was explosive. "Peter" had a caressing sound. Her voice loved to linger over it. She supposed the nickname was her father's way of saying that Peter was going to be let into the family, although her parents still seemed cold toward him. They weren't about to treat him like another son. They weren't giving him a hard time, either.

Two weeks later, they put on a tea to announce the engagement. A photographer came tooting out to the house and the next day, Rennie's picture was in the paper, looking, she couldn't help feeling, surprised by the whole thing. Her mother bought a ritzy new dress and was annoyed because Rennie wouldn't take time out from college to get one, too. That long, African print skirt and scoop necked white blouse seemed plenty good enough to Rennie, but her mother said she was so disappointed, the day was ruined. Rennie's brothers came with all their wives and kids. Each boy took her aside during the afternoon to tell her in a low voice that he thought Peter was a very nice guy.

Peter himself, all gussied up in his suit, with his hair cut, surrounded by a flock of new relations and everyone in Neville who was anyone, looked just plain mad.

"What does all this have to do with us?" he asked Rennie. "So we're in love. Why does that mean people have to pile into your house and yak, yak, yak?"

His parents weren't there. His mother sent Rennie's a note, ex-

plaining that because of the distance and Mr. Holland's health ——
Rennie wondered whether they didn't want to come. It wasn't
that far.

By Easter, which was late, Rennie's mother was snipping pictures
of wedding gowns out of magazines. After being the mother of
three bridegrooms, she declared, she was coming into her own at
last.

The Rosses didn't belong to a church, but they knew some of the
ministers in town socially. Which one did Rennie prefer? Reverend
Roberts? He was okay, she conceded, only she wouldn't be caught
dead getting married in his church — that pseudo-Gothic monstros-
ity. What about Dr. Johnson? *That creep?* Well, then, Pastor
Noyes?

Rennie suddenly remembered what Peter had said about being
married on a hilltop in blue jeans, without a minister. What did he
mean, anyhow?

"Pastor Noyes?" her mother repeated.

"Why can't we have a Quaker marriage? Then we wouldn't
need any minister. Would we?"

"*No minister?* There has to be a minister to pronounce the couple
man and wife. How else would the marriage be legal?" Rennie's
mother exclaimed, smiling indulgently, as if Rennie were still a
romantic little girl.

Was that true? Did there *have* to be?

Now that Rennie's mother had settled this matter, she switched
to other details — the gown, the veil, the bridesmaids.

It was all a familiar routine to Rennie. She'd been in each of her
brothers' weddings. Her closet was crowded with those bridesmaid
dresses she'd never wear again. Each time, the ceremony had
moved her deeply. Being in church was a rare experience that she
found awesome and strange and beautiful. Yet, each wedding had
made her feel the way she did about medieval art, when she took
that survey course, sophomore year — it was very beautiful, but it
had no connection with her life.

"Look at this, Rennie," her mother exclaimed, leafing through a bridal magazine. "An empire gown of white organza, worn over taffeta, with an attached train." This was the umpteenth model she'd suggested in a desperate attempt to rouse enthusiasm in Rennie. "How does that sound, dear?"

"What's organza? That slinky stuff?"

Rennie never found out, because just then her father came home from the office and inquired, but only rhetorically, whether it wouldn't be nice to invite some of his business associates and their wives to the wedding. The more he thought about the idea, the longer the list became.

"Peter and I don't even know them," Rennie muttered.

"You'll meet everyone at the reception. This will be an occasion for entertaining a lot of people we should have had to the house long ago. When Joe Pitkin's daughter got married, the whole plastics industry was there. It was like a convention. I bet some good deals were made over that champagne."

"But, Daddy, a wedding isn't a county fair or something like that."

Rennie's mother backed her up. "I think that's disgusting. A wedding should just be a sweet, pretty, joyful occasion. Ours was, Ed."

"Yes, I guess it was — can't remember too much. But your father had four daughters to marry off on a newspaperman's salary, during the Depression. I have only the one girl. I can afford to give her the best — always have given it to her, haven't I? Not that I'd agree to anything on the scale of the Pitkin wedding. Just happened to think of it. But I don't see what was so wrong about Joe's having his friends there. Don't forget, he's the one who had to pay for that shindig. So if it brought in a little something ——"

Rennie blew up. "A wedding isn't a shindig. It's something just between two people, and all those strangers with their minds on business have no right being there."

"Don't misunderstand, Rennie. I'm not talking about the ceremony. They were all solemn enough in the church. It was at the reception that the men quite naturally drifted together and

21

started talking shop. After all, who else was there to talk to? They didn't know the family. Anyhow, what does the Pitkin wedding have to do with yours?"

"Nothing."

"Mother and I will work on this list," Rennie's father said, dismissing the matter. "But until we find out the size of the church, we can't tell how many invitations to order and it takes weeks to get them engraved. I wish you'd make up your mind where you want to be married. How about Trinity? It's very spacious. I don't know the rector, but maybe if I spoke to him, he'd tailor the service to suit us."

"Why can't we have a Quaker marriage? You know — like the picture on the third floor landing. It *is* a real wedding, isn't it, Daddy?"

Her father looked at Rennie intently, as if he were trying to discover what lay behind the odd notion. "That old lithograph? I guess it does show the way Friends got married, a century or two ago."

So it *was* real, not just an illustration for a story! Peter was wrong.

"I found that picture among my mother's things," Rennie's father recalled. "Don't know where she got it, but it must have meant something to her or she wouldn't have saved it. There was no place to put it in this house and yet, I couldn't bear to throw it away. I was taking it up to the attic when I got the idea of hanging it on the third floor landing."

"Why can't I have a Quaker marriage?" Rennie repeated. "It would be appropriate, with my name."

"Isn't that a little farfetched?" her father exclaimed, obviously on the verge of losing his patience. "Your name is the only Quaker thing about you. Anyhow, there's no Friends meetinghouse in Neville. When I was a boy, my grandmother used to take me to one — funny little old place. I certainly wouldn't want your wedding to be held somewhere dinky like that."

"Besides," Rennie's mother objected, "none of our friends would know how to behave. I wouldn't myself. Would you, Ed? You scarcely remember anything about your Quaker ancestors."

"That's ridiculous, Joan. How can you say such a thing? I remember my grandmother very well. It's just that I lost touch with the rest of the family. I hope I'd know how to behave wherever I was. But I don't have the slightest idea what a Quaker type wedding's like." He shrugged.

Rennie pressed him. "Isn't there anyone you could ask?" She wanted to say, I'm not trying to bug you, Daddy. This is important to Peter. But she would have had to explain why and she didn't know. "Isn't there anyone?" she repeated.

"Not here. I suppose there are Friends somewhere in New York — all sorts of people there. I never heard of any in Neville."

"Have you, Mother?" Rennie asked, turning to her.

"There were no Quakers on my side of the family. Just Daddy's."

"Friends," Rennie's father corrected in a tone that indicated he had been obliged to bring this error to his wife's attention before. "I believe they prefer to be called Friends."

"Well, then, Friends," Rennie's mother repeated obediently, giving him an impatient glance. "I never knew any. But I always loved your grandmother's name — so unusual." She turned to Rennie. "Before each of the boys was born, I planned —— And finally," she exulted, reaching out and giving Rennie a hug, "you came."

Something about the curve of her mother's arm, the almost wistful way she reached out, made Rennie feel a kind of pity, as if, in a curious reversal, her mother were a little child and she, Rennie, the parent. She would have hugged back, only her father was saying things she didn't want to miss. Later ——

"Those old Friends went in for virtues when they named their daughters. One of my great-aunts was called Patience. The other one was Temperance. I wouldn't have named you after Temperance, Rennie," he declared, laughing.

"Serenity's beautiful," Rennie's mother exclaimed, withdrawing her arm. Even when she started leafing through the bridal magazine again, she still had that wistful look.

"I remember my grandmother very well," Rennie's father repeated, but whereas his voice had expressed annoyance before,

23

now it was nostalgic. He went to the coat closet to put his jacket away. Lost in recollection, he stood there, holding the wire hanger, forgetting what he'd started to do. "That woman," he murmured, shaking his head in wonder. "*She* really *had* serenity."

4.

Slowly returning to the present, Rennie's father finished hanging up his jacket. Then, with a contented grunt, he stretched out in his reclining chair and started to read the newspaper.

Rennie kept at him. "Where did she live, Daddy?"

He was scanning the headlines. "Who?"

"Your grandmother."

Turning to the stock market quotations, he murmured absently, "On the old family farm, down in Rhode Island."

"Firbank?"

The name seemed to trigger something. Rennie's father dropped the paper on the floor and looked at her. "Yes, Firbank."

"Where is it, anyhow? The way you talked when I was little, I used to think it was some pretend place — magical."

"It's eastward from Little Narragansett Bay, deep in the country. Nearest town's Kendal and that's minute."

"Did you know that your voice always gets moony when you speak about Firbank?"

Rennie's father laughed. "No. Does it?" He folded his hands over his stomach. "I guess the place is a bit magical for me, even now. We used to spend summers there when I was a little boy. Coming from New York —— Visiting Grandmother Serenity Otis was the event I waited for all year."

"Was she so nice?"

"I loved her! When I was naughty, she just took me on her lap and told me about the farm animals and the creatures living on the edge of Salt Pond, below the house. That was more effective than my parents' punishments."

"Isn't Salt Pond where you sailed the catboat? I remember your telling me ——"

"Yes. Grandmother let me hold the tiller. 'Thee steer, Edmund,' she said one day, when we were sailing across to the dunes. I was five. Nothing that's happened since ever made me feel so important. Grandmother died a couple of winters later and we never went back to Firbank."

"Why not? It sounds so neat."

"Mother didn't get along with her aunts. She'd taken up smoking and those old Quaker spinsters frowned on it. Turns out now, they were right. But at the time, no one knew that cigarettes were injurious. My parents had become real New Yorkers, caught up in a social whirl. The farm was pretty tame for them — only excitement a clambake or watching the steamer put in at Kendal. Father wasn't a Friend, anyhow, and all that thee-and-thy, going to meeting, never being offered a cocktail — well, we just didn't fit there."

Rennie's mother was of the opinion that things must be more modern now. "Remember, Ed, what you're talking about was over fifty years ago."

"I doubt if anything's changed. The kind of people they were, those old Friends, nothing would budge them. Time of Pearl Harbor, when I enlisted, Father's folks wrote to congratulate me. Even sent presents. But Mother's — I never heard a word from them. By that time, we'd pretty much lost contact with Firbank, anyhow. Friends have this thing about going to war. I don't know what else they thought a young man should have done when his country was being attacked. They're a pretty unrealistic lot."

Although Rennie knew she wasn't getting anywhere, she wouldn't give up. "Daddy, isn't there anyone in Firbank you could ask about a Quaker marriage?"

Her father shook his head. "The only one left is my cousin Oliver Otis — if he's still alive. Haven't heard from him in years. I guess I'd have been notified if anything happened. Oliver had a beautiful wife — forgotten her name — but he himself was always odd. Refused to fight in the First World War. He did go to France, though, as I recall — stretcher-bearer or some such assignment. He wasn't a coward. I never understood Oliver."

"What's so wrong with being a conscientious objector?" Rennie asked. "Some of the nicest guys at college ——"

"Oh, I know that these days a lot of young men — even Larry — but he was the only one of my three sons who wasn't willing to serve his country. Must have been the Quaker strain coming out in him, after all these years. He claimed he was eager to serve humanity, not to shoot it. What that boy didn't grasp was, if some of us weren't brave enough to defend humanity, there'd be none left to serve. Larry was so set against cooperating with the military that he didn't even want to register. We had quite a battle before I finally persuaded him to. You were so young then, Rennie, we kept it from you. But you might as well know now that if it hadn't been for me your brother would have gone to jail, instead of marrying Victoria and getting promoted to sales manager."

This wasn't the news to Rennie her father thought it was. Little happened in the family that escaped her. Actually, Larry had told her himself, at the time. Right now, he wasn't the person she wanted to hear about.

"Daddy, what's Oliver like? Couldn't you ask him about a Quaker marriage — write or even phone?"

"*Ask Oliver?*" Rennie's father shook his head emphatically. "We're out of touch. I can't even tell you much about him, except that he went to Harvard. His father was a professor there. After the war — I mean Nineteen Eighteen — Oliver married this English girl he'd met in France, a Friend who'd volunteered for nursing in a children's hospital. Wish I could remember her name — some nymph's. A very beautiful girl. I remember that." He paused, obviously enjoying the recollection.

Rennie, seeing her father look happier than he had in a long time, didn't have the heart to press him. She waited.

"A very beautiful girl," he repeated, smiling to himself. "The name suited her. Oliver brought her back to Firbank. At the time, people seemed to think he showed a little flair for writing, but that petered out. He never had a real occupation, as far as I know, only farming. Not," Rennie's father admonished her, "that farming's anything to look down on. Our ancestors did it. But Oliver and I wouldn't have had much in common, if we'd met, which we never did, except at family funerals. I always went to them. Last one was Aunt Temperance's. Must be going on twenty years ago, wouldn't you say, Joan?"

Rennie's mother nodded absently. Her mind was on other things.

"That's right! It comes back to me now," Rennie's father exclaimed. "Around Thanksgiving time, the year Rennie was born. I remember how cold and rainy it was — a real northeaster. It was late when I got to Firbank and I left as soon as the service was over. There was a man from our West Coast office in New York I simply had to see and it was a long drive — no superhighway in those days. Too bad. I would have liked to poke around the old place."

"We have to be careful about the flowers, Rennie," her mother announced, as soon as she could break in. "Choose colors that won't clash with your hair. Though, if you decide on a mantilla veil, your hair won't show."

"The house looked a bit shabby," Rennie's father remembered, disregarding the interruption, "much as I could make out, with all those people crowded into the living room. I hardly got a chance to speak to Oliver and his wife, just the usual 'how's the family?'. So you see, Rennie, I don't know what Oliver's like now. An old man, that's for sure, up in the seventies. He's fifteen years older than I am."

This seemed sufficient reason for not asking his cousin how to go about getting Rennie married the way she wanted to be. It was obviously an alternative her father had no desire to pursue. All he said was, still recalling his grandmother, "I wish some of that serenity had come down to us. Not one of us has it."

"Rennie," her mother put in, looking worried. "You simply must settle on your silver pattern. Here it is, almost May, not even two

27

months till the wedding. People will be asking me what you want."

"I don't want any silver. You're always complaining about having to polish it."

"Honey, if you just put it in an aluminum pan with a spoonful of baking soda — be sure it's aluminum ——" By the tone of her voice, Rennie's mother betrayed how hard she had to strain to control herself.

"I don't *want* any!"

It's true, Rennie thought, but why must I be so bitchy?

Rennie's father was still thinking of Firbank. "Now that you mention a Quaker marriage," he told her, "I remember, while I was down there that day, I saw the wedding certificate belonging to my grandparents, Edmund and Serenity Otis. He's the one I was named for, but I never knew him. Died before I was born. I always thought that was why Grandmother made so much of me — because I was his namesake. Now, I can see it was wishful thinking. I wanted her to like me best. The fact is, she was just as sweet with all the other children — my sisters and cousins, especially Oliver. Her last few years, she relied more and more on him. He was a grown man then, you see, and I was just a kid."

"You were talking about the wedding certificate," Rennie reminded him impatiently.

"Yes. It had more signatures than the Declaration of Independence — many more. Luckily, it was hanging on the wall near where I was sitting during Aunt Temperance's funeral, because there was nothing else to occupy my mind. People just sat there in silence. One or two stood up and spoke briefly about her, stressing her good points. Some woman read a psalm. Someone else said a prayer — he wasn't a minister; they didn't have any. No music, either. I never was one for sitting around and meditating. I can still remember how I used to fidget when Grandmother took me to Friends meeting in Kendal. I liked going with her, but not sitting still. So during the service for Aunt Temperance, I studied that certificate to keep from going stir crazy. It described the procedure of the wedding."

28

"What was it, Daddy — the procedure?"

"Can't remember, just that the wedding took place in Eighteen Seventy-four."

"That's a strange thing to do," Rennie's mother remarked, "hang a marriage certificate on the wall. Of course, it's an antique ———" She was still worrying. "Rennie, Daddy and I are fitting you out with household linens. But the heat's coming terribly early this year and you know how I hate shopping in hot weather. If you leave everything till the last minute ———"

What with all these arguments, day after day, and Rennie's trying to please her mother by deciding immediately which of her five nieces she was choosing for the flower girl, she hadn't done any work. She hadn't even opened her bulging, green book bag once, all vacation. That was serious. She had a fine arts quiz on Monday.

Sunday afternoon, an hour before she left home, Rennie got out her notes. Curled up in the den, she started to glance through them. This was her favorite course, the only one she really cared about, not for marks, but because she loved to lose herself in studying the pictures. Those Impressionists had a way of looking at the world that touched something Rennie felt deeply — a drive to reach the truth about what they saw, even though this didn't correspond to the outward image.

Studying the works of those artists — Monet, Sisley, Pissarro, Renoir — Rennie lost herself in pure delight. It wasn't the moment for her mother to come barging in.

"We haven't settled anything, Rennie. How can I plan? Here you are, going back to college, and you haven't told Daddy and me what arrangements to make. You ought to take a little responsibility."

Rennie had to clutch the book against her breast to keep from firing it across the room.

"It's *your* wedding," her mother reminded her.

"Then why can't I have it the way I want it? Why does everything always have to be what you and Daddy decide? Isn't there anything I can have my way? This time last year, he was making a big thing about my major. I hate those ed courses. I don't want to be a teacher. Art history is all I care about, but Daddy put his foot down. Now I'm getting married and I can't even have the wedding the way I want it."

This was too much for Rennie's mother. She looked both furious and hurt. "That's what Daddy and I have been trying to find out your whole vacation — how you want it — and you won't tell us."

Rennie was furious, too, but she couldn't answer back. What was this elusive thing she and Peter thought they wanted? She really didn't know.

She slammed the notebook closed and went up to her room. It was a total mess — clothes lying all over the floor. She couldn't stretch out on the bed because it was covered with records and stuff. She thought of straightening up, only now there wasn't time, what with her packing and leaving for college.

Priscilla was picking Rennie up in her car. She'd promised to arrive by four, though in this rain and with the Sunday traffic, she'd probably be delayed. Priscilla was always late, anyway.

Rennie collected her books. When she came downstairs, her parents started in again about the wedding. Time was growing short, they reminded her, and there were so many arrangements ——

It was a relief when Priscilla honked. Rennie kissed her parents quickly and rushed out, promising to talk to Peter and let them know definitely in a week.

"Maybe two," she called back, as she ran down the walk in the rain.

At last, she had broken away, leaving the hassle behind! But even as she got in the car, already looking forward to diving with Peter into that pool of completeness where all want is drowned, she was swept by desire for something else — she didn't know what.

Priscilla looked glad to see Rennie. "How was intersession?" she asked, switching on the ignition.

Rennie didn't answer. She was winding down the window, leaning out, letting the rain splash against her face, waving to her parents.

30

They were standing in the doorway, completely under cover, yet huddled together, as if they were out in the storm, clinging to each other for shelter.

"How was intersession?" Priscilla asked again. "Did you have fun?"

But Rennie was still watching her parents, ignoring the rain that trickled down her face, watching until they were out of sight. The way they clung to each other — less, she couldn't help thinking, out of affection than out of the need for shelter ——

5.

When Rennie got back to college, Peter wasn't there. It was late by the time he returned. His father didn't feel well and his mother needed the screens put up.

Rennie had a lot to tell Peter about her parents. "They just couldn't hear me," she cried. "They never even listened. I tried to get through to them that what you want is a Quaker marriage."

"I do? Who says? Don't even know what it's like."

"But, Peter, you told me you wished we could get married in blue jeans without a minister, just you and me. Don't you remember?"

"What's that got to do with a Quaker wedding? I bet even they don't wear blue jeans when they get married. Wouldn't want to, myself. That was just — I don't know — an idea. I'd have to have a lot more information about that ceremony besides the no-minister part before I'd agree to something that far-out. From what you say, your folks aren't for it and I don't see mine liking it, either."

"All I was trying to do was find out."

It was in that second that the idea came to Rennie. One moment, nothing was farther from her thought. The next minute, she had a plan.

"Peter! What if you and I went to see Oliver ourselves this weekend? Friday afternoon, we could borrow someone's car and drive down there; ask him what the wedding's like and will he help us get it — that's if we care for it."

"Who's Oliver?"

"This old cousin of Daddy's."

"Where does he live?"

"Firbank, Rhode Island. It's near Kendal, wherever that is. Do you think, if we called him up — asked Information whether he's listed ——? For all I know, he may be dead."

"Rhode Island!" Peter exclaimed. "That's a long trip. The way you talked, I thought he must live somewhere around here. I can't go to Rhode Island. Costs too much. Besides, I have studying to do, and if we're getting married in June, Rennie, I have to find a summer job."

"If we're getting married in June, Peter Holland, we have to find a church. All vacation, Daddy kept lecturing me about how we're not the only couple wants to be married then; how some churches were already dated up for June weddings last Christmas. I promised Mother and Daddy ——"

"Okay. You'd better fly. Otherwise you won't have enough time there. I'll borrow Jack's car and take you to the airport."

"You mean you won't come with me?" How could he let her go by herself? "Mother'll be scared. My plane might crash or get hijacked. That's what she'll be thinking the entire weekend."

But Peter didn't appear to be apprehensive about Rennie's flying. "I hope you can spend the night at Oliver's house," was all he said. "Where else could you stay?"

Rennie shrugged. She didn't know a soul in Rhode Island. She was thinking, If I wait now, if I wait just five minutes, I'll never do it.

"Be right back," she called over her shoulder, running out of Peter's room. She rushed down to the pay phone in the basement and dialed Information, only to find out whether the name was listed, whether Oliver was still living. "Otis," she repeated, shouting above the racket of her heart, "Oliver Otis, Firbank, Rhode Island. There *is*?"

She gave the operator the number of her father's credit card.

As if in echo, the name was spoken back to her — not "hello," quavered by an ancient voice, as she'd hoped, but "Oliver Otis," deep and crisp.

Taken by surprise, all Rennie could think to say was, You're alive! Instead, she murmured, "Mr. Otis?"

"Speaking."

"This is Serenity Ross. You don't know me. I'm your cousin Edmund's ——"

"Serenity!" he exclaimed with such resounding delight that the receiver vibrated. "Serenity Ross — of course, I know. I heard there was a child named for my grandmother."

"Right! The reason I'm calling — I wondered — would it be okay if I came over to see you Friday afternoon?"

"It would be first-rate. *First-rate!* Daphne and I'll be delighted."

He sounds as if he means it, she thought. Should I mention Peter? Just in case —— It would be embarrassing, turning up with him, when I hadn't said a word.

But suppose, after Rennie mentioned Peter, he wouldn't come? That would be embarrassing, too.

"You're sure it's convenient? Could I spend the night? Do you have room?"

"Oceans of room in this old house. Bring a friend."

"I'd love to. Maybe I will."

"Where is thee now?"

"What — what did you say?" Rennie couldn't have heard right.

"Where is thee calling from?"

"Oh! The men's dorm — no, I mean, I'm at Tilbury College. I don't suppose you've ever heard of it?"

"No."

"It's a hundred and seventy-five miles north of New York."

"Thee's coming a long way."

"Yes. I have a ride to Albany County Airport, only I don't know where to fly to."

"Hillsgrove. That's our nearest airport. But, Serenity, thee could come by bus. It would be cheaper, though a little roundabout."

"No," Rennie said. Peter had told her to fly. "I'll take a plane."

33

"Very well. But when thee comes down at Hillsgrove, thee'll still have to get a bus, the Bonanza. Stops right out in front of the terminal. Ask the driver to let thee off in Kendal. I'll meet thee there. Unfortunately, there's just one Bonanza in the afternoon. Leaves Hillsgrove at seven. Does thee think thee could make it?"

"Easily. I get out of class at noon on Fridays."

"That ought to give thee plenty of time. Serenity?"

"Yes?"

"Does thee have enough money?"

"Loads. Thanks a lot just the same, Mr. Otis."

"Oliver, to thee." Then, as Rennie started to say good-by, he repeated with an enthusiasm that made the receiver vibrate again, "Daphne and I'll be delighted!"

Rennie hurried back to Peter's room.

"Bonanza, organza," she sang, running to him and waltzing him around. "Bonanza, organza, we're going to Firbank on the Bonanza bus and I'll be married in organza, us, just us, the two of us, tra, la, la! You're invited, too."

Peter disregarded that.

"He called me 'thee,'" Rennie exulted. "Isn't that cool? And his wife's name is Daphne. Daddy was trying to remember. I'd phone and tell him, only he'd want to know how I found out. Everything would get complicated and Mother'd worry all weekend. I'll explain when I get back."

Peter got very businesslike. "Go over to the Administration Building. They have timetables in that alcove next to the registrar's office. Phone the airline. Be sure to get a reservation for Sunday. I won't try to meet you. There'll be a lot of people getting off planes and coming back to college. You can easily catch a ride. Have you got enough money?"

"That's just what Oliver asked, only he said, 'Does thee have?'"

While Rennie found this charming, it just amused Peter. "Guy sounds kooky to me."

"You don't understand," Rennie said, hurt. "It's Quaker language. Daddy's always telling me how his grandmother used to ——"

"His grandmother!" Peter snorted. "We're in the space age now." Then his expression softened. "Listen, you've got to grow up sometime," he said lovingly, running his fingers along Rennie's arm. "This quaint stuff ——" He stopped, turning thoughtful. "All the same, going there may be a good thing. Could give you a clue to your identity."

"What do you mean — my identity?"

"I think *I* know who you are. But I don't think *you* do."

Part Two

*S*o here was Rennie, all by herself for the first time in months, up in the air, sipping coffee, whizzing toward the unknown — Hillsgrove, Bonanza, Kendal, Firbank, Oliver, Daphne. When she got there, she'd be terrified. At the moment, cushioned on a cloud, securely fastened, she was weightless of worry.

The serenity she'd longed to leave with Peter seemed almost within her grasp. What made it so nearly attainable here? Did she have to go up in a plane to get it? Wasn't that a bit ridiculous? All along, she'd wanted Peter to come with her only because she was scared. Now she wished he were here so he could feel this quiet in her and share it.

It's the first really peaceful time I've had in months, she thought, closing her eyes. Why can't it always be like this?

Almost at once, the peace was shattered as a stewardess announced in a bellow that the plane was about to descend. On behalf of the captain, the rest of the crew and herself, she thanked Rennie for flying with them.

They were beneath the clouds, now, sailing slowly over woods and cultivated fields. The sun sparkled on a wide bay with countless coves. Miniature houses, woods, a white church whose steeple was like an inverted ice-cream cone — from up here, these reminded Rennie of that tiny toy village she'd found in the toe of her stocking one Christmas, years and years ago. It came in a golden net, like a spider's web, with a thread of a drawstring Rennie kept on her finger, carrying the toy village with her everywhere, cherishing each piece.

Then she began to leave the tiny houses and trees lying around. They got lost. She'd outgrown the village. Where was it now?

Even at that age, how could I have been careless of something I'd once loved so?

Unfastening the seat belt, Rennie picked up her book bag. It was heavy. Not that her clothes weighed much — only the tan shorts, the aqua turtleneck, sneakers. It was all those books that dragged her down and she hadn't even looked at one of them.

The blonde was brushing her long hair. Rennie fished out her pocket comb and ran it through her curls.

Oh, I forgot my toothbrush. Oh, well ——

The plane landed with a bump. Back on earth, Rennie was beset by worries again, afraid of the strangeness ahead. Would she find Kendal? What if Oliver wasn't there? What if he wasn't nice to her? Over the phone, he'd sounded neat, but —— Peter never should have let her go alone.

No, down here, Rennie couldn't grasp that serenity she'd glimpsed aloft any more than she could plunge into the clouds the way she'd plunged into her mother's whipped cream. It was just a childish illusion.

Surging forward, the noisy crowd filled the aisle. The blonde got up. So did Rennie, standing behind her, pressed against her dress like an upright sardine. That orange dress did nothing for the blonde, especially as the zipper was open halfway down her back, exposing a freckled skin with a big mole.

Gross, Rennie thought, turning away. I don't like her, anyhow. She studies and doesn't mind the motion. That zipper's none of my business. If she wants to run around looking like a slob —— Why didn't she dress herself decently?

But Rennie's hand had compassion. It reached out and slid the zipper up.

The blonde turned her head, flashing a warm smile at Rennie. "Thanks!" She wasn't so bad — quite nice, really. "Thanks," she repeated. "I'd hate to arrive looking a mess. My boy friend's meeting me. He goes to Brown."

I wish mine were meeting me, Rennie thought. It's going to be a long wait. What'll I do till that Bonanza leaves? I *could* study.

The airport was unimpressive. Walking behind the blonde toward the low terminal building, Rennie was suddenly overcome by her folly.

What am I doing here? How did I get into this? There must be some better way of finding out about a wedding than flying off into the wilds. It's the dumbest thing I've ever done.

She was always complaining about being pushed around by others. This was all her own doing. And yet, she'd been pushed into this, too — not by someone else, but by something inside herself that seemed to be running her life, as if she weren't much more than a spectator.

Following the crowd, Rennie found herself in a glassed-in, circular passage. It opened onto a lobby, where people stood waiting for their friends. A boy in a T-shirt reached out and grabbed the blonde.

I'm going right back to Tilbury, Rennie decided, watching them. Skip Firbank. It was a dumb idea. I'll go straight to the ticket counter, change my reservation to the next flight back, phone Oliver and tell him I'm sorry.

She bumped against a tall man wearing a floppy, white sun hat, the kind yachtsmen and tennis players wear. As she passed him, he stepped out of the crowd of waiting people and caught up with her, smiling eagerly.

"Serenity Ross?"

She stood still, startled, while the people behind her rushed by, jostling her with their bags. Pushing the sun hat back on his head in a gesture of embarrassment, the man drew away.

It couldn't be Oliver. He was meeting Rennie in Kendal and from what her father'd said, he was a feeble old man. This one was taller than her father, in much better shape, almost skinny.

"Oh, are you —? You're not Mr. Otis?"

He lifted the sun hat a moment, showing a bald scalp with a wisp of faded orange fuzz, and broke into a delighted smile. "So thee *is* Serenity! I knew thee must be. I'm Oliver." Taking the book bag from her, he reached out at the same time with friendly, searching eyes. His weathered face crinkled with pleasure as he sized Rennie up.

She was studying him, too, noticing that the collar of his white shirt was turned out over the tweed jacket; that his faded gray slacks and high leather boots belonged to the country.

"Welcome!" he exclaimed, taking Rennie's arm and guiding her into the terminal. "It was so fortunate — Mary Young came in to visit with Daphne, so I checked and found this was the only afternoon plane from Albany. Thought I'd run down and get thee — save thy taking the Bonanza. We'll go and claim thy baggage."

"This is all I have," Rennie said, pointing to the book bag. "Just for the weekend ——"

He looked surprised. "We thought thee was coming to spend the summer. Thee didn't say. So we just supposed thy father was sending thee to Firbank to become acquainted with the home of thy forebears."

"Daddy doesn't know I'm here," Rennie admitted, feeling a little uncomfortable. Maybe she should have called home and said where she was going. But then she'd have had to explain. Her mother would have been upset on account of Rennie's flying. Everything would have become complicated. "I'll tell him all about it after I get back."

For the first time, Oliver looked grave. "Serenity," he asked, peering at her intently, "thee's — thee's not running away?"

Rennie laughed. "Oh, no!" Running away! Running away from Peter?

"Not that we wouldn't be glad to have thee stay with us, anyhow," Oliver assured her, still grave. "But we wouldn't like to think of anyone's running away from home."

"I've got a reservation on the three o'clock plane Sunday afternoon," Rennie explained. "Classes aren't over till the end of May. I still have exams."

This seemed to set Oliver's mind at rest. He beamed on Rennie again.

They stepped out into the sunshine. It was a lot cooler here. The air was fresh and tangy. Across the street, in the small parking lot, Oliver stopped on the passenger side of an old pickup truck. Letting go of Rennie's arm, he opened the door of the cab. "Can thee hop up?"

When she was settled with the book bag on her lap, he walked around and hoisted himself into the driver's seat, slowly but with the ease of habit. About to put the key into the ignition, he turned toward Rennie, as if this were his first chance to get a really good look at her.

"How did you recognize me?" she asked, feeling shy, hoping he'd think she was okay. "There was a gang of kids getting off that plane."

"Thy hair," he answered, smiling. "It's the Otis hair. Mine was just like thine, when I was young."

It was hard to imagine. He really was old, only his face was so lively that one forgot his age. Peter needn't have worried about his being nice to her. Something already made Rennie glad she'd come. It was the way he looked at her — as though she mattered. She was used to people noticing her unusual coloring. But this man seemed to be looking past her face, searching beyond it.

His hand rested on the brake, ready to take off. Yet, for another few seconds, he went on looking at her. "So thee's coming home to Firbank," he said at last. "Wonderful! It's a good fifty years since we had a Serenity there."

2.

Oliver drove the truck out of the parking lot and onto a highway. His large, worker's hands, speckled with old-age spots, rested lightly, almost negligently on the steering wheel. But, pushing the floppy, white hat back on his head, he kept his eyes intently on the road.

Rennie, noticing his rather handsome profile, looked for a resemblance to her father. They were both clean-shaven and virtually bald. That was all they had in common. Not only were the features quite different; there was a striking disparity in their expressions and their whole bearing. Rennie thought she did see something familiar, though. Jonathan. From the side, Oliver looked a bit like Jonathan, her best-looking brother. No, on second thought, he didn't really. Jonathan was never this happy. Oliver must have a very carefree life.

The road was bordered by woodland with scarcely a house in sight, as if they were driving through a forest rather than on a highway. Although every car on the road overtook the pickup truck, Oliver never accelerated. He seemed to enjoy moseying along.

But Rennie felt urgency. With only two days for making all those arrangements —— It would be awful to go back Sunday with nothing settled. Should she explain now why she had come? It seemed a little pushy, plunging in right away.

"Everybody calls me Rennie," she said, temporizing. Oliver couldn't go on saying "Serenity" forever.

Without turning his head, he nodded, signifying that he had heard. But he never used her nickname.

"Reason I came," she finally told him, after such a long pause that she was beginning to feel uncomfortable, "is, there's this boy, Peter Holland, in my class at college. We're getting married the end of June and I thought we might have a Quaker marriage, only we don't know what it's like." Put this way, their intention – if it was an intention – sounded so childish that Rennie fished around desperately for something that would convey how mature she and Peter really were.

"Married?" Oliver exclaimed, before Rennie could think of anything sensible to say. "How old is thee?" He wasn't hiding his surprise.

"Nineteen."

"And Peter?"

"He'll be twenty this summer. He's very nice," Rennie assured Oliver. "You'd like him. I wanted him to come, but ——"

"Do thy parents approve?"

"It was their idea. Now they're trying to decide on a church for the wedding — we don't belong to any — and I wondered if ——" Rennie glanced sideways to see whether Oliver understood.

He seemed to be thinking. Then he asked, "Have you been in touch with Friends in your area — thee and Peter?"

"Daddy says there aren't any."

Oliver laughed. "There are Friends practically everywhere."

"You're the only one Daddy knows. That's why I came."

"I see," Oliver murmured, sounding a bit disappointed.

Rennie realized that she hadn't been tactful, telling him she'd come simply to get information about her wedding, not to visit, which was what he and Daphne had assumed. But it was true. Why else would she have come all this way?

Oliver quickly regained his good humor. "Thee'll meet a whole batch of Quakes here," he assured Rennie, grinning.

"Did you — did you say 'Quakes'?"

Oliver burst out laughing. "Yes. We joke a good deal among ourselves. Religion ought to be a purely joyous experience, but it's also terribly serious and if one doesn't look out one ends up taking one*self* too seriously. A dash of humor puts things in perspective. So we tend to poke fun at ourselves — not, thee understands, at others."

"Neat!" Rennie exclaimed. "Daddy's always correcting Mother because she says 'Quakers' and he thinks they want to be called 'Friends.' Wait till he hears that you said 'Quakes'!"

"Friends or Quakers — it's all the same. There was a time when people called us Quakers as an insult, so we disliked the term, but that's long past. A name makes no difference, anyhow; just what one is."

"Do Friends all speak the way you do?"

"Use plain language? No. It has practically died out. Old-fashioned Friends, like Daphne and me, still use it in the family or the Meeting."

"I like it," Rennie exclaimed. She was considered "in the family"! Just the same, she felt funny, riding with a man who had such far-out ideas.

"We don't foist our language on outsiders," Oliver said, "the way our forebears did. They were protesting the custom of making social distinctions. People used to address their betters as 'you' — it made the betters feel grander — and their equals or inferiors in the singular. So Friends dramatized their belief that all people are equal — not only men, but women, too; not only the old, but the young; not only free men, but serfs — by speaking the same way to everyone, saying 'thee' and 'thou,' even when they spoke to kings. Equality was a very revolutionary idea three centuries ago."

"But now," Rennie argued, "everyone says 'you' to everyone."

"Current speech is democratic," Oliver conceded, "but it isn't truth, addressing a single person in the plural."

Rennie'd never thought of this before. She could see why her father had called Oliver odd. But he was nice, too. She liked his absolute honesty, even if he was pernickety. It made her feel that she could trust him.

And he held the key to the Ross happiness. If he wanted to, he could fix everything up this weekend. She'd go back to college, tell Peter how the wedding was going to be arranged and call her parents. They'd order those invitations. Her mother could relax. Her father — what would her father say when she told him that she really was going to have a Quaker marriage?

But Oliver might not care to fix things. At the airport, he'd been so interested in Rennie. Now he rambled on as though she hadn't mentioned her problem. She felt annoyed. How far could she press him?

There was a long silence. Then, as they reached the crest of a hill, Oliver drove off the highway and turned into a little country road.

"We're almost home," he cried happily. "Daphne will be so pleased to see thee!" For an instant, he turned and glanced at Rennie gravely. "Did thy father tell thee about her?"

"Yes."

"Wonder how he heard. It's years since we've had any contact. But news travels."

Oliver stopped the truck before a long, white farmhouse with huge maples at each corner and wisteria hanging in fringes from the roof of a stately, semicircular porch. A lawn separated the house from the driveway. Behind the house, partly hidden by it, stood a white silo and a red barn.

Firbank!

Rennie jumped out of the cab before Oliver took his hand off the brake. A fresh smell of pine greeted her.

In her excitement, she didn't see a flat stone that protruded about a foot above the edge of the driveway and she stumbled, scraping her shin. The edges of the stone were worn smooth, so she didn't hurt herself. Anyhow, she was too excited to pay attention to anything but the house.

Firbank, her father's dream place! She saw at once that it really had the quality he always conveyed when he spoke of it. The house needed paint, but, touched by the setting sun, it had a misty, pink radiance, its outline blurring into the atmosphere, so that it was one with the earth, the trees and the sky that framed it.

That's what I've been missing all along, Rennie said to herself with surprise — beauty! That's the emptiness I feel sometimes, even though Peter and I have the best of both worlds.

A retriever and a little fox terrier came bounding down the porch steps and over the lawn to jump on their master in an uproar of adoration. "This is Lion," Oliver told Rennie, as if he were introducing an exuberant child, "and this little scamp's our Duffy."

Only interested in the house, Rennie saw that an old woman was standing at the door, smiling in welcome. She was terribly homely.

Rennie couldn't conceal her disappointment. "Is *that* Daphne?"

"No. Daphne can't come to the door. It's Mary Young." Fending off the dogs, Oliver looked at Rennie. His expression was troubled. "Thee said thy father told thee about Daphne?"

"Yes. He couldn't remember her name, but he kept talking about how beautiful she is."

"Thy father seems to forget that when he knew Daphne we were all a great many years younger. She's still beautiful in spirit and that shines in her face. Only, her appearance has changed," Oliver said slowly, looking at Rennie with such pain in his eyes that she felt forced to glance away. "I didn't think thy father could have heard about her stroke. It paralyzed her. Not quite three years ago. She's better now, getting around some, but her speech is affected. Don't think, though, that, because she can't talk, she doesn't understand what one says, or that her mind is failing. If anything, her perception is keener than before."

The dogs, rushing back toward the house, almost knocked Rennie over.

Oliver took her arm and started up the porch steps, swinging the green book bag by its webbed drawstring. "I used to have one like this at Harvard," he said, sounding cheery again.

He only spent a moment introducing Rennie to Mary Young, so eager was he to find Daphne. In the high-ceilinged entrance hall, he dropped his hat and the book bag on a chair that stood in the curve of a staircase.

"Just try to speak naturally," he urged Rennie, still holding her arm. "Before long, thee'll guess what Daphne wishes to say." He drew her into the loveliest room she'd ever seen.

It was lined with bookshelves, painted a soft gray green. Above the shelves hung a whole gallery of pictures. At the far end of the long room, in a bay window through which the last rays of the sunset streamed, Daphne sat in an armchair with the dogs at her feet. She was wearing a coral cardigan and a russet skirt. Her hair, coiled on top of her head, was touched with the rose of the sun. As Oliver crossed the room with Rennie, Daphne leaned forward. In that instant, her hair, no longer in the path of the sun's rays, turned pure white.

Devastating disappointment overtook Rennie: the face her father had remembered all these years for its extraordinary beauty was actually lopsided. Then she noticed Daphne's right arm, bent at the

48

elbow, motionless. Thin fingers, dangling limply from the wrist, covered one breast.

Disappointment, embarrassment in the presence of deformity, pity — or was it the thought that this might happen to anyone? — some disturbing uneasiness made Rennie start to draw back. But Oliver still had hold of her.

"This is Serenity," he told Daphne in the same affectionate tone with which he had just introduced the dogs. "Everyone calls her 'Rennie.' Suits her all right, doesn't it? Just the same, I like 'Serenity' better. She isn't staying as long as we thought, only till Sunday. Getting married next month. Can thee believe it?" He shook his head incredulously.

Daphne, smiling with one side of her face, reached out.

When the cold hand touched her own hot one, Rennie felt that disturbing uneasiness grip her again.

Then, without quite letting go of Rennie, Oliver bent and kissed Daphne.

A strange sensation, almost like an electric current, passed through Rennie. Linked to them both, she seemed to be joined in the circle of their love. And a comfortable sigh escaped her, as though she'd been holding her breath all her life and suddenly found she could release it.

3.

Daphne and Oliver let go of Rennie in the same moment.

"Yes," he said, answering Daphne's unspoken directive, "I'll take Serenity up to Heather's room. When she comes down again, supper will be ready. Mary said she brought a casserole. How nice of her!" Seeing Daphne's questioning look, he added, "She's gone home."

He turned to light the standing lamp beside Daphne's chair and another one near the couch. Rennie observed the almost ceremonial, joyous gesture with which he performed this ordinary act. He wasn't just pressing switches; he was bringing light out of darkness.

The room to which he took her then, leading the way up the curving staircase and through a long upstairs hall, was in an ell at the back of the house. It was a girl's room. A pale blue spread, sprinkled with irises and daffodils, covered the high brass bedstead. When Oliver turned on the bedside and desk lamps with that same joyous gesture, a silver-backed hand mirror on the dressing table and the andirons in the fireplace gleamed.

"This is the oldest part of the house," he explained, dropping the book bag onto a rocking chair. "Seventeen ninety-two. There was a little Friends school over in Kendal and my Great-great-grandfather Daniel Otis came here from Newport to be the schoolmaster. Let's see — what is he to thee?" Oliver interposed, grinning. "Thy great-great-*great*-grandfather! He built the original house — a story and a half, three rooms down, two up, with a central chimney. It was another hundred years before what we call the main wing was added. That's more pretentious, because with all their thrift and industry the family couldn't help becoming prosperous."

"I've never slept in any place this old," Rennie murmured, noticing how the wide floor boards sloped dizzily downhill from the fireplace to the dormer windows. A breeze was swelling the tieback curtains into balloons.

Oliver closed the windows and pulled down the shades, cautioning Rennie against bumping her head on the sloping ceiling. "We put thee in here because this was our daughter's room," he said. "Also, we thought thee'd like the back of the house best on account of the view. Wait till thee gets up tomorrow morning! These windows face the pond."

"Oh, Salt Pond! That's one of the things Daddy likes to talk about."

"Ed still recalls it, does he?" This seemed to give Oliver pleasure. "He enjoyed coming here when he was a small boy. I remember, the summer I came home from France, what a bouncy child he was, out there, fishing off the dock or collecting beach plums for Grandmother. It was a pity," Oliver murmured, shaking his head, "that he never came back, except to pop in when someone died and rush right off again."

"That's because of his business," Rennie explained, feeling she had to come to her father's defense, although Oliver didn't sound critical, just sad. "Daddy works awfully hard." Then, to her surprise, she blurted out, "Oliver, please help Peter and me." She hadn't meant to say anything like that; she'd lost her cool. Wasn't it information she'd come here for? Why was she suddenly asking for help?

Oliver took a step toward Rennie and placed a hand on her shoulder. "We'll do anything we can," he assured her and she could tell he meant it. "After supper, we'll sit by the fire and talk. Now, get ready and come down. Bathroom's next door. The towels on the rack are thine." He started to leave. "There's no one else in the house, just we three," he called back as he went down the hall, "so wander wherever thee wishes."

Left alone, upset because she'd blurted out more than she'd meant to say, Rennie had no desire to explore. She took her sneakers, the turtleneck and shorts out of the book bag. Unless she was going to study, that was all she had to unpack. Should she change or wait till morning to put on her other clothes?

There were pastel drawings in gilt frames on the walls, not the work of an amateur, Rennie figured, as she walked around the room, trying to decide what to wear. The drawings turned out to be a series of portraits, recording the childhood of the same little girl. In each picture, light and shadow surrounded the figure in such a way as to give it contour, texture and a mysterious personality. *Heather at six months* was written in pencil under one of the pictures and at the bottom of another *Heather's first birthday,* showing her with cheeks puffed, about to blow out a faintly sketched candle. There was *Heather at Cannes,* playing in the sand, and *Heather at Firbank, 1935,* a little girl of three or four.

Wow! Rennie thought, she's terribly old now.

Judging by the stuff on the bookshelves, Heather had been less a reader than a collector. There were dozens of tiny, carved wooden animals and some terra cotta figurines of a woman playing with a child or fondling it in her arms. As Rennie looked more closely at the delicate pieces of sculpture, she discovered that, in every one, the mother wore her hair piled on top of her head, like Daphne's.

That was what had made Rennie lose her cool — Daphne. It was Daphne who upset her — the lopsided face. Beauty was what Rennie'd been looking forward to finding here — how eagerly, she only now realized, experiencing this enormous disappointment. She'd come expecting to enter her father's dream place, to appropriate some of that magic herself. Instead ——

Even the shame Rennie felt at being turned off by someone's trouble couldn't overcome her reluctance to go downstairs. She'd have to talk to Daphne — "Just try to speak naturally," Oliver had said. She'd have to guess what Daphne meant to convey. Still, Rennie couldn't stay up here all evening. She was starving.

Deciding that she wouldn't change her clothes, she found her way back through the long hall and down the curved staircase into the living room. There was no one around. But Oliver's voice was audible, coming from a distant part of the house. Following the sound, Rennie passed through a brightly lit dining room with a table intended for a large family — not set for anyone just now — and a highboy reaching almost to the ceiling. In the big, warm kitchen beyond the dining room, Oliver, in his shirt sleeves, was standing at the stove stirring something. Daphne sat at a round table, doing nothing, with Lion and Duffy beside her.

"Come in, come in," Oliver called. "That's thy place, Serenity, on Daphne's left. Sit down. I'll dish up in a minute."

Rennie did as she was told, concentrating on the straw place mats, the beautifully polished wood of the table, a blue-and-white pitcher filled with flowers, the loaf on the bread board, the nicks in the old pewter teapot — anything to avoid looking at Daphne. Even when Oliver brought the casserole to the table and sat down, Rennie just stared at the indigo design rimming her white plate, which he began heaping with food. The fragrant steam touched Rennie's forehead. Without raising her eyes, she picked up her fork.

Oliver reached out and gently restrained the hand that held the fork. At the same time, he took hold of Daphne's paralyzed fingers and Daphne covered Rennie's other hand with her icy one.

Glancing up in astonishment, Rennie saw that they were both bowing their heads. Oliver's eyes were closed. He must be about to say grace. That made Rennie gulp. She wasn't used to this sort of thing. She waited anxiously.

But Oliver said nothing. There was, however, no mistaking his reverent expression. Rennie, sitting there in the eerie silence, not knowing what she was supposed to do, waited for words that didn't come. Then, her hands still held in theirs, she was once more overwhelmed by that feeling she'd had when she arrived, of being joined to Daphne and Oliver.

A second later, her hands were released.

Awkwardly, with visible determination, Daphne took up her fork. Oliver sliced the loaf and began eating, talking between mouthfuls about Mary Young's delicious casserole, the number of eggs the hens had laid, the lady's-slippers he'd found in the moist woods north of the house, the bluebirds nesting in the box outside the kitchen window, his delight in having immediately recognized Rennie at the airport.

"She looks exactly the way I imagined she would!" he told Daphne.

Listening to Oliver give an account of his day as if it had been a festival, observing the affection his eyes telegraphed to Daphne when he carefully set the teacup down within reach of her able hand, feeling the pleasure he communicated because Rennie had come, she felt reassured. This was a kind, caring man. He wouldn't let her go back to college without some solution to her problem. Coming here had been the right thing.

As she ate her first meal at Firbank, Rennie realized with surprise that she was happier than she could remember having been in a long, long time.

That's what we've been missing, Peter and I, she thought — joy.

4.

After the kitchen was tidied, Oliver left Daphne sitting at the table and ushered Rennie into the living room. She felt awful now. Unfamiliar with dishpans, she'd been clumsy and stupid about helping Oliver. Her experience was limited to sticking things in a machine. Rennie couldn't remember a time when her mother hadn't had the dishwasher.

Oliver took a small chair from under one of the bay windows and set it at right angles to the fireplace, explaining, as he stood watching the flames, that an old-time Kendal craftsman had made the diminutive captain's chair for Heather when she was a little girl. Her "inglenook," she used to call this corner. Small though it was, Rennie'd find the chair strong and comfortable. Would she sit here and enjoy the fire while he got Daphne ready for bed? She was feeling tired. Before long, Oliver promised as he left the room, he'd be down again.

So Rennie was going to have a chance to speak to Oliver without Daphne's disturbing presence. Greatly relieved, she tried out Heather's chair. From that low angle, everything in the room had an altered appearance. The chair fitted her body, but it made her feel different — younger than she was, still the kid she'd been before she started going with Peter, when her only worry was finding a store that stocked the right records.

Judging by the sound of things, getting Daphne upstairs was a major operation. Oliver could be heard, encouraging her step by step. "Try again, dear one. We're almost at the top. There! Thee made it!"

Looking around, Rennie remembered how her father had called the house shabby. It was. These armchairs needed reupholstering and the rug was worn in spots. It is shabby, Rennie admitted to herself. Still, this is exactly the kind of room I want when we're married — smaller of course, but with a fireplace, full of books and pictures. Peter would love it.

She'd never visualized their home before. Next year, they'd have one of those married students' apartments, but they'd mostly be eating in the cafeteria, just as they were doing now. It wouldn't be so different from living in the dorms, except that Rennie would be entitled to share Peter's room instead of staying in it more or less illegally. Beyond next year, where would they be? Peter was worrying so much about this summer, he couldn't plan. Summer jobs, he'd been told, were scarce.

For Peter to be worrying was unusual. That was one of the things that had first attracted Rennie to him — his easygoing, lighthearted approach. He still joked, the way he did when he took her to the plane, still teased her till she felt like socking him, but underneath all this was a new kind of seriousness that Rennie didn't know how to take and it frightened her. Was getting married going to change Peter?

It suddenly struck her that life had played a trick on them. The whole question arose in the first place because she and Peter talked about going camping. They probably never would have done it, anyhow. But that was what started her parents planning the wedding — so she and Peter would go off together respectably. Now, just *because* they were getting married, they couldn't even go. Peter had to work. This wasn't going to be a fun summer. Nothing seemed to add up.

Getting Daphne ready for bed was taking an awfully long time. Rennie could faintly hear footsteps through the ceiling. Their room must be directly overhead.

Unable to sit still any longer, she got up and walked around, looking at the pictures that crowded the wall space over the bookshelves. Light from the standing lamps didn't reveal details, but Rennie noticed oil paintings of flowers — bunches arranged in a blue-and-white pitcher, very much like the one on the table at supper. There were botanical plates, too, and a whole series of tiny water color drawings of children dressed in what Rennie presumed were Quaker clothes of long ago — probably illustrations for a picture book.

After these attractive little figures, it was a shock to come to a series of charcoal sketches that were so ugly Rennie tried not to look at them. They were the faces of brutalized people, with crazed eyes and gaping mouths, out of which one could almost hear screams coming.

Like Goya's *Disasters of the War*, Rennie thought, too disturbed by the horror of these sketches to look at them long. She felt relieved when she noticed something less disagreeable on the adjacent wall — a framed document written in an antique hand on a long, narrow scroll. Every *f* turned out to be an *s*.

Whereas, the document read, *Edmund Otis, son of Wilbur Otis and Elizabeth, his wife, all of Firbank, Washington County, State of Rhode Island* — Edmund Otis, the man Rennie's father was named for! — *and Serenity Millburn* — Serenity Millburn! — *daughter of Josiah Millburn and Sarah, his wife, of Kendal, having declared their intentions of taking each other in marriage, to Kendal Monthly Meeting of the Society of Friends, held at Kendal, Rhode Island, according to the good order used among them* ——

This was Rennie's great-grandparents' wedding certificate, which her father studied during that funeral!

Now, these are to certify to all whom it may concern, that, for the full accomplishing of their said intentions, this Ninth Day of the Fifth Month, in the year of our Lord Eighteen Hundred and Seventy Four, they appeared at a religious meeting of the aforesaid Society in Kendal; and he, the said Edmund Otis, taking the said Serenity Millburn by the hand, did openly declare: in the presence of the Lord, and before this assembly, I take thee, Serenity Millburn, to be my wife, promising, with Divine assistance, to be unto thee a loving and faithful husband, until death shall separate us.

A Quaker marriage! Rennie exulted. Here were the words that went with the picture on the landing at home! True, the wedding in the picture must have taken place years earlier than Edmund and Serenity's, judging by the clothes — the girl's bonnet, the boy's

56

knee breeches and courtly coat. But the action was the same. The boy in the picture was taking the girl by the hand, just the way this certificate said.

Then, in the same assembly, Rennie read on, *Serenity Millburn did in like manner declare: in the presence of the Lord and before this assembly, I take thee, Edmund Otis, to be my husband, promising, with Divine assistance, to be unto thee a loving and faithful wife, until death shall separate us.*

And in further confirmation thereof, they, the said Edmund Otis and Serenity Millburn, (she, according to the custom of marriage, adopting the surname of her husband) did then and there to these presents set their hands.

> Edmund Otis
> Serenity Millburn Otis

Intent on studying the signatures — Edmund's scrawl, Serenity's fine, carefully shaded penmanship, Rennie didn't notice Oliver return until he came up behind her and touched her shoulder.

"Did you know," she asked, turning to him in excitement, "that my middle name is Millburn?"

"Yes."

He was evidently pleased by Rennie's interest in the scroll. "It used to be the custom for Friends to frame their marriage certificates and hang them in the best parlor — perhaps," he remarked with a chuckle, "to remind themselves when they were angry at each other of their promise to be loving! It must have worked, for Quaker couples generally stuck together. Also," Oliver added, speaking seriously again, "it gave them pleasure over the years to see the names of their old friends on the certificate. All the guests signed it."

Oliver pointed to the text under the couple's signatures: *And we, having been present at the marriage, have, as witnesses thereunto, set our hands.* Then he ran his finger down columns of names that reached to the bottom of the scroll. "To this day," he said, "at a Quaker marriage, all the guests — even the children — constitute the legal witnesses and sign the certificate."

"Even children?"

"Why not? If they are present, they are part of the meeting for worship in which the bride and groom make their promises to each other. It wouldn't be unacceptable for a child to break the silence, as adults do when they feel moved to speak at a wedding. I've never known that to happen, but it would be in right ordering."

Rennie found this all very puzzling. When she was in her brothers' bridal parties, following the ushers through the church, counting between steps as she'd been told to do, trembling from head to foot, she had felt important and, she realized now, more grown-up than she actually was at the time. But it never occurred to her that she was involved in the marriage transaction.

"Thee sees," Oliver was saying, still pointing to the columns of names, "here Grandmother Serenity's two little sisters, my Great-aunts Patience and Temperance, affixed their signatures. Everyone present had the same importance, regardless of sex, age or position. A hundred years ago, that was considered outrageously radical."

"Is getting married in a Friends meetinghouse the same today?"

"The procedure is unchanged."

"Tell me more," Rennie pleaded. "What else happens at the wedding?"

"Come and sit down," Oliver urged, waiting for Rennie to return to the little captain's chair before dropping onto the couch. He looked bushed. "I suppose thee knows that, in a sense, a Quaker marriage begins long before the wedding day?"

Rennie tried not to show her surprise. Was he referring to pre-marital relations, like —— Bundling, maybe? Was *that* possible? Everything about these Friends was so peculiar. "Before the wedding day?" she repeated.

"Months before, the couple writes a joint letter to the Meeting, expressing the wish to be married under its care. In the words of the modern certificate, the prospective bride and groom 'declare their intentions of marriage with each other.' This is the first and perhaps the most significant step."

"Oh!" So he didn't mean —— Writing a letter — that was all he was talking about!

"At that moment," Oliver said gravely, "the commitment begins."

"The legal stuff?"

Oliver looked at Rennie curiously. "No," he answered, without elaborating. After that, he was silent, simply staring into the fire.

Had she asked the wrong thing? Rennie felt uncomfortable, not knowing what to say next. "It's true, isn't it," she finally ventured, "that Friends don't have a minister?"

"Kendal Friends don't," Oliver replied, still looking into the fire. "Some do, though few in this part of the country. Silent Friends, as we call ourselves — and we do an awful lot of talking — feel that every man is in direct contact with God. So we don't need anyone to do our praying for us. In our Meeting, no third person pronounces the couple man and wife. We believe only God can create such a union."

Now Rennie was way beyond her depth. All along, she'd known that God came into this somewhere, but she'd never figured out what it meant to her. For that matter, she had no idea what Peter believed. They'd never discussed it. Anyhow, she'd established the fact that they didn't need a minister. So no one would ask them any awkward questions.

Oliver turned to her with a kind, though sad, expression. "What reason do thee and Peter have for wanting a Friends wedding?"

Rennie told him how Peter had spoken off the top of his head about being married without a minister and how the idea had taken hold of her — she couldn't say why. "It's not really a reason," she admitted honestly. "We don't know that much about the way the thing is done. It's more a feeling. Partly my name, I guess."

She looked at Oliver anxiously, aware that one's name and some indefinable emotion weren't reasons.

His reaction took her by surprise. "A feeling may be a better reason than a well thought-out argument. It may be what Friends call a 'leading.' But," he added gravely, "thee should realize, Serenity, that it takes several months to arrange a wedding after the manner of Friends, even in the case of members, whom we know and have worshiped with over a period of time. Thee spoke of June."

Just when she thought she had won him over, he was blasting all her hopes.

"Can't it be done faster? I mean, don't Friends make an exception in some cases?"

Rennie's cheeks suddenly felt hot. What she had said, without considering the implications, sounded as if she were asking Oliver to use his influence. Or he might think she was pregnant. It had been unnecessary to beg like that. What difference did it make, putting off the wedding for a few weeks? She and Peter couldn't go anywhere, anyhow.

Oliver didn't seem ruffled. "Marriage is a lifelong commitment," he observed. "How can it be entered into hastily? It isn't only the couple's decision, but the continuing concern of the community in which they are married, of which they are part. To feel at home in such a community takes time — to get to know and trust the people in it. Without this fellowship, the solemnization of the marriage would seem a mere formality."

"Do you mean one has to belong to the church?"

"Nominal membership is immaterial. What counts with us is the experience of seeking together. Anyone is free to join the search. Centuries ago, a Friend Daphne and I greatly admire put this concept beautifully: *There is a principle which is pure, placed in the human mind, which in different places and ages hath had different names.*" Oliver's audible delight in the words he was quoting gave resonance to his voice. "*It is deep and inward, confined to no forms of religion, nor excluded from any, where the heart stands in perfect sincerity. In whomsoever this takes root and grows, of what nation soever, they become brethren.*"

Where the heart stands in perfect sincerity, Rennie repeated to herself. In whomsoever —— She wanted to remember those words.

But Oliver was asking, "Where were you thinking of holding the wedding?"

"That's what I want to know from you. Is there a Friends meetinghouse near Neville? If I had an idea where to find it, maybe I could persuade Daddy ——"

"No!" Oliver exclaimed with more vehemence than Rennie had heard him express yet. "Thee and Peter must make the application yourselves. Your parents' approval is important, but if you are married in meeting, thy father will not give thee away. Thee gives thyself to Peter and he gives himself to thee. You will enter the meetinghouse hand in hand. Your parents will already be sitting there, in the gathered silence, asking God's blessing on your union. The parents of the bride and of the groom have this very important part in the ceremony — an equal part."

How is Daddy going to feel about this? Rennie wondered. He's always looked forward to walking down the aisle with me on his arm. After being stuck in a pew at Eddy's and Larry's and Jonathan's weddings, he's really counting on it.

"I can tell thee where to inquire about the Meeting nearest thy home, Serenity," Oliver was saying, "but I'm afraid thee will find that Friends with whom thee and Peter have never had fellowship will be reluctant to undertake responsibility for your marriage. It's more than a ceremony with us; it's a deep and continuing concern for the permanence and rightness of the relationship. That's why a Friends Meeting first appoints a committee on clearness — two men Friends to call upon the prospective groom and two women Friends to call upon the bride. It's their responsibility to ascertain as far as possible that nothing threatens to interfere with the permanence and happiness of the marriage. When the committee is satisfied that the couple has clearness for marriage ——"

"Clearness?" Rennie broke in, appalled. "Do you mean like clearing customs when you've been out of the country?" She giggled, but she didn't think this at all funny.

Neither, apparently, did Oliver. "Not clearance. Clear*ness*. It's the Quaker term for establishing that nothing exists which might prove a hindrance; that both parties understand the responsibilities they are assuming and that they have every prospect of being happy together the rest of their lives. If, after exploring this with the couple, the committee on clearness feels comfortable about proceeding, the Meeting appoints another committee to have oversight of the wedding. These overseers are the Friends who take responsibility for seeing that the marriage is accomplished with reverence, dignity and simplicity."

Most of this was lost on Rennie. She was still floored by the clearness bit. Two strange women were going to come to see her and poke their old noses into her affairs — catechize her, maybe even examine her sex life. Putting the wedding off for a month hadn't seemed insurmountable, but this ——

"Forget it," she muttered. She wished she hadn't come. She wanted to go back to college this minute, get out of here. But how could she leave at this time of night? Oliver wouldn't be able to drive her all the way to the airport. Daphne —— Besides, he looked tired.

"Thee sees, Serenity," he was saying in a gentle voice, "until thee and Peter have known Friends and have shared in their spiritual search, you can hardly expect to understand what all this means to us. We have no forms or creed, placing our whole reliance on a common experience of the presence of God. This makes us one with our fellow human beings. The customs officer has no interest in people, only in spotting contraband in their luggage. Friends care deeply."

"Okay," Rennie exclaimed, unable to keep her voice down. "But marriage is something private, just between the guy and the girl. What right do others have to intrude?"

"That is where we differ," Oliver answered. "Marriage is a great deal more than an understanding between two people. It affects everyone around them, our whole civilization. Should the marriage break down, civilization will be that much weaker, just as the balance of nature is disturbed by our ecological carelessness. It affects the unborn children, for whom we wish to prepare a stable, harmonious home." Oliver paused a moment. Then he asked quietly, looking straight at Rennie, "If it's only yourselves you're concerned with, why bother with a religious ceremony? You could disregard these responsibilities completely and simply live together."

Rennie jumped. She hadn't expected this from Oliver.

5.

All Rennie could think of when she went to bed in Heather's room was getting out of Firbank. She hadn't had the nerve to break it to Oliver, as she left him standing at the bottom of the curving stairs, but, first thing in the morning, she'd ask him to take her to the airport or at least to Kendal. If she had to, she'd walk. The only thing that mattered now was getting away from here. Rennie wished she could have brought herself to tell Oliver when they were saying good night.

But it was too hard. After she'd left him and she was starting upstairs, he stopped her. Rennie, balancing between the first and second steps, felt a touch on her arm. Turning, she saw that Oliver's blue eyes, which were almost level with hers now, looked completely serene. "Way will open," he assured her. "Thee and Peter may have to search harder. But way will open. Not, perhaps," he added quietly, "as speedily as thy parents wish, or in the direction they've chosen. Still, it's worth pressing on for."

How could Rennie have told him then that she was leaving? To Oliver it would have seemed that she was running away.

Rushing up the remaining stairs as soon as he withdrew his hand, shutting herself in the strange room, she thought bitterly that she was going back to college without the solution she'd counted on and more mixed up than when she came. What did he mean, anyhow: "Way will open"?

Letting her skirt drop on the floor and leaving it there, not giving a hang, now, about those pleats, Rennie realized that the game she'd played so successfully with her parents all these years — avoiding every confrontation — hadn't worked in Firbank. In the light of

Oliver's super-honesty and deceptive simplicity, she'd felt exposed. Oliver was fifteen years older than her father. She'd expected, back here in the country, that he'd be fifteen years more naïve. Instead, he'd seen right through her. No need for any committee on clearness. He'd seen through her as thoroughly as the cop with the guillotine.

Rennie told herself that if she didn't get out of here fast, didn't return soon to the safe solidity of Peter's body, something terrible would happen. Feeling the way she did, she couldn't possibly sleep. She'd just read all night. What? She certainly wasn't going to study. Heather's bookcase didn't offer much. Rennie settled for a biography of Kate Greenaway with illustrations — delicate water colors of children in old-fashioned costumes, very whimsical — Nineteenth Century.

But, having slithered between sheets that smelled of outdoors, Rennie pitched the book back at the bookcase. How could she concentrate? The book missed, bouncing off a corner of the fireplace and landing in the middle of the floor. Rennie didn't care.

Not only had Oliver ruled out the possibility of a Quaker marriage; he implied that if all Rennie and Peter wanted was to live with and for each other, they shouldn't get mixed up in any religious ceremony. Oliver hadn't stated this didactically. He merely suggested it in the form of a question, asked in such a quiet, nonjudgmental tone that Rennie was shocked. His quaintness, his fantastically unashamed reference to God had led Rennie to expect that he'd be square, agreeing with her parents, who were not only determined to get her married, but married in a church — any church. That no one, except possibly Peter's parents, who weren't being consulted, cared about the views of the church seemed irrelevant.

To Oliver, getting married was obviously less important than how sincerely the fellow and the girl believed in the ceremony and how involved they were in the church or meeting. But how could people believe in something when they didn't know what it was? Maybe she, Rennie, was the naïve one, imagining that, because these

Friends dispensed with a minister, they wouldn't have religious ideas. Or that her name and a childish fantasy stirred by some old picture exempted her from taking those ideas seriously. As for being involved — it was one thing, getting excited in an election or over women's lib, very different having your marriage become other people's business. She and Peter would never tolerate that.

Turning out the little lamp on the bedside table, Rennie remembered Oliver's joyous gesture when he lit it. A nice man. He meant to help. Instead, he only upset Rennie, raising questions she didn't have time to face now, along with choosing a china pattern and passing her finals. Maybe later——

She wished she could get Oliver out of her mind; forget what he'd asked in that quiet tone. It didn't condemn Rennie, yet it told her firmly that, for himself, nothing less than premarital chastity would have been acceptable. Naturally, when *he* was young. But didn't he know stuff like that went out when the Pill came in?

Stop thinking about those things, Rennie scolded herself, turning her back on them.

They simply dodged around to the front of her mind, pestering and prying until she felt blasted clean out of her world. She was like one of those tumbling bodies in Michelangelo's *Last Judgment,* careening so wildly in space now that she had to clutch the blanket to keep from dropping into the unknown. Holding on for dear life, she shut her eyes so she wouldn't see the terrifying void below.

The next thing Rennie knew, sunshine was streaming into the room.

She jumped out of bed, still half asleep, went to the window and pulled up the shade. There, at the bottom of a field speckled with boulders, not a house in sight, was Salt Pond. A sand dune enclosed it at the back, cutting off the view of the ocean, just the way Rennie's father had always described it. Nothing was visible beyond but the horizon, making the little body of water a hidden, secret place on the edge of the world — sparkling in the morning sun, unpolluted, waiting for someone to come and discover it.

Leaning her elbows on the window sill, Rennie thought the pond didn't look nearly so big as her father had led her to believe it was when he used to tell her about his early exploits, sailing his grandmother's catboat.

Serenity, Rennie said to herself, trying to picture the woman with that tranquil sweetness, remembering how her father had observed sadly, when he spoke of her, "I wish some of that serenity had come down to us. Not one of us has it."

I want it! Rennie told Salt Pond. She felt like shouting, for suddenly she realized that she wanted serenity more than anything. It was awful, not matching one's name.

Turning from the window, she pulled on her shorts. To be serene about life; not to have another night like this last one, a tangle of nightmares! That bed of Heather's —— As Rennie's eyes emerged from the turtleneck, she threw the bed a sour look. Tonight, anyway, she'd be back in Peter's.

Would she? More likely, she'd have to return to her own dorm and sleep in her own bed. Peter was never going to put her out of his room, but she knew he didn't want her there as much as she wanted to stay. Something about him had a real need to be apart sometimes. When he was trying to decide about getting engaged, he had insisted on taking those long walks by himself. He liked being with his friends, too — playing handball and having a soda with them later. Other men's companionship interested him, whereas, these days, Rennie didn't care to socialize with the girls who used to be her best friends. Now that she was getting married, they no longer had anything in common.

It suddenly dawned on Rennie that Harriet and Priscilla and Audrey might be counting on being her bridesmaids. Didn't one always have some college friends in one's wedding? But it would be hypocritical, like inviting her father's business associates. Rennie thought, I don't want them. They don't trust marriage.

No, Peter wouldn't put Rennie out of his room. But that night, after she'd phoned to Oliver and asked about coming to Firbank, he'd tried harder than ever before to explain how he felt.

"If we go right on making love, what will getting married prove?

I don't think it should just be the legalization of an existing relationship. At least, I want our marriage to be more than that. You feel this way, too, or you wouldn't be trying so hard to get a wedding we can believe in."

"But the relationship does exist," Rennie argued. "It has since months."

"I know, At first, I wasn't thinking of taking care of you. I was just following instinct. But now you're going to be my wife. That's something special. Till you are, I'd just like to be friends with you — have more chance to explore your thoughts and feelings; my own, too. Let's face it — when we have sex, we don't do that. Will you try, Rennie? I may break down before the week is out, but let's try. I've felt bad all along because we put the cart before the horse — joined one part of ourselves before the rest knew what was happening. It ought to be a total thing."

He put his arms around her and stroked her hair with his cheek, holding her in a tender and protective embrace. Rennie knew then how strongly Peter meant this. But what would he feel tonight, when she got back, after she'd been gone all this time — ever since yesterday? Would he still ——?

It was nine o'clock. Rennie opened the door of Heather's room and crossed the upstairs hall. There was no sign of Oliver or Daphne.

In daylight, the hall was different. Looking through open doors, Rennie noticed tall headboards on old-fashioned bedsteads, a white-and-indigo homespun coverlet, a red-and-yellow patchwork quilt. Sunlight bleached the bare wood of the floors. Each room was so neat, you'd think nobody lived there. Even Daphne and Oliver's bed was made. Curious about their room, Rennie stopped at the head of the stairs to peek in. Like the living room below, it was crammed with books and pictures. On either side of the Franklin stove were armchairs covered with some flowered stuff. The rug was frayed but colorful.

Struck by a weird thought, Rennie lingered. This must have been Serenity and Edmund's room. Had they, repressed Victorians, made love in that big four-poster with the pineapple finials? Were their babies born in that bed, planned or unplanned? Did Edmund die there and, years later, Serenity? The thought gave Rennie goose pimples.

As she went down the stairs, awed by all this, running her hand along the smooth curve of the banister, she felt an almost seductive pull. The house was tugging at her, appealing to her to remain. Everything about it was inviting and beautiful, with a character of its own. The house seemed to be enfolding Rennie like Peter's arms — not one of his bear hugs — more the way he had held her that time, in a tender and protective embrace.

But Rennie's mind was made up. There was no use staying now. Oliver was undoubtedly a remarkable man, only, so far as Rennie was concerned, he'd turned out to be a complete washout. Until this moment, when the full force of her disappointment got to her, she hadn't realized how much she'd counted on him. Loving the house just made her feel worse.

She had to find Oliver and announce the change in plan. That was all — say it coolly. No explanation was called for. He must be in the living room. Rennie could hear the vacuum cleaner. But when she looked in from the doorway, she found it wasn't Oliver. A girl in bluejeans with stringy hair was running the machine — no, it was a boy.

He couldn't hear her above the sound of the motor, but noticing her shadow cross a bar of sunlight on the floor, he turned and switched off the vacuum. Pushing the hair out of his eyes, he grinned up at Rennie. Who was he?

A second boy appeared suddenly, carrying a canvas sling filled with fireplace logs. "Hi," he said without really looking at Rennie. He went to the wood box and set down his load.

Rennie wondered whether these were Heather's children, helping their grandfather. The way they took her presence for granted, it was clear they'd been told she was here.

Still looking for Oliver, she walked through the dining room and bumped into a woman coming out of the kitchen. "I just put a roast

68

chicken in the refrigerator. They might like it tonight." The woman hurried toward the front door. "Sorry, I have to run."

She went before Rennie had a chance to ask about Oliver. If he'd gone out, wouldn't Daphne be here? There wasn't even a dog.

Early though it was, the kitchen had been straightened. That pernickety Oliver — didn't he ever leave things around? There wasn't a single dirty dish in the sink. On the counter, baking dishes and platters, covered with transparent wrapping, contained a variety of tempting foods — lots more than three people could consume in a weekend. Had Oliver been cooking all night?

He'd left a note for Rennie, a large, stiff sheet of paper, torn out of a spiral book. It was propped against the sugar bowl on the table. Instead of writing out her name, he'd made a little sketch of Rennie's head — not a line drawing, but a real portrait in delicate color, produced by just a few, expert strokes. Beneath it, Oliver had written with a felt-tipped pen:

> We hope thee slept well. Help thyself. Coffee on the stove, eggs in the pan, cereal on the counter, bread in the toaster, fruit in the fridge. When thee's broken fast, Daphne would be pleased if thee dropped in to see her. She's in the woodshed beyond the back hall.

The woodshed! Rennie said to herself. What on earth can Daphne be doing in the woodshed? She read on:

> Then will thee come and find me in the Vietnamese Forest? Follow the little path behind the barn. We hope we can make this a happy day for thee. *The sun is but a morning star.*
>
> O.O.

6.

The last words of Oliver's note were puzzling. "The sun is but a morning star." What did that mean, anyhow? And why had Oliver written it? This was as strange as the Vietnamese Forest in Rhode

Island and all those people milling around the house. But Rennie was too fascinated by her picture to wonder very long.

In the picture, her hair made a cloud around her head, just the right shade — cadmium red with a touch of burnt sienna. The eyes, however, had an expression Rennie didn't associate with herself. Her father had said deprecatingly that Oliver was just a farmer. Little did he know! Only a real arist could have made this sketch. When? It must have been from memory, after Rennie went to bed. She felt impressed and terribly pleased.

She didn't want any breakfast, merely coffee, but she sat at the table a long time, studying the sketch and sipping slowly to postpone the moment when she'd have to look for Daphne. Shouldn't she go upstairs first and put her stuff in the book bag? Maybe she ought to make the bed. And the airline — she had to phone and change her reservation. But she went on sitting there.

A woman came in, carrying a pie plate in one hand and a cookie tin in the other. With a friendly hello, she placed both on the counter, surveying the dishes that were already lined up. "I brought a cherry pie and some meringues," she told Rennie.

"Are they having a party?"

"No. Since Daphne's stroke, we women of Kendal Meeting have looked out for their main meals. Most of us do our baking on Saturday and we each stick in an extra pie or sheet of cookies for the Otises. Somebody fixes a casserole or roast. Midweek, one of us brings in something fresh. With their food mostly taken care of and the First Day school keeping the house clean, Daphne and Oliver manage beautifully now."

Rennie hadn't wondered about the mechanics of the household. Food had been provided for her, the bed she slept in was made up, fresh towels hung in the bathroom. Everything in the house was inviting. Who filled the wood box so she could sit by a cheerful fire hadn't interested her. But she did wonder about the kids working in the living room.

"Are those Heather's boys vacuuming in there?" she asked, watching the woman hang a clean dish cloth over the sink.

The woman turned to her. "No. Heather lives in England. She has one boy, but we're all the family Daphne and Oliver have over here — I mean, the Meeting is."

They have us, Rennie started to say. We're their cousins. But then she thought, Daddy doesn't even know about Daphne. Oliver should have told him.

"We're a lot like a family," the woman was saying, "and with everyone in the Meeting doing a little, it's no trouble for any one person. It's been an absolute blessing for our children. We were beginning to have some problems with these youngsters — you know — like everybody else. Then this happened to Daphne. The whole Meeting just grieved. We love Daphne and Oliver. The sudden blow made us feel helpless, till we realized how much there was to do. Oliver's wonderful, but he couldn't manage everything — nurse Daphne — she needed so much bolstering at first, as well as physical care — cook, clean, look after the farm, their business affairs ——"

"He's an old man, too," Rennie put in.

The woman laughed. "A pretty spry old man. But it was too much for one person. So the Meeting divided up the Firbank housekeeping. We put it to the children — whether they'd be responsible for the cleaning — make it their project. It's a big house, you know. But with all of them pitching in —— We'd been paying them for doing chores at home, most of us, and still we had to keep after them if we were going to get anything done. Now we asked them to work here purely out of love. I wish I could tell you how they rose to it. They must have been secretly yearning for grown-up responsibility — something to give them pride — while we kept treating them like children or hired help. We've learned more from this than the kids," the woman added, laughing.

She'd barely left when a couple of little girls — junior high, Rennie figured — burst into the kitchen. Their hilarious shrieks died when they saw Rennie. They sounded like best friends and made a comical picture together — the one short and dark and curly-headed, the other tall, with straight, blond hair.

"Hi," Rennie said, as they stood in the doorway, sizing her up. She noticed the admiration she evoked in them and smiled encouragingly. But she felt a little envious. To be that age, finding life nothing but a joke! "I'm Rennie," she said.

"We know. Oliver Otis told us. We're Nancy and Sandy."

They took a pail and mop out of the broom closet.

"Do you do this every Saturday?" Rennie asked, as the girls started sloshing soapsuds around. Would any kid give up part of her weekend to wash someone's floor for love? Rennie couldn't believe it.

"No," they answered together.

"Just once a month," the big girl explained.

The short, dark one went on. "We take turns. All the bigger kids in First Day school do something. It's a schedule we made up. If we didn't pitch in," the girl added with evident pride, "the Otises wouldn't be able to get along. They'd have to leave Firbank."

The other girl looked at Rennie gravely, as if she wondered whether this glamorous college student appreciated how indispensable she and her friend really were.

"You're terrific," Rennie told them magnanimously. "You both go to First Day school?"

"Yes."

"What is it, anyhow?"

"Sunday school. Quakers call it that because, see, it's the first day of the week."

"Plain language?" Rennie asked, amused. She was getting to know her way around this peculiar place. "But you don't say thee and thy."

The girls giggled.

"Nobody does," the short one explained, "except Oliver and Daphne Otis — well, she *used* to. Mary Lancashire, three or four others —— We're studying the Gospel of Matthew this spring, see? And you know where it says, like, I don't remember the exact words, I was hungry and you gave me something to eat, I was thirsty and you gave me a drink?"

"No," Rennie admitted. "I never read it."

"Well, anyway, it goes on, sick and ——"

"A stranger," the other girl put in. "That comes first, Nancy, I was a stranger and ye took me in; naked and ye clothed me."

"Okay. Never mind. *Then* it says, I was sick and you came over to my house. When we read that, we felt it was like Daphne Otis talking to us and we were those people in the Bible."

As the water level began rising, Rennie pushed the coffee cup aside and stood up. It was definitely time to leave. "Is this the way to the woodshed?" she asked.

"Yes, but don't go in now. Daphne Otis is there."

"I know."

"It's the only rule here," Nancy said. Her eyes implored Rennie to abide by it. "We can do anything we like in the house, go anywhere, read their books, swim off their beach, even sail their boat. Only, we *never* go to the woodshed when she's in there. You mustn't."

You mustn't, Rennie felt like saying. Oliver's letting *me*, even if I can't spout the Bible. But, after all, she wasn't a kid any more. "It's okay," she assured them. "I'll only stay a minute."

She didn't want to go. There was something spooky about the whole thing. What, she wondered, as she walked timidly toward the back hall, could Daphne be doing in the woodshed that was so mysterious? She moved slowly, noticing the coats and snowshoes hanging from wooden pegs and the row of boots on the floor. The back door still had a huge, old hasp and lock. Just inside the door stood a sack of bird seed. Some had spilled. Rennie felt it crunch under her sneaker.

The back hall opened directly into the woodshed. Instead of firewood, Rennie saw an easel standing in the middle of the floor and dozens of canvases stacked against the unplastered walls. She stopped short. There sat Daphne, wearing a faded violet smock. In front of her was a little table with an open sketch book, brushes, tubes and pans of paint, a jar of water.

So *Daphne* was the artist!

She sat very close to the shed window, with her useless arm facing Rennie. Something on the other side of the small panes attracted her attention. Was it a bird up in the tree? After a few moments, Daphne glanced down at the sketch book. She dipped a brush into the water, ran it lightly over a pan of paint, and started dabbing the paper with short, decisive strokes.

Rennie, almost holding her breath as she followed the progress of the brush, wondered why Daphne didn't notice her. Then the truth struck her: with that side paralyzed, Daphne's eye probably didn't move and she couldn't see out of the corner. Unless she turned her head, she'd never know Rennie was there. Rennie ought to say something. But apart from calling out, "Good morning," which would sound stupid and only startle Daphne when she was concentrating so hard, Rennie couldn't think of a thing to say.

She was still overcome with surprise at discovering that Daphne was an artist, obviously the one who made the little sketch on Oliver's note. No doubt she'd painted all those pictures around the house. The way Daphne worked showed she was a professional, or had been, before —— All Rennie'd felt for this woman until now was pity. Suddenly she was filled with enormous respect. She'd never known a real artist. To have a chance to see one at work!

The dabs on the water color paper were beginning to take shape. Rennie saw that what Daphne was trying to capture was the light of the sky filtering through the leaves of the tree. Some of the leaves appeared to let light shine through brilliantly. Others were painted a deeper shade. Sometimes part of a leaf was much darker than the rest. Since these were all leaves on the same tree, Rennie was puzzled until, crouching down far enough to look out through the window herself, she saw that, where the light had to penetrate more than one layer of leaves, it was still bright, but a deeper green. Leaf on leaf created a pattern of subtly shaded color that Daphne was reproducing with amazing faithfulness. Transferring another brushful of paint from its little pan to the paper, she made the cloudless sky between the leaves a dazzling blue. Then she sketched in the fine branches and twigs. Rounded by light and shadow, they didn't look like sticks jutting out from the tree so much as part of the surrounding air.

Fascinated, Rennie stood there watching the picture emerge, tingling with excitement, feeling as though she were present at a momentous birth. There was something *happy* about Daphne's picture, bright and vibrant with the beginning of mysterious life.

If it was me, Rennie thought, glancing at the crippled arm, I couldn't ever be happy again.

Amazed by magic that evoked such beauty from blank paper, still unable to believe that poor Daphne should turn out to be an artist, Rennie stood there in the doorway, watching the left hand create a startling interplay of light and color.

Suddenly the hand stopped moving. Looking up, Rennie found that Daphne had turned her head and was smiling at her.

"Hi," Rennie said.

Daphne beckoned her in, pointing to a chair on the other side of the table. When Rennie sat down, Daphne rested the brush on top of the water jar and looked eagerly at her, clearly waiting for Rennie to speak.

Say something, Rennie commanded herself. *Say something!* But nothing came out.

"Oliver left me a note," she managed finally. "He told me to drop in for a minute and see you. But the kids said —— Is it all right?"

Daphne nodded happily.

"You're the one who made that little sketch of me, aren't you? I thought it was Oliver. You painted it on that same paper."

Daphne nodded again. Then she looked down critically at the picture in the sketch book.

"It's nice," Rennie said. After that, she just clammed up.

Holding the book at arm's length and squinting, Daphne began to smile to herself. She placed the book on the table again and turned toward Rennie, looking at her earnestly. Suddenly she opened her mouth.

Rennie's heart stood still. Daphne was about to speak! This was why the picture was so happy. A breakthrough!

But no sound issued from Daphne's throat and she closed her mouth again. She pointed to Rennie, to the sketch book, then to Rennie again, pleading with her eyes for some sign of understanding.

What was going on? It couldn't be, could it, that Daphne was offering to *give* Rennie that picture? Would she really? But the picture wasn't finished and Rennie had to leave. She wondered whether she ought to tell Daphne. No. Things might get complicated. Oliver'd better take care of that.

Looking disappointed and frustrated, Daphne reached for a pencil and writing pad. Then, seeing that Rennie was getting up to go, she dropped the pencil and simply held out her hand. Rennie gave it a tap, pulling back quickly, as if she were testing a hot iron, and hurried to the door. "I'm going down to the Vietnamese Forest, whatever that is," she told Daphne, relieved to have an out. "Oliver said I should come."

Running out the back door to avoid the lake in the kitchen, Rennie found herself between tulip beds, great masses of pink and yellow flowers. The bluish gray slates of the roof on the red barn made a lovely pattern as they caught oblique rays from the sun.

Rennie stood still a minute to look back at the house. It was plainer on this side than in front. In a way, she liked it better. Over the kitchen were two dormers — that was her room. And beyond the kitchen was the woodshed. Rennie saw something moving behind the window. Daphne was waving to her.

Daphne, the house — everything was ganging up to make Rennie stay. Although she couldn't see the pond from here, she knew it was tugging at her, too. But her mind was made up.

Oh, I forgot to call the airline! Oh well —— Planes can't be that crowded on Saturday. I'll get a seat.

Waving back, Rennie turned and walked around the barn. It smelled — not of manure, but deliciously of hay. A little further on, she found the path and followed it into the woods.

7.

The air had a fragrance wholly unfamiliar to Rennie. It smelled of pine, bayberry and other shrubs she couldn't name, all seasoned with salt spray. She felt light and momentarily carefree, as she followed the narrowing trail, wondering where it led. This evening she'd be back with Peter! But before she left, she wanted to ask Oliver what he meant about the sun being a morning star. And she must be sure to see Salt Pond, so she could tell her father about it.

How could an insignificant body of water, which he hadn't laid eyes on in fifty years, have such a hold on a grown man? He was prosperous and successful. He had a big house and a pretty decent family. Yet, clearly, he'd never been so happy as in his childhood, when everything was larger than life and Firbank a veritable paradise.

Rennie was actually in this paradise of his, inhaling the spring fragrance, feeling the freshness of the air on her skin, looking up at the sun shining through the leaves and seeing the interplay of light through Daphne's eyes. In spite of all their troubles, Oliver and Daphne had a serenity that the Ross branch of the family lacked. Maybe the place rubbed off on their souls.

Was this what Peter meant when he said that Rennie might find a clue to her identity here? At the time, she was miffed. How could she not know who she was? That was ridiculous; Now, she wasn't so sure.

If she could just bring Peter here sometime, maybe he'd help her figure out why the place meant so much. After they were married, if they took a short trip, couldn't they come here? Peter and Oliver would hit it off. But what excuse would there be for coming? Rennie began to wonder whether she ought not to stay until to-morrow. There might never be another chance. No. That was absurd. Her identity wasn't in a place. It was in her genes.

She had to get back to Peter. How could she have thought of

leaving him all weekend? What would he do? Was he still in the cafeteria, lingering over breakfast, sitting at that table near the window, sitting there all by himself? Maybe that girl in his math class, the tall, skinny one — she was always trying to get him to notice her. Now that Rennie wasn't around ——

Suddenly, Lion and Duffy came running at her, jumping up in a tumult of recognition. Oliver must be nearby. A few steps further on, Rennie saw him. He was in a group of men, digging around the roots of a tree. Now that Rennie saw him, she couldn't remember what she'd wanted to ask before she left.

"Serenity!" he called. "Come and meet these friends."

When she reached them, he introduced her, his face expressing what Rennie could only interpret as pride. The men grinned and held out their earth-stained hands for her to shake. She was too confused to catch their names.

"This is a great day," Oliver exulted. "We think we've discovered the technique we've been searching for to make trees bloom again in Vietnam! Thee knows, the ecological damage caused by American defoliation chemicals during the war is incredible. More than a third of the mangrove forests along the coast were destroyed and those herbicides scarred the inland forests extensively. If we've really succeeded in revitalizing soil, what a great day this is!"

The other men reflected Oliver's satisfaction.

"Come," he said, handing the shovel he was holding to one of them and taking Rennie's arm. "I want to show thee more of Firbank. The Vietnamese Forest covers only a few acres." Waving to his friends, he drew Rennie away. The dogs scampered beside them.

"Is this what you call the Vietnamese ——?" It was just woods. What had Rennie expected? Disney-type rice paddies, water buffaloes, exotic temples in Rhode Island? She stopped in mid-sentence. Oliver wasn't listening to her.

He stood still, cocking his head. "Hear that?" he whispered. A smile overspread his face. "A blue-winged warbler, stopping to rest in our hemlocks on the way north! Hear the buzzy bzzzz-brrrr?" He looked, Rennie thought, as if a long-lost friend had suddenly returned. Even when he began walking again, the smile lingered.

"Why," Rennie asked, as Oliver continued through the woods, "why Vietnamese? It looks just like the rest."

Oliver laughed. Rennie could see that he was laughing at himself. "That's just my private name for those acres," he explained, looking a little embarrassed. "Before the Civil War, they used to be known as The Shelter, because this was where slaves, who'd escaped from their masters and were being pursued by law enforcement agents, found shelter. We don't know exactly where the hiding place was — everything had to be kept so secret that there are no records — but this was definitely a busy station on the Underground Railroad. Grandmother could remember how terrified she was as a girl, when her father and other Friends who acted as 'conductors' risked imprisonment, helping those fugitives. They were brought in — ragged, hungry, frightened to death — and given sustenance and comfort. After dark, they were loaded into the wagon, covered with hay, and driven to the next 'station,' ten miles north of here. Eventually, it was hoped, the slaves would reach Canada and freedom. At that speed, just think how long it took them to get there."

The Underground Railroad! Rennie had read about it in American Civ, but no one had ever told her that her own ancestors took part in this illicit traffic. She was proud of that. Listening to Oliver, she thought, Peter's got something. I'm discovering my identity. My roots are in this place.

But couldn't this prove to be a trap? Oliver's lifestyle belonged to another era — as dead as the dodo. If Rennie paid too much attention to him, she'd quickly be out of step with her generation — a dodo herself, at nineteen. Just because Oliver was so likable — so very likable — didn't mean he was right.

"This part of Firbank has always been set aside for the relief of suffering," he was saying. "In the Depression, when the mills in Kendal closed, we divided The Shelter into little gardens and gave them to the men who were laid off, so they could come out from town and grow vegetables for their families. During the Second World War, when there was rationing, we did the same thing. There was a long strike later and the gardens again helped to nourish people. Then, when those bombers first began defoliating the trees of Vietnam, I was so distressed that I had to find a way to counteract the damage. A tree, Serenity, is as sacred, in its way, as a person. Someday, I said to myself, there will be an end to this destruction. When the time comes that we pray for so fervently, we must have a formula ready for making the contaminated soil capable of nourishing life again. I went over to the university to consult the forestry men. Thee knows, this is hardly the same climate as Vietnam's," Oliver admitted wryly, "but it's where I live and the only land I own. I learned from those foresters that, here at home, where herbicides had been used as weed killers in lethal doses, the soil could be restored with activated charcoal. So I destroyed life in the old vegetable patches, then experimented with the charcoal and finally planted seedlings — covered them in winter, even made smudge fires in the worst weather. Nursing those trees was pretty hard work, along with running the farm. But until Daphne's stroke, I managed somehow. Then friends rushed in to help. As thee sees, they're still helping."

"Yes."

"For years," Oliver continued, "it was discouraging. People thought we were crazy, because we were trying to simulate growing conditions for tropical vegetation in New England. But we kept at it. And now," he exclaimed jubilantly, "I think — I *think* we may be on the track. It will have to be proved, of course. But I'm hopeful."

He looked it. To Rennie, though, his whole plan sounded crazy. She wondered whether he might be senile.

The field they came to was dotted with boulders. How did anything grow in the stony soil? This was the field she'd looked out on when she woke up. And there, at the bottom of the slope, lay Salt Pond.

"Oliver," she asked suddenly, "what was your grandmother like? You must remember even better than Daddy. He was wild about her."

"We all were, not only as youngsters, though she responded with

80

instinctive understanding to children and animals, but grown people sensed a special quality in her, too. When Daphne came here as a bride to a strange country, still haunted by the suffering she'd seen during the war, it was Grandmother who did most to make her feel at home."

"She had security, didn't she?"

"Does thee mean financial independence?"

"No. Was she sure — you know — of herself, not scared half the time?"

"Yes, but I think she would have called it faith. It was a deep trust that there is something divine in every human being; that we can rely implicitly on that light for guidance. Thee'll understand this better when thee sees her portrait. Daphne painted it shortly after we were married. I'll show it to thee when we go back and tomorrow thee'll see the house in Kendal where Grandmother was born. Now, we'll get in the dory and row across to the dunes."

"Let's!"

Rennie's father would ask whether she'd stood on those mounds of sand, knee-deep in coarse grass and beach pea, to watch the surf come pounding in.

Oliver led her past a boathouse, out onto a small, stone dock, where the dory waited. The bottom of the shallow water was covered with eel grass and clam shells.

Rennie watched Oliver pull in the painter. As he squatted, holding the side of the dory against the dock so she could jump in, he glanced at his watch. "Gracious! It's later than I thought. Daphne will be waiting for us." He looked disappointed. "I'm afraid we can't row over after all, Serenity," he said sorrowfully, letting go of the painter and standing up. "Some other time. Thee'll simply have to come back to Firbank. Come back and bring Peter."

"Oh, Oliver, I'd love to!"

"Now let's hurry to the house and prepare lunch. Daphne must be hungry, after working all morning. No doubt thee is, too." .

This was it — the moment to tell Oliver. Rennie mustn't postpone it any longer. She tried the words over in her head so that she'd make the announcement coolly. I'm sorry. I've changed my plans. Right after lunch, I'm leaving ——

But Oliver took her breath away.

"Daphne would like to paint thy portrait. Will thee sit for her?" Without giving Rennie time to reply, he exclaimed, "Won't they be handsome, side by side, the two Serenitys?"

"My portrait? You must be kidding!"

"She's dying to do it. Unfortunately, there won't be time for oils, just pastels. But if thee would pose for her this afternoon —— Daphne thinks she can finish it in one sitting."

To have one's portrait painted by a real artist — wouldn't that be something? Peter'd be impressed. So would Rennie's parents. But she had to leave. She couldn't go through another night in Heather's bed. Or was a portrait — a portrait of herself! — worth sticking it out for? This was too much for Rennie. The struggle must have showed in her face.

Oliver saw her hesitation and pleaded. "Do, Serenity. It would mean a lot to Daphne. Thee sees, it isn't very often that a young person comes to the house who stirs her imagination."

"But there are all those kids up there, vacuuming and scrubbing."

"The First Day school youngsters? Oh, Daphne and I couldn't get along without them. They keep us going, polishing every Saturday. Does us the entire week. They gladden our hearts, too, those young Friends, with the outpouring of their love. But, Serenity, it's thee Daphne wants to paint. She felt this the moment thee arrived. It was thy coloring at first, like Heather's — when she was young, that is," Oliver put in. "Heather's hair is going gray now, though her complexion's still fresh. But to get back to Daphne — at supper she found she was seeing beyond thy surface beauty to the woman unfolding in thee — its boundless promise. That's the beauty she wants to portray. She thought about it half the night."

Rennie was stunned. Daphne could see right through her, too. But instead of being put off by what she saw beyond that surface "beauty" — no one had ever used the word in connection with Rennie before — she found promise. No one but Peter had ever liked Rennie that much. Her parents loved her, of course, but they kept wanting to improve her. Daphne seemed to like her the way she was. Could Daphne really be thinking all this, or did Oliver just make it up to hide her handicap?

"This morning," he was saying, "she told me thee reminds her of a leaf on that maple outside the woodshed window. Was thee in there with her?"

"Yes."

"Then thee saw she's doing a little water color sketch of those leaves — the way they look from underneath, seen through the glass, all new and tender green, luminous against the sky. She often expresses her feelings about people in terms of nature. This is how she sees thee."

So that's what Daphne was trying to tell Rennie when she pointed to her! How was Rennie to know?

"Thee's given Daphne an eagerness to paint she hasn't had in years," Oliver told her. "Not since she fell ill. She's worked hard, learning to use her left hand, but without zest. Her eagerness this morning is something of a miracle, just like old times. I never expected to see it in her again. Wait till I write Heather!" He looked ecstatic, but there was a note of anxiety in Oliver's voice as he asked, "Thee will sit for her, won't thee?"

How could Rennie say no?

Oliver reached for her hand and squeezed it. "Thank thee," he said. Then, whistling for the dogs, he led the way across the field, back to the house.

8.

When Rennie first saw her great-grandmother's portrait, she was taken aback.

She'd expected it to be like those massive pictures on the walls of the Administration Building at college — the dead deans and presidents, dressed in their best, black suits, who sat in somber offices, staring pompously down on the students.

Rennie knew Serenity wouldn't be pompous, but she wasn't prepared for what she saw when Oliver led her into his study and showed her the portrait.

It was airily framed and much smaller than those of the deans and presidents. The whole picture shimmered with light. Although Serenity's dress was austere — pale gray, the color, Oliver explained, that many Quaker women of her generation wore — it was made of some glowing material — silk or taffeta — and the fichu around her neck was so white one could almost feel the sun touching it. Sunshine picked out the strands in her silver coronet of braids, too, and lit the whole background — the leafy, budding world of Firbank in springtime. So it wasn't really surprising that, over her shoulder, Serenity should be carrying a jaunty, little, bright pink parasol — just different from what Rennie had expected.

Serenity's face was different, too. Yes, she had what Rennie called security, but it was a daring kind. It would risk trusting someone, even someone disappointing. It would trust the unknown, too, and do what seemed right, without counting the cost. Despite, or perhaps because of, this cool courage, Serenity looked incredibly lighthearted. Daphne had caught her in the act of smiling tenderly at something not visible in the picture, something close to the ground — a child, maybe, or a dog.

"Daphne's acceptance by leading American critics of the Twenties began with this portrait," Oliver was saying. "It was exhibited in New York and instantly acclaimed. Commissions began pouring in. Her future was assured. Thee sees, up to that time, the popular idea of an old person's portrait was something dark and solemn."

"Like Rembrandt," Rennie put in.

"Yes. This showed a warmth and gaiety that were exceptional. Daphne's experience in France had given her an understanding of people, not just of their characters, but of their predicaments, and we're all in some sort of predicament. Even Grandmother, with her spiritual strength, was constantly in a fix because she cared not only for her family and her lovely friends, but also for the most unlovely people — youngsters caught by the police; drunks, as they were called in those days, who had no home to go to; young girls in trouble. Firbank seemed always to be awaiting the arrival of some fatherless baby. The humor and sympathy with which Grandmother ministered to these people, the conviction she held that it wasn't up to her to pass judgment on anyone, inspired Daphne. And the picture communicates this. From the moment it went on exhibition, people responded to it."

So Daphne had had a successful career! And this successful artist wanted to paint Rennie's picture — how fantastic!

"We're thinking of hanging thy portrait here," Oliver was saying. He pointed to the adjacent wall space. "It'll make a companion piece to Grandmother's. Won't they be beautiful together!" Joyfully anticipating, he clapped his hands like a child. Then he went off to prepare lunch.

Feeling guilty because she wasn't in the kitchen, helping, Rennie lingered, turning back to Serenity, seeking some rapport, like those conversations she used to have with the bride on the landing at home, when she was small. No way — she was grown up now, past the age of fantasy. Her courses trained her to look at pictures critically, to analyze techniques, recognize periods and schools, not to walk through the canvas, into the world of the subject.

Look at me, won't you? Rennie pleaded. I'm your namesake. I'm alive!

But Serenity showed no interest.

The wall space beside the portrait was bare. Very soon, though, Rennie herself would be looking down from this very spot. The thought made her tingle. *Her* portrait would answer when she talked to it, if she ever came back to Firbank after it was hung. Only, Rennie didn't care about that. Her great-grandmother — that's whom she wanted to make friends with. Wasn't it ridiculous that the woman, responding merrily to the inanimate child or dog at her feet, paid no attention to Rennie?

Look at me! Say something, *please!*

It was no use.

After lunch, while Daphne rested, Oliver brought the drawing board and a box of pastel crayons into the living room. Rennie had expected to pose for Daphne in the woodshed. (In her opinion, it should have been called the studio.) But Oliver explained, as she followed him into the living room, that the afternoon light was better here. He turned the back of Daphne's chair to one of the bay windows and, facing it, the little captain's chair for Rennie. Then he moved away a few steps to survey his arrangement.

"Heather sent those from England," he said, noticing Rennie's interest in Daphne's rainbow crayons. "Thee sees, they're square — easier to grip than her old, round ones."

Rennie nodded. What changes in routine this illness demanded!

"I'm going to put on my skirt," she told Oliver. Maybe she ought to ask where he kept the iron. Those pleats were a mess.

"No need to," he murmured, glancing at Rennie as though he were noticing for the first time what she had on. "The blouse thee's wearing is a lovely color and the shorts just suit thee. This picture isn't going on the society page of the *Kendal Sun*," he assured her, laughing. "Daphne wants thee to feel comfortable — be thyself." He adjusted the position of the little chair until it satisfied him. "She'd like thee to talk to her while she's drawing."

"*Me?*"

Rennie was already nervous. If she had to hold a conversation with a dumb woman, too ——

"Oliver, what about?"

Was Daphne going to pry, like those clearness women?

"Peter. Daphne wants to hear about him."

That was okay. Rennie wouldn't mind talking about Peter. She could go on about him all day.

"Daphne says, ever since thee came, I've monopolized the conversation. She insists thee hasn't had a chance to tell us anything about thyself or about Peter." Oliver grinned sheepishly, as though he were apologizing.

"You'll be here, won't you?" Rennie cried. "You're not going anywhere?"

If he left, it would be like this morning, when Daphne looked so disappointed because Rennie didn't understand what she was trying to tell her.

He seemed to sense her fear, for he said very gently, "Those men are waiting for me down in the Forest."

"But how am I to know ——? How do *you* know what Daphne's saying? Can you really tell?"

A second ago, Oliver was laughing at himself in that endearing way he had. Now, his whole expression changed. He turned to the window and gazed out. "How can I tell?" He was silent a moment. Then he said, "We've loved each other, rejoiced together, endured pain, worked and worshiped together for well over fifty years. How can I help knowing what Daphne wants to say? And it's very important to listen to her, to make her believe — truly believe — that she's still the person she was before the stroke. For a long time, although she was improving physically, she appeared to have become somebody else. The wonderful companion I'd known since she was nineteen seemed to have died. Another, less lovely, had taken her place."

The sting of held-back tears suddenly bothered Rennie's eyes. To have the person you were married to change overnight, to go on loving that person, contending not only for her body, but for her whole personality —— As Oliver spoke, Rennie had the queer feeling that she was inside his pain, so shattered by it that tears seemed frivolous. She hadn't grasped the core of this pain before, terrible though it appeared on the surface.

"Illness is devastating," he was saying, "because it erects a barrier between the patient and the rest of the world, even those who care most. It requires that one concentrate on one's body instead of on other people's needs. For someone like Daphne, who'd been concerned with others all her life, this had a diminishing effect. She felt unworthy because the functioning of her limbs and speech became the focal point of her attention. Contempt for this preoccupation with her own person depressed her. Fortunately, I was always able to reach her innermost self and hold on to it tightly till she emerged from those shadows."

"It's so cruel!" Rennie cried. "I mean — losing her speech and not being able to write what she wants to say, either. Why did it have to be her right hand, too? It isn't fair!"

And this man talked about God.

"It does seem overmuch," Oliver agreed. "But that's the way the nervous system is hooked up, crossing the body. When the right side's paralyzed, the speech center, in the left part of the brain, is affected. At the time, I realized that the most important thing was to get Daphne painting again. As soon as her strength came back, we started training her left hand. Just holding the brush was agony. Getting those muscles used to a new job took infinite patience. Sometimes it seemed all we had to work with was faith. We did have that. Also, we had so much support from Heather and our friends that I often wondered, Did we have to have this affliction in order to discover the depth of their love? Well," he said, turning to Rennie with an expression that was suddenly radiant, "all that's past now. Only the love that sustained us remains." He started toward the door. "Wait here, Serenity. I'm going to get Daphne. If she doesn't begin soon, there won't be light enough to finish."

Evidently struck by another thought, Oliver came back and placed both hands on Rennie's shoulders. "Thy coming has meant a great deal to us," he said, looking into her eyes and smiling affectionately. "Thee knows, Heather's our only child and she lives in England. Married a Yorkshireman, Stephen Thirsk, the son of Daphne's classmate at the Academy of Design. Stephen came here to study engineering in Cambridge and took our Heather back with him. We find it hard, living so far apart. When Daphne was stricken, Heather flew over and nursed her until we'd passed the worst. Then she went home. Her family always spends the summer with us. They'll be here July first. We can't wait."

It wasn't the moment, but Rennie suddenly remembered what she'd wanted to ask earlier. "Oliver, that thing you wrote in the note — what does it mean, the sun's a star, or something?"

He let go of Rennie and stepped back. "The sun is but a morning star? Those are the last words in *Walden*."

"Oh! *Walden* — I read that, freshman year."

Rennie recalled very little, except that the man who wrote it — Thoreau — built a shack on Walden Pond and made pencils. She'd gone through the whole book the night before a quiz, swiftly running her eye down the center of each page, reading the first and last sentences of paragraphs, the way she'd been taught to study. If those were the last words in the book, she must have read them. But she didn't remember.

"When I was a boy, ten or eleven," Oliver was saying, his face lighting, "my father and I spent a week following after Thoreau, along the Concord and Merrimack rivers. It was beautiful. Those rivers weren't quite so polluted then. This is the anniversary of Thoreau's death — May sixth. That's what made us think of *Walden*, when we woke up and looked at the calendar. Thoreau died young, but what he wrote went right on living. Now, more than a century later, those glorious words are still vital. *Only that day dawns to which we are awake. There is more day to dawn. The sun is but a morning star.*"

Rennie wasn't sure what it was all about, but the enthusiasm in Oliver's voice was so vibrant that she felt herself sharing it without understanding why.

"There's another reason Daphne and I thought about those words early this morning," Oliver said, a little reluctantly, as if admitting something he hadn't intended to say. "They express the way we see thee — more poised for flowering than thee thyself has any idea of." Flashing another smile in Rennie's direction, he left the room.

9.

Stunned, Rennie tried to figure out what Oliver meant. All she could really be sure of was that, in some strange way, these people, whom she hadn't even known yesterday morning, were beginning to love her as she'd never been loved — not on account of what she was, but for what they believed she was going to be. Even Peter didn't think of her in the future.

How close she'd come to leaving! If Oliver only knew. She was terribly glad he didn't. It would really hurt him and Daphne. That her coming meant anything to them had never occurred to Rennie, or she probably would have been willing to stick it out, regardless. Why had she wanted to leave, anyhow, when everything here was so fascinating? Just because a Quaker marriage was out? Because Heather's bed gave her nightmares? Could a bed?

It struck her that when she asked Oliver how he understood what Daphne was trying to say, he described that total thing Peter claimed he wanted with Rennie, except that, once the wedding arrangements were settled, there was no reason why they should ever again have to endure pain until they were very old and one of them might be sick. As for worshiping — that wasn't for Peter and her, either. But they'd love, rejoice and work together — take turns cooking and washing the dishes.

Daphne was wearing the violet smock when she came into the living room on Oliver's arm, proceeding slowly, with a kind of majesty, in spite of the fact that her right leg swung sideways at every step instead of striding forward. Her beautiful hair was freshly combed. Until then, it hadn't dawned on Rennie that, of course, it had to be Oliver who did it for her.

"Thee sees, Serenity," he said, perhaps to distract her attention from their painfully slow progress, "this is how we walked into the meetinghouse at York, the day we were married — arm in arm. Nowadays, everything's less formal and couples are apt to come in hand in hand. It makes no difference."

Daphne turned and smiled at him. The way her large, gray eyes shone, she didn't need speech.

Rennie thought, I bet that's how she looked at him that day. All these years! Why can't Peter and I ——?

She could see the moment Daphne was settled in her chair how excited she was about doing the portrait. Her cheeks were pink and there was elation in the way she twisted the paper till she had it placed on the drawing board at an angle that pleased her. Oliver fastened the corners with thumb tacks. Thoughtfully Daphne chose her crayons, looked at them, put some back, chose others.

Rennie, sitting down on the little chair, was glad to discover that she had a view of the side lawn through the bay window. She'd have something to focus on during the long, boring hours. Then, looking at the room again, she saw how different everything appeared from this low perch. It was as if she were a child, sitting at Daphne's feet. Her eyes were only just level with the drawing board and Daphne's face was foreshortened, quite different, almost normal.

Turning her head, Rennie had a scare. Oliver was already leaving.

"Be sure to remember everything Serenity tells thee, dear one," he called in from the entrance hall, "so thee can tell me later. I want to hear about Peter, too." He opened the door. Then he was gone.

Forcing herself to do her part, fixing her attention on the lawn outside, Rennie took a deep breath. "His whole name," she began "is Peter Hallburt Holland. He comes from a little town in eastern Ohio — Charlesbury. It's about as opposite as you can get to Neville, where I live — suburban New York and sophisticated. You know? We're not rich, just — we don't have to think about money. But the Hollands —— Charlesbury isn't country like this, either, just small town, very conservative. Most people still go to church. So when Peter first got to college, he had sort of an identity crisis — he had to decide where he stood on a lot of issues — with the folks back home, whom he'd respected all his life, or with the kids at college, who were rebelling. Our eyes were opened fast, freshman year."

Rennie stopped and glanced at Daphne, wondering whether, in her condition, at her age, back here in Firbank, she had any idea what Rennie was talking about, how different their lifestyles were.

"For me," she went on, looking down at her own curled-up fingers and studying them intently while she spoke, as though she'd never seen them before, "coming from Neville, it wasn't so much of a shock. But it threw Peter. He almost quit college. Both his parents are school teachers. They'd been so proud of Peter getting into Tilbury. It's a good little college, even if it isn't Ivy. They'd made a big investment in him. There isn't much money and they have two other kids to educate. They kept reminding Peter how, ever since he was a little boy, he'd wanted to be an astronomer. How could he just drop out? I guess it was all pretty traumatic. That was before I knew him and he's never told me much about it. By the time we met, beginning of junior year, Peter had things under control, even made Dean's List last term, and those astrophysics courses are hard. Then, when his parents objected to our getting married, he flunked his math exam. But he's done well again since his parents backed down. Only thing, he can't go to grad school, unless I get a job."

Doing what? Rennie wished she knew. What was there she could do? With the teacher shortage there used to be, she thought she had it made, majoring in education. Then appropriations were cut back. Many of last year's graduates hadn't even found jobs.

"Now Peter's worried about *me* finding *my* identity," Rennie confided, glancing at Daphne to see whether she understood. But Daphne was concentrating on the picture, studying Rennie for a moment, then glancing down at the drawing to sketch in a line. "It was Daddy's idea that I major in education. As a matter of fact, I was interested in art. Not like you; I can't draw a straight line. But art history. After taking that survey course freshman year, I was so excited about the Impressionists, I thought it would be fun going to museums, traveling — all that. But Daddy wouldn't let me. I think he felt this thing I have about pictures is childish — sort of going off into a dream world — that I'd get over it when I grew up. He said art history wasn't practical — what could I do with it? Teacher training would give me something to fall back on. I was mad at the time. Why should Daddy decide on *my* lifework? Then again, he's the one who's paying for my education, so I guess he has the right to decide. But this morning, when I was watching you paint, I felt gypped again."

Rennie looked at Daphne, wondering whether she was listening. She didn't appear to hear a single word.

"What Peter's most worried about is getting a job for this summer. I wish he'd settle that so he could put his mind on the wedding. There's this service station in Charlesbury. The man who runs it thought he could use Peter, but then it turned out he had to lay off some of his help. Peter didn't really want to spend the summer fussing with cars. Still, he'd have been glad to get anything. A lot of kids are having trouble this year."

Rennie had the feeling that she was just talking to herself. It didn't matter what she said — Daphne was so absorbed in her work.

"It was funny, how we met," Rennie went on, staring out the window again, but visualizing the scene so vividly that she giggled. "We were in the cafeteria at college. I was carrying my tray full of dinner to a table in the far corner of the room, where these girls from my dorm were sitting. None of us had a man then. That's why we ate together. Well, somebody had spilled pea soup on the floor, and I had my eyes on the tray, so I didn't see it. Wowee! I slid right across the room, tray and all. But instead of falling flat on my face, like I felt I was going to do, I landed in this strange guy's arms. We'd never seen each other before. He just happened to be sitting there and he caught me. The whole cafeteria clapped. Then the guys whistled and made those noises — you know, wolf calls. Peter was embarrassed. I guess he thought the way to cover up his embarrassment was to do something smart, so he kissed me in front of the whole student body. I was in his arms, anyway. He was full of the devil in those days," Rennie added wistfully. "Now he's turned awfully serious."

Daphne was looking at her. Was it because Daphne was interested in the story or was she so intent on studying Rennie's features, striving for a likeness, that she hadn't heard a word? She just stared, then looked down at the drawing board and made some strokes on the paper.

Did she really see through Rennie to that person Rennie was going to be? Daphne had captured the character of Serenity Otis, giving her a kind of immortality. Was she doing the same thing now? What would it be like, this portrait? How much of Rennie's secret self would show? She wasn't so sure that she liked having her portrait painted, after all. A snapshot might catch you at a bad moment, when your hair was a mess or you were squinting in the sun, but it didn't give away how your self looked inside, like this.

"I never did get to eat with those girls," Rennie concluded, trying to keep her mind from wandering. It was hard, sitting still so long.

Daphne was staring at her again, but, this time, Rennie was sure she was following the story. What happened next? the large gray eyes asked plainly. Rennie was having no trouble understanding Daphne now. What happened next?

Why had Rennie started to tell this? She certainly couldn't go on.

Daphne opened her mouth. What happened next? her eyes repeated.

We went to his room, Rennie answered, not out loud, just to herself.

But Daphne was staring at her intently. Rennie's heart started to pound. She couldn't sit here another minute. She had to get up, run outdoors. Too bad about the portrait — she was already running, running as fast as she could from Daphne's large eyes, even though her muscles wouldn't move. She had gripped the arms of the little captain's chair and she couldn't let go. She leaned forward tensely, but her fingers clutched the wooden arms more and more tightly. Her cheeks burned. The tears that unexpectedly started spilling over them weren't cooling. They burned, too.

Daphne turned her eyes from Rennie and dropped the crayon she was holding into its box. She slammed down the lid. Without looking at Rennie again, she took hold of a rag and rubbed her fingers on it. Her face was white.

"No," Rennie screamed suddenly. "I'm not going to tell you." She didn't just think the words, didn't just say them, she screamed them at the top of her voice. "As long as nobody got hurt——"
This was one of those nightmares, when she kept calling for help.

Daphne's head fell back against the chair. Her eyes were shut.

Trembling, Rennie jumped up. Had she given Daphne another

stroke? She stood looking at the motionless figure, the grotesque, white face. With the eyes closed, it had no life. What should Rennie do?

She didn't notice Oliver rush into the room until, pushing her aside, he took hold of Daphne's good hand.

"Dear one," he said calmly, yet his voice confirmed Rennie's anxiety.

Daphne opened her eyes and smiled. She was still white.

"Thee's done too much for one day," Oliver told her, sounding relieved. "It's tired thee. Come." He drew her slowly to her feet, glancing over his shoulder to reassure Rennie. "Supper's nearly ready," he said. "I was just putting the kettle on." He helped Daphne across the room. "Thee'll have a tray, all cozy in bed."

Terribly shaken, Rennie watched them leave. Each step seemed to take them an eternity. As they reached the entrance hall, Daphne stood still and looked back. She detached her arm from Oliver's and held it out toward Rennie.

What did she want?

"Please come, Serenity," Oliver said, smiling for the first time since he'd entered the room. "Daphne would like to tell thee something."

What? Trying not to sniff, Rennie went toward her.

The elation Daphne had expressed when she started the portrait glowed in her again. She reached out and, drawing Rennie to her, gave her a kiss. Then she took Oliver's arm and walked slowly toward the stairs.

10.

During the night, it rained. Waking in bright sunshine and running to the window, Rennie was surprised to find that the leaves were sparkling. She must have slept so soundly that she never heard the downpour. Now, the air was clear, promising a day of opening buds, but it was still early. Rennie shivered. Pulling Heather's quilt around her bare self, she knelt by the window and rested her folded arms on the sill, trying to imprint the view on her memory.

It didn't register. She was thinking of the portrait — how, when Daphne and Oliver started their journey upstairs late yesterday afternoon, she ran back to the drawing board, so impatient to see her picture that she fumbled with the switch before she lit the standing lamp. Then she stopped in her tracks, not daring to look. Those troubled feelings that had surprised her by breaking out — mightn't they show, give her away? Torn between fear and curiosity, Rennie finally forced herself to face the portrait.

At first, she couldn't take it in. There she was, exactly the way she thought she looked, in the aqua turtleneck and tan shorts, sitting on the little chair, staring out the window. The shape of her features and her coloring were absolutely true to life. And there was a simplicity about the whole thing, an economy of line, an ambience, as if she belonged to the room. But the eyes — minutes went by before Rennie grasped what they conveyed. Then she was dashed. They were blue enough; it was their expression that shattered her. She'd been braced to find them clouded by conflict. It was much worse! They were neutral, devoid of emotion, empty. Did she look like that?

Am I like that? Am I really?

Hearing Oliver come downstairs, Rennie had run out to the hall and asked anxiously, "Is Daphne sick?"

"Just tired. A night's rest will restore her. She went right to sleep."

"What happened?"

"She says thee ran away."

"I didn't! I wanted to, but I stayed right there, on the little chair."

"Thy body did. That was no use to Daphne, who was trying to paint thy spirit. It had fled. She said it wearied her, looking at an empty body, so she just closed her eyes." As Rennie followed him into the kitchen, Oliver exclaimed, "I'm so relieved! When I heard thy cry —— It's good thee called and that I was here. I hadn't been in long."

Although Rennie couldn't get herself to admit that she'd simply lost her cool, she did try to tell Oliver she hadn't called him. Taking the casserole out of the oven, he had merely murmured offhandedly, "Oh? I thought thee did."

He knew very well, Rennie told Salt Pond now. He was only trying to make me comfortable, like Daphne when she kissed me. Or had Rennie really screamed, the way she was always trying to do in those nightmares? Oliver didn't fake.

While they were eating supper, she'd asked him how he and Daphne met.

During an air raid in Paris, he'd told her, toward the end of the First World War. "In the midst of bombs and flying debris, I spied her uniform, which was like mine — gray, with the red-and-black Quaker service star on the brassard. We were both in the Mish, thee knows — the Anglo-American Friends Mission." He had gone on to explain that Daphne happened to be in Paris, on leave from her volunteer job at the hospital in the Marne Valley. He himself, after being court-martialed at home and confined to barracks for refusing to bear arms, had finally been allowed to sail to France, where he'd helped to rebuild houses and restore the vegetation. "In the Verdun area alone, we planted twenty-five thousand trees, mostly fruit."

Trees, Rennie thought. All he ever does is plant trees on account of wars. I wish Larry knew him. Oliver'd understand Larry, instead of fighting him, like Daddy.

After supper, Oliver had taken Rennie into the woodshed and had shown her some portfolios of Daphne's drawings and paintings, beginning with the botanical plates she'd made as an art student, then examples of what he called her "unfolding period" and finally the mature work, done in her free, unique style.

"When she recovered enough to start painting again, she was helped by her memory of Auguste Renoir," Oliver explained to Rennie.

"Daphne *knew* Renoir?"

"Yes."

What an experience! It didn't seem possible that anyone now living ——

"Until her illness, our life together had been influenced by someone very different — John Woolman, the Quaker farmer from Mount Holly, New Jersey, who went about the American Colonies in the Eighteenth Century, appealing to slaveholders to realize their humanity. Daphne and I literally followed after him, walking the roads he walked. But when she was recovering from her stroke, it was Renoir who inspired her. In his last years, he was so crippled by arthritis that he couldn't use his right hand. Yet, in this period, he painted some of his finest canvases."

"I know! *The Bathers.*"

Oliver had glanced at Rennie approvingly, evidently pleased to find that she was up on Renoir. "After the Armistice, Daphne went to see him. By that time, she had been transferred to Savoy, near the Swiss border, where another Quaker team was helping to repatriate prisoners — undernourished Frenchmen going home to die, many of them on stretchers, or insane. It was a satisfaction to Daphne to give them a little comfort as their convoy passed through — a bowl of soup extended with that smile of hers, the unaccustomed solace of a kind word. But it was such heartbreaking work that every night she had to draw to preserve her equilibrium. Those charcoal sketches to the left of the couch in the living room — has thee noticed them?"

Rennie nodded. She didn't want to admit that she'd rushed past quickly.

"Horrible, aren't they? Those were the types Daphne saw in the convoys. It still hurts me to look at them."

"Me too."

"What makes those pictures so terrifying is that they're not the faces of Frenchmen or any other nationals. They have no ethnic characteristics, only the mark of suffering common to prisoners, whether they've been captured in war or by a society that drives certain people to lawlessness, or whether they're victims of their own phantoms. Daphne revealed something through those agonized faces that's in many of us. So we find them unbearable."

I thought they just stirred pity in me, Rennie said to herself. Was I scared, too?

"As soon as Daphne had a few days off, she went to the south of France to see Renoir. He was seventy-eight and only able to paint with his left hand. It was emaciated, so tender that it had to be bandaged before he could hold a brush. Yet, his spirit overcame everything. The day he died, he said he was just beginning to understand how to paint! I shouldn't wonder," Oliver had added thoughtfully, "if this may not turn out to be Daphne's finest period, too. Thy portrait will probably rate as one of her very significant works."

My portrait! With those eyes?

Rennie shivered. Kneeling by the window, remembering last night, she had been so absorbed that she didn't notice the quilt slip off her shoulders. Gathering it around her again, she wondered whether she'd been too fresh when she asked Oliver why he'd chosen farming instead of a more prestigious career. He didn't answer immediately.

Collecting some drawings he'd been showing to Rennie, returning them to their portfolio, tying the faded red tapes that held the covers together, Oliver said finally, "Daphne and I made a pilgrimage. It was a couple of months after we were married."

"A pilgrimage?" In this day and age!

"Yes. All we thought we were doing was traveling south in Grandmother's Model T. It turned out to be a great deal more." The recollection drained expression from Oliver's face, as if he'd left the scene for the past. Then he smiled at Rennie, aware of her presence again. Putting the portfolio down on the drawing board, he leaned back in his chair, curving his fingers around the arms. "Because of the war, I'd been obliged to leave college in my junior year. After I got back from France, I returned to Harvard and graduated with the class of Nineteen Twenty, hoping to go into publishing. But conscientious objectors weren't getting the best jobs. Many employers felt they weren't deserving."

"How unfair!"

Oliver nodded. "It was September before I finally landed something — publicity work in the promotion department of a jewelry firm. Thee can imagine that, with my bringing up, of all the jobs I might have found, this one — to encourage ostentation — was the least appropriate. But it paid well. If I did a large volume of business, I'd earn a commission. The job wasn't to start till the first of the year, so, in high spirits, I left for England and married Daphne. A few weeks later, we came to Firbank. Grandmother had invited us to stay till we got a home of our own. I dreamed of our home — the fine studio Daphne'd have and the room where I'd write. I was completing the first draft of my novel." The recollection made Oliver look a little sad.

But Rennie was elated. A novel. He'd written a novel! Wait till I tell Daddy, she thought. That "flair for writing" he belittled didn't peter out.

Oliver had turned to the window, though nothing was visible out there, in the dark. "Daphne and I were deeply happy together," he murmured, "and yet we were troubled, too. We'd seen such suffering during the war that we wondered whether we had a right to be so happy."

That Daphne and Oliver could ever have been uptight was inconceivable to Rennie.

"We were anxious about our future, too," he had added, facing her again. "We believed in ourselves and each other, but we still had to prove our worth. One isn't accepted as an artist till one's had shows. One isn't an author till one's published. Daphne wouldn't find it easy to make her way in American art circles. And how was I going to finish my book, once I became a businessman?"

"You were lucky! You had a job. Peter ——"

Oliver didn't seem to hear Rennie. "Daphne had a cough she couldn't shake. At the end of October, Grandmother urged us to go south for a few weeks. She offered to lend us her car. When we packed the paint box, the typewriter and the binoculars, we never guessed we were setting out on a voyage of discovery. But Grandmother may have hoped so, for she suggested we stop at the Woolman House in Mount Holly when we got to New Jersey. 'Who knows?' she murmured as we said good-by. 'This may prove to be a pilgrimage.' I was wondering what she could possibly mean when she added, 'A pilgrimage leads back to the place from which the traveler started, doesn't it? And yet, the person who returns isn't quite the same as the one who left.' Daphne and I weren't. When we came back six weeks later, we'd made a decision that changed everything. We've never regretted it."

A pilgrimage! Rennie said to herself again.

"We went to Mount Holly and stayed at the house John Woolman built for his daughter when she married, shortly before the Revolution. We thought of it merely as a charming and inexpensive place to spend the night. But the next morning, when we woke up in our snug room under the eaves, I did something seemingly unimportant that was to alter our lives. Wedged between the high brass bedstead and the big central chimney was an old-fashioned bookcase. I opened the glass doors. Inside were early editions of Woolman's works. I'd never read his Journal. Daphne hadn't even heard of him. I reached out for a volume, only to glance through it."

Picturing the little room, Rennie could just see Oliver leaning out of bed, reaching for the book, while Daphne snuggled beside him.

"Opening the Journal, I read the first sentence aloud: *I have often felt a motion of love to leave some hints in writing of my experience of the goodness of God and now, in the thirty-sixth year of my age, I begin this work.*"

Oliver had paused, studying Rennie's face, as if to determine whether she grasped the tremendous significance of these words. "Thee sees," he spelled out, "in the very house Woolman built for his own newly married children, he was talking to Daphne and me about the goodness of God — talking to us, who'd seen so much evil during the war that we couldn't quite believe in that goodness."

Now, kneeling at the window, seeing the pond sparkle in morning sunshine, Rennie remembered how she'd tried to look attentive last night, while Oliver spoke about the goodness of God. All she'd really been thinking about, though, was Oliver in that brass bedstead, leaning against the pillows, reading, with Daphne lying in the crook of his arm. He would have had all his hair still — that bright red fuzz, like Rennie's — what he called the Otis hair. And Daphne —— But Rennie couldn't picture her.

"Wait," Oliver had told Rennie, getting to his feet. "I want to show thee something." He went to his study.

That's how it'll be for Peter and me once the wedding's over, Rennie had thought, still visualizing the couple in bed. We'll be relaxed and happy.

Oliver came back with a book that was bound in worn leather, splitting along the spine. Opening it carefully, he held it out to Rennie. *The Works of John Woolman*, she read, taking the book. At the bottom of the title page was a date: 1775.

"Wow!" Rennie had exclaimed. A real antique, a treasure! Two hundred years old.

"That's the house in Mount Holly," Oliver told her as she glanced at the frontispiece. His next words made her look with greater interest. "Daphne painted it that morning. When we got back, she gave the little water color to Grandmother, who pasted it into her copy of Woolman, the one she'd had since she was a girl. Second edition." He caressed the book. "Not many around any more."

It *was* a treasure! Rennie had studied the picture — a plain house of weathered rose brick with a wide porch, a well sweep, trees at each corner, all enveloped in beckoning radiance. This wasn't just an old farmhouse. It was the record of Daphne's mood that day. Closing the book reverently, Rennie handed it back.

"What attracted us," Oliver told her, running his fingers lovingly over the worn leather, "were Woolman's simplicity and humility. And he had compassion, not only for the oppressed, but for young people, whom he considered to be victims of the economic system."

"So are we!" Rennie had cried. "Don't you think so?" But then she asked herself honestly, Where would I be without Daddy's credit cards?

"In Woolman's day," Oliver had reminded her gravely, "the system included slavery. While he was still in his twenties, apprenticed in a shop, he declared his stand against it. His boss expected him to wait on customers and draw up legal documents, but not to have opinions. One day, Woolman was asked to write a bill of sale for a black woman. He refused. What courage! He soon left the job and didn't take another. As he gave his reasons, he seemed to be speaking to me, urging me to consider my future."

Opening the book again, Oliver read, *"I had several offers of business that appeared profitable, but did not see my way clear to accept of them; as believing the business proposed would be attended with more outward care and cumber than was required of me to engage in. I saw that where the heart was set on greatness, success in business did not satisfy the craving, but that commonly with an increase of wealth, the desire of wealth increased."* Oliver looked up from the book. "This, I thought, didn't apply to me," he told Rennie. "All I wanted was to support Daphne. Then why did the words jolt me?"

"What was wrong with your wanting to make a decent living?" Rennie had cried, rushing to defend Oliver against that old Woolman.

"Was my heart set on greatness? Woolman had overtaken me at a moment when I wanted to be left alone. *Things that served chiefly to please the vain mind in people,* he wrote, *I was not easy to trade in.* Neither am I, I realized suddenly, squirming so that Daphne looked at me in alarm. Not wishing to worry her, I read on. The farther I went, the worse I felt."

"You should have told Daphne!"

Turning pages, Oliver didn't seem to hear. *"The increase of business became my burthen,"* he read on. *"For though my natural inclination was toward merchandize, yet I believed truth required me to live more free from outward cumbers; and there was now a strife in my mind between the two."* Oliver looked at Rennie again. "So Woolman gave up shopkeeping and farmed, doing some tailoring, too. He says, *I believed the hand of Providence pointed out this business for me; and was taught to be content with it, though I felt, at times, a disposition that would have sought for something greater.*"

As Oliver relived that morning in Mount Holly, his eyes showed how far he was looking into the past. "Unable to bear any more," he recalled, "I said to Daphne, 'Let's have breakfast.' When I put that volume back, my hand was shaking."

Rennie pictured them jumping out of bed. What was the matter with Daphne? She should have seen that Oliver was upset.

"I didn't yet know how tenacious Woolman could be," he had told Rennie. "Downstairs, on a table in the room with the corner fireplace, were modern reprints of his Journal and Essays. A card announced they were for sale. I put down the money and slipped our first copy of Woolman into the knapsack. After breakfast, we sat in the flower garden. It was a beautiful, sunny day. While Daphne painted this little picture of the house, I read her Woolman's account of his first southern journey. There was nothing disturbing about it. He simply appealed to the planters to realize their humanity; to consider what slavery was doing to their children — whether it mightn't lead to war. Daphne and I were deeply concerned about racial justice, too. We turned to each other suddenly and, being of one mind, said at the same moment, 'Let's follow him.' We consulted the *Journal* for his route. Even then, we weren't aware of what was happening to us. But that was the beginning of our pilgrimage."

Recalling the events of last night, Rennie had forgotten about the time. The grandfather clock in the entrance hall informed her softly that it was eight. Oliver had asked her to be down by then. She sighed as she tore herself away from the window and, flinging the quilt onto Heather's bed, began to dress.

While she combed her hair, she studied the face in the mirror, wondering what reflection Heather had seen when she stood here and went through the same motions.

Above the Franklin stove in Daphne and Oliver's room, there was a full-length portrait, which Rennie had stopped to study yesterday as she looked in from the landing on her way downstairs. She knew it was Heather's on account of the hair, which was the color of her own but not so fuzzy. Heather must have been about Rennie's age at the time, tall, skinny, very serious.

What was she like inside then? A mess, too? No, not with parents like that. Rennie envied her. She tried to picture Heather's face in the mirror, but all she saw were her own eyes. Were they really empty of emotion, the way Daphne'd painted them?

If, Rennie told herself, slowly going downstairs, her portrait really rated as one of Daphne's significant works, then the empty eyes reflected accurately how she looked. Utterly depressed by this thought, she simply couldn't face Oliver and Daphne. Why not just sneak out of the house and thumb a ride to Hillsgrove?

11.

They were waiting for her at the kitchen table. Daphne looked better. Color was back in her cheeks. She was wearing a soft blue shift, which brought out the beauty of her hair, and a fascinating necklace of real acorns, split and mounted in gold, linked together by tiny gold oak leaves. Oliver had on a white shirt, complete with tie. The food before them was untouched.

Rennie'd never considered breakfast a regular meal, which people enjoyed together, only a foggy, solitary time for coming to, over coffee. So she was surprised that they took her hands again and bowed their heads. But this unfamiliar interlude, the momentary suspension of activity, the touch of their hands eased Rennie. Maybe, in daylight, the portrait wasn't all that bad. After breakfast, would she have the courage to sneak into the living room and look at it again?

When they'd finished eating, Oliver carried the dishes to the sink. Rennie jumped up, but he asked her to remain at the table. From the shelf above the hutch, filled with what Rennie had assumed were all cookbooks, he took a heavy, antique Bible and a small book with a faded cover.

"First Days," he explained, "we always read before washing up." Sitting down again, he opened the Bible to a section devoted to names and dates, written by different hands, mostly in old-fashioned script. For over a century, he said, the births and deaths of every member of the family had been recorded. Turning the pages until he found a name he seemed to be looking for, he pointed it out to Rennie. With a start, she saw it was hers, followed by her birthday.

"How did you know?" she cried. "Daddy said we were out of touch. He wasn't even sure you were still alive."

Oliver grinned wryly. "If it had been otherwise, thy father would have visited Firbank again. He never misses any of our funerals."

Why does he come then, of all times? Rennie wondered.

"We tried to get both thy parents to join us on several happier occasions, such as Heather's wedding and Aunt Temperance's ninetieth birthday. She was the last of that generation. But thy parents were always engaged. I can't recall how we heard about thy arrival." Oliver turned to Daphne. "Does thee, dear one?"

Rennie glanced at Daphne swiftly, curious to see how she was going to answer. For a second, there was no sign of response.

Dear one, Rennie repeated to herself. It isn't sugary. It has dignity.

Daphne reached across the table to the bulky Bible. She ran her left forefinger down the page on which Rennie's birth was registered. Near the bottom, the finger stopped and indicated a name: *Temperance Mary Millburn, January 6, 1865–November 29, 1954.* This had been inscribed with a flourish, in the style of Lincoln's time, all but the date of death, which was added in a small, contemporary hand, probably Oliver's.

"That's right," he exclaimed. "I remember now. When Ed came for Aunt Temperance's funeral, he told us about the new baby." Giving Rennie an affectionate nod, Oliver added, "That was thee."

I was only two months old, Rennie figured, the last time Daddy saw Firbank, and he was in a rush that day. If it had been me, spending summers here when I was a kid, I'd have wanted to bring my own kids sometimes.

Oliver was turning the pages of the Bible till he came to a frayed ribbon. "This," he announced, settling back in his chair, "is from the Book of Proverbs. We read the beginning of the chapter last week. *Attend to my words; incline thine ear to my sayings. Let them not depart from thine eyes; keep them in the midst of thine heart. For they are life unto those that find them, and health to all their flesh. Keep thy heart with all diligence; for out of it are the issues of life.*"

Judging by Oliver's voice, one would have thought he was much younger. He read slowly, enunciating each word as though he were listening to it and enjoying the sonority. At the cadences, he paused and looked off into space.

To Rennie, the whole thing was a riddle. *Keep thy heart with all diligence.* What did it mean?

Oliver had closed the Bible. He was leafing through the book. It didn't look recent. Still, maybe it would be easier to understand. Rennie leaned forward and twisted her neck to read the title: *Letters of Early Friends.* No, she probably wouldn't catch on to it, either.

"This," Oliver said, when he found the page he was looking for, "was written in Sixteen Sixty by one of the first Friends. He was describing their mode of worship, which has come down to us essentially unchanged. It was so revolutionary, so different from that of the established church, rejecting ritual, clergy and consecrated buildings, that the English became alarmed and imprisoned Friends. Thousands died in those filthy Seventeenth Century jails."

"Why didn't they simply come to America, where there was freedom of worship — like the Pilgrims and Puritans?" Rennie broke in. "That would have made more sense than dying."

Oliver looked at her strangely, with a gesture of impatience, as if he really thought Rennie didn't know what she was talking about.

"The freedom of worship the Pilgrims and Puritans found in the New World, Serenity, they denied to any who disagreed with them. In Connecticut, Quakers were branded. In Boston, they had their ears cut off. Four were hanged on the Common. Of all the colonies, only Rhode Island practiced religious toleration. That's why our ancestors settled here."

Rennie'd always felt, even if she knew it wasn't factually true, that, really, the world just began in the Nineteen Fifties — events of significance to her, at any rate. With the exception of the Impressionists — before man's conquest of space, women's lib, the Pill — what was there? Now Oliver was talking about people who lived three hundred years ago, people Rennie was vaguely connected with, who'd had hair-raising experiences. It gave everything another twist.

"I'm choosing this passage to read today," Oliver was saying, "so that, when we go to meeting, thee'll understand a little about the silence and thee'll feel at home in it."

Meeting! This hadn't occurred to Rennie when she decided impulsively to come to Firbank — that Friends meeting would be part of the deal, though she should have known. If she'd thought of it, she'd have been scared off and probably wouldn't have come.

"The first that enters into the place of your meeting," Oliver read from the book, *"turn thy mind to the light, and wait upon God singly, as if none were present but the Lord; and here thou art strong. Then the next that come in, let them, in simplicity of heart, sit down and turn in to the same light and wait in the spirit; and so all the rest coming in, sit down in pure stillness and silence of all flesh. Those who are brought to a pure, still waiting upon God in the spirit are come nearer than words are."* Keeping his finger on the place, Oliver looked up from the book for a few moments, as if to savor what he had read. Then he continued. *"In such a meeting, there will be an unwillingness to part asunder, being ready to say in yourselves, It is good to be here."*

Listening to Oliver read in the sunny kitchen, Rennie felt deeply moved. Not that the words meant much to her. Simple English though this was, it might have been a foreign language, so far as her understanding went. The words spoke of experiences Rennie had never had. It was the poetic style, the rhythm, Oliver's calm, precise voice that moved her, not, she thought, the substance of the passage.

Oliver closed the book and laid it on top of the Bible. He sat quietly for some time, looking out at the tulip bed under the window. Rennie wondered whether he saw the flowers or whether he was turning his mind to the light. *Simplicity of heart,* she thought. That's what he has. I can see why Daphne left Yorkshire for him. How does one get that way? All those how-to books about having sex — there ought to be some manuals about having simplicity of heart.

Daphne seemed to be moved, too. She sat very still. In repose, her face was less distorted than when it was trying to express something and frustration smoldered in her eyes. Oliver was right — Daphne was still beautiful in spirit. It shone in her face now.

Finally, Oliver pushed back his chair and went to the shelf to replace the books. Then he helped Daphne to her feet. Taking his arm, she walked with him into the woodshed, followed by the dogs. Her right leg swung sideways, as if it were loose at the hip.

Watching them until they were out of sight, Rennie thought, *Valiant,* that's what they are. She looked around, wondering what she could do to help. But even after Oliver returned, only to disappear again down cellar, Rennie just stood there, dreaming.

Dear one, she repeated to herself. I wish Peter —— But he'd think this as kooky as plain language.

Lion and Duffy returned to the kitchen. They stood by the cellar door, whimpering, waiting for Oliver to emerge.

He came up with a bushel basket of apples. "The last of the crop," he announced, puffing. "We'll take them to Kendal for the fellowship meal. After meeting, we have that unwillingness to part asunder that those early Friends spoke of. It's good to be there. So we stay and eat together. Everyone brings something. Once in a while, there's an unanticipated multitude. Students come over from the university to worship with us. They aren't Friends, but they're in accord with our Peace Testimony and want to join in the experience from which it springs. We invite everyone present to share our meal, even when we're not sure there's enough. There always is. We eat and are filled. What time does thy plane leave?"

"Three ten."

Oliver nodded. "Take thy belongings to the meetinghouse. Thee'll be going directly from there."

To the bus? Or was he driving her to the airport? Who'd stay with Daphne? Rennie had learned enough about this place to realize that Mary Young didn't just drop in on Friday. She came when she heard that Oliver wanted to meet the plane.

Lion and Duffy kept getting underfoot.

"It's because we're going to meeting," Oliver explained. "They know. We never read aloud after breakfast except on First Day. When they hear that, they know it'll soon be time for us to leave and they'll be home alone." He stooped to pat them.

They rolled over on their backs with their paws in the air. Oliver, crouching down to scratch their stomachs, looked up at Rennie. "Daphne would like to work on thy portrait again."

"I thought it was finished!"

"Not quite." Getting to his feet a little stiffly, Oliver asked, "Will thee go in and sit for her till we leave? There's about an hour."

"No! No, Oliver, I can't."

He looked at Rennie gravely. "Has thee seen the portrait? Daphne doesn't want thee to see it till it's finished."

"I didn't know I wasn't supposed to. You never said."

Oliver nodded. "We *were* a bit upset last evening. And it doesn't matter, unless thee's disappointed."

"Is that really how I look?"

"With expressionless eyes?" He laughed. "That's why Daphne needs thee to pose again — so she can put thy spirit into the eyes. It eluded her yesterday." Coming over and taking Rennie's hand, he said softly, "Thee needn't be afraid of Daphne. She's seeing way beyond thy present confusion to the person she believes will emerge. But thee was hiding thyself yesterday and so she couldn't do the eyes apart from just their color. Thee may not like the finished portrait, either. To become the person Daphne sees will make demands thee may not care to accept. But, if not for thy sake and Peter's, Serenity, do this for Daphne and me. Last night, after thee went to bed, I studied the portrait a long time and I think thee is inspiring her to do something lasting. It's much more than the likeness of an individual. It's the dawn of that day we hope thy whole generation will wake to."

"Do I — have to talk about Peter?"

"Of course not. Before her stroke, Daphne liked having conversations with her subjects. It relaxed them, took away the feeling that they were posing. And for a good portrait, she had to know about their lives, not just their features. That's why she wanted thee to talk. But we communicate at the highest level in silence. So speak or not, as thee feels moved."

"Oliver, what does it mean — that thing you read from the Bible — 'keep thy heart'?"

" 'With all diligence.' By 'heart' Solomon meant one's self, the center of one's life, which one gives to the person one loves. Thy heart is the only lasting gift thee has to give to Peter, the only manifestation of love that can endure as long, the marriage promise puts it, as you both shall live."

Rennie was still baffled. "What," she asked, "does diligence have to do with love? It means working hard, doesn't it? Love isn't something one works at. It just sort of happens."

"I think not. Love is the human counterpart of God's caring for us. It's not a little bird that suddenly appears in springtime, alights awhile, then flits away when the weather or the season changes. We have to strive very hard sometimes to keep our hearts ——" He glanced anxiously at the clock. "Do come," he pleaded.

Still holding Rennie's hand, he drew her gently toward the back hall.

12.

In the woodshed, the sun was blinding. Daphne sat with her back to the window, twisting a kneaded eraser between her thumb and forefinger. Her face was in shadow, but a crown of sunshine rested on her head. Concentrating on the eraser, she didn't look up when Rennie came in to sit on the little chair that Oliver brought from the living room. He placed it at such an angle that Rennie looked straight out, over Daphne's head, into the maple tree beyond the glass.

Light filtered through layers of leaves, just the way it did yesterday, only then the air was still. This morning, a breeze tugged at the leaves, twirling, blowing, pushing them around. Joyfully, it seemed to Rennie, they bobbed with the air currents, knowing they were securely fastened to their twigs. At this season of the year, no wind could detach them. They were having a wonderful time, dancing, roller-coasting, turning into a tangle of bright green kites.

As the patterns of light shifted and tumbled, Rennie had a sudden flash of understanding. If this was how she appeared to Daphne, it must be that when Daphne looked right through her she didn't, after all, see the mess inside — the fears and frustrations and ugly things Rennie couldn't talk about, her whole crisis-ridden life — or, if Daphne did see the mess, she disregarded it. With the heightened perception Oliver spoke of, Daphne had simply watched light from some outside source — what source? — shine through Rennie. She'd transferred the variety of hues she thought she saw to her sketch pad — a beautiful combination of brilliance and shadows spread out against the sky.

This was the person Daphne and Oliver seemed to think Rennie would be someday, though they knew she was confused now. She couldn't wait to get back and tell Peter. Wasn't this the identity he'd hope she'd find? What words would describe her experience here? She just knew one way to communicate with him intimately.

He wanted something else from her now. He wanted her to be strong, not a pushover; a person in her own right, not one who felt secure only when she was making love with him, believing — and she really did believe it till she came to Firbank — that to be-dependent-on, to make-love-with was to love.

There's a lot more to it than that, she told the flying green kites. *Keep thy heart with all diligence* — how am I going to explain this to Peter?

Daphne was studying a pastel crayon, rejecting it, choosing another. Because the light was behind her and Rennie was facing it, Daphne's features seemed blurred. That made it almost possible to imagine how she looked in her twenties, when she and Oliver began their pilgrimage.

They'd often stopped on the road to study the birds, Oliver had told Rennie last night. Sometimes Daphne painted. "I sat beside her on the grass with the typewriter but wrote little, gazing at the horizon, wishing I didn't have to go to work in that office. As a writer," he'd confessed in a self-deprecating tone, "as a writer, I'm what thee'd call a dropout. I never finished that book."

Unable to conceal her disappointment, Rennie had cried, "Why not?" Then she was sorry. Oliver's face, usually radiant, had become downright sad.

"As we traveled south," he'd explained, "we saw people working in the fields. It seemed to us that, for the poor, conditions weren't much better than in Woolman's time. All the way home, we talked about the poverty we'd seen. Just before we crossed the Connecticut River, we stopped to picnic by the lighthouse at Cornfield Point, where the river flows into Long Island Sound. While we ate, I read to Daphne from Woolman's *Plea for the Poor: To turn all the treasures we possess into the channel of universal love becomes the business of our lives.* I put the book down. Looking out across the channel in the Sound toward Plum Gut, where the current runs hard, I tried to take this in. All the treasures — *all.* Was this the business of our lives, Daphne's and mine? What had it to do with the jewelry business?"

To Rennie's surprise, it wasn't Oliver but Daphne who came up with the answer. "Why can't we stay at Firbank?" she had demanded. "Grandmother wouldn't mind. Thee can run the farm. It's too much for her now and she's worried about what will become of it after she's gone."

"Me? Farm?" Oliver had cried. "I didn't," he'd told Rennie, grinning, "say, 'Me, a Harvard man?' But farming was the last thing I'd ever thought of doing." He had reminded Daphne that farmers lead a hard life; that he wanted her to have every comfort.

"I want thee to be happy," she'd retorted. "And thee's not going to be, competing in the business world. All those outward cumbers! I'm a countrywoman. Farming doesn't frighten me."

"But thy painting!" Oliver had protested. "Thee has so much talent."

"I'll paint, too," Daphne promised. "At Firbank, it'll be easier to turn all the treasures we possess into the channel of universal love, won't it?"

As Oliver described this scene, his expression changed. The lightheartedness that impressed Rennie when she first saw him returned. "Ever since that morning in Mount Holly," he confided, "Woolman struggled with me. For six weeks I managed to resist him. But I couldn't resist Daphne. I suddenly felt so eager to break the news to Grandmother that I threw everything into the car and started to speed. Through Old Lyme, New London, Mystic, Stonington and Westerly we dashed at twenty-nine miles an hour! When we got to Firbank and told Grandmother, she simply smiled, as if she'd known all along this would happen. She'd never said a word about that job, but it didn't please her. All she answered, when I asked whether I might run the farm instead was, 'Woolman once remarked that if the leadings of the Spirit were more attended to, more people would be engaged in husbandry.' So we stayed at Firbank."

Oliver had started, then, to take Serenity's little book back to his study. In the doorway of the woodshed, he stopped. "There was no time for writing," he explained, turning to Rennie. "But I'm glad we made the decision then. Grandmother died the next winter, only a few months after she posed for her portrait. When it went on exhibition, Daphne got so many commissions, she was soon earning more than I would have done in that job! We installed kerosene stoves, and with only two fireplaces in use we didn't need a lot of cord wood. I cleared this place out for Daphne. It isn't the spacious studio I dreamed of, but she loves it."

So do I, Rennie thought, looking around at the canvases stacked against the unplastered walls and the old potbellied stove in the corner. She was so absorbed, trying to picture Serenity posing, that she forgot she was posing herself. Suddenly she felt rather than saw Daphne staring into her eyes.

"You know," Rennie told her, "to love the way you and Oliver do, one first has to have security in one's self and one can't have security unless one loves that way. So how does one break into the circle?"

The moment the words were out of her mouth, Rennie regretted them. She'd asked a question, forgetting that Daphne —— Rennie would have to give the answer herself.

"I guess — well — to begin with, like Oliver said, one has to start working at it. I used to think that just meant taking turns washing the dishes. But now ——You and Oliver can't understand how hard it is. You don't need to work at loving. With so much love, you can afford to share it, let it spill over onto other people. I ——"

Turning her head, Rennie saw that Oliver was standing in the back hall, looking in. "Time to leave," he announced, as if he were sorry to interrupt. He glanced anxiously at Daphne, then at the drawing board, last of all, at Rennie. "We don't like getting to meeting late," he told her. "It disturbs the Friends who've already begun to center down. Are thy belongings packed?"

"No. I'll run upstairs." Standing up, stretching, Rennie didn't dare look in the direction of the portrait.

"We wish thee weren't leaving," Oliver said, giving her that affectionate nod she loved.

"So do I! Maybe I can come back with Peter after exams. Would that be okay? No, we'll be busy with the wedding — all those arrangements. We still don't have a church. Daddy's going to be awfully mad because I said I'd let him know last week. But right after the wedding — could we come? Unless," Rennie added doubtfully, "Peter finds a job. It might be a long way off." She almost wished he wouldn't find one so she could bring him to Firbank. That was mean, when he was so worried.

Rennie walked to the door and Oliver came in to help Daphne out of her chair. But Daphne waved him aside, reaching toward Rennie. Oliver understood.

"Before thee leaves, Serenity, Daphne would like thee to see the portrait. She may alter a little something after studying it awhile, but it's essentially finished. I'll make a frame." He looked at Daphne questioningly. "Narrow gilt to match Grandmother's?"

Daphne agreed happily. But Rennie, standing in the doorway, felt rooted to the spot. She couldn't face those eyes in the portrait. And yet she had to. Daphne was still holding out her hand and Oliver stood by the drawing board, smiling encouragement to Rennie.

She took a step forward. It was the hardest thing she ever had to do.

Oliver gave her an understanding glance. "It's humbling," he acknowledged, "though only in a creative way, to see oneself as someone else —— But thee'll like this. Thee knows, dear one," he exclaimed, turning to Daphne, "there's a marked resemblance to Grandmother! I hadn't seen it till this instant."

Rennie leaped forward and looked. The eyes were alive! This was a real person, a happy one, who really did have her great-grandmother's expression — lighthearted, trusting, courageous — and that tenderness with which Serenity looked down and laughed at the child or dog at her feet. But, except for the turtleneck and shorts, the shape and coloring of the features, it was another person — somebody else — not Rennie Ross.

Oliver was helping Daphne out of the chair. He gave her his right arm. With the left one, he reached for Rennie's. "Come," he said, drawing them both toward the back hall. "If we don't leave soon, there won't be time to stop in Kendal and see the house where Grandmother Serenity grew up." Feeling Rennie's reluctance to part from the portrait, he added, "On thy next visit, thee can study it longer. And someday, when thee comes to Firbank — someday, thee'll suddenly find it's a true likeness."

Rennie didn't really know what happened after that. All the way to Kendal, she was in a fog. She must have gone upstairs and got her stuff because the book bag was lying on the seat of the cab. She remembered coming out of the house and finding the truck in the driveway, parked beside that flat-topped stone she'd tripped over when she arrived. Daphne was balancing shakily on the stone, gripping Oliver's shoulder.

"Grandmother's old horse block," he told Rennie as he helped Daphne into the cab. "We're lucky she insisted on keeping it in its place after she gave up riding. It's just what Daphne needs."

Rennie was looking toward the back of the house, the red barn, the white silo, wondering whether she'd ever see Firbank again. How long would it be before she resembled the girl in the portrait? She didn't think she could come back till then.

The leaves of the maple outside the woodshed were still bobbing about. Naturally, Rennie thought, they can let themselves be blown around and enjoy it. They know they're securely fastened to those twigs. I'm fastened to Peter. Why can't I feel secure, too?

Oliver had let down the tailgate of the truck and placed a short plank against it, reaching to the ground. "Does thee mind walking the plank and sitting on the floor?" he asked Rennie. "It's all we have to offer. Will it ruin thy clothes?"

Rennie didn't mind. Her skirt needed pressing, anyway. She thought it fun to climb up and sit with her back against the cab, as Oliver told her to do. But all she could think of was getting a last look at the house.

Oliver put the plank back. Fastening the tailgate, he rested his hands on it a moment and leaned toward Rennie. "Grandmother left Firbank to all her descendants," he told her. "I happened to be the only one of the lot who was willing to farm. But wherever thee

117

settles with Peter, wherever thee happens to live, remember that Firbank's thine, too, waiting for thee to come home to, any time in thy life."

13.

Bouncing along toward Kendal in the back of the truck, her hair blowing like those leaves, Rennie finally saw the ocean. It was breaking in slow ripples on the beach at the foot of a sea wall. Those graceful birds, circling and diving over the water, that Rennie had taken for gulls, were terns, Oliver explained, shouting back to her from the cab.

Rennie remembered the emotion with which her father described standing on the dunes at the outer edge of Salt Pond, when he was young, and watching the surf. In his recollection, the ocean was always wild. She wondered whether it happened to be unusually calm today — Oliver said the tide was low — or whether her father recalled only the storms — times when a little boy would have been scared.

The road left the shore and turned inland. From the town line on, it paralleled the Kendal River, running between a steep, grassy bank and houses that looked old and dignified, set wide apart on lawns shaded by huge trees.

Oliver stopped the truck for a moment, letting the motor idle. He twisted around so that, through the sliding window at the back of the cab, he could point out a yellow house to Rennie. "The one with the veranda and those big stone urns of geraniums on either side of the steps — see it? That's where Grandmother was born."

"Oh."

"It was the time of the gold rush," Oliver added, "Eighteen Forty-nine. Many Kendal men were boarding brigs from a wharf over there. They sailed into Little Narragansett Bay, around Cape Horn to San Francisco. They didn't find much gold, but, back here in Kendal, my Great-grandfather Josiah Millburn prospered. He owned a shipyard downriver a way. The discovery of gold in California created a sudden demand for deep sea vessels. With his reputation for honest workmanship, Josiah couldn't help getting rich. That worried him so much that when Serenity and her sisters were still very young, he gave up shipbuilding."

"Getting rich *worried* him?" Rennie cried through the sliding window. With the motor chugging, she must have misunderstood. Or was Josiah another Woolman?

About to release the brake, Oliver twisted around again so Rennie could hear him. "Josiah wasn't comfortable being rich while others were poor. After selling the shipyard, he had just enough for his family to live on plainly. The rest of his life he devoted to the needs of the town, the Friends Meeting and rescuing slaves. Even so, he and Sarah were so thrifty, money just accumulated."

"I don't think I've ever heard of anyone worrying about getting too rich," Rennie called to Oliver, laughing at the thought, "except around income tax time." She began to understand why her father said his family didn't fit with his mother's people.

"No," Oliver shouted, driving on. "There aren't many folks around today like Josiah and Sarah."

Up a steep hill the truck labored. Oliver turned into a crescent-shaped street and called back to Rennie, "Here we are!"

It can't be, Rennie said to herself — that little building without a steeple, those ordinary windows — is *that* the Friends meeting-house? She'd expected something a lot more impressive. Cathedrals, like Chartres — just seeing the radiance of that glass and the grandeur of the vaulting projected on a screen could move Rennie. This insignificant building ——

Plain clapboard, joined to the earth by a thick, green hedge, Kendal Meetinghouse was the color of Serenity's dress in the portrait — pale gray, very austere, yet, like the dress, it glowed with sunshine. Children were running about the yard. The older people talked and laughed, the way wedding guests do when they come out of a church, only these people were moving toward the door of the meetinghouse. The place didn't look Sunday-solemn, but almost festive.

Two men stood beside the drive, holding a wicker armchair between them.

Oliver stopped the truck. "Sam! Jorim!" he exclaimed in greeting. "That's Serenity Ross in back. You met her yesterday at Firbank."

The two men grinned at Rennie, as if they were old friends. Then they helped Daphne out of the cab. Lifting her into the chair like experts, they carried her between them down the walk, up three stone steps and through a wide open door. Progress was slow because they had to keep stopping. Everyone wanted to speak to Daphne. Rennie recognized Mary Young, the dumpy, old woman who was at Firbank when she arrived, and the two who came in with food.

Oliver drove on to park behind the meetinghouse. Getting out, swinging the book bag, he opened the tailgate and started tugging at the plank.

Rennie stopped him. "I can jump."

"Sam and Jorim have never failed to be there, waiting for us, by the syringa bush," Oliver told her when she was down, "not one First Day since we began coming to meeting again after Daphne's illness." Noticing that Rennie's attention had been caught by a long shed with a row of open stalls, he explained, "In the old days, Friends left their horses there during meeting."

He took Rennie's arm and started up the drive but stopped a second later to look at the sky. "Those gulls flying over the ridgepole of the meetinghouse followed the tidewater up from the Bay this morning and ——"

Panicked, Rennie blurted out, "What do you — what am I supposed to do in meeting?"

"Listen."

"But you said there was just silence."

Oliver looked down at Rennie, smiling reassurance, yet when he spoke, it was gravely. "Yes, mostly we simply listen for God's presence, wait for guidance. Then, a Friend who has a fresh insight may feel moved to share his or her thought in words. Thee'll find the strangeness wearing off after a bit. Thee may even find the silence comforting."

To Rennie, it seemed only terrifying. How could she listen for some "presence" when she didn't even know what it was — whether it existed?

Two girls were running toward her — a short, dark one and a tall blonde — Nancy and Sandy, who'd swabbed the kitchen floor yesterday. Coming alongside in a spasm of giggles, the girls tugged at Rennie's hands.

"Sit with us," they begged.

Oliver glanced at Rennie. Sensing that she preferred to stay with him, he told the girls, "If Serenity sits with you, she'll be left alone on the facing bench when you go out for First Day school."

"True."

"Whom will she have to shake hands with, then, when meeting closes? Besides, Daphne Otis and I were counting on having Serenity ourselves. What about lunch? Why don't you invite her to sit between you at lunch?"

"Will you?" Nancy pleaded. Without waiting for the answer, she let go of Rennie and ran off again. "Come on, Sandy, we're late."

"See you then," Sandy called back.

Oliver was smiling. "Things are very different these days," he observed. "When I was a boy, only elders — my grandparents and Friends of their generation — sat on the facing benches. That's what we call the low gallery at the front of the meeting room. We children would never have dared to sit up there. Now that we're old, we prefer being in the body of the Meeting with everyone else. So, for years, the facing benches were left empty. Then the children took them over — out of defiance, chiefly. They knew it was against tradition and they thought their parents or older Friends would object. But we encouraged them. There's nothing about our customs that may not be changed, if change seems indicated. That's how it came about that the younger children sit up there during the first half hour, when they worship with us, before First Day school."

At the door of the meetinghouse, Oliver stood aside to let Rennie walk in ahead of him. She had to restrain a ridiculous impulse to reach up and put her hand in his.

14.

They were in a vestibule lined with books. Beside the coat rack, Daphne's wicker armchair waited for her the way horses used to wait out in the shed. Oliver dropped Rennie's book bag on the chair and took her into the quietest roomful of people she'd ever been in. It was bare. Nothing but benches — not an altar, or a lectern, not even a bunch of flowers. The sun, streaming through the tall, clear windows, brought out the grain in the blond wood of the benches and illuminated the features of the still worshipers. They looked like figures in a painting. There was a Post-Impressionistic kind of vacancy about their gaze, as if their souls had left their bodies. How different from the animated scene outside, moments ago!

Oliver led Rennie to the bench were Daphne was sitting and stood aside again. Daphne gave them a welcoming glance. Then she returned to her meditation.

The bench was hard, not just the seat. The back stabbed Rennie between the shoulder blades.

People kept coming in. Rennie wondered what they came for — nothing to look at, nothing to listen to, no program to read —— But it was supposed to be a solemn occasion. She tried to focus on that. Wasn't this what Oliver meant by "centering down"? Why couldn't she control her mind? Just to bug her, all it came up with was: *Little Miss Muffet sat on a tuffet.* She hadn't thought of that since she was a baby. Why now, for goodness' sake? What's a tuffet?

If I were at college, I'd look it up in the dictionary.

Where's Peter now? Still in bed, probably. Or is he out someplace? Where? I've got to know.

She hadn't been running, but she felt that way. She took a deep breath.

Stop wriggling. Find a comfortable position and stay in it.

Settling herself on the bench, Rennie wished she'd remembered to bring Daphne something. Her mother would have thought of that. If Rennie had told her parents she was going to Firbank, her mother would immediately have asked, "What are you taking as a hostess present?" Why hadn't this occurred to Rennie before she left Tilbury?

I just used Daphne and Oliver, she realized, horrified. Till I got here, I never thought of them as persons, except to be afraid of. I don't even have a paperback with me that they'd care about, just course books.

Something wonderful seemed to be emanating from Daphne. Her spirit shone in her face.

Maybe, Rennie said to herself, she feels easier here, where everyone else is silent, than where people are talking all around her.

But Rennie felt uncomfortable, left out.

Turning a little to peek at Oliver, she found that he'd withdrawn all expression from his face. The vitality that made it so striking was missing, now, and he was a long way off, beyond Rennie's reach. He and Daphne had both forsaken her. Though she was sitting between them, she was excluded, stark alone. Why did they want her to sit with them if they were going to run out on her?

In desperation, Rennie looked up at the row of kids in the gallery, hoping to catch Nancy's or Sandy's eye. Even they seemed remote, practically dead. Was this what Friends called centering down? How did such little ones do it — keep still so long? They looked cute, especially the five- or six-year-old girl who kept yawning. Rennie noticed that the older boys—the ones who vacuumed the Firbank living room and filled the wood box — were sitting near the door. Too grown up to show their defiance by taking the facing benches, she thought. I wonder what they did that bugged their parents. Couldn't be drugs or sex — not here. But one never knows. Mother and Daddy wouldn't dream that I ——

How come she was thinking of sex, now, when she was supposed to be listening for God's presence? Or was God more permissive than people? Did He understand?

What would Oliver say if he could read Rennie's thoughts? Not daring to look at his face again, she studied his hands — those large, brown, expressive hands, which were always so busy at home. Now they rested quietly on his knees, with the fingers curled in relaxation.

He wouldn't mind, Rennie said to herself. At least, he never seems to set himself up in judgment. All he asked was that I listen, and if that's what I heard ——

From under the sleeve of his jacket and the white shirt cuff, Oliver's wrist watch stuck out far enough for Rennie to see that it was only twenty minutes past eleven. *Forty* more to go.

So this was what a Friends meetinghouse looked like on the inside. Rennie remembered how her father, coming here with his grandmother, had hated sitting still. Rennie certainly took after him in that! Her father would never agree to holding the wedding in such an undistinguished little place. She herself — would she want to walk down this short, gray-carpeted aisle with Peter, stand before the Meeting, and promise, with divine assistance — what did that mean, anyway? — to be loving and faithful as long as nobody got hurt? No! Those weren't the right words. They were what kids at college said about having sex outside of marriage — it was okay, as long as nobody got hurt. The Quaker marriage promise was: *as long as we both shall live.*

Rennie almost laughed out loud at the funny slip. What stopped her was the realization that the promise was anything but funny. How could one make it in absolute sincerity? Even if one meant it at the time, how could one know what would happen later? If somebody got hurt, a marriage was done for, no matter what people had promised.

124

Right now, Rennie thought, Peter and I are loving and faithful without having promised anything, and nobody's hurt.

Is nobody hurt? she wondered suddenly, startled by the very possibility. What a crazy idea! She and Peter were both okay.

Against the silence, the question kept echoing, Is nobody hurt? It was roaring now so that Rennie wanted to stick her fingers in her ears to keep out the sound, *Is nobody hurt?*

But the sound was inside her head. Her fingers wouldn't stop it. She tried to confront it, argue it away, only she seemed to have lost the power to reason. Part of herself had taken off, without even saying good-by.

It isn't only Daphne and Oliver who've left me, she thought suddenly, very frightened. I've left myself! She pressed her knuckles against her lips to stifle a scream. I've left myself!

If she let the scream out, would her self hear it and come back — the self that was drifting away on the silence, calling plainly to her as it receded, Is nobody hurt?

All that remained, she saw with a jolt, were the roles she played: the teacher-to-be who professed an interest in kids she didn't possess; the bride-to-be, about to walk down the aisle of some church — any church — on the arm of her father, who would give away a daughter he didn't possess — a daughter dressed in white, with a veil, signifying a virginity she didn't possess, who was marrying a man who craved something more than what she kept offering him — something she didn't seem to possess, either.

Oh, but I do! she cried inside herself. Isn't that what Daphne was saying in the portrait?

This was momentary panic, like a nightmare, because part of herself had run away across the silence, leaving her naked, a person who went through life just wearing roles.

Is nobody hurt?

Unable to bear this another minute, Rennie wondered whether it would be okay if she got up and walked out — pretended she had to go to the john. Squeezing past Oliver's long legs was going to be a problem, and Rennie didn't know where the john was, but she couldn't stay here any longer. She really did have to go.

There was a small rustle, then a scuffle of feet. Looking up, Rennie found that the children were stepping down from the low gallery and filing out. Nancy and Sandy winked at her as they went by.

Could Rennie slip out with them and not be noticed, except by Oliver and Daphne? Something held her back — she mustn't run away, leaving part of herself out there, in the silence.

As soon as the children closed the door, they exploded. Their voices and the clatter of their feet as they went downstairs resounded through the meetinghouse. But the hush in this room was impenetrable. Only Rennie seemed to have noticed the welcome diversion.

Now that the children were gone, there was nothing for her to look at. She counted the benches, set in a hollow square so Friends faced one another. Five on either side of the aisle, each seating eight at a pinch — that made eighty, plus thirty-two in the gallery. One hundred and twelve in all. The preliminary guest list Rennie's parents had made up, just roughly, already went into the hundreds and Peter's parents hadn't even been asked yet how many people they wanted to invite.

For the wedding, this meetinghouse would be inadequate. But today, the benches were only partly occupied. Rennie studied the people opposite. Their clothes had a certain style — strikingly simple but not pseudo, like the raggy, brightly patched jeans kids wore at college.

Fidgeting, she told herself that she was actually wasting time. This was her first opportunity in months to think about those patterns her mother kept harping on — the silver and china and the material for the bedspread. Her mother was right — choosing them carefully was important, even though they seemed trivial, when Rennie was trying to get a Quaker wedding. Now, that was out of the question and, really, making the right choices *was* important, because those were the spoons and forks and plates she and Peter were going to have to look at every day, the spread she'd fold up every night — if she ever made the bed. So they'd better be beautiful. Well, she and Peter wouldn't use their best things all the time. Still, if, out of indifference now, Rennie settled for something that didn't express the beauty she and Peter wanted, she'd be sorry later.

The sun had shifted. It was no longer slanting through the windows, sharpening the faces of Friends with glare and shadow. A gentler radiance suffused every face and made even the benches beautiful. For the first time, Rennie noticed how carefully they were crafted — maybe it was Josiah, the shipbuilder, who'd made them when Serenity was young — functional, free of curlicues, a visible simplicity of heart.

That was exactly what Peter seemed to crave from Rennie — simplicity of heart, joy, beauty. These were the gifts she wished she could bring back to him from her journey, like the candy bar he'd given her when she left, because he knew she loved it.

The Chocomarsh! Till this moment, Rennie'd forgotten she still had one. As soon as meeting was over — when people shook hands, the way Oliver said they did at the close — she'd run back to the vestibule, fish the Chocomarsh out of the book bag, and offer it to Daphne — providing it wasn't melted by this time, or squashed. Not much of a present, but it was all Rennie had to give and specially precious, because Peter had given it to her. Surely, Daphne would understand.

Already visualizing the pleasure Daphne's eyes would express when she took the candy bar in her good hand, Rennie felt easier. Looking out at the trees in the meetinghouse yard, she suddenly noticed that the birds were singing. Would the voices of his friends bring Oliver back from that far-off place he'd retreated to? Turning slowly toward him, Rennie peeked again. He was still away. She herself gradually slid off into thoughtlessness.

Drifting dreamily, she jumped when a man's voice broke the silence. He was just behind her, evidently standing, because she could feel a slight tremor, now and then, as his hands gripped the back of her bench.

127

"In our family reading this morning," he said, without raising his voice, as though he weren't addressing a roomful of people, but only speaking to Rennie, "we came across three quotations that are strikingly similar. They've stuck in my mind during meeting. The first two were written by Friends in Sixteen Sixty and Seventeen Sixty; the other by a Jew who died in the Nineteen Sixties."

Rennie could hear the pages of a book being turned. Curious, she wanted to twist around and look at the man. It seemed polite to face him when he was talking to her. But she noticed that no one else changed position. Friends seemed to be listening to his voice as a sort of accompaniment to their meditation, rather than giving it full attention.

"This is what they wrote," the man said. *"There is that near you which will guide you. O wait for it and be sure ye keep to it.* These are the words of Isaac Penington." The man paused, as if to savor them, the way Oliver had, when he was reading after breakfast. Then the man went on. "Here," he said, "is what John Woolman wrote: *There is a principle which is pure, placed in the human mind, which in different places and ages hath had different names. It is, however, pure and proceeds from God. It is deep and inward, confined to no forms of religion, nor excluded from any, where the heart stands in perfect sincerity."* The speaker paused again. At last he said, "And here are the words of Martin Buber: *Everyone has in him something precious that is in no one else. This precious something in a man is revealed to him if he truly perceives his strongest feeling, his central wish, that in him which stirs his inmost being."*

The speaker began to discuss these quotations. Rennie stopped listening. She was trying to hold on to the words. What Oliver read at breakfast was puzzling, but there was nothing mysterious about something that guides you, a principle which is pure, confined to no specific forms of religion, where the heart stands in perfect sincerity, something precious that's in no one else.

Oh, Rennie said to herself, feeling she'd made a discovery, that's the trouble with those how-to books on sex! They're like the driver's manual in Mother's new car. If you follow the instructions, you'll get top performance — the same as everyone else who owns that model. There's nothing unique about it. What Peter wants is the precious thing that's only in me. Wistfully, Rennie thought, If we were starting now, if we were meeting tonight for the first time, things would be different.

Like how?

I'd listen, for one thing. I'd listen to Peter — not just to what he says, but to what he feels.

"It's the bride's family that decides about the wedding," she remembered his saying when she told him of her parents' plans for the reception.

She'd heard the note of bitter resignation in his voice at the time. As long as he hadn't protested, she'd disregarded it.

Peter's parents care about him, too. Why shouldn't they have some say?

If we were starting now —— But we're not.

"That," the man behind Rennie was saying, "is why I find the connection between these three quotations so meaningful."

Rennie had missed his reason, thinking about Peter. And yet, she'd been listening, too — not as she did in her role of student, busily taking notes while the prof lectured so that, without ever letting his ideas become hers, she could give him back his words on the exam. She had listened unconsciously, seeming not to pay attention, yet feeling the force with which these odd phrases clarified her needs.

Where the heart stands in perfect sincerity, Rennie repeated to herself, as the man stopped speaking. She'd heard the words before — yes, Oliver had quoted them when he explained why she and Peter couldn't just walk into a Friends meetinghouse and ask to be married.

Make a wish, she thought then, a *central* wish.

She squeezed her eyes shut the way she used to do as a child, when she blew out the candles on her birthday cake or saw the first star shining in the evening sky and her mother would urge, "Make a wish."

What should Rennie wish for? She wanted so much — serenity, mostly. But was that her central wish? Didn't serenity spring from something deeper? What was the precious something, which stirred her inmost being? What was it she must wait for? Why wait?

A faint sound broke the spell. Rennie opened her eyes. Some girl across the aisle — she couldn't be more than twenty-five — was standing up. She began to talk, very softly and hesitantly, hunting for words, as if she were drawing them from deep inside herself. "As Jesus was on his way to Jerusalem, the Pharisees asked him when the kingdom of God was going to come. He answered, *Not with observation. For behold, the kingdom of God is within you.*"

Rennie was annoyed by the girl. Why did she have to go and break the spell? It seemed imperative that the wish be made fast, before the magical moment evaporated, as it always did, once the candles were blown out or the sky was suddenly full of stars. Rennie refused to listen or look at the girl any longer. She shut her eyes tightly again, ignoring her, wishing and wishing for that precious, nameless thing.

Suddenly Rennie jumped. Someone had touched her hand. Opening her eyes swiftly, she saw that Oliver was sending her a message with his handshake — conveying a relationship that had nothing to do with their being first cousins once removed. His eyes told her how happy he was to have her there.

And Rennie *was* there. Her fragments had come back together. For better or worse, the self that drifted off on the silence was once more joined to the rest of her. She was whole again.

All around the room, people were shaking hands.

As Oliver let go, Rennie turned to Daphne. Reaching out, she took the paralyzed hand in her own warm one and gently pressed it.

Part Three

*H*e had said he wouldn't come to the airport to meet her, but there he was, waiting. Although eagerness shone in his face, Peter didn't kiss Rennie, the way he did when she left. He simply grabbed her hand and drew her toward the exit.

"Have you got the address?"

"No. A Quaker marriage is out. I don't know why I was so dumb, thinking we could just walk in and buy a wedding. Their procedure is complicated. Takes months — committees on clearness and stuff. We wouldn't really want it."

Rennie glanced at Peter anxiously, hoping he'd understand.

"That's okay with me," he said. "Frankly, it didn't sound like the right church for us. Only reason I went along with the idea was, you seemed to have your heart set on it. What's Oliver like? As kooky as he sounded on the phone? Was he nice to you?"

"Was he ever! He's *not* kooky. Plain language is democratic — that's why he uses it. Peter, wait till you see Firbank! It's the greatest. And you know something? It belongs to *me*, too! I can go back there any time. I bet even Daddy doesn't know that."

"You have to phone him. Soon as we get to college. He was trying to reach you all weekend. Kept ringing your dorm. Called mine, finally. Was he uptight!"

"What about?"

"Thought you'd gone off for the weekend with me."

Rennie giggled. "Did you tell him it was just Oliver?"

"Yes. That's when he really exploded. 'Pete,' he shouted, 'Pete, you mean — you don't mean Rennie would go to *Firbank* without *telling* me?'"

Peter was a wonderful mimic. Rennie could just hear her father. " 'She went to see *Oliver?*' " Peter repeated in that outraged, incredulous tone Rennie knew all too well. Then, in his natural voice, he asked, "What was so bad about your doing that? Guy's old, isn't he? Related to you, even."

"I should have phoned home Friday," Rennie admitted. "I'll do it before supper. Peter, could we spend a little while in Firbank this summer? It wouldn't cost anything. You'd hit it off with Oliver. Could we?"

Peter's face clouded. "Depends."

"Any nibbles? That printing place you heard about Friday?" At once, Rennie was sorry she'd asked. She knew without being told that nothing had changed for Peter.

"The city would be ghastly in the summertime, anyhow," she said, hoping to make him feel better.

He was more worried now than when she left, while she was so happy, bursting with all she had to tell him. How could she communicate her terrific experience when he concentrated on the job that refused to come his way? He'd only said one word — "Depends" — but the tone implied that his failure to land a job was due to a deficiency in himself. Everybody was having trouble, Rennie thought, though not everybody was getting married, too. Maybe she ought to consider baby-sitting. But having to wrestle with kids all vacation ——

"You were sweet to come for me," she said as they crossed the parking lot, looking for the car Peter had borrowed. "It's just like Oliver coming to Hillsgrove. He told me to take the bus. Remember? Instead, he came himself. Mary Young happened to drop in. Well, I think she planned it so Oliver could leave Daphne."

But Peter knew nothing about Daphne's stroke or who Mary Young was or that Austin and Judy, Mary's son and daughter-in-law, had driven Rennie back to Hillsgrove Airport after the fellowship meal.

134

"We had this neat dinner in the First Day school," she told Peter, when they were in the car. "I wish you could have been there. It was like one of those primitives of country people — you know, sitting at long tables with checked cloths, heaps of food, everything plain, but so good. The people were like that, too — simple, full of fun, and yet they have this tremendous dignity. Even the kids are great. A couple of little girls were snowed by me. I had a good time, after I got over being disappointed about the wedding. That dinner was neat. People *enjoying* each other ——"

"Was this when you got there?"

"No. Today, after meeting, before I left."

"Meeting? You went to Friends meeting? Start at the begining," Peter urged. He drove through town and onto the Tilbury road. "Tell me everything as it happened. Oliver met you and then ——?"

Rennie suddenly felt terribly tired. She rested her head on Peter's shoulder. Reaching around, he drew her to him for an instant, but swiftly replaced his hand on the steering wheel.

Impatient as she'd been to tell Peter everything, now that she was with him, Rennie didn't know how to begin. It was going to take more effort to convey the deep meaning of Firbank, the love she'd seen in Oliver and Daphne, than she could put forth at this moment, when she was bracing herself for her father's anger. Why should he mind her going to see Oliver? It was strange. But Rennie had expected some such reaction. That must have been the reason why she didn't phone him before she left — that and her mother's fear of flying.

"Daphne made this little water color of the maple leaves outside the woodshed window," she told Peter. "Daphne's a marvelous painter, though she's had a stroke. The picture shows how I look to her, full of promise."

Rennie glanced up at Peter, hoping he wouldn't laugh. Repeated like this, words that had seemed wonderful and exciting, when Oliver spoke them, sounded corny. Peter didn't laugh.

"It's like the portrait. Oh, I haven't told you the most important part — I had my *portrait* painted, Peter. By a real artist! Maybe someday it'll look like me. You were right about my finding my identity there."

This wasn't starting at the beginning. But Rennie felt certain that if she could just describe Daphne's pictures Peter'd grasp something of what she'd experienced. Or if, when they reached college, they'd —— That way, Rennie could tell Peter best. There'd be no need for finding words.

Rennie recalled how, this morning, while she posed for Daphne again, she had watched those maple leaves outside the window, bobbing about like kites. She'd wondered then how she was going to explain *Keep thy heart with all diligence* to Peter. Apparently, it took words like these — antique, mystifying words that Rennie had never heard anyone use in ordinary conversation before — to communicate what she had learned about love over the weekend. Spoken by Oliver, the words were okay, beautiful even, but for Rennie to use them in speaking to Peter really would be kooky.

Why couldn't she tell him about it naturally, in her own words? She didn't know how.

Peter was the only person Rennie'd ever wanted to talk to about her feelings, yet she had never tried to articulate them. She had let her body speak, not her heart. And now she was unable to talk to Peter about what mattered most.

This morning, in the woodshed, while Daphne studied the expression of her eyes — her *spirit*, Oliver called it — Rennie had realized that there was more to love than making it with someone. She still thought so, but even as she visualized the crown of sunshine resting on Daphne's head, even as she repeated silently what she'd said about having to work at loving, all Rennie could *feel* was her need to love in the same old way.

Imagining the relief of being joined to Peter, Rennie felt a rude jolt when the car stopped and she found, looking up, that they'd already arrived at her dorm. Girls were sitting on the steps in the late afternoon sunshine. Like a detached observer, Rennie saw herself mounting those steps, stopping to yak with the girls, going to her room — the room that always seemed less home to her than Peter's — phoning her father.

You went to *Firbank* without *telling* me? You went to see *Oliver?* The happiness that filled Rennie when she landed, when she tried to tell Peter about Firbank, turned to pain, such furious pain that she started to cry.

Peter had already opened the door of the car. He slammed it again. With his other arm, he reached around and held Rennie tightly. "What's wrong?" he asked, as sobs began to shake her. "I thought you had a good time."

"I did. It's just —— I don't know. I hurt."

"You scared that your father's changed his mind about letting you get married?"

"He wouldn't do that. I don't *think* he would. Anyway, I'm nineteen."

She started to sob again. Peter rubbed his cheek against her curls.

"I loved it there," she managed to tell him finally. "They loved me. Everything's different here. It's not your fault," she assured him. "I'm just not the same person I was in Firbank. I liked myself better. But ——" She sniffed. "Here is where I am."

Struggling to pull herself together, Rennie looked at those girls sitting on the steps of the dorm. How can I walk past them? she wondered. My face must be a mess, all streaked and swollen.

Everyone would pounce on her, want to know what was the matter. She might even run into Mrs. Oldbody — that would just be her luck. The housemother would take Rennie into her apartment, find her a Kleenex, make her a mug of coffee, try to get to the bottom of her trouble.

A nice woman, Mrs. Oldbody, in spite of her name — not nosy, always on the side of the girls, fighting their battles with the dean. She probably knew that Rennie's bed was empty most nights, but she acted as if what Rennie did was her own business. A good woman, and yet, what could she do? What could anyone do?

"You're being romantic, Rennie," Peter was saying. "You were only in Firbank a couple of days, as a visitor. If you had to stay there and work, you'd feel about it the way you do about Tilbury."

Rennie didn't argue with him. She just shook her head. Peter couldn't understand, any more than that housemother.

Oh, but he did! Stroking her arm rhythmically, he said, "Let me take you over to my place first. Wash your face before you have to talk to all those girls. You can phone your father from the men's dorm."

Rennie swallowed. If she went to Peter's room now, feeling like this ——

When they got there, he tossed her a big, slightly used handkerchief. Then he wet his wash cloth, tipped up her chin, and dabbed her face — hard, the way a boy would do. That almost made Rennie laugh. "There," Peter said, "now run downstairs and call home."

"Not now." Looking around, Rennie observed, "The room's just the same. Nothing's changed."

Peter laughed. "What did you expect? You were only gone two days."

"A lot might have happened," Rennie said, remembering how afraid she'd been that that girl in his math class —— "What did you do while I was gone? You haven't told me anything. Did you sleep late?"

"No. Too much work. Walked this morning over the Ridge."

Rennie hardly dared ask, "By yourself?"

"A bunch of us went." That was all he told her.

But she knew that he loved her, that he wouldn't go off with another girl just because Rennie was in Firbank. Why did she worry?

She sat down on Peter's bed, feeling better the minute her backside encountered those lumps in the mattress that it had tried to dodge all year. She was in her world again, where she knew her way around.

"My selves are back together!" she announced. "This morning, in meeting, part of me drifted off. I was upset about that. But I got myself together again. You can't imagine how creepy that silence is. In a way, though, it's comforting, too. I got to thinking, during meeting, that if we were starting tonight — like, if we'd only just met — things would be different."

"How?"

138

"I'd listen to you. Not so much to what you say — more to what you feel. I've never really done that, have I?"

By way of answer, Peter sat down on the bed beside Rennie and took her in his arms, almost crushing her, though she could feel restraint in him, too. Her heart raced. She closed her eyes, abandoning everything, all her selves, to Peter. At last, she could tell him what she had felt at Firbank, without having to find words.

What she had felt at Firbank — it wasn't this, the same old thing, was it? There'd been all that stuff Oliver talked about. "Thy heart is the only lasting gift thee has to give to Peter," he'd said this morning.

But if, Rennie thought, not opening her eyes, just waiting, if Peter wants to —— Was that really restraint she imagined she felt while he held her so tightly? Or was he already breaking down, before the week was out? If he is, Rennie decided, I'll just forget the whole thing — Firbank and all that. If he wants to ——

Letting go, Peter stood up.

Rennie's eyes flew open. A sigh escaped her. She didn't know whether she was relieved or disappointed.

"Run down and phone," Peter urged. "Your father has something very important to tell you."

"What?"

"He wouldn't say. I kept asking him for a message, but he said he had to tell you himself. Go on," Peter said, pulling Rennie to her feet. "The sooner you get it over with, the better."

Slowly, Rennie moved toward the door. "Maybe Victoria's had the baby," she said, playing for time. "I hope it isn't twins. She sure looked like it. Remember, at the engagement party, how huge she was already?"

"No. I don't remember a thing about that party, except how I hated it. Once we're married, Rennie, we're going to do things *our* way. That's for sure. Now, go!"

2.

It was the same pay phone Rennie'd used only a few days ago, when she thought she was just going to find out whether Oliver was still alive and had ended up arranging to visit Firbank.

In spite of her reluctance, she was glad to be calling home. Her father would sputter at first, but then Rennie could tell him about his dream place, about Daphne's stroke and that he was all wrong about Oliver. He's not the least bit kooky, Daddy, she'd assure him, simply very honest and kind. As for the Vietnamese Forest — Rennie didn't think she'd mention that. Her father'd only laugh at Oliver's naïveté — anybody would. But he'd be so eager to hear the Firbank news! Rennie could scarcely control her impatience.

He must have been sitting by the phone, waiting for her call, because he answered on the first ring. Impatient himself, he ignored the operator when she asked whether he'd accept the charges. "Honey," he cried, while she was still talking to him. "I have the most wonderful thing to tell you!"

"Is it twins?" Rennie broke in quickly, so the operator wouldn't think her father was being fresh. How long would he go on talking before she could begin to tell him about Firbank?

"Is it *what?* Cut out your hippy lingo, Rennie. I don't understand that kind of talk and I have too much to tell you. Been trying all weekend to get through and you weren't there. Did you *really* go to *Firbank?* I just can't understand it. How could you have gone there without *me?* If you'd only *said* something, I'd have driven you over. You know how nervous Mother is about flying."

"That's why I didn't tell you — so she wouldn't worry."

"To think of your going to see Oliver behind my back!"

"Daddy!" Rennie cried, appalled. It had never occurred to her that she was doing anything sneaky. "I didn't dream you'd feel that way. I'm sorry."

"You know how much the place means to me, Rennie."

"I just wanted to find out how Quakers get married and you said Oliver was the only one you knew. So I went to ask him about the procedure. I guess it isn't really the kind of marriage we want."

"Of course not. I told you right away. If you'd only listened to me, you would have saved yourself the whole trip."

"But it was nice there, Daddy. And wait till you hear — Daphne painted my portrait!"

"That's it! That's her name — Daphne! On the tip of my tongue all along. A very beautiful woman."

"Except," Rennie said, dreading the effect on her father, "she's had a stroke."

"She has? Too bad."

"It's so awful. You should see her ——"

"Tell me about it when you come home. This is a toll call and I have important news — your wedding. It's settled! June twenty-first. West Neville United Church. Isn't that wonderful? I knew you'd be delighted. No need for you to do any more shopping around. I've got it all arranged."

"*You've* got it — ? I thought I — Peter and I ——"

"Yes, honey, I know. But the time kept getting shorter and shorter and you couldn't make up your minds what you wanted, so I simply had to take matters into my own hands. I phoned two or three churches in Neville — the big ones, like Trinity. But, of course, they were booked solid. Then I had the bright idea of trying some churches in West Neville and I called the minister at United. We were lucky. Just the day before, this couple had broken their engagement, so the church was available. I bet the minister was delighted to get another wedding on such short notice. It's all working out beautifully."

"I wonder why they broke the engagement," Rennie murmured.

"That other couple? Don't know. They have nothing to do with you, anyhow."

"Maybe not, but I'm sorry for them just the same. Suppose it had been us. Daddy, why didn't you tell Peter, when you spoke to him? He asked you to give him the message."

"The bride's family always decides these matters. Standard

operating procedure. Time enough, when you're married, for him to make decisions."

"He's planning for us both to."

"Now stop arguing, Rennie, and listen to me."

She didn't. "We don't know a soul who belongs to that church, do we, Daddy? How can Peter and I be married by total strangers?"

"Don't be silly. The people who belong to the church aren't the ones who'll marry you. It's the minister."

"We don't know him, either."

"That's what I'm getting at. If you'd only *listen* to me! Dr. Mifflin — that's the minister at United — makes a practice of interviewing couples three or four times before the wedding. He wants you and Pete to go and see him so he can discuss your ——"

"Clearness," Rennie broke in. "I know all about that." Apparently, this was standard operating procedure, too. She and Peter had no choice. To get married, they had to submit to some investigation.

"No," her father shouted, exasperated. "Not clearance. The man's already said he'd do it. He isn't one who'd go back on his word."

"I said clearness."

"Okay. Skip what you said. Just write down the address of the church. Fifth and ——"

"I don't have a pencil. I'm calling from a pay phone."

"Well, you can remember. Fifth and Linden streets, West Neville. You know where the Old Sachem's Trail comes in, by the library? It's across the street."

"Are there a lot of steps leading up to the door of the church?"

"I don't remember. Why? You want me to go and count them tomorrow?"

"Never mind."

Rennie wasn't about to tell her father that she had to be sure Daphne could get into the church. But it wouldn't be a problem. Two of Rennie's brothers — Larry and Jonathan, probably — would just have to be told to bring a porch chair from home so they could carry her out of the truck.

"Mifflin's expecting you this Saturday at three P.M. sharp," her father was saying. "Please don't be late. He's a busy man."

"*He's* busy! Peter and I have *exams*. We both need to study next weekend. Why can't we wait till college is out? Does Peter have to come, too? He wasn't planning to be in Neville till the wedding. His folks want him home. This'll be the last time."

"I told Mifflin it's a tough moment for you children, but he seemed adamant. Maybe if I phoned again, he'd waive those interviews. Just a formality, anyhow. No need for them, really, because I explained a husband's responsibilities to Pete myself, back in March, and Mother can have a heart-to-heart with you."

What about? Rennie wondered. The Pill? She knew a lot more on that subject than her mother.

"Right now, she's worried to death about getting everything done at such short notice," Rennie's father admitted, sounding worried himself. "The invitations, the gown, the bridesmaid business — all that."

Rennie could picture her mother throwing herself into this production, making lists, telephoning from morning to night, running in to New York to shop, enjoying herself so much that she was exhausted and irritable.

All because of me, Rennie thought, awed.

"You know how Mother has this unfortunate habit of getting fussed by social things," Rennie's father was saying. "But she always comes through. Anyhow, you'll be home soon and then you can cope with those details — take them off her hands."

"*Me?*"

"It's your wedding, isn't it?"

"No. I mean, yes."

"Okay. Would you like me to phone Mifflin and put the heat on? Tell him we don't need those interviews?"

"If they go with getting married in that church, how can *you* put the heat on, Daddy?"

How different he was from Oliver, who'd really tried to understand and help Rennie, even if there was nothing he could do. If she could only talk to Oliver now, she herself would see things more clearly. She'd been so dumb the other night, very much like her father — completely obtuse. And Oliver had listened patiently. Even the silence of Friends meeting would have been welcome in this hassle. Rennie'd learned a lot at Firbank, only now it was too late to communicate it to her parents. If she and Peter wanted a wedding, they'd have to settle for this one.

"About the gown," Rennie's father was saying. "Mother's picked out several very attractive models. I think you'll like them. She wants you to choose one on Saturday and get it fitted, after you've been to see Mifflin. Sunday noon, Mother and I thought, as long as you and Pete are going to be here, we'd have a few people in. Nothing elaborate, just some of our old friends."

Poor Peter, Rennie thought. Aloud she said, "Sunday? Oughtn't we to be going to church in West Neville? I mean, if we're going to be married there ——"

"I hadn't thought of that. Guess you're right. Well, some other Sunday. We've already invited a few people. If we go to West Neville, we won't be back in time."

"What do they believe in that church, anyhow, Daddy?"

There was a pause. "I don't know. Usual thing, I guess. Nothing extreme or embarrassing. Only trouble is, it seats fewer than we'd planned to invite — three hundred and fifty at the outside. But there's plenty of parking space. It's handy for the reception, too. The country club's only a block away. Oh, I haven't told you about that piece of luck. The Club steward agreed to squeeze us in although he has two other weddings that afternoon."

Rennie remembered the way Peter looked at the engagement party and she wondered how she was ever going to get him to that reception. Trying desperately to picture him on the receiving line, shaking three hundred and fifty hands, smiling politely at all those strange faces, Rennie suddenly had a scary thought. When they left the church, heading for the country club, they'd already be completely married, wouldn't they? Peter had warned her that, once they were married ——

"You don't appreciate how lucky we are, getting all these breaks," her father was saying plaintively.

144

Why must he make a spectacular out of the wedding? What was wrong with him, that he needed this so badly? How little he understood the person in Rennie! Maybe she didn't understand the person in him, either. Maybe if she listened ——

"I'll tell Peter," she promised, wishing she hadn't given her father such a hard time. "I'll see how he feels about it."

At that, Rennie's father blew up. "Too late now for a lot of discussion. Everything's settled and I don't want any further arguments. We've had enough shilly-shallying."

It's Peter's wedding, too, Rennie started to say, but her father sounded as if he couldn't take much more. She suddenly felt sorry for him. He'd been so elated about fixing up his only daughter's wedding in the style he'd always dreamed of and Rennie couldn't express enthusiasm or gratitude. For the first time in her life, she felt sorry for her father.

"Thanks, Daddy," she made herself say. "It was sweet of you to take all this trouble. Maybe Peter will stop in Neville on his way home. Then we can have at least one interview with Dr. Mifflin. That wouldn't be enough, though. He said three or four, didn't he?"

"I'll call him," Rennie's father promised, sounding relieved. "We'll work things out somehow."

"Yes," Rennie said without much conviction. "Way will open."

"What's that mean? You talking like a hippy again?"

"No, Daddy. Like a Quake."

3.

By the time Rennie got back to Peter's room, the cafeteria had closed. It was all the same to her. She wasn't hungry. Her father's announcement and the expression on Peter's face, when she relayed the news to him, had taken away her appetite. But Peter said they had to eat, so they went down to the corner and had hamburgers at that place they called The Grease Spot. It wasn't a festive meal.

Jammed into the tight, dim booth, Rennie felt a stinging lone-liness. They were isolated, the two of them against the world, wedged in here with the damp, sticky table between them, while, outside, their lives were being directed by others. Their profs were preparing the exams they would pass or fail, employers were scan-ning Peter's job applications (maybe) and rejecting them, Rennie's parents and that minister, the steward at the country club, the florist, the dress designer and her three sisters-in-law, each of whom had her own opinion, were cooking up that wedding. The only part Rennie and Peter would have in the whole affair would be to say, "I do."

A childish fantasy floated through her mind — suppose instead of murmuring "I do," she were to shout "You'd better believe it!"

Brine from the pickle oozed across the paper plate. Before start-ing on the hamburger, Rennie wanted to reach out and take Peter's hands, the way Oliver and Daphne took hers when they bowed their heads. But, of course, she couldn't do a thing like that — not here, in the booth, anyway. How was Peter to understand? Rennie didn't herself. She only knew that, as she sat at the polished kitchen table with Oliver and Daphne, joined in the circle of their love, she felt happy.

Now she felt depressed. So, obviously, did Peter. He said very little when she reported her conversation with her father. It was the way he looked that made Rennie want to do something desperate.

Surprisingly, the only thing that didn't upset Peter was the minister's insistence on those interviews.

"I told Daddy you don't have time," Rennie assured him, while they were eating. "He's going to ask whether we could skip them."

"Getting there's going to be a problem," Peter agreed, frowning. "But speaking to that minister's our only chance to find out what his church stands for. I'm not going to be married in a church I know nothing about. Your father doesn't care what it preaches, but I do. Suppose we're expected to say things we don't believe. How could we?"

"I don't even know what I believe. Do you?"

Hesitating, Peter said finally, "Maybe not altogether. But I sure know what I don't."

"You think that minister is just going to talk to us about religion?" Rennie cried suddenly. "I thought he wanted to examine our sex life, and when he found out, he'd refuse to perform the ceremony, tell Daddy —— Maybe that's all the committee on clearness was going to do — tell us what we had to know. I was afraid —— That's why I gave up on a Quaker marriage. Peter, you really would have gone for some of the things Oliver said."

"Like what?"

"He talked a lot about truth. The way he spoke of it, you'd almost think the *t* was capitalized. I don't know exactly what he meant — something more than just honesty, sort of like God, even. And he was always quoting, but not showing off. Bits from books are simply part of his conversation. It's hard to tell when he's quoting and when he's making things up. The first night, he said something about a principle that belongs to all religions. No one church has a monopoly on it. Men of all nations who cultivate it become brothers."

"Rennie, how great! Tell me more."

"The actual words are even more beautiful — like poetry, though not really. Someone quoted them again in meeting. They're by Woolman, I think. He's an old character Oliver and Daphne are nuts about — lived a couple of centuries ago. They made a pilgrimage to places where he went — backpacked. I wish I could remember the words." Rennie rummaged in her recollection. *"Where the heart stands — where the heart stands —"* but she couldn't remember where that heart stood.

Looking at her intently, clearly eager to find out where, Peter exclaimed, "He's a farmer? Sounds literary."

"That's what he really is — a writer, only he dropped out. If he'd finished his book, telling about their pilgrimage, the way he told me, it would have been as great as Woolman's. But he was too busy, taking care of people — the unemployed, the strikers, Daphne — and farming, planting trees, always planting trees."

There were many things Rennie could tell Peter about Oliver — how he'd said that a Quaker bride isn't given away by her father, but gives herself to the bridegroom, who gives himself to her; how Oliver had floored her by saying that if she and Peter were concerned only with themselves and not with being part of a religious community, why bother with a religious ceremony? That they were living together hadn't seemed to perturb him, only their getting married in a church with which they weren't involved.

"What an ass I was!" Rennie exclaimed. "I thought of those clearness people as meddlers. Actually, they'd have made us feel part of their community, the way Friends made me feel this morning after meeting. I *belonged* at that meal. It was nice."

Rennie told Peter about the Vietnamese Forest, about how Oliver had almost taken her in the dory across the pond to the dunes, only it was time for him to get Daphne's lunch.

"What he said was, 'Thee'll simply have to come back to Firbank. Come back and bring Peter.'"

It was harder when Rennie tried to communicate the outpouring of Daphne and Oliver's love; to explain that they had so much, they could afford to let it spill over onto other people. Even if she had found words to say this without sounding corny, it wasn't the moment. The mood Peter was in, speaking of love would only make matters worse. Rennie didn't see any relation between love and the wedding her parents were planning.

What had made her think that Oliver and Daphne would come? Daphne couldn't travel all that distance in the truck or any other way. Besides, they'd hate the whole performance. But it would have been a comfort to know that they were there, in the church. It would have made the whole occasion more *pure*, somehow.

"Hasn't he any faults?" Peter asked suddenly.

"Oliver? Oh, I guess so. He's terribly pernickety — that's why he speaks plain language. He says it isn't truth to address a single person in the plural. And the house — you'd think nobody ever slept there. The beds are always made, just like at home, only Mother doesn't have anything else to do. Oliver has the farm and taking care of Daphne. Even so, he polishes the kitchen table so hard, you can see yourself in it."

"Do they have any children?"

"One — Heather. She lives in London, so they just see her in summer. I wonder," Rennie murmured, surprised by her own curiosity, "I wonder what Heather's like."

"That Vietnamese Forest idea," Peter was saying. "It doesn't sound too good."

"No. Judy Young called it 'quixotic.' Austin's a potato farmer, so I guess she knows what she's talking about. Still, faults wouldn't take away from Oliver's wonderful simplicity of heart, would they? I mean, little faults?"

"You're sure hooked," Peter said, laughing at her.

"I wish you had come. Then you'd understand."

But it wouldn't have been the same, Rennie had to acknowledge to herself.

Why? Did she need to be apart sometimes, too? Until now, she'd always clung to Peter. Was going to Firbank for her what those long walks were to him? Did he and she have to be whole persons separately, as well as joined? Wasn't that a contradiction? The tall, skinny girl in Peter's math class wasn't any real threat and Rennie knew it. Insecurity just made her latch on to the girl — the fear of losing Peter. But Firbank — it couldn't be, could it, that Oliver would come between them now — not Oliver the person, but his views on life?

The thought that she might have to give up all that Firbank had become to her this weekend or lose Peter made Rennie hurt again, the way she did when they drove up in front of her dorm and she realized that she was back in a world she didn't like. She had wanted to get out, rush back to Firbank with Peter. And now she wondered whether she'd be happy with him there.

He was standing up. Reaching for Rennie's hand, he pulled her to her feet. "Come on," he said, "back to the books. Better get to bed early, too. You looked bushed."

"I — am," Rennie answered shakily. "But I've got to work. Didn't do a thing in Firbank. How was I to know we'd have to go to West Neville next weekend, just before exams?"

They spoke little as they walked to Rennie's dorm. On the doorstep, she thought, At least, after the wedding, we won't have to live apart any more.

"It'll be like taking the exams," she called to Peter as he was starting to leave.

"What will?"

"The wedding. Terribly painful, but once it's over we can live happily ever after."

In her room, Rennie turned the book bag upside down and shook the contents out over her bed. On top of the pile of books and clothes, there was the Chocomarsh.

Oh! I forgot to give it to Daphne!

Rennie could have cried. The candy bar was such a little thing. Still, she'd wanted Daphne to have it. During the silence, she'd planned to fish it out as soon as she could. But when meeting closed with all that handshaking, Friends surrounded Rennie, introducing themselves, telling her how happy they were to have her there. A couple of old folks remembered her great-grandmother. Some man said he'd grown up with her father's mother. Rennie'd been invited to sign the guest book, which lay open on a little table in the vestibule. She'd barely done that when Nancy and Sandy rushed over, tugged at her arms and dragged her away to the First Day school. They wanted, they explained, to be sure of getting three seats together for the fellowship meal. With all that happening, Rennie'd forgotten the candy bar.

And those other gifts she'd thought about during the silence — what she wanted to bring back to Peter: simplicity of heart, joy, beauty —— She hadn't given them to him, either. Where were they?

Carrying an armful of books from the bed to the desk, Rennie suddenly stood still. She was holding something that didn't belong to her — a package done up in corrugated paper held together with rubber bands. How had this got into her bag? Had she taken it from Peter's room?

150

She dropped the pile of books on the desk and fumbled with the rubber bands. Her great-grandmother's copy of Woolman! That's what she was holding! Had she picked it up by mistake? Embarrassed, she thought, I must send it right back. Could the mails be trusted?

Standing there, feeling the nap of the worn leather with her finger tips, Rennie recalled how reverently Oliver had handled the book. She looked for Daphne's water color, but the book opened at the fly leaf. In the upper corner was Serenity Millburn's name. Under it, Oliver had added:

> For our cousin, Serenity the Second,
> whose coming has brought great joy to
> Daphne and Oliver

Rennie gasped. They were giving her their treasure! Secretly, Oliver had slipped the surprise into her book bag. Daphne had signed her name. Rennie knew what effort went into shaping those six letters.

She wanted to run across the campus right away and show this to Peter, but first she flopped across the bed, just to look at the book a minute. Turning the page, she came to Daphne's little water color — the rosy brick house with the well sweep and those huge trees at the corners. Daphne had painted more than a farmhouse. She'd created a mood, backward- and forward-looking at the same time — nostalgic and expectant.

On the next page were those words that Oliver had read to Daphne as they lay in the high, brass bedstead: *I have often felt a motion of love* . . .

Rennie could hear Oliver reading in that surprisingly young voice, pausing from time to time to look off into space. It was as if she were back in the woodshed at Firbank, among the portfolios and canvases, enfolded by those plain, unplastered walls.

4.

All three of Rennie's sisters-in-law telephoned first thing Monday morning, one after the other — Jane, then Matty, then Victoria. That's what woke Rennie. The reading lamp was on, shining in her eyes. She reached out quickly and turned it off.

Lying there, listening to the phone ring, Rennie wondered what she was doing, sprawled on top of her bed, still wearing the blouse and skirt she'd put on yesterday in Firbank. Serenity's book lay beside her, opened at the first chapter. Before Rennie'd even finished the first page, before she could run to Peter's room, she must have fallen asleep. As for spending the evening studying ——

"Rennie?" Jane cried.

"Mm."

"Anything wrong? I've been ringing and ringing. Must be five minutes. I was afraid you were dead or something. You sound funny. Not a hangover, I hope. Forget it, I was just kidding. I know you wouldn't go smoking pot or anything like that. There's this boy across the street from us, got picked up for possession of drugs. I couldn't believe it. Very fine family. Father's a ——"

"What's up, Jane?"

"I just called to ask — were these orchid bridesmaid dresses your idea? I didn't think so. The most godawful color — swears with everything. Never mind. It'll be a fun wedding anyway. Get yourself some coffee, kid."

Jane had barely hung up when Matty called to say that Jonathan objected to hiring those striped pants and a monkey jacket. Why was Rennie putting on the dog, for goodness' sake? At *her* wedding, the ushers wore ——

"How's Peter?" Matty asked in closing, without giving Rennie a chance to answer. "Has he cheered up yet? I never saw such a sad sack as he was at that engagement party. Anyone'd think it's a shotgun wedding."

Rennie was just going back to sleep when the phone rang again. Victoria was in a state. Her mother-in-law! Now the woman was insisting that the bridesmaid dresses be ordered right away.

"You know how she is, Rennie. Why can't she wait till after the baby's born? There'll still be time before the wedding. How am I to tell what size I'll be then?"

Victoria proceeded to give Rennie a detailed rundown of statistics — her waist and bust measurements before and after each of her previous pregnancies, the weight she'd gained, the weight she'd lost — as proof that ordering her dress now was absolutely insane. Rennie was to call up her mother and prevail upon her to be reasonable.

"Me?" Rennie managed to put in. "What can I do? She never listens to me."

"But it's your wedding! If you can't have things your way at your own wedding, when can you? Believe me, after you're married, you're never going to. Your in-laws will call the shots." Victoria was becoming hysterical.

"Okay," Rennie said, simply to shut her up. "I'll try."

Rennie decided to get out of the room fast, before her mother squeezed her call in. But first she had to clean up her bed. That Chocomarsh — if only she hadn't forgotten to give it to Daphne! She must have fallen asleep reading. Rolling over on the candy bar, she'd squashed it till the wrapper split. Now the whole thing was one sticky blob, streaked across the bedspread, Rennie's blouse, her skirt and both arms. The gooey stuff was all over the place, revolting. A shower — that's what Rennie needed first. She could hardly keep her eyes open long enough to find the bathroom.

Oh, the library!

Those books Rennie'd dragged all the way to Firbank and never opened were due by nine-thirty. How was she going to get to the library so soon? She couldn't concentrate. She hurried, but she didn't know what she was doing. Getting dressed, running across the campus, sitting through that conference with her adviser — these were all just painful delays she had to endure until she could show Peter her treasure.

When she finally reached his room, he was working. She didn't dare interrupt. But, after lunch, they spent an hour in the college garden, lying on their stomachs under a tree, looking at the book.

"It must be worth a fortune," Peter observed, when he saw the date on the title page. "Do you realize that this was printed the year the American Revolution began?" He ran his fingers over the brown stains at the edges of the title page. "When these old books get damp, the sizing runs."

Rennie drew his attention to the frontispiece, explaining why the house in Mount Holly had so much significance. Peter nodded gravely, as if he understood.

"We could go there ourselves sometime," Rennie said timidly, wondering how he'd respond to this. "I think the house is still standing. Oliver didn't say it wasn't. One never knows, though," she added anxiously, "with urban renewal and all that." There was no assurance anyplace, no stability, even in bricks and mortar. All of a sudden, without warning, an old, familiar skyline changed completely. Here today, gone tomorrow.

Why should this thought provoke anxiety? Rennie had a mad desire to snatch the book and hold it tightly against her breast. She couldn't, because Peter was looking at it. Trying to be rational, she told herself that at least she had Daphne's water color. For her, the house would always stand, indestructible, a landmark.

Peter wasn't listening. He had begun the first chapter. What would his reaction be to that bit about the experience of the goodness of God? Rennie hoped he wouldn't be put off by it. But he was way past that now, already in the second chapter, grunting assent as he came to the part Oliver had quoted to Rennie.

Reading on, Peter stopped suddenly. "That makes sense!" he exclaimed. "Woolman believed that slavery didn't just hurt the slaves, but that it hurt the slaveowners, too. I bet he was the only one who saw that. He says that by forcing blacks to work, the planters were actually victimizing their own children. The parents made it possible for their children to live in ease, but they also passed trouble on to them. The craving for luxury and idleness, instilled by the parents, would lead to war. It did!" Peter read on. "*Children feel themselves encompassed with difficulties prepared for them by their predecessors.*"

"That sounds like me," Rennie murmured, smiling wryly, but sighing at the same time. "Encompassed with difficulties. My predecessors — Mother and Daddy — they're the ones who've got us into these difficulties about the wedding. Not only you and me, but Jane and Matty and Victoria and the boys — the whole family, in fact. Nobody's happy."

Absorbed in reading, Peter paid no attention. Rennie felt a jab of jealousy. She wanted him to like the book, but she felt she was being left out, just the way Daphne and Oliver had left her out during the silence in meeting, when they seemed so far away.

Recalling the strange power of that silence, Rennie thought, It isn't true. Mother and Daddy didn't get us into this trouble. Peter and I did. We got ourselves into it. We'll have to get ourselves out.

Peter had found some folded sheets of paper that had been put in the book. They looked very old. Rennie noticed how carefully he spread them open.

"Great-grandmother must have written that," she told him. "See? It's the same handwriting as in her name on the flyleaf."

But Peter didn't turn to the front of the book. He was reading the top sheet aloud: "*Wealth is attended with power, by which bargains and proceedings contrary to universal righteousness are supported; and here oppression, carried on with worldly policy and order, clothes itself with the name of justice and becomes like a seed of discord in the soil.*"

Peter let out an enchanted whistle. "Beautiful! That's exactly how things are right now." He read on to himself. Coming to another sentence that struck him particularly, he repeated it for Rennie. "*May we look upon our treasures, the furniture of our houses, and our garments and try* — I guess," Peter put in, "that means judge — *whether the seeds of war have any nourishment in these our possessions.* Beautiful! It doesn't mean the stark poverty of Saint Francis or socialism, just a voluntary scaling down to essentials. This house Woolman built doesn't look like a slum! All he's saying is, everybody should decide for himself what's most important and give up the luxuries."

The chapel chimes struck two. Peter had a class. Reluctantly, he closed the book. Then he opened it again and took out the folded sheets, hunting for a sentence that had impressed him. To Rennie's surprise, it was the same one that had jolted Oliver. *"To turn all the treasures we possess into the channel of universal love becomes the business of our lives,"* he read. "Beautiful! The business of our lives — I want to remember that. This guy's real."

"Why can't we be?" Rennie cried in agony, turning to Peter, imploring him to tell her how they could become so. But, of course, he didn't know, any more than she did.

All week long, this question recurred to Rennie: Why can't we be real? Each day, she seemed to be more separated from her self. This had troubled her in Kendal. Now, she was actually glad of it. Part of her had floated away, leaving the other part playing those roles — the docile student, appearing to listen raptly to her adviser as he prescribed the education courses she'd have to take next year, when she didn't give a damn about them; the docile daughter assenting to her parents' proliferating plans for the wedding, when she hated them more and more.

The whole week long, Rennie went around in this dutiful haze, accepting everything because she was persuaded that her real self was someone else — not this role player, who acquiesced to what she didn't believe in. Her real self was way off in a place where the heart stands in perfect sincerity.

On Thursday, her father telephoned to say that Dr. Mifflin was obliged to cancel the appointment for Saturday. "He has a funeral. Very inconvenient, but people can't help dying. That interview was just a formality, anyhow."

"Peter finally managed to borrow some guy's car," Rennie wailed. "Seemed as if everyone was going away this weekend. He had an awful time. And now ——"

"That's all right. You have to come home anyhow to choose your gown."

Strange, uncalled-for words echoed in Rennie's head. *May we look upon our garments. . . the seeds of war . . .*

"And there's our party Sunday noon," her father was saying. "Mifflin doesn't know when he can see you now. The only free time he has is after the service, but you can't go then."

"Why not? It's important."

"I just told you. All these people are coming. They want to meet Pete."

"But he wants to talk to Dr. Mifflin."

"What about? It's not his wedding. I mean, I'm arranging it."

Now this! Rennie cried inside herself. Instead of clearness, it's cocktails. How am I going to tell Peter?

"By the way," her father added, as she was about to hang up, "there's a letter here for you. I didn't forward it because you're coming."

Who'd write to Rennie at home?

"It's not from the Dean of Studies, is it?" Was he giving her the gate? He wouldn't do that before exams. Anyway, her marks weren't *that* bad. "It's not from college, is it, Daddy?"

"No, it's from Kendal."

"Kendal! From Oliver?" He'd written to her! Just when she was longing so to talk to Oliver, he'd written!

"No. Somebody named Young. A. Young. Periwinkle Farm. Who's that?"

"Austin. Mary Young's son." Rennie was disappointed. Only Austin.

"One of your Firbank friends?" There was a touch of jealousy in her father's voice.

"Not exactly. I just met Austin and Judy at meeting. After lunch, they drove me to the airport. I don't know what he'd write about. Can't be very important."

"Would you like me to open it? I'll read it to you."

The unmistakable eagerness in her father's offer brought out the negative in Rennie. "Never mind," she said. "I can wait till Saturday."

5.

"So just because of Dr. Mifflin's funeral," Peter was saying with a cynical edge to his voice, "we can't find out what gives in that church."

"It's not his funeral," Rennie explained. "He isn't dead. He's just the one who's doing the talking at it."

She had tried not to look at Peter's face when she told him about their having to go to Neville anyhow on account of the gown and that party. It wouldn't have surprised her if he had balked, but he said nothing.

On Saturday, he got the car that he'd arranged to borrow and they left right after lunch. Less than half an hour from Neville, Peter suddenly turned off the highway and parked at the side of an ice-cream shop. Rennie thought, Why now? We're almost home.

"Let's get some cones," he said. "It's hot."

He's putting it off as long as he can, Rennie thought sadly. How he hates going home with me! And suddenly she asked herself, Why do I do this to him? I love him. Shouldn't I be making him happy instead of ——

They sat at the counter, swiveling on high stools.

"What'll you have?" he asked. "French vanilla? Dutch chocolate? Burnt almond? Maple walnut? Black raspberry?"

Slowly, he read off the flavors painted in a long list on the wall behind the counter, turning to Rennie questioningly after each one — fifteen in all. As he read, she followed the list, unable to decide.

"Cape Cod cranberry? Butter pecan? Strawberry mouse?"

"Mousse!" Rennie corrected. Then she thought, I'm just like

Daddy, jumping on Mother when she says "Quakers." What difference does it make?

"Mousse," Peter repeated, grinning.

Rennie saw that she'd been caught. Peter had said "mouse" to tease her; he knew better. A flicker of his old fun-loving self twinkled in his eyes, but it was just a flicker. Then he returned to the serious business before them. "Orange sherbet? Lemon? Pineapple?"

So many exciting flavors! Which did Rennie wish for *most*?

My central wish, she thought, recalling the words she'd heard in Kendal and how she had tried to make a wish during the silence, tried with all her might, not knowing what it was she wished for.

She turned and swiveled till her knee touched Peter's. "Do you realize," she asked, "that everyone has something precious in him that's in no one else? To know this secret self, one only has to make a wish, but it must be a *central* wish."

Here, in the ice-cream shop, with the juke box playing, those words didn't convey what they did in that quiet meetinghouse. Maybe they had to be quoted correctly and Rennie couldn't remember.

"Marshmallow fudge?" Peter continued, running down to the bottom of the list, as if he hadn't heard Rennie's question. "Maine blueberry? Canton ginger? Peppermint stick?"

He had come to the end. Now he just sat there, looking at Rennie, waiting, not pressing her to make up her mind.

She'd heard each flavor as he read it, tried out the taste on the tongue of her imagination, asked herself whether that one was what she wanted more than any other. All the while, she was hearing something else — Peter.

With each flavor, he was sending her an SOS, wasn't he? Stringing out the simple business of buying her an ice-cream cone in order to delay getting to Neville.

"What'll you have?" Peter asked again.

And, suddenly, Rennie thought she knew what it was she wished for. "You," she told him. "I don't want a cone. I want you — you

159

feeling good about things, the way you used to. Let's get out of here." She was losing control of her voice.

The waitress stared at her across the counter.

Like an animal fighting its way out of a cage, Rennie jumped down from the stool and escaped through the swinging door.

Outside, Peter grabbed her arm. "What's the matter? You sick?"

"I've got to go somewhere quiet and think."

There was a picnic table at the edge of the parking lot. They climbed over the bench that was bolted to it and sat down, side by side. Beyond the table stood a row of trash cans.

Rennie ignored them. She was trying to find words for her feelings. "When I saw all those flavors," she explained, "it hit me. There's more than one choice. We can have anything we want, can't we? Why do we have to take that wedding? It isn't —" Rennie hesitated to use the word — "truth. You know — real."

Peter's face lit up. "You mean —— Are you saying, you'd be willing to wait? Oh, Rennie!" He had looked at her lovingly, longingly for months, but never like this.

"I don't know what I'm saying, just that if it weren't for the wedding, everything would be peaceful. I'm not studying. They'll throw me out of school. We're simply being pushed around."

"That's for sure!"

"Oliver and Daphne took things into their own hands, as you said we would after we're married. Why can't we start now?"

Peter was still looking at Rennie in a way that convinced her she'd made the right decision, but then he turned anxious. "What about your folks?"

"I know. It's going to be rough."

"Mine'll be in heaven," Peter admitted. "They just couldn't see me marrying without a job and another year of school. It didn't make sense to them and I've been feeling for a long time that they're right, only I promised you and I wasn't going to go back on my word."

"Peter! Why didn't you say so? It's not fair, keeping things from me."

A guilty look crossed his face. He said, "It was the only way I could be with you this summer. If they'd just leave us alone! Let us wait till fall, give us time to work out a better kind of wedding —— By the end of the summer, I'll have a little money — I hope. It would be different if I had landed a really good job, one that paid decently. Then I'd have been willing to face that wedding — get it over with. As it is ——"

"Stop worrying about money," Rennie begged. "I've got plenty. My allowance ——"

"Yes," Peter broke in bitterly, "and your father's credit cards."

"Where could we go for the summer?" Rennie asked. "Someplace that wouldn't cost." She didn't need his reply. "Firbank!"

"No," Peter said emphatically. "I'm not going to Firbank. This summer I'm working, even if all I can get is mowing lawns. Plenty of people in Charlesbury would give me lawn jobs."

A different thought popped into Rennie's mind. It made her suddenly shy. "Peter?" She dropped her head and stared into her lap, almost afraid to whisper, "Could we maybe make a pilgrimage?"

He put his arm around her shoulders and brought his head down to the level of hers. Their curving bodies formed a kind of shelter, a nest. From the center of it, Peter asked, "Where to?"

Rennie hesitated.

If she had been able to see him, she wouldn't have dared answer this way. But in that little nest, so close that they couldn't see each others' eyes, she found the courage, when he repeated softly, "Where to? What would we be going after?" to whisper back, "Our humanity."

Still holding her, Peter answered in the same hushed voice, "Our whole life is going to be a pilgrimage to find our humanity, Rennie, starting now, today, this minute."

"I mean," she said, "couldn't we backpack, like Daphne and Oliver, when they walked the roads, seeking the direction their lives should take? You and I are seeking, too."

They were still so close that Rennie couldn't see Peter. Surprised, she thought, We're joined now as we've never been before.

But then Peter let her go and straightened up. "We're seeking, all right," he said gravely, "but we can't take six weeks out just to bum. Your folks wouldn't like it and I'm not playing with you anymore while your father picks up the tab. We can stay in Charlesbury. My folks would love to have you, now that we aren't ——"

Charlesbury! Amusing Peter's little sisters all day while he was out mowing lawns; helping his mother with the housework. Mrs. Holland would soon discover how useless Rennie was. To spend the whole summer in Charlesbury ——

Raising her head, Rennie took in the trash cans. They were filled to overflowing and the covers didn't fit. There were crushed paper cups and remnants of ice-cream cones strewn on the ground. Above the cans, the air was black with flies.

First, Rennie thought, you have a choice of all those yummy flavors.

6.

Leaving the ice-cream shop, Peter stepped on the gas. Earlier, he'd dawdled, putting off their arrival in Neville. Now he seemed eager to get there. Rennie, hiding her face in his sleeve, was the one who wanted to dawdle now. How was she going to break the news to her parents? Did she really have the courage?

Suddenly she drew back and looked at Peter anxiously. "What about the apartment? We've paid the deposit. If we aren't legally married ——"

"Don't try to cross that bridge yet, Rennie. I may still land a good job this summer. Then we'll get married before we go back to school."

Relieved, Rennie was about to nuzzle against his shoulder again when another thought struck her. "You don't mean, do you," she asked incredulously, drawing back, "you don't mean, if we aren't getting married, we're never, ever going to have sex, the *whole summer?*"

Peter didn't answer.

"Do you? How can we stand it?"

All Peter said was, "My folks are trusting. If we sneak off while we're staying with them, they'll feel I've let them down. They'd worry about the girls, too. Try to hide something from my little sisters! To them, I'm someone pretty great, someone to take after."

"I think you're great, too! Maybe you've got something. I mean, perfect sincerity —— But I always thought, as long as nobody gets hurt ——"

"Somebody would get hurt and I don't want it to be my parents. Matter of fact, you and I are hurt, Rennie, with your parents insisting on this rotten wedding, just because they suspect we've been up to something. They're hurt, too."

"*They're hurt?* Do you really think so?"

"Of course! You know yourself they're not happy about you. Could be, that's why they want this big show — to put a good face on things. And if you don't think there's anything wrong, why are you feeling guilty?"

"I'm not!"

"You said yourself, when you told me about Daphne painting your portrait, that you panicked because you didn't want her to know. You must have felt guilty."

Rennie looked down into her lap. Guilty? Is that how she felt when she screamed and Oliver came running? No. It was just that she thought Daphne wouldn't understand. She didn't want to appear like that to Daphne.

"Besides," Peter was saying, "I want us to determine what we're doing, not just to be at the mercy of our emotions all the time. I don't want to be pushed around anymore, by your parents, by sex, anything. That's what's so great about Woolman — he was in control of his life, not a pushover for his boss or his desires."

Rennie looked at Peter. She had the feeling she'd thumbed a ride with a stranger — he was so different. When they'd started out, he'd been willing to accept the wedding, the reception, the whole package. And now —— Rennie herself was responsible for this — her realization that there were many options. If Peter was turning out to be somebody different —— Hot though it was, she shivered.

When they reached the house and started up the walk, dragging their feet, they were both grim.

Suddenly, Rennie had a thought that made her giggle. "Jonathan's going to be mighty pleased!" she exulted. "He won't have to rent that monkey jacket, after all. And Victoria can relax."

They both laughed. But when they entered the house and Rennie saw how happy her parents were to see her, how warmly they welcomed Peter, her heart sank. Incongruously, she thought of Firbank, of the grandfather clock in the entrance hall and the chair at the foot of the stairs, where Oliver had dropped her book bag when she arrived — he'd been so impatient to take her in to meet Daphne. The entrance hall in her parents' split level was entirely different, half filled by that hideous rubber plant and the massive, wrought-iron banister. Why should Rennie be reminded of Firbank here?

Her mother had made some lemonade. She brought the pitcher into the living room. Rennie's father followed, pressing Peter for his opinion as to which team was likely to win the pennant.

"I'm just going up to my room for a second," Rennie announced, hoping Peter wouldn't feel deserted. "Be right back." As soon as she came down again, she'd tell her parents.

"Don't take long," her mother begged. "The manager of the Bridal Boutique is waiting for us. She's giving this gown personal attention."

Her mother's words hit Rennie like a slap. She could barely make it up the stairs. On her bureau there was a letter, addressed in what looked like a high school boy's writing. The Kendal letter! Rennie tore it open and read:

DEAR RENNIE,

Hope you got back to college okay. Judy and I stayed and watched your plane go up.

The man who drives my tractor broke his leg yesterday. He wasn't on the tractor, on his motor bike, going to the beach. It's a bad time for me. Oliver says the man you are marrying is looking for a job. Would he want to work on a potato farm? If he's interested, tell him to phone me right away collect.

Judy says hello.

Your friend,
AUSTIN YOUNG

Rennie rushed to the head of the stairs. "Peter! Come here. Right away! Peter!"

He bounded up, looking anxious, evidently thinking she was hurt. She handed him the letter.

Rennie's parents came rushing to her room.

"What is it? Rennie, what's the matter?" her mother cried before she reached the landing.

Her father followed, climbing the stairs more slowly. He took in the situation. "It's that letter from Kendal. What's it about?"

"Austin Young's offering Peter a job!" Rennie cried, rushing toward her parents and giving them each a hug.

"Running his tractor," Peter explained. "Gee, I'd love to work outdoors all summer. Mr. Ross, could I use your phone to call collect? Right away?"

"I hope it's not too late," Rennie murmured, wishing she had let her father open the letter the other night.

Maybe I should tell them now, she thought, while Peter's calling Austin. Then he won't have to take the first blow. But it suddenly dawned on her that if Peter got the job they might get married, after all. He'd said that he'd be willing, if he had a decent summer job. Why couldn't they live at Firbank, like Oliver and Daphne, when they were first married, staying with Serenity? Had Peter seen this, too? The whole picture was suddenly changed.

It seemed no more than a minute before Peter came bounding up the stairs again, two at a time, calling to Rennie, "It's okay!" He looked jubilant. "I'm going next week, right after my last exam. He needs me pretty badly. There's a room in the loft I can use."

Rennie thought, *I'm* going — that's what he said. Not *We*.

"When will you be back?" Rennie's mother asked. "There's the rehearsal dinner and our boys will want to get together with some of your bachelor friends before the wedding."

"What's more," Rennie's father put in, "I have an awful feeling Mifflin will insist on those interviews."

For a minute, Peter just stood there, looking at Rennie's parents, then at Rennie. At length, he said, speaking only to her, but loud enough for her parents to hear, "It's a good job. If you want to, you can still change your mind."

"Change her mind about what?" Rennie's mother cried.

"Getting married," Rennie told her. "I mean, not getting married." She turned to Peter. "Do you want to?" She remembered how Oliver had said, in describing the moment when he and Daphne began their pilgrimage, that they were "of one mind."

"It's up to you," Peter answered, looking at her in a way that told her he was giving her the choice, yet it left no doubt about his preference.

"What is?" Rennie's father demanded. "Not getting married? What are you two talking about?"

Rennie disregarded him. "We're of one mind," she told Peter, taking him by the hand.

He turned and faced her parents. "Mr. and Mrs. Ross," he announced, not as if he were making a big speech, delivering earth-shaking news, just matter-of-factly, "Rennie and I have decided to put off our marriage. We're not breaking up. This just isn't the time. In the fall ——"

Rennie was looking intently at the wall-to-wall carpet in her room, absorbed in following the lines where it was stitched together. It was sewed so neatly that the piecing hardly showed.

"But we've ordered the invitations!" her mother cried. "It's too late. They put through a special rush order."

Rennie's father took a step toward Peter. "You can't do that!" He sounded furious. But then, surprisingly, he broke into a laugh. "Many couples get these last-minute jitters," he said, thoroughly amused. "Seems to me, now that I come to think of it, something like this happened to us, too. Didn't it, Joan? But I never would have given in to it. That's not manly of you, Pete. Let me tell you children, you're making a big mistake, acting up like this. You'll regret it later."

With the most tremendous effort, Rennie managed to detach her attention from the lines in the carpet. "We're not acting up, Daddy," she assured him. "We mean it. We're going to get married, only not June twenty-first."

"Of course you're getting married June twenty-first," her father shouted. "Everything's settled. I don't want to hear another word."

"What about the wedding presents?" Rennie's mother asked in that deceptively placid tone she always used when she was particularly agitated. Her thumb rubbed the tips of her fingers nervously. "My cousins didn't wait for the invitations. The guest room is already cluttered with boxes of presents you haven't even looked at. If you call off the wedding, you'll have to send them all back, Rennie. Write everyone notes, explaining." Her voice took on a bitter overtone. "Don't expect me to help you."

Write notes? With exams coming up? Mother must be crazy.

Rennie went over to her. "I know you're disappointed," she said as calmly as she could. "I'm sorry. But Peter and I can't face it right now." Rennie turned so that she was speaking to her father, too. "All that stuff that has nothing to do with the business of our lives —— We want to live more free from outward cumbers." She reached up and put her arms around her father's neck.

He didn't draw away, yet she could feel his tense body expressing irritation and she knew she had used the wrong language. Why couldn't she just speak like herself? She didn't blame her father if those words got to him.

"In that case," he said sternly, "you're staying with us this summer. We'll take you to Europe. You've always wanted to see the Louvre. I'll try to get some time off."

"No," Rennie cried, letting go of him. "I want to be in Firbank. Heather and Stephen will be there and I can help. I have a right to go. The place belongs to me."

"It does nothing of the kind!"

"Your grandmother left Firbank to all her descendants. Didn't you know? It's yours, too, Daddy."

"It's Oliver's, no matter what Grandmother wrote in her will. But never mind about that. I don't want you running around with a man you're not married to." He gave Peter a warning glance. "If you're both going to Kendal ——"

"We won't do anything you don't want us to, Daddy. I'll be okay."

Rennie's mother didn't hear this. She had run out of the room.

"I'll be okay," Rennie repeated. She might falter, but Peter was determined.

Reaching up and putting her arms around her father's neck again, Rennie looked at him, pleading for understanding, trying to make him see that she didn't mean to hurt him, that she simply wanted her heart to stand in perfect sincerity.

She'd never looked at him so lovingly, so eager to have him back her up in a decision she knew was right. Then she had a shock. This was the first time she'd ever seen her father cry.

Part Four

*T*he dunes that separated Salt Pond from the ocean were covered with clumps of coarse grass and beach pea. Stepping barefoot from the soft, warm sand onto the prickly grass, Rennie and Peter got a stinging surprise. Oliver had told them that the dune grass took its revenge this way when it was trodden on. But the beach pea — that delicate mauve flower, like a small sweet pea — simply died.

"And we need it," he explained. "This sparse vegetation is all that keeps our bulwark of sand from blowing away. If we lost the dunes, the ocean would engulf the pond and flood the farm."

Every afternoon when Peter finished work, he biked over to Firbank. Then he and Rennie rowed across the pond.

It was awesome, after beaching the dinghy on the mud flat at the edge of the pond, to climb to the top of the dunes and behold the ocean. Rennie and Peter stood there, hand in hand, leaning against the breeze, watching the surf pound and break along the shore. After the stillness of the pond, ruffled only by the plaintive call of a piping plover, they found the roar exciting.

The beach stretched as far as they could see, east and west. Apart from the terns circling overhead and an occasional surf caster in high rubber boots, there was no one.

"The beach belongs to us," Rennie exulted. "To you and me!"

Lying side by side on the sand, gently toasting, they were close enough to touch, but it was only with their eyes that they communicated love. They were content to wait. Like the beach, their lives stretched endlessly before them, all theirs now, free of outside interference. They were free, too, of that frantic greediness they'd been consumed by at college. It seemed out of place here. They had forever and their frenzy was slowed to the rhythm of the ocean — deliberate, constant, measured against eternity.

They'd never taken time before to put their feelings into words. Now, with all of life before them, they talked endlessly, telling about themselves, about things that had happened, as if they'd only recently met.

"Just when I thought I had my identity as an astronomer finally fixed," Peter said one afternoon, picking up a fistful of sand and letting it run slowly through his fingers, "I go and find I'm happy farming. Austin's made me see how much more there is to it than just weeding and spraying. Don't worry. This isn't another identity crisis, like that time, end of freshman year."

Hesitantly, finding it hard to speak of this, even now, Peter told Rennie why he'd wanted to leave college then.

"All that cynicism! Not really trusting anybody —— In Charlesbury, there are plenty of bad guys, but until they've proved it, you believe they're decent. Generous, too. I couldn't get used to this dog-eat-dog, every-man-out-for-himself stuff at college. Another thing — we have so much fun at home. My father kids a lot. He's never unkind. It's just that he has this way of seeing the funny side of things, even the most serious."

"Like Oliver!"

"I guess so. Hadn't thought of that. It's what makes Dad such a great teacher. I'm used to cheerfulness. Then I get to Tilbury and there are all those guys and girls going around depressed, not bothering to comb their hair, psyching each other out, wondering why they came, unable to decide what they want from life, everything's awful. It got to me finally."

Rennie thought, That's past! He's happy now.

But, in the back of her mind, there was always something Oliver had intimated when she'd phoned to ask whether she might spend the summer at Firbank. He'd been delighted about that and about the postponement of the wedding.

"Thee and Peter have won freedom to make your own decisions," he exulted.

"Yes!" Rennie had sung out joyfully. "And they lived happily ever after!"

At that, the telephone went dead. Were they disconnected? No, this was one of Oliver's silences. "It will depend," he'd said then, "on what you do with that freedom. Firbank will help. The pond and the dunes and the ocean will counsel you."

So Oliver thought this was just the beginning of their problems, not the end. Rennie couldn't bring herself to tell Peter. They were so happy.

She did confide how very nearly she had run away, when she came to Firbank before. "I guess I was trying to escape from myself. I didn't understand what was going on inside of me. I wanted what Firbank offers. But I was scared of it, too. And that clearness bit! If it hadn't been for Daphne ——"

The one thing neither of them mentioned was Rennie's portrait. She avoided going to Oliver's study so she wouldn't have to confront it. Peter was obviously fascinated. Hardly a day went by that he didn't look in for a minute or two and stand before it, but when he came out, he said nothing. Rennie felt shy about asking what he thought. She knew it would be years before she looked that way — if ever. So the portrait got to be a thing between them, a subject she was afraid to discuss.

But one day, on the beach, she blurted out, "You can't imagine how I felt when I was posing for Daphne and I thought I'd given her another stroke! She looked so white, leaning back with her eyes closed. I was sure I'd killed her."

Peter stared at Rennie in horror. How was it possible that she had never told him the whole story?

"The funny thing was, afterward, when I knew Daphne was okay, I felt good about her, even though I'd spilled all those things I didn't want to tell anyone, like how we made love. Well, I didn't *tell* her, but she knew."

Those afternoons were so perfect, why was it that Rennie would invariably have to remember suddenly how her father cried when she and Peter announced they weren't getting married yet, and how her mother had barely spoken to her since? She tried not to think about her parents, but they had a frightening way of disrupting her contentment. Strangely enough, when she thought of them in meeting, they troubled her less. The silence really was comforting.

Peter seemed quite willing to go to meeting, though he didn't feel at home there. "It's not the silence — I don't mind that," he observed, rolling onto his back in the sand and clasping his hands behind his head so he could look at the sky. "It's a do-it-yourself religion. I like that part — not having anyone tell me what I'm supposed to think and say. But it's so stripped down! No impressive architecture, no flowers. That much I can take. It's the music I miss. I sang in our choir till my voice changed. To me, going to church means singing."

The absence of music in meeting didn't present any problem to Rennie. She never went to church, so she didn't miss it. "What I hate," she admitted reluctantly, "is the plainness of the meeting-house. Remember the fabulous course in Gothic architecture I took last year — French cathedrals, Thirteenth Century? That's the grandeur I keep hankering for."

Peter got to his feet. "There's something else," he said, grinning sheepishly. "I can't get used to women speaking as part of the service. I guess that makes me a male chauvinist. Seriously, I'm not against women having a part in anything. You know that. It's just — well, in my church, it could never happen. My family's belonged there for generations and I guess this attitude of my ancestors about women's place in the church is pretty well ingrained." Peter was clearly trying to tell Rennie the truth about himself.

Pulling her up, he shouted, "Come on!" Then he let go and started sprinting along the beach so fast that Rennie couldn't keep up.

174

"I'm glad *my* ancestors weren't sexist," she taunted, pelting him with dead-men's-fingers, the dark green seaweed that the ocean washed up at high tide. "That's one thing to be proud of. I wouldn't want your ——"

A clump of seaweed silenced her, narrowly missing her cheek and landing in her hair. Before she could get hold of the slimy ribbons, Peter ran back to her and pulled them off, kissing her at the same time.

"Look out," he commanded with masculine authority. "Watch what you're saying! Your children are going to get my ancestors."

The sharp *plick* of a sanderling flying overhead made them look up. Then they dove, laughing, into the water, splashing each other without mercy. They swam till they were exhausted. At last, they climbed over the dunes again and rowed back.

Sometimes, as the stillness of the pond settled on their souls, Peter shipped the oars and let the dinghy drift noiselessly, nowhere in particular. Exams were over. He had a job he liked. Rennie was blissful at Firbank. All those worries about the wedding, the hectic preparations, the violating of their sense of fitness, were gone. For the present, they had no further wishes. In the fall, they told each other, they'd get married their own way — whatever that was. They weren't thinking about it any more. For such a simple wedding, they didn't need to plan and prepare. One day, they'd just get married.

In the fall —— Now, the whole, beautiful summer was endlessly theirs, or seemed to be, though the calendar said it was slipping away.

Even when Rennie got her marks in the mail, along with a notice from the dean announcing that, because she'd flunked two education courses, she was on probation — even this wasn't terribly disturbing. A month ago, it would have seemed like the end of the world.

"It just means," she said to Oliver, shrugging, "that I'll have to take two extra courses before they let me graduate. So?"

Actually, Rennie was pleased. She had demonstrated her lack of talent for teaching. Maybe her father and the dean would recognize this and let her change her major. Not easy to do in one's senior year. But if she was willing to work her head off, why should they object?

"And I am willing," she assured Peter. "Everything's going to be different next year. I'm really looking forward to it."

Daphne was giving her a whole new conception of art history. The approach was exciting. Instead of assessing a work objectively, as scholars were trained to do, Daphne entered the creative core of a fellow artist's feeling and thinking. She saw his output as an interpretation of his personal life and the world around him. In her view, current social or political events determined the character of a particular work, even though the subject might not suggest any outward connection with the artist's life and times. To Daphne, every painting was an autobiographical note on canvas.

In men like Van Gogh or Toulouse-Lautrec, the connection was obvious to anyone. But Daphne saw cause and effect in the experience and production of many other artists, whose work had never been understood that way. Leafing through books that Oliver had taken off the shelves for her, she spent hours showing Rennie prints of one painter's work, then a page in his biography or in a contemporaneous history. These, she believed, revealed the sources of his inspiration. Even the biographer hadn't always been aware of a connection. With her own brush, Daphne reproduced the artist's palette to show Rennie how he mixed his colors and why he juxtaposed them.

Occasionally, Rennie remembered that this woman, who conveyed more than any lecturer, actually couldn't talk. But Rennie had grown so used to it that she seldom noticed any more, except on those rare occasions when Daphne's enthusiasm outran her patience and she opened her mouth to speak. Then the silence struck at Rennie's heart.

Back in May, after she'd phoned Oliver to ask whether she might come and spend the summer at Firbank, Rennie had rushed to the college bookstore to get a present for Daphne. But nothing seemed altogether appropriate. The recent releases wouldn't be to Daphne's taste, except the art books and they were far too expensive. As for the gifts — so much useless stuff!

It was really something deeper that kept Rennie from finding the fitting present for Daphne — a gulf so wide between that beautiful spirit and the material offerings in the store that Rennie felt anything she might buy would be unworthy, almost an affront.

Well, I'll just bring me, she thought finally, leaving empty-handed.

As soon as she arrived at Firbank, she knew that was all Daphne and Oliver really wanted — her. Moreover, she wasn't only welcome; she was desperately needed. Heather's family had had to call off the annual visit. Stephen was changing jobs and couldn't get away. In August, Oliver told Rennie, Heather would be coming by herself for a couple of weeks. He made no comment, yet his disappointment was obvious. Some of that irrepressible joyfulness Rennie had found so winning before was absent.

"There's a lot of work here in summer," he warned Rennie. "Thee mustn't do more than thee wishes to. When Heather comes, she'll put us to rights."

When Heather comes ——

Rennie found she was looking forward to this almost as much as Oliver and Daphne. She had a hunch that, at last, she was going to have a friend, someone as wonderful as they were, but young; someone who'd understand. And she longed for such a friend. The girls at college were more mixed up than she was. What she'd always wished for was an older sister. With all those brothers ——

Not one of their wives had ever treated Rennie like a person. To them, she was just a kid whose behavior was incomprehensible, if not downright revolting. "When I was your age ——" Jane or Victoria or Matty was always saying, not to inform Rennie about the past, but to rebuke her for failing to follow their examples. With all the griping they'd done about the wedding, they must have been secretly looking forward to it, because now that it was off they were even less pleased than when it was on. They acted as if Rennie had cheated them out of something.

Under the circumstances, Matty declared as soon as word got

around that the wedding was canceled, *under the circumstances,* she didn't see how Rennie could very well *not* get married. Victoria complained that she'd already begun a cute little flower girl's dress for Vicky, as if that fact compelled Rennie to go through with the ceremony. And Jane had some other grounds for disappointment — Rennie didn't even listen to her. These reactions came as no surprise. Her sisters-in-law were always like that.

"When Heather comes," she told Peter, "I'll have the first real girl friend I've ever had. I just have that feeling. She'll take over the housekeeping, too. Will I be glad!"

Rennie was working harder than she'd ever done in her life. In addition to the usual chores, there was preserving at this time of year. All of Oliver's garden and orchard seemed to be ripening at once.

"Wait till you taste the pie we're having tonight!" she told Peter. "Cherries from that tree near the horse block — what the birds left. I'm getting to be a neat cook, you know it?"

At the outset, Oliver had informed Peter that Daphne expected him to have supper with them every evening. They ate on the back porch, shaded by the grapevine, which was so thick with leaves that they could hardly see the barn. To Rennie, the evening meal in this green bower seemed like a continual celebration.

As she held Peter's and Oliver's hands during the moment of quiet before they began eating, she sometimes recalled her first meal here — how happy she suddenly felt that night after having been so scared. She remembered thinking that that was what she and Peter had been missing all along — joy. Now, peeking up at his nice, thoughtful face, she said to herself, We have it at last! Don't we?

And they lived happily ever after. How could Oliver possibly think their problems were only beginning?

2.

Oliver kept bringing in fruits and vegetables — far more than Rennie could cope with, even after he'd showed her what to do.

"We don't string our rhubarb," he said. "Just wash and cut it up with those scissors. It's the strings that make it pink when it's cooked."

Tomatoes to can, beans to freeze, beets to pickle, berries — Rennie didn't know where to begin. Not that Oliver expected her to do anything, but every time he came in he had another bushel basket full of stuff. The kitchen counter was so heaped with young carrots, zucchini, golden summer squash and tangles of early corn tassels that there wasn't room to prepare supper.

"When Heather comes," Oliver murmured, surveying the mound of produce, before going out to collect more, "she'll take care of everything."

"But she isn't coming for weeks," Rennie complained to Peter. "This stuff can't wait. It'll spoil. How am I ever going to ——"

Although Peter pitched in and helped, they couldn't get ahead of that garden.

"Austin says Oliver ought to retire. Sell out."

"*Sell Firbank?* Peter!"

"I know. But Austin thinks he's too old. And that Vietnamese thing! It's crazy, according to him. Even experts aren't trying to figure out ways of restoring that land. At least, he's never heard of any."

"That's why Oliver has to!"

"It's probably hopeless, or academic types would be working on it."

"Oliver doesn't think anything's hopeless," Rennie cried, angry at Austin for putting these ideas in Peter's mind. "He may be old, but he's no fool. Matter of fact, the head of the Forestry Department at the university phoned yesterday. He's bringing over some visiting scientist to see Oliver's plants. Austin doesn't know what he's talking about. Sell Firbank! Peter, don't ever say anything like that again."

The paring knife had raised a blister on Rennie's thumb. It hurt and she was dog tired. But suddenly, looking up to estimate how much there was left to do, she had a flash of pleasure that dissolved her fatigue. The sun was hitting those vegetables on the counter, highlighting the earthy beets and carrots, outlining the seeds hidden in the bean pods.

"What Renoir would have done with that! Daphne'd do even better — she'd communicate the goodness of the earth. And," Rennie added thoughtfully, "of this house."

She felt an impulse to touch everything, not as she'd been doing — washing and peeling for preserving — but for sheer delight. Picking up a plump, ripe tomato, she rubbed away the grains of soil that clung to it. For a moment, she held the exotic-looking thing in her palm as though it were a sacred object, reverently running her fingers over the smooth, red-gold skin, seeing, experiencing beauty in a vegetable for the first time. Then, smiling at Peter, she handed him the tomato. "Feel," she said.

While it sometimes seemed to Rennie that all she did was cook and freeze food, actually, housekeeping was only incidental. A large part of her day was spent helping Daphne prepare for her Fiftieth Anniversary Exhibition, scheduled for next April.

The invitation came as a complete surprise. When it arrived, Oliver was jubilant. "Recognition is welcome to an artist any time," he told Rennie. "But to think, to think that this should come to Daphne now, after all she's been through! The Museum of Contemporary Art. The leading one in the country! Isn't it wonderful?"

The museum asked for an inventory of all Daphne's works. She was to mark with a star the pictures she especially wished to exhibit. The curators would select from these. They would need the inventory by the end of August, at the latest.

"We'd always intended to make one," Oliver told Rennie, looking worried now. "But we were too busy. While Daphne was well, she thought only about creating, not of tabulating. Since then —— It will take weeks to go through the canvases in the woodshed and the stacks we have in the attic. Then there are her sketch books, catalogues of shows she's exhibited in over the years, all those port-folios —— With the garden and the Forest to care for I —— If only Heather and Stephen had come! He'd have helped outdoors while Heather worked on the inventory."

To Rennie, this seemed the chance of a lifetime. "Could I — would you let me do that? I mean, if you showed me how ——"

"Serenity! To have thee do it would make Daphne particularly happy. Did I tell thee she wants the exhibition to begin with Grand-mother's portrait and end with thine? In fact, that's going to be the title of the whole exhibition: *The Two Serenitys.*"

"*My* portrait in *that* museum? Well, it doesn't really look like me."

Rennie's disclaimer seemed to strike Oliver as extremely funny. "Peter thinks it does."

"Do you mean it? Has he told you so?"

Instead of answering, Oliver patted Rennie's shoulder and went on about the inventory. The first thing, he told her, was to build a file, entering each work by title and date on three-by-five cards. He brought out a shoebox from the cupboard in the back hall. It would hold the index cards, at least for a start. To give Rennie a large working surface, he put leaves in the dining room table.

"We haven't used this room in years," he told her. "Thee's going to make it important again." When he brought in an armchair for Daphne, the room was ready.

Rennie felt like one of those people who work in museums. This was better than any paying job. With the artist herself looking over her shoulder ——

Sitting beside Rennie, watching the number of index cards in the shoebox grow, Daphne signified approval with her large, gray eyes. Since the day she painted the portrait, she'd made it clear that she wasn't put off by anything in Rennie. But now something else seemed to be happening. Daphne didn't simply accept Rennie; she *depended* on her. She was turning over the whole sum of her creative production to a girl who had no training, who hadn't even finished college. Awed by Daphne's unbelievable trust, Rennie thought at the same time, I can do it!

Help — abundant help — suddenly arrived.

Rennie's little friends, Nancy and Sandy, dropped in one afternoon, hoping to take her for a swim. But, seeing the huge mess of string beans Oliver had just picked, they settled down in the kitchen and helped Rennie instead. When they went home, they must have reported that extra hands were needed at Firbank because, from then on, hardly a day passed without some woman — usually two or three — arriving unannounced.

There were two Marys, both about Daphne's age — Judy Young's mother-in-law and Alice Hill's mother, Mary Lancashire. Those women who'd stocked the Otis kitchen when Rennie came the first time returned. There were some with toddlers. Nancy and Sandy brought their mothers.

In threes and fours, these Friends spent the afternoons on the back porch, working together until they'd disposed of all those fruits and vegetables, drinking the iced tea which Rennie had spiced with mint from the bed in the dooryard. They brought Daphne the Kendal news. The Ashaway baby was sick. John Ludlow thought it might be meningitis. The library had been given a collection of rare books. Billy Green, who, it turned out, was only sixteen, had stolen a car.

This got to Rennie. So a Quaker home and First Day school were no guarantee that a kid wouldn't rip off.

The whole Meeting seemed to feel responsible for Billy. "Where does thee think we made mistakes?" Edith Ellis asked Rennie. She explained that Billy was the age of her son. The two boys had gone through school together. "What ought we to have done?" she asked sadly.

How should I know? Rennie felt like blurting out. Why ask me?

But then she felt flattered. A grownup was turning to her for advice! Very different from Rennie's mother, who'd been saying for the past six years, "I can't wait for you to get out of those teens. Then you'll see I'm right."

One afternoon, Betsy Klein asked, "Will you and Peter have dinner with us tomorrow? I'd like Henry and the children to know you."

A few days later, Alice Hill, whose husband moored his schooner in Little Narragansett Bay, invited Rennie and Peter on board for supper and a moonlight sail.

"Only a Midwesterner could appreciate how excited I am," Peter declared, when he heard this. "Till I came here, I'd never seen the ocean. Now I'm going out on it. I'll see how the land looks from the water!"

When they arrived at the dock, they found Neil and Alice and their children ready to cast off. The *Katrina* was old and beamy. She'd been washed ashore in a hurricane, Alice explained as they went on board. The hull was completely stove in. Neil had towed her to his boatyard and repaired her, so that she was not only seaworthy again, but she had regained the dignity that was characteristic of the old schooners built on this coast.

For Rennie, just watching Peter as he scurried up and down the deck helping Neil hoist the sails was a joy. He was more than happy; he obviously admired Neil and liked being with him. As soon as they were clear of the Bay, making for Fisher's Island, Neil asked Peter to take the wheel. Peter sent Rennie a proud glance. He was the helmsman!

They dropped anchor in a little cove. Alice went below to prepare supper. Looking down the companionway into the galley, Rennie noticed how shipshape everything was. She liked Alice. If Heather was like that ——

They ate in the cockpit, watching the sun go down and the moon come up. Little Denny Hill named the lighthouses that sent beams out all around them: Stonington, Watch Hill, Point Judith, Block Island, Montauk. Sitting with a boat cushion at her back and Peter's arm around her shoulders, Rennie looked up at the stars. She was completely happy.

Why did Alice have to go and spoil the perfectness by reporting to Neil that little Simeon Ashaway's condition was worse this evening? John Ludlow only gave him a fifty-fifty chance now of pulling through.

Rennie didn't know the Ashaways, but she did know the doctor. The first Sunday she and Peter were in Kendal, John and Clara Ludlow had invited them to a cookout in their yard after meeting. And a few days ago, they'd asked them to come for dinner the night Heather was due to arrive.

Neil turned to Rennie and Peter. "Ben Ashaway works for me. I know what that family's going through. But if anyone can save Simeon, It's John Ludlow. He's the best pediatrician there is."

The children added their boisterous endorsement.

In spite of the serious situation, Neil chuckled. "Did you hear about the hamster?"

Rennie shook her head.

"Simeon's two and a half, you know. All he wanted when they rushed him to the hospital was his hamster. But, of course, his parents weren't allowed to take it in. John did, though, smuggling it in in his pocket! Every time he makes rounds, he brings the hamster so the kid can hold it while he examines him. Who but John Ludlow would do a thing like that?"

"The head nurse came in one day and caught him," the little Hill girl, whose name Rennie'd already forgotten, put in, giggling. "Was she ever mad!"

Laughing, Alice mimicked the nurse. " 'Doctor Ludlow! You know this is against hospital regulations.' John just looked her in the eye and answered, 'Miss Hardy, maybe it is. But I'm obeying a higher regulation.' And he went right on bringing Simeon his hamster! Only," Alice added anxiously, "this morning, the poor little boy didn't seem to care."

This definitely put a damper on what otherwise would have been a perfect evening.

When Rennie told Daphne and Oliver about the hamster the next morning, Oliver exclaimed, "John's just like his father. Philip Ludlow was the most wonderful man I've ever known. Hadn't been for him, Neil Hill never would have come to Kendal. Did Neil tell thee how it happened?"

"No."

"As a boy, he lived in an apartment in New York. It was pathetic because all he dreamed of was sailing — building boats and sailing them — and there he was, cooped up in the city. His mother happened to come here on business and she was so won by Philip's beautiful spirit that she brought her whole family to live in Kendal. That was over twenty years ago. The first time Vaughn Hill came, she stayed at Mary Lancashire's. Alice was the oldest girl, must have been about fourteen then. When Neil finished school, he opened a boatyard downriver, not far from the place where Josiah Millburn built his ships, and married Alice. None of this would have happened if it hadn't been for Philip Ludlow."

"Will it be okay if we go to the Ludlows' Tuesday night? That's when Heather's coming. I mean, wouldn't you like me to get supper?"

Oliver gave Rennie a grateful smile. "We'll manage," he assured her. "John probably figured it would be less of a strain for Daphne, not having so many people at once when she's excited, as she will be, the night Heather arrives. Go, by all means. I'm glad thee and Peter will have a chance to get to know John."

"I never thought I'd want to know another pediatrician. Used to be scared to death of mine."

Remembering the silly way she used to howl, when she was little, just riding down to Dr. Appleby's office — probably, Rennie realized now, more to bug her mother than from fear — she suddenly saw how far she'd come. Her childhood was like another life, light-years away, receding rapidly, almost unreal.

When her father telephoned, she found it painful to turn her thoughts back to Neville. Her mother seldom spoke to her. If she did, it was no longer in that placid tone that betrayed anxiety. She sounded polite and detached now, the way she did at cocktail parties, if she was obliged to be civil to some woman she couldn't abide.

"She's written me off," Rennie told Oliver, after a most unsatisfactory conversation.

He looked at her gravely. "That's impossible."

"You don't know my mother."

"Serenity, thee'll have to help her understand why thee acted as thee did. Thee can't let her go."

Rennie's father wasted no time chatting with Oliver when he called up. He immediately demanded to speak to Rennie, as if there were some emergency. And indeed he sounded more anxious as the summer progressed. *How* was Rennie?

"Okay." Why all this concern about her health? She was never sick. If it was Peter he worried about —— "I'm okay," Rennie repeated. "I told you — you needn't worry about me."

When was she coming home? Hadn't she grown tired yet of cooking for Oliver and his wife? "Mother says, she didn't think you knew how. All you ever made for us was instant coffee. You never wanted to do anything for us. How come you're the Otises' unpaid housekeeper?"

"They need me."

"Your parents need you, too, Rennie. Mother deserves a vacation. The heat is something this year. And those wedding presents —— You haven't written half the notes. I don't see how ——"

"Daddy, why don't you and mother come here? It's lovely and cool and there's plenty of room."

"Come to *Firbank?*"

"Why not? Oliver and Daphne always wanted you to visit them, since before I was born."

What had Rennie done now? How could she invite her parents? They'd be out of place here.

But her father acted as if he hadn't heard her. He simply asked again, as he was ringing off, "When are you coming home?"

Home?

Firbank was home to Rennie now, certainly more than Neville, where her room, crammed with the relics of childhood that her mother dusted and cherished, seemed more strange and unconnected to her each time she returned. It was nothing but a chrysalis out of which her expanding self had broken. She'd left it behind, flown away. Her room at college had never felt like home, either. It was only the place to escape from into Peter's. But Heather's little room in the ell was home, with Rennie's record player on the desk and her books on the shelves. Serenity's Woolman lay on the bedside table. Rennie hardly ever opened it and then only to look at Daphne's water color, but she liked having the book there.

Coming back to Heather's room had been coming to a familiar place, one where Rennie fitted, where she belonged. She'd feared that, when Heather arrived, she would want the room. But Oliver assured Rennie that Heather and Stephen had used the big one in the main wing for so long, Heather would feel quite at home there, too.

Oliver never came into the ell. Just the same, Rennie tried to pick up her stuff from the floor and make the bed sometimes, simply because she knew that was how he liked his house to be.

When Peter came up there, he would survey the room as if he, too, felt it was home. The little terra cotta figurines intrigued him. He took them up, one after another, and held them carefully, studying the details, running his thumb over the surfaces, absorbed in a way even Rennie hadn't been the first time she saw these statuettes of the mother and her child.

Rennie knew now that Daphne had modeled them for Heather when she was small. Fragile though they were, Daphne made them expressly to be played with.

"Beautiful," Peter murmured.

"Daphne thinks toys should be works of art, too. Even if they're soon broken, they should give tactile pleasure and delight the eye. In fact, she believes that a child will take better care of something with aesthetic quality than a tough, ugly toy."

"Beautiful," Peter repeated, putting down one figurine and taking up another. He was fascinated.

Watching him, Rennie thought, Now I understand why he didn't want to make love at his house. I wouldn't want to here, myself, not in Heather's room.

Somehow, it wouldn't feel right. Rennie'd only want to do things here that she'd be willing to have Daphne and Oliver know about. Anyway, she'd assured her father ——

But, high above the beach, the night before Heather arrived, Rennie was released from this constraint. So, apparently, was Peter. Or maybe it was the very opposite of what he meant to do. It just seemed to happen, taking them both by surprise in the soft fold of a sand dune.

3.

Daphne kissed Rennie once more.

They'd been working in the dining room all afternoon, going through a stack of canvases without really putting their minds on them, simply marking time till Heather arrived.

Oliver was in the garden, picking corn for supper. He'd been up since dawn, polishing the saucepans and the silver till their gleam reflected the joy of his anticipation, doing a day's work outdoors, cutting his finest roses to put in Heather's room, then dressing Daphne in her go-to-meeting best — the soft blue shift with the necklace of acorns.

All along, Rennie had looked forward to Heather's coming with the same eagerness, though hers was tempered by suspense. Would this really turn out to be her first honest-to-goodness girl friend, a marvelous person — like Daphne, only younger; someone who would talk to her? Rennie tried to remember the generation gap: Heather was old enough to be her mother. That made no difference! She'd be everything Rennie's mother was not — relaxed, cheerful, handsome, attentive to people's feelings and needs.

But now that, any minute, Heather would be driving up in the car she'd rented at the airport in Boston, Rennie wondered whether having her here was really going to be all that nice. Oliver and

Daphne would withdraw their attention, wouldn't they? Transfer it to Heather.

I mustn't be jealous, she warned herself. They'll be completely wrapped up in her. Natch! She's their daughter, isn't she?

Still, Rennie was so accustomed to feeling at the center here that she hated having to take a back seat. Both eager and apprehensive, she kept listening for the strike of the grandfather clock. Four! It wouldn't be long now.

Going over to Daphne's chair, she held up a canvas. "Is this one you'd like them to put on exhibition? Does it get a star?"

It was a seascape. The picture belonged to what Oliver always referred to as the "unfolding period" in Daphne's artistic development — more stylized than some of her later work, yet beautiful, Rennie thought.

She studied Daphne's expression, trying to read the answer to her question. But Daphne wasn't concentrating. She hardly seemed interested in the picture, glancing at it only briefly, then at the door in expectation. After that, her eyes came to rest on Rennie's face. They revealed such tenderness, overlaid with sadness, that Rennie was forced to look away and fix her attention on the canvas she was holding up. As the details began to sink in, blood suddenly rushed to her cheeks. That sand dune in the foreground — it was in this very hollow that she and Peter lay on their backs last night, looking up at the stars!

He had pointed out constellations she'd never heard of and traced the path of the Milky Way. Over a thousand years ago, he'd told her, Charlemagne, enthralled by the mystery of the firmament, followed that galaxy westward, clear across Spain to Cape Finisterre, the End of the Earth.

"If he'd gone much farther," Peter whispered, reaching out in the dark for Rennie's hand, "he would have fallen into the sea."

Then the mystery of the firmament had enthralled them, too. The lapping of the waves at low tide dissolved their wills and their intentions, drawing them into the rhythm of Nature, as she busily renewed herself, replenishing the planet. The life-giving impulse that governed all the other creatures in that vast, starlit universe washed over them, too, till their beings concurred with the ebb and flow of the ocean.

Rennie tried to push this memory away, to slam the door of her mind on last night. Staring at the canvas, she kept her face averted, so Daphne wouldn't see it was red.

Suddenly, Rennie jumped. Her head was being encircled and drawn down to the level of Daphne's. Cool lips touched her burning cheek.

Why did Daphne do that? Could she really see through people? Or had last night's events left their mark on Rennie's features the way the ocean left its imprint on the sand, long after the tide went out? Somehow, Daphne'd guessed. And she wanted Rennie to know that she loved her. All this Rennie realized even before Daphne let her go.

Turning away quickly, Rennie dropped the canvas on the table, determined to run out of the dining room. Then she stopped, frozen. A tall woman in scarlet stood at the door, taking in the whole scene.

Instinctively, Rennie turned to Daphne again. And she saw how redundant the power of speech would have been at that moment. Daphne's eyes expressed a joy that needed no confirmation in words.

As Heather walked across the room and bent over her mother's chair to embrace her, Rennie felt acutely disappointed. This wasn't the girl she'd dreamed of at all. That scarlet pantsuit with the frilly blouse sticking out from the neck of the brass-buttoned blazer, the hairdo, which had sprayed the Otis fuzz into a silver nimbus — how could this cool chick have been hatched at Firbank?

Rennie was still so upset by the dune in the picture, by Daphne's kiss and Heather's abrupt appearance, that when Heather straightened up and smiled at her like a guarded stranger, asking, "Where's Father?" Rennie almost answered stupidly, In Neville.

I promised him, she was thinking miserably, I promised him I wouldn't —— What will I say when he calls?

"Where's Father?" Heather repeated, smiling encouragingly now, as if she thought Rennie was a shy kid, afraid to answer. She didn't seem to place her. Hadn't Oliver written about Rennie's coming to Firbank?

"Picking corn," she said finally. "I'll go get him."

It was a relief to be out of there.

At the back door, Rennie bumped into Oliver. He'd just seen Heather's car. Bursting with excitement, he brushed past, barely noticing Rennie.

She didn't return to the dining room. Nobody needed her now. She walked around the house. The air felt good. Slowly going down the lane to wait for Peter, she wondered what kind of mood he'd be in after last night. If he withdrew from her, too, she wouldn't be able to take it.

But he was sweet. When he pedaled into the lane and saw her standing by the Otis letter box, waiting for him, he broke into a happy grin. Dear Peter! Rennie could count on him.

Sitting astride his bike with his feet on the ground, he put his arm around her waist, not passionately but lovingly, the way she'd seen men do at the station in the evening, when their wives came to meet the commuter train. All the way to the house, he kept his hand on Rennie's shoulder while he pedaled slowly, wobbling on the sandy road.

"Who's here?" he asked, seeing the strange car.

"Heather. She's arrived."

"Oh! What's she like?"

"Different. Not at all as I pictured her. Not like Oliver or Daphne."

Their eyes were almost level. Peter's searched Rennie's. Obviously trying to make up for her disappointment by switching to something agreeable, he asked, "Isn't this the night we're supposed to have supper with the Ludlows? You like them, don't you?"

Rennie smiled. It didn't make her feel better, but she loved Peter for trying. "Sure," she said. "They're great. Oliver's letting us take the pickup."

When they reached the house and entered the dining room, they found Heather sitting in Rennie's chair. She had pushed the shoe-box and canvases to the end of the table to make room for the gifts she'd brought her parents: a sky blue cashmere cardigan for Daphne, a camel's hair sweater for Oliver, a tin of custard powder.

"After all these years in the States, Daphne's still an English-woman at heart," Oliver told Rennie, laughing affectionately. "She loves her custard sauce."

Heather's youngest girl had made a little patchwork cushion for her grandmother and the boy had put together an intercom so Oliver could talk to Daphne when she was upstairs and he was down.

"What thoughtfulness!" Oliver exclaimed, examining the inter-com. "What ingenuity!"

He must have filled Heather in. When Peter was introduced, she was almost cordial. Yet, even with her parents, Heather conveyed a certain reserve. This far and no further, her closed-up smile seemed to say.

Rennie thought of the figurines in her room, of the warmth ex-pressed by the mother as she played with her child. No reserve there. Was it because Heather lived in England that she wished to keep her distance? Was this a foreign trait she'd acquired, like the British inflection that colored her Rhode Island speech? Was it like the disconcertingly cosmopolitan aura that overlay her Firbank personality?

From her handbag, Heather drew a pile of photographs, passing them around, identifying her children for Rennie and Peter, talking rapidly, as if she didn't feel quite at home.

Later, driving to Kendal in the truck, Rennie said to Peter, "I don't understand her. That reserve — when she was showing them the snapshots, it was almost as if she was placing her husband and children between herself and her parents, like a shield. If she had parents like mine —— But Oliver and Daphne!"

"I'm sorry. I know you were counting on her being a sort of older sister. She still may. First impressions ——"

Rennie shook her head. "I don't think so." Then she murmured,

"I hope she hasn't messed up my index cards. Why did she have to park her stuff right there, for goodness' sake?"

As they stood at the door of the Ludlows' house, it suddenly struck Rennie that Peter hadn't said a word yet about last night. Why should he? They never used to discuss it afterward. But Rennie recognized the same turbulence in his face that Daphne had observed in her own.

Clara Ludlow came to the door. Dainty and pretty, she had the fresh complexion of someone who lives near the ocean. Rennie felt drawn to her. John, she said, would be down directly. "I urged him to take a little rest before dinner. He was at the hospital all night."

The house was unusual — an old New England saltbox with Oriental atmosphere. Chinese pictures and artifacts decorated the living room, all but one wall, which was devoted to a collection of sea shells.

"John's whaling forebears brought the Canton ware back from China," Clara told Rennie, observing her interest. "The other things he got himself, when he left Chungmou."

"You mean," Peter asked, impressed, "he's been to China?"

"Yes, but it was a long time ago — Nineteen Fifty, during the Civil War. He was with a Quaker medical unit, caring for civilians. Sometimes they were behind Nationalist lines, sometimes in Communist territory. Whatever side they happened to be caught on, people needed help."

John came downstairs, looking tired but very pleased to see Rennie and Peter.

During dinner, the Ludlows asked about life at Tilbury. Although their children had finished college, they were interested in education. In the middle of this conversation, Peter suddenly asked them how one went about getting married by Friends. The question took Rennie by surprise. She didn't know he was considering this. Why hadn't he told her?

"Friends don't perform marriages," John explained. "They're simply the witnesses when, in the presence of God, a man and a woman take each other as lifelong partners."

Clara began to describe the procedure.

It was all just what Oliver had told Rennie the first time she came. The letter of application, the committee on clearness, overseers ——

"But one has to belong," Rennie put in. "Not be a member, necessarily, but part of the religious community. Oliver said so."

"You belong," Clara assured her, laughing.

"All summer, you've been part of our community. Haven't you felt it?" John asked.

"Yes, but ——"

"That's all Oliver Otis meant. Ask him whether it isn't."

"How should the letter be worded?"

Peter was serious about this!

So were the Ludlows. "There's no fixed form," Clara replied. "Just state your wishes to be married under the care of Kendal Meeting. Both of you must sign it. I'm sure Friends will be pleased. We've enjoyed having you with us."

In the presence of God, Rennie thought. Could she, in perfect sincerity ——

This didn't seem to faze Peter. "How soon can it be arranged?"

"Ordinarily, it takes at least two months for a couple to 'pass meeting,' as we call it," John told him. "Are you in a hurry?"

The question made Rennie smile. Being a doctor, she said to herself, he thinks —— "I'm not pregnant," she assured him. Then, seeing his unflapped expression — the same nonjudgmental look that made Oliver so endearing — Rennie cussed herself out for being a fool. That thought probably hadn't been in John's mind at all when he asked the question. Why was she acting like a silly kid?

"It's only that we'd planned all along to get married before we go back to school," Peter explained. "We have an apartment in the married students' quarters. But I guess we could wait a couple of months."

"That will be more acceptable to the Meeting," John declared. "The reason our procedure takes so long is simply that Friends wish the couple to avoid acting impulsively and also to allow plenty of time for discussion. Because the Meeting will feel a continuing responsibility for that marriage in the years to come."

Peter was only half listening to John. He had turned to Rennie. "How about it?"

She didn't know what to answer.

Sensing her uncertainty, Clara quickly changed the subject, apologizing for the dessert. Rennie was so fussed, she wasn't sure whether it had turned out too stiff or too soupy.

After they moved back to the living room, Peter told John he had found a shell on the mud flats around Salt Pond that he couldn't identify. John slid open the glass door that protected his collection. "I started this when I was a little boy," he said, "long before I became a scientist interested in zoology. Just beachcombing it was, then. Nowadays, I don't have much time, but I still add a shell occasionally. The ones in this section all came from Salt Pond."

Clara went back to the dining room. She blew out the candles and cleared the table. Rennie stood beside Peter, watching him scan the specimens in the collection as he looked for one that resembled the beautiful little fluted shell he had found on the flats last week.

"There it is!" he exclaimed, pointing.

"That's an oyster drill," John told him. "Very pretty, but tough on oysters. It bores in and kills them. Rennie, how do you like this?" He carefully picked up a tiny, tiny, rosy shell, only half the size of her fingernail, and dropped it in the palm of her hand. "Delicate tellen," he explained. "And here's a salt marsh snail."

John's face interested Rennie more than the shells. This was a highly competent man. Parents placed their children's lives in his hands. But, for the moment, he was a child himself, back among the treasures of his boyhood. Tired though he was, he looked radiant.

"Here's a ribbed mussel. This is a false angel wing that's been drilled by a moon shell." John laughed wryly. "Bad as people, aren't they?"

When Clara returned, she showed Rennie pictures of her children and grandchildren, explaining where everyone lived and what they were doing. The whole family sounded interesting.

Why isn't Heather like this? Rennie asked herself sadly. Clara's everything I hoped Heather'd be.

It was a beautiful evening — over too soon — but all through it, Rennie kept wondering what had made Peter suddenly decide on a Quaker marriage. Was it perhaps that he wished theirs might be as good as the Ludlows'?

When they were on the doorstep, saying good-by, John murmured, "Tell Oliver Otis ——" He hesitated. Under the outdoor light, Rennie saw that he looked different now — not radiant, as he had been when he showed them the shells, quite the opposite. He looked defeated. "Tell him Simeon Ashaway died this afternoon. There's going to be a meeting of thanksgiving Friday at two in the Kendal Meetinghouse."

The hamster, Rennie thought. What's going to become of the hamster now?

"Thanksgiving?" Peter blurted out indignantly. "When a little kid dies, what's there to give thanks for?"

"His life — what there was of it. A meeting of thanksgiving's our term for a memorial service."

Looking at John, Rennie saw that the term seemed as inappropriate to him, in this instance, as it did to Peter.

4.

Heather took everything over — not only the housekeeping, but the inventory as well. Thanking Rennie for beginning the job, she promised to get it finished before she went home, evidently convinced that Rennie wished to be relieved of it. How was Heather to know that she was taking away the most exciting project Rennie'd ever worked on?

"I tried to tell her that I like it," Rennie complained to Oliver, "but she doesn't seem to understand."

"Her ideas are a bit different," he admitted, looking embarrassed. "She thinks her method is more efficient. She's reorganizing the file."

"*Reorganizing?*"

After all the work Rennie'd put in! So Heather didn't think she'd done it right. She couldn't speak to Daphne about it because Heather was always there.

Overnight, Rennie became a fifth wheel at Firbank. For the past weeks, she'd been run off her feet. Suddenly, she had nothing to do. Bored to death, she watched the children, who still came and did the chores, even though First Day school wasn't in session. Nancy and Sandy had been longing for her attention. Billy Green, the boy who stole that car — did Rennie think he'd go to jail? With a police record, would he ever be able to get a job? Was there anything they could do to help him?

They expected Rennie to have all the answers. Ben Ellis and Charley Fiorentino, who cleaned the living room, wanted to know about Tilbury. Was it hard to get in? Did it have a good science department?

"I don't know. Peter's the one to ask. Why don't you come some afternoon and talk to him?"

These kids touched something in Rennie. They needed her. Wasn't the very goodness of their bringing up, that love for mankind, instilled in them from childhood, a hazard? They were too innocent. The desire to serve made them vulnerable. Rennie wished she could protect them against the evils that were waiting to pounce, the moment they left home. She listened. She tried to give straight answers. After all, didn't she know a lot more about the world the kids were going to encounter than their gentle parents?

If she had just had an older friend, when she was their age! Her sisters-in-law merely regarded her as a built-in babysitter, thoughtfully provided by the management, whenever they dragged their brats over to visit the grandparents.

"Run upstairs and play with Rennie," they'd command, the minute they entered the house.

"I don't wanna."

"Go on. I have something to tell Grandma."

Maybe that was why Rennie had so little interest in small children. But these teen-agers were fun. After all, she was still one herself, though not for long.

Oliver sensed that Rennie was suffering from the change in her status at Firbank. He tried to make her feel as welcome as before, though he wasn't about to tangle with Heather. Besides, he was seldom indoors. The Forest claimed his attention. Those scientists from the university had given him a lift. After their visit, he merely reported that they thought his experiments were promising. But Rennie was on to Oliver now. This was an understatement. The scientists had been impressed.

"Wait till Austin hears what they said!" Rennie gloated to Peter. "He won't dare call Oliver quixotic again. Or too old."

The days only began for Rennie now in the late afternoon, when Peter arrived. Then they rowed across the pond and swam, staying later than they used to because Rennie didn't have to cook supper. Even so, time was no longer measured against eternity. It pushed them again. Summer was almost over; Kendal Friends were meeting for business the week after next. If Rennie and Peter wanted their application for marriage considered, they'd have to submit the letter soon. Why was it so hard to write?

"It really isn't that complicated," Peter argued. "The Ludlows said just to state our wish to be married under the care of the Meeting."

Rennie looked at the ocean. Peter expected her to say something, but she couldn't.

"Isn't that what you wanted all along — a Quaker marriage?" he argued, sensing her hesitation and baffled by it. "Isn't that how the whole thing started — why you came here in the first place? Hadn't been for your wanting a marriage like the one in that picture on your third-floor landing, we wouldn't be here. Right?"

"Right."

"What's the trouble? The ceremony couldn't be simpler. We

198

don't have to do a thing except make that promise and sign the certificate."

"In the presence of God. I don't know what that means. When I get up and promise, I want my heart to stand in perfect sincerity. And if I don't know what God is, how can I say ———"

"You're taking me on faith. Why can't you take God?"

"That's different. How can I *promise* to be loving and faithful till one of us dies? How can I tell what's going to happen? I mean — so many people promise and break up."

"One promises on faith, too," Peter cried. Suddenly, he blew his stack. "I can't be around you any more and not make love! No matter how hard I try ——— But when I sleep with you, Rennie, I want to be your husband. If we hadn't started so early, it would have been better."

"You mean you're sorry?"

"Of course I'm not sorry. Don't be an idiot. Well, maybe I am a little sorry that we messed things up so. That's why I want to get married soon as we can. If I'd finished school I'd feel right about the whole thing. But with Dad's heart condition, I might have to help out. If anything happens to him, how are the girls going to get their education? Mom couldn't swing it all. That's what I meant when I said it would have been better if we'd met later. The least I can do for my folks now is behave with you the way they'd want me to, the way I want to myself. We have to make some compromise," he muttered, "don't we?"

"Compromise? Never!"

They were quarreling. What about? They both wanted to get married, didn't they? Or were they, without knowing it, about to break up? Rennie shivered.

The shore birds had already come back from the north, anticipating winter, hovering over the beach grass on the dunes. The snowy egret was skimming the pond. How did the birds know when it was their season for nesting? Why didn't humans have a built-in timetable?

When Rennie woke up the next morning, it was raining. The

199

pond looked desolate. Standing by the window for a second before getting dressed, she remembered that this was the day of that memorial service.

There had been a time when, thinking of Oliver and Daphne, Rennie had believed their troubles simply came with old age; that she and Peter wouldn't have to face anything major for years and years. Now, suddenly, she saw this might happen anytime. Even a baby could get sick and die. The realization filled her with anguish. It was the first time she'd thought about death coming close to her personally, about dying.

Her hands gripped each other desperately. She pulled them apart, but they wouldn't let go.

And when the crunch comes, she said to herself, what do you do?

Death was a subject one took care not to mention in Neville. Rennie's mother didn't want to hear about it. If one of her friends "passed away," as she put it, she tried to push the event out of her mind as soon as possible. Rennie'd grown up with this attitude and assumed it was general. So how would she ever get an answer to her question: What do you do?

Sitting around the house all morning, Rennie thought how right Oliver was about Peter and her not living happily ever after. She had hesitated to write that letter because their marriage might not last as long as they both lived. Now she wondered whether they'd even make it to the wedding. *This afternoon*, Peter had declared when he left last night, *this afternoon* they were going to write that letter, definitely. Rennie told herself she'd have to stop shilly-shallying, as her father would say.

What would her father say when she told him they were going to be married in that homely little meetinghouse? And Rennie's mother!

They're not going to like it. They're not going to like it one bit.

After lunch, when Oliver was starting off for the memorial service, leaving Daphne with Heather, Rennie had a sudden impulse to climb up into the truck. What else was there to do till Peter came?

Oliver welcomed her with his usual warmth, but he seemed surprised. "Thee doesn't know the family, does thee? They've been so taken up with Simeon, we haven't seen much of them at meeting. It isn't necessary for thee to attend."

"Oh, I'm not going to *that!*" Rennie assured him, recoiling at the very thought. Even if she had known the Ashaways, she wouldn't want to be present at anything so morbid. "I'm just coming along for the ride. While you're there, I'll bum around Kendal, maybe go to the library."

"Thee'll get wet."

"That's okay."

As they sloshed along the shore road, Oliver pointed to an osprey perched on top of a pole. "Ten years ago," he told Rennie, shaking his head sadly, "there were a hundred and fifty osprey nests in Rhode Island. Now there are only seven. We're driving our friends away."

Alone with Oliver, Rennie wondered whether she should take advantage of the opportunity to tell him how troubled she was. But he was having a hard time steering the truck through puddles and his expression was so sad that she kept still. What were her problems, compared to someone's dying? The rain made the whole scene more melancholy.

When they reached the meetinghouse and got out, Oliver looked downright diminished — old and lonely. Rennie didn't have the heart to desert him. Contrary to her intention, she followed him in.

The vestibule was crowded and smelled of damp clothing. Rennie brushed against Daphne's wicker chair. In the meeting room, there were more people than on a First Day. Otherwise, everything looked the same, except that a vase of flowers stood on the sill of each tall window — no florist's arrangements. Friends had simply gone out into their gardens and picked their loveliest flowers. Then, with a trust Rennie envied, they gathered here, seeking comfort — all but Rennie. She was the only one who wasn't mourning, because she hadn't known the child. A detached observer. Maybe that was why the bench stabbed her in the back — to remind her that she was an outsider.

But Oliver was happy to have her beside him. When he saw she meant to stay, he sent her a grateful, loving message with his eyes. Then he withdrew to that inward place where she couldn't follow.

All the First Days Rennie had come here with Oliver and Daphne! She felt as at home in this meetinghouse now as she did in the ell at Firbank, or *had* felt, before Heather arrived. Until then, Firbank was perfect. Now it was no longer paradise. But how could the place have changed, simply because someone else arrived? It was still the same place, wasn't it? Daphne and Oliver were still the same people. They felt the same way toward Rennie.

Could that be why Heather didn't like her? Ever since she left London, Heather must have been looking forward to the pleasure her parents would express on her arrival. But when she entered the house, her father wasn't even there and her mother was kissing a strange girl.

Oh, Rennie said to herself, I never thought of that. If it had been me getting home and seeing another girl with my mother —— I wouldn't have liked that myself. Still, she's old. Can one be jealous at her age? Then Rennie put her hand over her mouth to stifle a giggle. If Heather only knew *why* Daphne kissed her!

The meetinghouse was full now. Even the facing benches were occupied. Latecomers were standing at the back. Rennie recognized a lot of people. Surprising, how many friends she'd made this summer.

Neil and Alice Hill were sitting across the aisle with Mary Lancashire, Alice's mother. Whenever Mary saw Rennie, she beamed on her with extraordinary pleasure. "Thee looks so much like thy great-grandmother!" she would exclaim happily, recalling her youth, forgetting, no doubt, that she'd said exactly the same thing last time.

"Do I really?" Rennie always asked her. "You're not just saying it?" But, of course, looking like Serenity wasn't what Rennie cared about. She wanted her confidence.

At my age, maybe she didn't have it, either.

Down front, there was a whole group of people Rennie didn't

recognize. These must be the Ashaways, mother and father and three young children; grandparents, uncles and aunts, friends, maybe some of the workers from Neil Hill's boatyard. They looked stunned, as if they were at a loss to understand how God could be so cruel as to kill a little boy.

And yet, they must be taking His love on faith, as Peter phrased it, otherwise they wouldn't have come here, running for comfort the way Rennie used to run to her parents when she was small and she fell and hurt herself. Her parents would kiss the bump and right away it felt better. The hurt remained, but that kiss made it bearable.

The magic of love! When I was born, Mother and Daddy were so happy to get a girl, after all those sons. Not that they didn't love the boys, but they'd always wanted a child to name Serenity. They still love me. They don't understand, but they love me. They really do.

Oliver seldom spoke in meeting. Rennie was startled when he stood up and looked off into space, as if he weren't quite sure what he was going to say. Then, in a conversational tone, he announced, "We're gathered in the presence of God to give thanks for the life of our dear little friend, Simeon Ashaway." He paused a long time.

In the presence of God! So already, without even getting as close to the wedding as writing that letter, Rennie was there. Was all of life in that presence?

"Even as we give thanks for the joy it was to have him among us," Oliver continued, "we cannot deny the question that is in all our minds — why a child should not have been allowed to grow to maturity. Everything in us argues that Simeon should have lived."

How like Oliver! With his simplicity of heart, standing in perfect sincerity, he'd put into words the sorrow and bewilderment everyone must be feeling. He wasn't trying to tranquilize the parents with pious words. He acknowledged their outrage, which must be far, far greater than John Ludlow's or Peter's.

Rennie glanced at the Ashaways. How were they taking Oliver's message? Mrs. Ashaway had one arm around a restless little girl. Her other hand was clasped in her husband's. Turning away quickly, Rennie told herself their feelings were none of her business. Private.

"So we have to accept without understanding," Oliver was saying. "And for beings like us, who live by our wits, that's close to impossible. Nevertheless, we trust, we *know*, that the ordering of life is right, however wrong it may sometimes look to us. If we had more understanding, we'd stop measuring a life by its length, only by the fullness of its love, which radiated so abundantly from little Simeon."

Oliver's voice trailed off. He'd finished. No, turning to the tall windows, where rain was zigzagging down the panes, he felt moved to add something. *"In that glistering circle in the firmament which we call the Galaxy, the Milky Way,* John Donne wrote, *there is not one star of any of the six great magnitudes."*

Rennie jumped. The Milky Way! How come Oliver mentioned that?

"It is a glorious circle, Donne said, *and possesseth a great part of heaven, and yet is all of so little stars, as have no name.* Our little star had a name. It was like that of the just, devout man, who took the child Jesus in his arms and blessed God."

Oliver slowly let himself down onto the bench and rested his hands on his knees with the fingers curled in. Rennie turned to him. She felt such a need to communicate the emotion swirling in her that she had to restrain an impulse to put her hand in his, the way she did in the silence before meals. His assurance that all of life was lived in a presence one couldn't understand, but which he trusted — how did this connect with the mystery of the firmament that had overpowered Peter and her?

They'd upset the ecology — wasn't that the trouble? — divorced mating from nesting. They were caught by Nature's steamroller determination to replenish the earth.

Through her thoughts, Rennie heard Neil Hill speaking about Simeon, telling about the hamster in the same way he'd told Peter and her on the boat. He wasn't literary, like Oliver. He simply described Simeon's love for the tiny animal — the way he laughed when it cocked its ears and scampered over the bedclothes; the way he tried to stroke its whiskers.

Though Rennie'd never seen the child, she could picture him in the hospital, playing with his pet.

Neil was talking about the tides now — how they rose and fell according to some celestial plan no man could alter or control. But Rennie was only half listening. She was thinking that someday — not next year, or even the year after, but someday — it would be fun to have a baby. She'd go off the Pill and some night she and Peter would will her to conceive. Instead of being just a little afraid, as they always were — never quite sure that there mightn't be some slip-up — instead, they'd hope. The procedure would be the same, but their feelings —— No, it wouldn't be at all the same. They'd be acting in harmony with Nature instead of thwarting her, inviting another being to share their lives and become part of their love. There'd be an element in the procedure that Peter craved, an abandon and life-giving joy they'd never known.

Unable to imagine that joy, Rennie sank into the silence that followed Neil's message. She felt a strange contentment, an ease of heart, though nothing had changed.

It would have been good to go on savoring this precious quietude, but old Mary Lancashire was standing up, clutching her skirt nervously with one hand. In the other, she held a book. "I should like to read from the fifty-fifth chapter of Isaiah," she announced, sounding as if she might break down any minute. She held the Bible up before her, but she must have known the passage by heart because she scarely glanced at the page. As she spoke, her voice grew steady and something very like rapture overspread her kind, wrinkled face.

"For my thoughts are not your thoughts, neither are your ways my ways, saith the Lord.

For as the heavens are higher than the earth, so are my ways higher than your ways, and my thoughts than your thoughts.

For as the rain cometh down, and the snow from heaven, and returneth not thither, but watereth the earth, and maketh it bring forth and bud, that it may give seed to the sower, and bread to the eater:

So shall my word be that goeth forth out of my mouth: it shall not return unto me void, but it shall accomplish that which I please, and it shall prosper in the thing whereto I sent it.

For ye shall go out with joy, and be led forth with peace: the mountains and the hills shall break forth before you into singing, and all the trees of the field shall clap their hands."

Rennie'd never heard these words before. Why hadn't anyone brought them to her attention? The mountains and hills breaking forth into singing and the trees clapping their hands for joy! Wait till I tell Peter, she thought. *Beautiful*, that's what he'll say.

Oliver'd once remarked that love isn't a little bird which suddenly appears in springtime, alights awhile, then flits away when the season or the weather changes. If that were true, maybe Rennie *could* promise —— If she really loved Peter — oh, I do! — then her love wouldn't ever flit away, would it?

The meeting was over. Oliver turned his back on Rennie and shook hands with the man on his other side — some stranger, whom he obviously wished to welcome. Then he swiveled around and took Rennie's hand, looking into her eyes with such tenderness that she knew he understood everything.

"Way will open," he whispered. This was just what he'd predicted the first time Rennie came to Firbank.

Friends were standing around in little groups, visiting together or speaking to the Ashaways, reluctant to leave one another.

Oliver took Rennie's arm as they walked down the steps of the meetinghouse and made for the truck. He looked like his old self. His face was upturned so the rain could fall on it.

"Oh, how good! How magnificent, after our weeks of drought!" He stuck out his tongue to catch the drops. "My seedlings will be so glad."

"Yes," Rennie sang out, skipping along beside him. She could just see the trees clapping their hands for joy. "Wait till I tell Peter!"

5.

At their Monthly Meeting in Eighth Month, Kendal Friends appointed a committee to determine the clearness for marriage of Serenity Millburn Ross and Peter Hallburt Holland.

The committee, Oliver told Rennie when he came home from Monthly Meeting, was to report at the next session, which would be held on the twenty-ninth of September. It was hoped that Rennie and Peter would be present. "We don't like discussing people in their absence," Oliver explained. "Thee's welcome to stay at Firbank till then. Peter, too, if Austin doesn't need him any more."

"We can't. College opens the fifteenth. But I guess we could sneak back for a couple of days. Borrow some guy's car."

"If the report of the committee on clearness is satisfactory, you'll pass meeting. Kendal Friends will then undertake responsibility for the marriage."

Oliver went on to describe the next step. Yet another committee would be appointed — overseers, who were to ensure that the ceremony was conducted in reverence and simplicity. At the wedding, one of them would read the certificate aloud. "As soon as the Meeting has appointed overseers," Oliver concluded, "thy parents will be at liberty to issue the invitations."

"Not before?" Now that Rennie'd decided it was possible to make that promise, she couldn't wait. She'd call her parents tonight. "Not before?"

Oliver shook his head.

When Rennie had broken the great news to him on the way home from Simeon's memorial service — that she and Peter planned to be married in Kendal Meeting as soon as possible — she'd expected him to exclaim, "First-rate!" He hadn't and she was disappointed. Now, as he described the arrangements in a cautious, almost tentative tone, she was furious.

What? *Furious with Oliver?* She'd always been so starry-eyed about him. "Aren't you pleased?" she blurted out. "You kept saying way would open."

"It will. I'm confident. As for the timing — the committee on clearness will help you decide that."

"We *have* decided! We wrote that letter, remember? You said yourself it's the most significant step. That's if we pass meeting," Rennie added, suddenly uncertain. It was by no means a foregone conclusion. She'd better not tell her parents yet.

But she felt easier when Oliver announced that the committee consisted of the Ludlows and the Hills. "Four of our most concerned members. Thee and Peter will find them helpful."

"We like them best, too."

"Thee'll hear from Clara about arrangements for the interview."

Until recently, Oliver explained, it had been the custom for the two men Friends on the committee to talk with the prospective bridegroom and the two women with the bride. That was because it wasn't considered proper to discuss matters relating to sex in mixed company. But times had changed. In the opinion of Kendal Friends, it was in right ordering for the entire committee to interview the couple together.

Rennie felt relieved to hear that Peter would be with her. Just the same, she began to have that sinking feeling she always got before an exam. She could picture herself and Peter in the almost empty meetinghouse, trying to guess what answers the committee wanted them to give to loaded questions. Like Firbank after Heather arrived, the meetinghouse would be transformed from a place she had come to love to an unsympathetic one. It would become a courtroom. She thought of Joan of Arc being tried by all those religious, then burned at the stake. Rennie knew it was silly. The Ludlows and the Hills — why would anyone be afraid of them? But she was.

If only she could have talked to Daphne! Rennie wouldn't have minded admitting to her how apprehensive she was. But Daphne was never by herself now. Heather monopolized her completely. They sat in the dining room the whole day.

Heather was having trouble with the inventory. It was taking longer than she'd anticipated. She was afraid it wouldn't be finished, after all, by the time she had to leave. Rennie felt like gloating, Serves you right! You should have left my file alone.

All week, Rennie hung around, waiting to hear about the interview. John and Neil were busy men. It seemed they were having difficulty settling on a time when they would both be free.

Friday morning, Rennie was sprawled on Heather's bed, studying a set of Botticelli prints she'd found downstairs, when Heather appeared in the doorway. She was wearing her scarlet pantsuit. This was the first time she'd been in the ell this summer.

Rennie looked up quickly. Was she being called to the phone? But she saw at once that there was no urgency.

"Would you mind," Heather asked hesitantly, as if she hated to impose on Rennie, "would you mind keeping Mother company this afternoon? Father wants to take me to Kendal to call on some old friends."

Would Rennie mind? To have Daphne to herself again!

Even after Rennie agreed, Heather lingered, looking in from the doorway with a puzzling expression. Was she trying to find an excuse for coming in?

"You brought your gramophone."

Heather'd spotted the one sizable object in the room that wasn't hers. Maybe the clutter bugged her. Or was it that she wanted to be young again, living here? The wistful way she looked around touched Rennie.

"Come on in."

Heather didn't need to be coaxed.

Rennie slid off the bed and transferred her sweat shirt, jeans and sneakers from the rocking chair to the top of the bureau.

"Olly always uses this room when he's here," Heather told her, sitting down. "I wish I could have brought him and the girls. Stephen didn't think we ought to spend the money this year. Actually, the children are a bit much for Mother now — all that racketing around. But they were disappointed. They love it here. When I was their age," Heather added, "I just wanted to get away. It seemed confining."

Like my room at home, Rennie said to herself. This was Heather's chrysalis. Only, how could anyone want to break out of Firbank?

"The inventory's almost finished," Heather announced.

So that's what she really came for — to crow.

No. Quite the contrary. "I couldn't have done it without the start you made, Rennie. Turned out, your system was really better. In the end, I went back to it. If I hadn't, it would have taken forever."

Rennie flopped down on the bed. This was the first nice thing the woman ever said to her. And it wasn't all.

"You've done a great deal for Mother, apart from the inventory. The portrait — I think it's even better than Great-grandmother's. Don't you?"

"I — don't know. I try not to look at it."

"Why?"

Rennie shrugged.

"After her stroke, Mother lost interest in painting. She learned to use her left hand to please Father, but it took too much effort. Then you came. Your stirred something in her. The letters Father wrote about you! I was a bit jealous," Heather admitted, looking at Rennie shyly.

So I was right, Rennie thought. It's not that she doesn't like me. She just doesn't want her parents caring for someone else. Who can blame her for that? She must have felt awful the day she arrived, when she walked in and her mother was kissing me.

Reaching for one of the terra cotta figurines, Heather ran her fingers over the surface, the way Peter loved to do. She shook her head incredulously. "Imagine making a work of art like this for a small child to play with! I wasn't more than three or four. Who but my mother ——?"

"You're so lucky! Mine never would let me touch her things for

210

fear they'd break. Ever since I first came here, *I've* been jealous of *you.* I kept wishing for parents like yours."

"They've mellowed," Heather conceded. "They're better than they used to be."

"Better? They must have been wonderful to start with."

"Oh, they were. Only, as an adolescent, I didn't always think so." Heather smiled faintly. "Maybe I'm the one who's mellowed. But it wasn't much fun here for an only child. I was lonely and I wanted more attention than Mother gave me. All she ever did was paint. She had to. It was as necessary to her as breathing. Besides, we depended on it. Portraits were our cash crop, like potatoes or those Christmas trees Father raised. He didn't have much time for me, either." Heather put the figurine back on the bookshelf.

She wants to rap, Rennie decided. That's why she came. She has this urge.

"I should have been a boy," Heather murmured, arranging the figurines a little differently. "Not that Father ever made me feel he was sorry. Far from it. He loved me dearly as I was. I just knew that, with all the work on the farm, a son was what he needed."

Rennie thought of Austin's telling Peter that Oliver ought to sell out. That was ridiculous this year, next year. But someday, wasn't it bound to happen? If there'd been a son to take over the farm, Firbank could have stayed in the family. This must be on Heather's mind.

"I used to keep a jackknife in my pocket," she recalled, "the way a boy would do, so if Father wanted one, I'd have it handy. I tried to anticipate his wishes, like Mother. They were so close, those two. I knew they loved me as much as they loved each other, but I *felt* excluded. I guess I wanted to be first with both of them. My own children don't feel like that, at least, I don't think so. Stephen and I have a good marriage, but it isn't so all-encompassing as Mother and Father's."

Rennie felt sorry for Heather. How could she ever have thought that Oliver and Daphne excluded her from their love? It was utterly ridiculous. Heather knew that, too — now. She was a mature woman. And yet, a shred of that childish dissatisfaction lingered. Did one carry it around all one's life?

"You think your parents are bad!" Rennie cried. "You should have mine — wow!"

Or is it just because they *are* my parents that I feel this way? she wondered suddenly. They gave me plenty of attention — smothered me. Still, with no one but those big brothers, I was lonely, too.

"I'm a full-time mum," Heather declared earnestly. "Always available. And yet," she admitted, "my children aren't above grumbling, either. They want their independence. I'm patient, though — more patient than Mother was. She had so much temperament. The stroke flattened that. But when I was a child, she could get very angry — still does, when she wants to say something. If she thought a person or an animal was being ill treated —— Or something beautiful — it would rouse more emotion in her than in other people. I used to envy girls who had stolid mothers."

Rennie laughed. But she could well imagine that, in her early teens, Heather would have wanted her mother to be like other women.

"I never quite got over her being so different," Heather confided. "When she put on her smock — not another woman in Kendal would have gone around like that."

"Weren't you proud of her? I wish my mother did something interesting. It would take her mind off me. She wouldn't be left with nothing to do, now that her last child's grown up."

"Indeed I was proud! At exhibitions, I'd wander around the gallery, listening to people's remarks. When they admired a picture, I'd have to control myself not to cry out, 'My mother painted that!' But at school, the other girls wore fussy frocks and lipstick and dated. I wasn't permitted to."

That's why she wears mod clothes now, Rennie thought. She and my mother would hit it off great!

"And plain language," Heather was saying. "If any of my classmates heard my parents speaking to me, I was mortified."

"I think it's cool."

"That's because your parents didn't use it. For me, it was another of those peculiarities that set us apart. Besides, it's ungrammatical and undemocratic."

"Heather! It's frightfully democratic. That's the whole point. Your father explained it to me."

For an instant, all her childhood annoyance blazed in Heather's eyes. Then, a grown woman again, she laughed. "I guess there are some things I'll never come to terms with," she said, getting up to leave. "You see, plain language was democratic in the beginning. Right up to Great-grandmother's time, Friends upheld this testimony of addressing everyone the same way, although other people thought they were barmy. I could admire that."

"It's great!"

"But Friends of Mother and Father's generation didn't want to isolate themselves from other people and they adopted a double standard of speech: plain language in the family and Meeting; regular English with everyone else. That makes a distinction between the in-group and the outs. Not," Heather muttered, as if she felt a little silly, "that it really matters. I expect I'd be sad if Mother and Father gave up the plain language."

She had reached the door.

Rennie detained her. "Heather, your father talks about taking Daphne to New York for the exhibition. Is she up to it?"

"I don't know. She seems more frail this summer than a year ago. But Father thinks seeing her pictures in the Museum of Contemporary Art will make Mother so happy, it's worth the risk. She'll certainly get very tired."

"They could stay in Neville with my parents," Rennie suggested. "Drive into the City from there. It might be quieter than a hotel."

But would Rennie's parents want them?

Heather didn't respond to this. She started down the corridor. "Anyhow," she called back, "Mother has something nice to look forward to. I hope Stephen and I can come for the opening. The children will be away at school."

She cares about her mother, Rennie thought, as Heather disappeared around the landing. She cares so much. Why can't she lay those ghosts and let her love pour out the way Daphne's does?

It couldn't have been five minutes before Heather called to Rennie from the downtsairs hall that she was wanted on the telephone. "Take it in Mother and Father's room," she suggested.

Clara Ludlow, Rennie thought, excited. We're going to be interviewed!

She felt strange, entering that room, the sanctum of so many couples — generations of them. And stranger when she heard the voice on the other end of the line. It was Priscilla Munro, calling from New York. What for? They hadn't been in touch since college closed.

"What's up?" Rennie asked.

"I'm getting married."

"No kidding!"

"I want you to be my bridesmaid — you and Harriet and Audrey."

"You're getting married?" Rennie was having a delayed reaction. "You mean, you've finally gotten the nesting impulse?" She giggled.

This didn't seem to strike Priscilla as funny. "I can't wait for you to meet Mac," she said gravely. "We met in Easthampton at the beginning of the summer and, right off, we just clicked. He comes from San Francisco. That's where we're going to live."

"You're quitting college? Oh, Priscilla, you shouldn't do that."

"Don't be a nut! Tilbury isn't the only educational institution in the country. I'm transferring to Santa Rosa U. Mac says it's even better than old Til. Have I told you the date? September twelfth at the Murray Hill Church, but you have to be at the rehearsal and the bridal dinner the night before."

"The twelfth," Rennie repeated. "Yes, I guess I can. We're being married ourselves at the end of October. That's if we pass ——"

"You are? How neat! But, Rennie, I can't be in your wedding. I'm awfully sorry. California's too far."

"That's okay."

"Listen, don't worry about the dress. Mother's ordering everything. Just send me your measurements." In closing, Priscilla threw in, "Peter'll get invited, too."

Rennie ran downstairs to tell Daphne and Heather. "If you knew Priscilla!" she exclaimed, laughing. Then she said, suddenly aware of the great seriousness, "I wonder what kind of guy this Mac is? He must be pretty special."

6.

That afternoon, it was like old times. They sat on the back porch, just the two of them, Daphne sipping iced tea through a bent straw because the right side of her mouth couldn't negotiate the glass.

Rennie was happy. "Won't you be excited," she exclaimed, "walking into the museum with Oliver and seeing your pictures hanging in room after room — the ones we starred?"

Daphne smiled.

Could be the lopsidedness, Rennie said to herself, but it looks like a pretend smile. She doesn't believe she'll go.

"Heather told me how proud she used to be at exhibitions. I'll feel the same way. I'll want to say to the people standing there, '*My* cousin painted those!' "

Was Daphne really more frail? After the initial shock, Rennie had become so accustomed to her handicap, so interested in her personality and her art that she scarcely paid attention to her physical condition. If Daphne thought she was slipping, she never let on. Except when she longed to speak, she was always serene — none of that temperament Heather made so much of. If she was slipping ——

Rennie had an impulse to reach out and take the paralyzed hand, to guard it, to ward off anything that might befall. Instead, she said the thing she knew would please Daphne most: "I like Heather."

A few hours ago, Rennie couldn't have said it, not in perfect sincerity. But now it was true. Behind the slick façade and arm's-length reserve, she'd seen a lovable, though humorless and rather pathetic woman.

Rennie didn't reach out, but Daphne did, giving Rennie's arm an appreciative pat. Yes, nothing Rennie could have said would have pleased her so much.

"Funny, isn't it, that Heather and I never met before? Second cousins — you'd think ——"

All the summers Rennie's family might have spent here!

"I wish Mother and Daddy'd drive up before I leave. If the committee on clearness passes us and the Meeting approves, we could have the wedding the very next weekend, couldn't we? Well, I guess there'll have to be time to send out those invitations. But why must they be engraved? I can write them. Anyhow, when Mother and Daddy see the meetinghouse, they'll understand that with our family and Peter's and all the Kendal Friends there won't be room for outsiders."

How Rennie's nephews and nieces would wriggle during the silence! Never mind. It was a lovely thought — her family surrounding her in the little meetinghouse where their ancestors had worshiped.

All at once, her happiness became panic. She turned from Daphne and stared out across the dooryard. They'll come, won't they? They wouldn't refuse to come to my wedding, just because it's different? They wouldn't do that to me, would they?

Turning back, Rennie saw her doubts reflected in Daphne's eyes.

"I guess," Rennie said slowly, "I ought to try to tell them why I want to be married here. That was always my gripe — that Mother and Daddy never gave sensible reasons for decisions they made. When I was small and I kept asking, 'why?' they'd say, 'because.' Now it's 'standard operating procedure.' Sounds sophisticated, but as an explanation it isn't any better."

Come off it, she said to herself. You sound as bad as Heather.

"I owe them a decent explanation," she told Daphne earnestly. "As soon as the committee on clearness passes us — *if* they pass us —

I'll phone home and ask Mother and Daddy to drive up right away. They wouldn't come when I asked them a couple of weeks ago, but maybe now, because of the wedding —— They can have the room next to the one Heather's in, can't they? Will that be okay? I'll make up the bed."

Daphne nodded eagerly.

"It'll be my chance to show them Firbank — row Daddy across the pond. No, I guess he'll want to do the rowing. He was so proud, as a little boy, if Great-grandmother let him handle the boat. I can just see his face, when he stands on the dunes and sees the ocean! We'll go clamming on the flats."

Meanwhile, what would Rennie's mother do, back at the house? Would she try to talk to Daphne? Or would she just sit in some corner and take out her crocheting, dissociating herself from the scene?

Of course not. She'd be in an absolute fever, making plans for this imminent wedding — the gown, the veil, the bridesmaids. She'd start compiling those lists. When she got home, she'd rush to the Bridal Boutique. The whole routine would be set in motion again.

Oh no! Rennie cried to herself. I can't face it. Bad enough, being in Priscilla's wedding.

"As soon as Heather comes back," she told Daphne, "I must have her take my measurements so Mrs. Munro can order the bridesmaid dress. It seems such a waste. I already have three hanging in my closet at home, only worn once. But, of course, they all have to be alike. It's funny — bridesmaids don't do anything, just march and get their pictures taken, so why do they have to look alike?"

Rennie had a sudden inspiration. That bride in the picture on the third-floor landing at home didn't have any attendants.

"Daphne, do I have to have bridesmaids and a flower girl?"

Daphne shook her head.

"A veil? Do I have to wear a veil?"

Daphne shook her head again.

Realizing that she had nerve, proposing this to such a great artist, Rennie still couldn't resist asking, "Would you design my wedding dress? You know — the kind that's right for a Quaker marriage. The Bridal Boutique wouldn't have the faintest idea." Rennie held her breath.

It was one of those moments when speech would have been redundant. Daphne's face radiated pleasure.

"Wait," Rennie said, jumping up. She rushed to the woodshed and returned with Daphne's Bristol board under her right arm, the water-color box in that hand and the brushes in the left. Then she took the water jar to the kitchen and filled it afresh. She was so excited that she had to grip it hard to keep from spilling.

In the palest blue gray, Daphne sketched a shadowy outline of Rennie's figure, topping it with red fuzz. She proceeded to clothe the outline in a long, simply flowing gown, rounded at the neck. Cocking her head, Daphne held the paper up before her.

"I love it," Rennie declared, "just the way it is."

But Daphne had another idea. She placed the paper on the table again and started a new sketch. Rennie, sitting beside her with her elbows propped on the table, watched a whole series of sketches emerge, each one a little different. As Daphne finished one, she turned to Rennie for her reaction. Then she began another, to see whether Rennie would like it better.

"I love them all," Rennie cried. "I wouldn't know which to choose."

There was something mysterious about them — more dreamlike than real, reminiscent of the expression of the eyes in Rennie's portrait — something only Daphne envisioned. No material, however gossamer — not even organza — could possibly translate these sketches into actual garments; yet for the completely spiritual occasion Rennie wanted her wedding to be, nothing less would be suitable.

"We don't have to have a big reception, do we, like the one Daddy arranged at the country club? I know Friends won't want champagne served, so why can't we just have punch and wedding cake out on the lawn behind the meetinghouse? It'll still be pretty warm. The First Day school tables can be set up in that shed where the horses used to wait."

Daphne didn't seem to be listening. She was gazing at the woods beyond the dooryard. Then she made an even more fanciful sketch. This gown wouldn't stun the wedding guests like a dress designer's creation. Just the opposite — breathtakingly beautiful though it seemed to Rennie, it was unobtrusive, a natural part of that self she'd give to Peter at their wedding. In this sketch, Rennie was holding a tiny bunch of flowers — one of those unpretentious, old-fashioned bouquets, so small that she carried it just by curling her fingers around the stems.

"The bouquet!" Rennie cried, recalling those big, stiff arrangements her sisters-in-law balanced on their forearms at their weddings. "I want that sweet, little bouquet."

In a corner of the paper, Daphne made an Impressionistic painting of the bouquet as it would appear to Rennie when she held it and looked down — a harmony of concentric colors — cerulean merging with rose madder and vermilion, pale yellow with aquamarine and viridian — transparent, flowing into one another. Then, running down the margins of the paper, Daphne reproduced the individual flowers in quite a different style — life-size, precise, detailed, like those botanical plates she'd done as an art student.

Rennie didn't know much about flowers. She wondered whether Daphne took into account the fact that it would be fall. Would these be obtainable? Or was Daphne just playing make-believe with her? No. She wouldn't do that. She knew how seriously Rennie was taking her wedding.

Daphne was still working on the flowers when Heather and Oliver returned. Heather went to the kitchen to start supper. Oliver, stooping to kiss Daphne, looked fascinated as he saw what she was doing.

"My wedding dress," Rennie explained, pointing to the last sketch Daphne had made. "That's the one I'm choosing. Isn't it neat? And that's the bouquet I'm going to carry. Would you tell me the names of the flowers so Mother can tell the florist?" Simply because Daphne had decided on them, it became terribly important to Rennie that she have just these, no others.

Taking the chair on Daphne's other side, Oliver produced a

pencil from his pocket and began writing under each detailed flower in his small, careful writing: *blue flag, marsh marigold, robin's plantain.* Halfway down the line, he stopped, looking puzzled, and turned to Daphne.

He doesn't know the names of the others, Rennie thought.

But as Oliver exchanged glances with Daphne, the puzzled look disappeared and a little smile began to form around the corners of his mouth. Without saying a word, he'd asked her something and she'd answered. They were sharing a secret. If they had whispered, holding their hands up before their mouths so Rennie wouldn't hear, she couldn't have felt more left out.

Now I know what it was like for Heather, she thought, hurt.

Oliver had turned back to the Bristol board and was writing in the rest of the names: *star flower, coral honeysuckle, birdfoot violet.*

That's a wildflower, Rennie realized. Is it out so late?

When he'd finished, Oliver smiled at Rennie. "It'll be the most beautiful wedding," he exclaimed, his eyes shining, "at the loveliest time of year!"

He looked at Daphne again and that same secret passed between them.

7.

The interview didn't take place in the meetinghouse, after all.

Daphne and Oliver were still looking at each other, sharing that secret, when the telephone rang. Clara Ludlow wanted to speak to Rennie. She was sorry to be calling so late, she said, but she'd only just found out that John and Neil would both be free this evening. Would Rennie and Peter have supper with them at the upper end of the beach?

As soon as Peter came from work, he rowed Rennie over. They walked along the shore until they found the Ludlows and the Hills, sunning themselves, with a mess of picnic things around them.

After they'd all been swimming and had played a game of Frisbee, John started a fire. Rennie and Peter went with Neil in search of more driftwood.

"What do you call this?" Peter asked Neil, pointing to a silver-gray, lacy plant growing out of the sand.

"Dusty miller."

"And that crazy-looking stuff just above the water line with all the seedpods that are fun to pop?"

"Sea rocket."

"Neil," Rennie asked, "do violets grow around here in the fall?"

"No. End of May."

"What about marsh marigold, star flower, blue flag, robin's plantain — do they come out in the fall?"

"Those are all spring flowers. Last of May, beginning of June, the Firbank woods are full of them."

How strange that Daphne shouldn't know!

Their arms loaded with branches and old planks that had been washed ashore, they returned to the fire. Clara was heating a huge kettle of chowder. Alice had baked biscuits. Corn from Neil's garden was laid in the embers. A feast! But first they stood in a circle, silent, watching the crimson sun get ready to slide into the sea. Neil and John reached for Rennie's hands. She dug her toes into the still-warm sand, thinking that, in fact, they were reaching for her soul.

These people weren't about to grade Peter and her. Their function was to find them, catch up with them where they were, walk along a little way — be their companions on this pilgrimage.

That's what it is. A pilgrimage! We're trying to realize our humanity the way Oliver and Daphne —— One doesn't have to backpack.

One could make a pilgrimage standing in a circle, digging one's toes into the sand while the sun went down.

They sat around the fire, eating all they could hold, joking. It was more like a joyous family celebration than an interview. As Rennie watched the Ludlows and the Hills licking ice-cream sticks for dessert, she thought, They seem as young as we are.

Even bundled in a bulky fisherman's sweater, Clara moved with grace, as if she had her limbs under perfect control. Rennie wondered whether she was a dancer. In contrast, Alice was tall and moved slowly. Her personality, like her voice, was low-keyed — quiet, but decisive.

"I can still remember how scared I was when I met with my committee on clearness," Neil said. He stuck out his tongue and ran it along the ice-cream stick. "Don't know why. They were my friends, though they were so much older — Philip Ludlow and Oliver Otis, the two men I admired most. I wasn't afraid of them. I guess I was just leery of what I was getting into." He grinned wickedly at Alice.

"I wasn't scared," she murmured, unruffled by his teasing. "I had Diligence Smith on my committee."

Diligence, Rennie repeated to herself. Never heard that name before. It's like Serenity. *Keep thy heart with all diligence.* I wonder if she did.

"I can't remember the name of the other woman who interviewed me," Alice was saying. "She wasn't much use. I guess her marriage hadn't been too satisfactory. But Dilly was marvelous. She knew what she was talking about — been widowed a long time. Then, late in life, she married Durand, a charming man."

"They were beautiful together," Neil recalled and John agreed.

Alice was gazing into the fire. "Dilly reminded me that Neil and I didn't have to go it alone," she said softly. "In making our promises, we were counting on divine assistance, weren't we? So what was there to worry about?"

Rennie envied Alice's assurance. She'd also have to declare her reliance on divine assistance at her wedding. Could she, in perfect sincerity? If so, why wasn't she just as relaxed?

"Clara and I weren't subjected to any clearness committee," John said. "We were married in her church."

"I wasn't a Friend then," Clara explained to Peter and Rennie. "John and his father and brother were the only ones I knew. They were such special people, I couldn't be sure I'd feel comfortable worshiping with the others. So I waited till after we were married."

"How long did it take you?"

Peter's interest surprised Rennie.

"Till Philippa was born. Up to that time, it didn't seem to me that it made any difference. I loved the church I was reared in. But when our baby came, I felt a great desire to be joined to John in worship, too — for her sake. It wasn't till later that I understood how much meeting meant to me for itself."

After the chowder bowls were rinsed in the ocean, everyone gathered around the fire again. No one spoke for some time. It gradually dawned on Rennie that this wasn't because the Friends couldn't think how to begin. They were trying to focus on what was important, collecting their forces. Perhaps they were even now falling back on divine assistance.

Looking up, Rennie saw her first star. She shut her eyes. Make a wish! *Let us pass meeting. Please let us pass* —— Even before she opened her eyes again, she knew this was too small to be her central wish.

Peter seemed frightened. On the point of whispering, Are you afraid they won't pass us? Rennie held back. She had a suspicion his answer might be, No, I'm afraid they will.

What's come over him? He was the one who was so crazy to write that letter. He couldn't wait to be my husband.

Maybe he was worrying about the insurance again — how he was going to pay those premiums. After the engagement party, when Rennie's picture was in the paper, an agent had come to Tilbury and looked Peter up to explain the necessity of his carrying substantial life insurance, now that he was getting married, so that, if anything happened to him, Rennie'd be provided for. Those premiums had been on his mind the past few days.

John was explaining that the original function of a committee on clearness had been to determine that the man and the woman who wished to be married were "clear of all other engagements" — not engaged to someone else, or even married.

"We're not," Peter assured him solemnly.

"Didn't think so," John replied, amused. "Nowadays," he added, becoming serious again, "the committee's job is to make sure the two people are clear in their minds about the sacredness of the step they're taking." He looked searchingly from Peter to Rennie. "Why do you want to get married?"

"We love each other," they cried together. They were of one mind!

It seemed a foolish question — the pediatrician asking routinely, "Does it hurt?" when he knew perfectly well that it did.

But, in the flat half-light, Rennie could see expectancy on all four of the faces that were turned to hers and Peter's. She thought, What they're asking is, how will it be different?

In spite of their simplicity, these people were with it. They didn't need to go into Rennie and Peter's sex life. They could guess. They weren't criticizing; they weren't approving. Like Oliver, they made it clear without saying a word that, for themselves, Rennie and Peter's lifestyle wouldn't be acceptable. But they believed that there is something near one which can guide one; that this something would guide others as well as themselves. No need for them to preach or meddle.

How *would* it be different?

Peter'd feel better — that was the main thing. They'd be respectable. Their parents would like that. They'd be entitled to the apartment in the married students' quarters, though Rennie wouldn't cook. With two extra courses, she'd be swamped. If she had to keep house, too ——

"I think I know what you mean," Peter was saying. "And I guess the answer is, we don't know. We want the kind of marriage you have and it'll take a lot more than we're putting into our relationship now. Maybe that's because we're young. I've got this hang-up about supporting Rennie and helping my family, if they need it. I'm sick of playing house, like a couple of little kids. But we've got another year of school. It would have been better to wait till we graduate. We can't. It's too hard."

"You're young," Neil observed, with a nod of approval. "But you're speaking like a man. Still, need shouldn't be the whole reason for marrying. John and I need Clara and Alice, but if that had been our only reason for getting hitched to them, we probably wouldn't be here now. We'd have busted up."

Clara asked, "How do your parents feel about your getting married?"

"Mine want me to, though not in meeting, probably. Peter's don't really, but they're being nice about it."

By the light of the fire, Rennie discerned unease on the faces of Friends.

"Maybe," Clara suggested, "you need to discuss this with them further. It takes time for a meeting of minds. If you're married in the next few weeks, they'll hardly have a chance to understand what it means to you or to us. We wouldn't feel very comfortable, you know, if it turned out that your parents weren't in accord."

Now why did Rennie have to go into all that? Would they flunk them, just because their parents —— *Would* they?

"I like your way of doing things," Peter was saying. "From what Rennie told me, I didn't think I would, before I came here. All but Woolman's *Journal*; that's great. But Oliver sounded sort of — well, I'd never heard of anyone like him. Soon as I came here, of course, I knew I'd met up with somebody pretty special. You folks are honest. I go for that. One of my profs is always telling us the chief quality an astronomer has to have is accuracy. I guess accuracy in one's work is the same as honesty in one's life."

Alice looked as though she were about to speak, but she seemed to be weighing the words first. Finally, she asked, "Are you familiar with our Queries? Have you heard them read?"

"No."

"We don't have a statement of belief, you know, only a set of questions relating to personal conduct. From time to time, these are read in meeting. The Queries are searching. They remind us of what we want our lives to be. So when we haven't been living up to our potential — and who does? — they make us dissatisfied, though we're only answerable to ourselves, in the silence. The Query on marriage sums up my ideal: *Do you make your home a*

225

place of friendliness, refreshment and peace, where God becomes more real to those who dwell therein and to all who visit there?"

Rennie thought, Where God becomes more real! How can I make it that? *Friendliness, refreshment and peace* —— She and Peter had known all three of these at Firbank. Still it had never occurred to her that that apartment was supposed to be more than a place to sleep and have snacks in. Regular meals they'd eat in the cafeteria, as they'd always done. Maybe sometimes their friends would come in for a rap. But to make that apartment another Firbank!

It was being laid upon them to transform four walls into a place of the highest significance. Someday, maybe, when they'd graduated, they could put their minds on this, but senior year, and with those extra courses! Just as Daphne had led Rennie past the surface of a canvas, past the composition of forms and spaces, the choice of pigments — past all these to the living personality behind them — so now Rennie was being led to a new dimension, the envisioning of an ideal beyond anything she had imagined for next year, or ever.

When the sun went down, the sea breeze died but the air grew colder. So did the sand. Rennie thought suddenly, That's how I'd be if Peter left me. No! I have to generate my own power.

When he was trying to decide whether he wanted to marry her, Peter had asked her to stay away a whole week. She'd had no one to fall back on then but the girls in the dorm, not her self. Now she was about to give that self to Peter. Did she really possess it? Was it secure? She had told Daphne that, to love, one first had to have security and one couldn't have security unless one loved the way Daphne and Oliver did.

Maybe all along, I didn't really love Peter. Is that possible? Wasn't I just hanging on to him for dear life? But now —— Now!

"As far as I'm concerned," Clara was saying, turning to John and the Ludlows, "Rennie and Peter are clear for marriage."

"I approve of that," the other three said.

Rennie reached out to hug Peter. They had passed!

"As for the date," John said slowly, "perhaps you will give that a little more thought."

This was all. The interview was over. But they stayed sitting by the fire, gazing at the embers a long time. It was a silence like the one that always preceded the close of meeting, a feelingful time.

Rennie exulted to herself, They said we can get married in meeting!

But they had also appealed to her and to Peter to perceive their strongest feelings, their central wish. They'd urged them to wait for that which was near them, which could guide them. In different words, they were saying exactly what others had said the first time Rennie went to meeting, when she'd resolved to listen to Peter.

I'm listening to him now! I hear what he's saying. He doesn't want to marry me yet, but he can't help himself. I asked for it. I begged to be dependent. I have to let go now, even if it should mean ——

John reached out and took her hand. The others shook hands with each other. It really had been a Friends meeting, here, by the fire.

The men stood up and stretched. They gravitated toward the water's edge. Neil and John listened as Peter described the extragalactic sources of radio emission. "Quasars," he was saying, "are way, way out there, at the rim of the observable universe. They're receding from the earth with tremendous speed."

Rennie, kneeling by the fire, helped Clara and Alice pack the dishes and the kettle into a canvas ice bag. As she glanced from one to the other, she thought, I feel about them the way Nancy and Sandy feel about me.

She stopped working for a minute and looked up. It was such a clear night, she was sure she could see every one of those eighty-eight constellations and five thousand stars that Peter said were visible to the naked eye. And there, extending all the way around the celestial sphere, was the Milky Way.

Suddenly, Rennie felt a surge within her, an irresistible impulse to wish on that whole sky full of stars, every last one. She didn't shut her eyes. They were trying to encompass the universe. This was her central wish — she had it at last! Nameless, infinite, beyond her grasp, yet real, as real as herself, it stirred her inmost being.

This was such a secret wish, how could she share it with Peter?

It would take a whole new medium to express it, a whole lifetime to define, to live out the glowing perfection that Rennie envisaged now.

If divine assistance — whatever that was — could see Peter and her through marriage as long as they lived, why wouldn't it see them through the next few months, till they graduated? Why wouldn't it help them to wait till Peter had the independence his manhood craved?

Only I can give it to him, Rennie realized suddenly. Only I can give it to myself.

Once they both had this independence, then — *then* they could depend wholly on each other, couldn't they, like Oliver and Daphne?

Daphne! That's what she was trying to tell me with those spring flowers! Oliver got the message right away. All along, they had reservations about our getting married before we graduate, but they weren't about to tell us what to do. They wanted us to come to it ourselves.

Letting go of the ice bag, Rennie jumped up. She didn't run to the water's edge; she flew.

Seeing her coming, Peter opened his arms wide.

"We can wait," she whispered, as he held her close. "It's only nine months till graduation. When we want our baby, we'll have to wait that long."

By the time Peter got through kissing Rennie, John and Neil had discreetly withdrawn and joined their wives. They were getting ready to go home, dousing the fire, heaping sand on the smoldering embers.

Part Five

*O*n the way home, Rennie got to thinking about Larry.

If he'd only known Oliver and John and Neil when Daddy made him register for the draft — some men who had the same views about participating in war — he wouldn't have had that awful feeling of standing alone.

After the army turned Larry down on account of his knee, everybody expected him to be grateful that he didn't have to go either to Vietnam or to jail. And yet, Rennie remembered, he wasn't. He just complained that people whose values were different from his were running his life.

It was the same for him as for Peter and me, when everyone was arranging that wedding we didn't want. Seemed as if we were being processed. But wasn't Daddy right about Larry? What would have been the good of going to jail? I wouldn't want my son to.

The whole question was more complicated than it appeared when Rennie's father referred to it, back in March. Then she'd blamed him. Now she saw that he was being true to *his* convictions — as true as his Great-grandfather Josiah, when he broke the Fugitive Slave Laws.

Nothing was simple anymore; nothing was all good or all bad. Even Daphne and Oliver. How could such a perfect marriage as theirs have had negative side effects? Yet, it was a fact that, much as they loved Heather, when she was young they'd failed her.

So it isn't surprising if Daddy failed Larry.

Rennie decided to go and see Larry and Victoria while she was home. It was ages since she'd been to their house. She'd tell them about Firbank and beg them to drive over sometime. She'd break it to Victoria that she wasn't having any bridesmaids; that Vicky wasn't going to be a flower girl.

I'll go and see everybody, Rennie decided — Matty and Jonathan and Jane and Eddy. It's important for all of them to know what's going on. Wait till Jane hears that a Quaker bride is treated the same as the groom! With her consciousness raised the way it's been lately, she'll wish she'd had a wedding like that.

The bus took forever. Rennie was used to whizzing around in planes, not to riding and changing, riding and changing again, as she had to do to get from Kendal to Neville by bus. But it was a lot cheaper. From now on, that was how she intended to travel.

You do get to see the country.

Last spring, when her father spoke about Larry, Rennie wasn't being processed yet. In all fairness, she had to admit that her parents were reaching out to her then. "You're still our little girl," her father had said. "Mother and I love you very much." And her mother kept repeating, "We just want you to be happy." It troubled them that they couldn't give Rennie the security she needed. She had come close to breaking down, then, and telling her parents everything.

Instead, she'd clammed up. "Quit worrying about me. I'm okay."

If she had just given her parents a chance, they might not have tried to push her into marriage before she was ready.

It wasn't only the countryside Rennie was seeing as she bounced along in that bus. She suddenly saw why her parents wanted a spectacular wedding and why her father broke down when she and Peter rejected it.

Her parents had been worrying about her lifestyle. To try to reason with Rennie would have been useless. So they decided that the way to give her security was to get her married with a big splash, overlooking the fact that Rennie scarcely knew what marriage was all about.

I ought to have let my own parents come along on my pilgrimage, she thought miserably, looking out at a shabby trailer camp. But I pushed them away. I didn't think they'd understand. Well, they wouldn't have. Still, not telling them only made things worse.

Now she was returning to Neville firmly resolved to change all this. Her original plan had been to stay at Firbank until after Labor Day. Austin wanted Peter to work that long. Then they were each going to spend a week at home before college opened. Rennie was going to Priscilla's wedding. But when they were writing their second letter to the Meeting, she had this sudden impulse.

"Daddy's been begging me to come home," she told Peter. "Give Mother a break. With all I've learned this summer, I can easily take over the house. It'll make them happy to have me there on my birthday. Next year, I'll celebrate it with *thee!*"

"And every year thereafter," Peter declared happily.

In their second letter, they informed the Meeting that they didn't plan to be married till May thirty-first. Would Friends postpone considering their marriage till January? They'd be able to come to Kendal during intersession.

Rennie hoped Oliver and Daphne wouldn't feel she was running out on them. "It's just that I have this sudden impulse to explain to Mother and Daddy."

"What Woolman would have called a 'motion of love,'" Oliver observed.

Rennie could see that he was as delighted about her concern for her parents as he'd been about the postponement of the wedding. But he'd miss her help, he said.

"I used to think nobody needed me," she told Peter, "and now so many people —— I feel bad about ditching Oliver just when Heather's going back to England."

Peter shrugged. "No problem. I'm still here, aren't I? Every afternoon and every weekend. I can do a lot for Oliver."

Rennie hugged him for that.

"Look," he said, "I can't take you to Priscilla's wedding."

"Of course not. It's okay." Rennie had another impulse. "Peter, after we get back to college, if we ever have a free weekend, could we go to Charlesbury? I'd like to talk to your parents about — well, just rap."

That pleased him.

On the way home, in those buses that drove all around Robin Hood's barn, in those hot bus stations where she waited, Rennie told herself how glad she was that she'd made this decision.

When she finally got to Neville, dog-tired and stunned by the heat, nothing was quite the way she'd pictured it. She offered to cook supper and was told to set the table. Her mother wasn't about to turn over her kitchen to anybody. In spite of what Rennie's father had said, that wasn't the kind of vacation she wanted. Paris — yes. If he had offered to take her to Paris, she might even have risked flying. But just to sit in her own living room while her daughter took charge ——

"I'm getting on," she said, "but I can still run my house, thank you."

Was it because Rennie'd never offered to do anything before that her mother didn't understand? It was the same with the plans for the wedding.

"What will there be for *me* to do?" her mother asked. "If you're not having any attendants and no proper reception, just fruit punch in the *horse stalls* —— Who ever heard of serving nothing but fruit punch at a wedding? Our friends will think ——"

"They're not going to be there. The meetinghouse is too small."

"You said it seats over a hundred. Even with the two families and those overseers, there'll be room for the Dixwells, the Goffes, the Whalleys ——"

"No, Mother. Kendal Friends will fill every bench. There'll be Oliver and Daphne, the Ludlows, the Hills, all the Youngs, Mary Lancashire — she remembers Great-grandmother — the Ellises, Nancy and Sandy and their parents, the Kleins, Charley Fiorentino, who cleans Firbank, Sam and Jorim and their wives, the Ashaways and Billy Green. He's the kid who ripped off a car. Peter's been spending a lot of time with him."

"You mean," Rennie's father exclaimed, "Pete's keeping that

234

kind of company? It's not just the lingo I object to. If that's what Pete ——"

"All the younger men in the Meeting are doing things with Billy," Rennie broke in. "Trying to act like his big brothers. If we don't have another soul at our wedding, we want Billy Green."

"Daddy and I don't know any of those people," Rennie's mother complained.

"Joan, let's not make this hard for Rennie. She's got new friends. Oliver's given her ideas." There was a touch of bitterness in those last words. Then, as Rennie's father turned to her, she saw that his love superseded all else. "Maybe we did overdo it a bit, when we planned that June wedding. We only have one daughter. We wanted to give her the best. But if you prefer to be married in Kendal, we'll go along with their mores, even about omitting the champagne. Won't we, Joan?"

Rennie's mother assented.

"With one exception, Rennie. I insist on giving you away. Every father does that."

And Rennie, who wanted so much to sound like an adult, blurted out, like an adolescent, "You don't own me, Daddy. How can you give me away? I'm giving myself to Peter. He's giving himself to me. At Quaker weddings, the guy and the girl come into the meetinghouse the same way. Friends always believed in the equality of the sexes. It's no new thing with them."

Rennie's father looked hurt, as if she had accused him of not regarding women as equals. If he didn't, why would he protect and treat them with courtesy? It had come as a shock to be told by Jane, who was into the women's movement and making her father-in-law the target of her crusade, that the chivalry his own father had instilled in him was nothing but the rankest male chauvinism.

Rennie could see that her father was having to struggle not to blow his stack. He put his arm around her instead. "Look, honey, your wedding's rescheduled now. A lot may change in nine months. You said the Friends Meeting isn't going to finalize the arrangements till January. We're not supposed to send out invitations till then, right? Very well. Let's forget the whole thing till next year."

Forget the whole thing! Rennie'd sacrificed herself, leaving Firbank — Peter, Daphne, Oliver, Heather — so she could give her parents insight, and now her father wanted to forget the whole thing! His tone suggested that by January, or May at the latest, the whole thing might be off.

This got to Rennie. How could her father think that she and Peter —— She couldn't take it. She simply went upstairs.

Reviewed in the privacy of her room, her remark about her father not owning her seemed pretty stupid. Of course he didn't. He never said he did. If she wanted to be so literal, it was a fact that he had earned practically everything she owned. Even her body wouldn't have survived if he hadn't provided nourishment.

But that wasn't the point at all. Rennie, who was so eager to make her marriage deeply spiritual, had missed the significance of the act to which her father attached such importance. She'd assumed it was only pride that made him insist on walking down the aisle with her on his arm in the presence of his friends and associates, when, all the time, it was the significance of this act that he regarded — his responsibility for his daughter. He'd taken this responsibility all her life and only he could hand it over to Peter.

But this is going to be a *Quaker* marriage, Rennie argued, as if she were still downstairs.

Sighing, she began to unpack. The Bristol board with Daphne's sketches she propped on her bureau. Someday, she'd show her mother the sketch of the dress she intended to wear. She'd explain that there was no need to order flowers. Peter'd simply go out to the Firbank woods on the morning of the wedding and pick a little bouquet. At the moment, though, Rennie wasn't in the mood to show her mother Daphne's sketches.

It struck her then that, in spite of her resolve on the bus, she hadn't leveled when her mother asked what there was for her to do at the wedding. Oliver'd made it clear that all four parents had a very important part in the ceremony, an equal part. When Rennie and Peter entered the meetinghouse, they would be sitting there,

236

"in the gathered silence," Oliver had said, "asking God's blessing on your union."

How could Rennie have communicated this to her mother? Such expressions came naturally to Oliver, but they'd never been used in this house. Coming from Rennie, they would have sounded phony.

Her room didn't feel like home, even with Serenity's Woolman on the bedside table, the way it used to be in the ell at Firbank. Rennie wished she were back there. She wanted Peter. Rushing home had been a mistake.

She got into bed and turned on her transistor. Those Wounded Knee Indians were demanding that the government honor the treaties made with their ancestors. Indians reminded Rennie of what Oliver had told her about Woolman's going to visit a tribe on the Susquehanna River in the Seventeen Sixties, when many Indians were on the warpath. The year Heather was ten, she and Daphne and Oliver wanted to follow the wilderness trail Woolman had walked over, only to find that it had become the roadbed of the Lehigh Valley Railroad.

As Oliver told the story, Woolman's journey was exciting — the gentle, frail white man following his Indian guides along a path so narrow that they had to walk single file; the hardships of camping out in winter; the tomahawks that were brandished all around them.

Homesick for Firbank, Rennie opened the *Journal* and looked up Woolman's account of this journey, beginning with his reason for undertaking it.

Love was the first motion, and thence a concern arose to spend some time with the Indians — like some incantation, the antique language carried Rennie back to Firbank — *that I might feel and understand their life, and the spirit they live in, if haply I might receive some instruction from them, or they be in any degree helped forward by my following the leadings of truth amongst them.*

To understand, to learn from, to help — not aggressively, however well meant, but simply by following the leadings of truth — if

237

a man belonging to a race that was exterminating the Indians could travel safely among them, armed only with that outreaching love, why couldn't a girl follow those leadings with her own parents?

Long after she turned out the light, Rennie pondered this, repeating Woolman's words: *Love was the first motion . . . I was made quiet and content.*

2.

The day before she went back to college for her senior year, Rennie celebrated her twentieth birthday with her parents. "I'm not a teen-ager any more!" she exclaimed, counting the candles on the cake her mother had baked.

"Make a wish."

Rennie filled her lungs. My *central* wish, she thought anxiously. Before she could formulate it, she had to let her breath go.

Her mother watched the candles she'd lighted one by one being extinguished with a single puff. "You grew up so fast," she observed wistfully.

For seven years, she'd looked forward to the day when Rennie's turbulent teens would end, yet now, forgetting the frustration, she already looked back to them nostalgically, convinced the future held no comparable joy.

Rennie's father went to the den and returned with his arms full of packages and cards. That manila envelope — it came from Firbank! Before looking at anything else, Rennie had to open it.

"Oh," she cried. "Daddy, look! It's a water color Daphne made of the house." She ran over to his place and held it up. "Isn't it lovely?"

He looked at the little picture a long time without betraying any feeling. Then he turned away. "Hasn't changed in twenty years," was his only comment.

Rennie felt let down. "I thought you'd like it. You always used to be so moony ——"

Her mother was reading a humorous birthday card in a very loud voice. But, as Rennie tucked the picture back in its envelope, all three of them were silent.

Tomorrow, Rennie comforted herself, I can show it to Peter. *He'll* like it.

When her bus rolled into Tilbury, he was waiting, his bright yellow head thrown back as he scanned the windows. It seemed forever before Rennie reached the door and jumped down. She was with him again!

He took her bag and put his arm around her shoulder, bending a little to smile lovingly at her, saying nothing.

"I thought I'd never get here." That was all Rennie could think of.

Too happy to speak, they crossed the campus. It was crawling with students. The upperclassmen acted as if they owned the place, but those freshmen looked lost.

"Poor kids," Rennie murmured. "I'm glad I'm not young any more."

Peter laughed. "How was your birthday?"

"Mother and Daddy gave me an electric skillet. Daphne and Oliver must have looked up the date in the family Bible. They sent me a little water color of the house. It's in my bag. I'll show it to you later. When I opened it, Daddy —— I don't think he likes my being friends with Oliver. It's almost as if he feels Oliver's seduced me — you know, charmed my love away from him. It isn't true!"

The gentle smile Peter gave Rennie was clearly meant to heal any hurt she might ever sustain. "I have something for you. Couldn't risk sending it through the mail. Anyway, I wanted to give it to you myself."

"What *is* it?"

"Wait till we get somewhere that isn't so public."

When they reached the college garden, Peter drew Rennie to a

239

bench and took a small package out of his pocket. His eyes shone. She untied the white ribbon slowly, smoothing back the tissue paper, savoring her anticipation.

"It was my mother's," Peter explained, as Rennie looked down on an amethyst set in a narrow, gold ring. "She wanted you to have it."

"Oh, Peter!"

"You don't have to wear it," he assured her quickly, "if you'd rather not, though it isn't showy. But it has a lot of meaning, coming from Mom."

Rennie looked at the ring, then at Peter, then at the ring again. He reached out for it and took her left hand. "This is only the first one I'm going to put on your finger," he declared.

As he was kissing her, some girls walked by. He pulled back quickly.

The violet stone was sparkling in the sunlight. It made Rennie's hand seem strange, as though it belonged to someone else.

"Did you tell your parents I'd like to go home with you sometime?"

"Yes. They were pleased. Are they ever glad that we're not getting married till we graduate!"

"Is a Quaker wedding okay with them?"

"They said just so it's genuine for us, that's all they care about."

But *your* father isn't being gypped out of giving you away, Rennie thought. It doesn't matter that much to him.

"Dad said he never expected to see the day when I'd be excited over how many bushels of potatoes a given acre can produce! We talked a lot."

"What about?"

"You and me, mostly. That was good. Everything's clear between us now. So if he dies suddenly ———"

Rennie turned to Peter in alarm.

"He may, any time. If he does, I won't feel I held out on him. From what he said, we're not the first couple who've found sex a problem." Grinning, Peter squeezed Rennie's arm. "What was Priscilla's wedding like?"

240

"Beautiful. I was surprised. It's a handsome church — Nineteenth Century, one of the few old buildings in that part of New York. It looks small and lost among the skyscrapers. The stained glass is second-rate, naturally, but with the sun shining through it there were lovely pools of color on the white canvas in the aisle. And the music! It was so beautiful!"

Peter looked at Rennie quickly. "You're not sorry that we —— It isn't too late to change. Friends would understand."

"Oh, no, Peter. That kind of wedding isn't for us. I want it to be serene, and they were so uptight. The best man had this list of reminders he kept pulling out of his pocket — his duties — and Mrs. Munro ran around the vestibule before she went into the church, fussing with our dresses, straightening our bouquets, telling Audrey and Harriet and me that we looked adorable and remember to start on the left foot. I don't want some guy pronouncing us man and wife. *I'm* marrying you and I want *you* to marry me."

"That would suit me best," Peter admitted. "What's Mac like?"

"Nice, easygoing. Not good-looking — just an ordinary guy. I think he's great but I can't understand what Priscilla sees in him. I mean, the way she used to talk about getting married! And she turns out to be the first one. I guess people never know what they'll do when they fall in love."

As they neared her dorm, Rennie confided, still thinking of Priscilla's wedding, "I got giggly during the processional. I was so nervous about balancing on my front foot and remembering all the instructions. But I really liked that wedding. It was just right for Priscilla and Mac — their idea of how they wanted to be married. What matters is how the couple feels — if they really believe in it. Don't you think so?"

"What you're trying to say — I think it's what Woolman meant, only he said it better. *There is a principle which is pure, placed in the human mind* — something-something — *confined to no forms of religion, nor excluded from any.* Remember that?"

"Yes! *Where the heart stands in perfect sincerity.*"

When Rennie got to her room and started to unpack, her hand still looked strange. She didn't think she'd wear the ring — not now, anyway. If her friends were still here, she'd be rushing down the corridor to show it off, but Audrey and Harriet had graduated and Priscilla was on her honeymoon.

It was such fun seeing them again at the wedding! Now, though, Rennie felt ashamed as she recalled the moment when Mr. Munro gave Priscilla away and the bridesmaids were lined up at the side of the chancel. Instead of being suitably solemn, Rennie had sung to herself, *Three little maids from school are we, filled to the brim with girlish glee. I'm glad Priscilla's getting married here and not me.* How could she have been so flip?

While Priscilla and Mac were taking their vows, Rennie had thought of what Oliver'd said about it being the parents' job to ask God's blessing on the union. Maybe bridesmaids were supposed to do that, too, as well as march and look adorable. At the rehearsal, they'd been given a lot of instructions for their feet — not to make the processional too draggy, keep in step, put the weight on the forward foot. They'd been given no instructions for their souls.

In a rather frightening voice, as if he dared anyone to contradict him, the minister had declared Mac and Priscilla to be man and wife. Then, while he was blessing them in a quite different tone, fervent and exalted, Rennie was thinking, I just hope it'll be a good marriage. I hope ours will, too.

And the organ added heartily, Amen.

In the recessional, Priscilla's brother marched out beside Rennie. "Man!" he exclaimed as they reached the vestibule. "When you're married in church — man, *you're married!*"

Reliving that wedding, Rennie took off the amethyst ring and hid it in her bureau drawer under the aqua turtleneck.

Writing the thank-you letter gave her a hard time. Mrs. Holland was an English teacher and English had never been Rennie's best subject.

If I make a mistake in grammar, if I sound like an eighth-grader

———

By return mail, she got a letter that quieted her fears. Peter's mother gave an amusing account of the whole family's activities,

242

ending with such warm affection that Rennie surprised herself and wrote again. After that, she got a letter from Peter's mother every week, just the way he did. It was also signed, *Mom*.

Carrying the two extra courses turned out to be harder than Rennie'd foreseen. She worked all the time. So did Peter. They saw little of each other during the day because they'd decided that Rennie was staying out of his dorm. At the far end of the reading room in the library, there was a row of tall windows, each with a cushioned seat beneath it, set between book stacks. That was where they studied every evening.

Switching her major in her senior year, Rennie expected to be way behind, but she'd learned a lot about art during the summer. She was constantly being struck by the relation between an artist's work and his life, discovering for herself the truth of Daphne's theory that a painting is an autobiographical note on canvas.

Before she knew it, Thanksgiving recess arrived. "I wish I could go home with you," she told Peter, "but Mother and Daddy would be hurt."

The day after Thanksgiving, Rennie took the train from Neville to New York and did her Christmas shopping. For Peter, she got a facsimile of some ancient treatise on celestial navigation; for Daphne and Oliver, a book about French cathedrals that she would have liked to keep herself.

When she'd taken care of everyone else, she remembered Peter's sisters. What could she get in a hurry? Because, if she didn't catch the four o'clock train, she'd hit the rush. What would be appropriate? At twelve and fourteen, Beth and Evey were as unsophisticated as Nancy and Sandy.

The children's books were enticing — the colors, the designs, the imaginative treatment. And the profusion! Many of Rennie's old favorites were there, books she hadn't thought about in years. For so long, she'd been straining to grow up fast, to read far-out stuff, to scan pages rapidly for information, never listening to the language, never reading to enjoy.

The Wind in the Willows — her father used to read that to her when she was small! Remembering happily, she browsed. Just for a second ——

"Nice? It's the *only* thing," said the Water Rat solemnly, as he leant forward for his stroke. "Believe me, my young friend, there is *nothing* — absolutely nothing — half so much worth doing as simply messing about in boats. Simply messing," he went on dreamily: "messing — about — in — boats; messing ——"

"Look ahead, Rat!" cried the Mole suddenly.

It was too late. The boat struck the bank full tilt. The dreamer, the joyous oarsman, lay on his back at the bottom of the boat, his heels in the air . . .

"Whether you get away or whether you don't; whether you arrive at your destination or whether you reach somewhere else, or whether . . ."

By the time Rennie managed to get away from Rat and Mole, she'd missed the train.

3.

In no time, Christmas vacation arrived.

When Rennie got home, her mother was in tears. She had bursitis in her right shoulder. The doctor had immobilized her arm.

"What'll I do?" she wailed. "The whole family's coming Christmas Day — Larry and Victoria, Jonathan and Matty, Eddy and Jane, all the children. I was looking forward to it so. How can I cook with one hand?"

Rennie's father stood by, troubled, completely helpless. His executive genius stopped short at the kitchen door.

"No problem," Rennie declared, laughing. "After the summer at Firbank, I'm equal to anything."

This time, her mother was more than willing to let Rennie take over the household.

"You're so competent!" she exclaimed, as Rennie stuffed the turkey on Christmas morning. "I'm amazed."

It was rather fun, showing off. Rennie spared no effort, baking gingerbread men, going overboard with fresh cranberries, candied sweet potatoes, creamed onions, turnips, hot rolls. Her mother sat at the kitchen table, watching her in awe.

Rennie's father brought her old highchair down from the attic for Larry's baby. Then he placed telephone directories on the dining room chairs for Edmund the Third, Vicky and Jocelyn. The other three children, he said, were big enough now to behave like adults.

There were sixteen of them at dinner — absolute bedlam, with all the kids notifying Rennie at the same time about their pet aversions.

"Okay, I won't give you any potatoes. Want some onions?"

"Yuk."

"How about turnips?"

"YUK!"

Lawrence Ballantine Ross — just like Victoria, Rennie thought, to foist a pompous name like that on such a little guy. Defenseless, too. But wait till he grows up! Lawrence Ballantine was in the highchair, picking up morsels with his chubby fingers and stuffing them in his mouth. Rennie smiled, recalling how upset Victoria had been before he was born. The bridesmaid dress, her measurements, et cetera.

That's one worry this family doesn't have any more, Rennie thought happily — outfits for the bridal party. There isn't going to be one.

But, looking around the table at her parents, her brothers and their wives, she had a moment of anxiety. Would they understand? To them, the pageantry was the best part of a wedding. Would they sense the significance of utter simplicity? The silence would just make them itchy, wouldn't it? How was Rennie going to explain?

She had no time to consider this because little Edmund was demanding ketchup on his turkey.

Vicky and Jocelyn left the table and started running around, tearing through the kitchen. Their parents took this in stride, but it got to Rennie.

When I have kids, she thought, almost tripping over Vicky as she carried in the flaming plum pudding, when I have —— But she stopped herself, recalling how obnoxious she'd been, not too long ago. No wonder her mother was fit to be tied half the time!

Nobody finished the plum pudding because the children suddenly made a dash for the presents under the tree. There was no restraining them. It was an orgy. The wrapping paper, chosen for its beauty and tucked in with care, the rosettes, the gay cards, the ribbons, the affectionate messages — everything was torn apart as if by wild beasts and sent flying across the room.

Rennie received enough kitchenware, silver spoons, towels and knickknacks to set up housekeeping on the spot. But Peter had sent her the reproductions of Daumier caricatures that he knew she wanted. And Larry had chosen his present for her himself, instead of leaving the job to Victoria, as he usually did. It was a new edition of *Walden,* illustrated with magnificent colored photographs of the pond and surrounding woods in all seasons.

Only that day dawns to which we are awake, Rennie thought, turning to a picture taken in the early morning. The pond, studded with lily pads, shimmered. *Only that day* —— Am I just now beginning to wake up?

Deeply moved, Rennie went over to Larry to thank him and to explain why his present meant so much to her, but it was impossible to talk to him. He was trying to appease Lawrence Ballantine, who had reached the limit of endurance hours ago. Thinking she might be more successful, Rennie started to take the baby out of Larry's arms. This precipitated a real crisis.

It was a relief when everyone went home. After Rennie had disposed of the mutilated wrappings, the spurned gifts that the children simply left, the broken candy canes they'd parked behind the television; after calm returned to the house, Rennie sat down on the couch beside her mother and explained her reason for choosing

246

the present she'd given her. It was a beautifully illustrated book on early American crafts.

"You're interested in antiques and I thought, if you'd learn more about them and discover the angle that appeals most, you might get into some fascinating project. There are lots of great volunteer jobs at the museums. Now that your last child's leaving home, what's to stop you from going to New York a couple of times a week?"

Rennie half expected her mother to balk at the suggestion. She didn't. She examined the plates thoughtfully and thanked Rennie again. That was all.

But Rennie's father, sitting in his reclining chair, pretending to be glancing through the book Peter had urged her to give him — a study of the American Constitution — Rennie's father had been taking everything in. He looked at her over the rim of his glasses and smiled approval. Then he got up and locked the front door.

After her parents had gone to bed, Rennie stayed downstairs. She turned out all the lights except the ones on the tree. There was something special about this Christmas that she wanted to think over, to hold on to, to savor.

With all the uproar the kids had made, it was still beautiful, precious, Rennie's last Christmas at home. She missed Peter, but not the way she did when she thought she'd die without him or worried about his falling for some other girl. There was no ache now. Inexplicably, she had seemed to carry him with her all day. Things he'd said came back to her as she moved about the house, working so hard and so happily.

He had become politicized during the summer. That was Judy Young's doing. It wasn't enough, she'd told him, to be honest oneself. Honesty in government had to be won, too. In Judy's opinion, modern Friends ought to dramatize the nation's crying need for truth by reverting to the plain language!

"Judy's made me see that I've been so preoccupied with what's happening in the heavens, I've ignored what's going on on earth," Peter had explained to Rennie shortly before vacation. "You know," he added thoughtfully, "Judy's idea about Friends going back to 'thee' and 'thy' — she just may have something. In the old days, they wouldn't use titles, like Mr. and Mrs. or Miss. If we went back to that, who'd need Ms.?"

Recalling this made Rennie giggle.

In a week, it would be January. Her father's implied prediction of last summer — that the wedding might be permanently called off by then — was proving unfounded. Peter was coming New Year's Eve! On the second they'd leave for Firbank.

Rennie couldn't wait to tell Daphne about her art courses. She was doing a term paper on portraiture. Holbein, Franz Hals, Velasquez — how they conveyed character and a particular life situation, merely with a few pigments! It wasn't just the Impressionists who succeeded with this. In fact, the early masters had set a standard which few of their successors surpassed. Rennie began to realize that the whole history of art was one unbroken continuum. Artists took what was handed down to them and perfected or rejected it. With time, their followers perfected or rejected that. What was perfected in one age was rejected in another, only to be reinstated later.

A year ago, Rennie couldn't see that much of anything earlier than Mid-Twentieth Century bore any relation to her life. What an ego trip! How had she thought it all evolved, if not from the past? Recalling the Hals portraits, she asked herself whether anyone painting today could convey greater character. The way those laughing boys caught your eye, communicated their exuberance, carried you into their world!

There was something in the faces of the women, too, that jolted her former opinions. From Rembrandt's portarits to Sargent's, the women subjects expressed an inner vitality that refuted the notion she'd always held — that they were poor, downtrodden chattels. Some undoubtedly were, but most of them looked less unhappy than a lot of so-called liberated women Rennie knew and, in spite of those ridiculous dresses, those stays and crinolines, wiser. Rennie wondered whether the restrictions imposed on them hadn't, perhaps, given women of the past more security than modern women enjoyed in their limitless world, so undefined that it was confusing and terrifying. Instead of competing, most of the women in those old portraits seemed to be concentrating on the art of living. This was such a subversive idea that Rennie decided she'd better keep it to herself. She was certainly not going to tell Jane. But Daphne would understand.

She's the most liberated woman I know, Rennie thought, even now, when she's physically dependent. At my age, she was going out to the war zone, not to prove anything, simply to help. That was so long ago, women didn't even have the vote.

Through her thoughts, Rennie was vaguely aware of a sound in the distance. It grew louder. Carolers! They didn't usually come around on Christmas night. These people must be feeling the way she did — eager to share their joy.

Rennie ran to the door. They stood at the bottom of the steps, a little bunch of high school kids, zipped up in parkas, frozen and ecstatic. Devils, probably, every last one of them, but as they sang their hearts out onto the frosty air, they looked like those angels in the *Singing Gallery* of Della Robbia.

"Joy to the world!"

Rennie rushed to the kitchen for the platter of gingerbread men. Mittened hands reached up and grabbed. Rennie was thanked with radiant smiles. Those kids really did look angelic, transfigured by the season. Next week, they'd be ornery again. Why couldn't the Christmas spirit be preserved, like those fruits and vegetables Rennie put up at Firbank? Why couldn't it be kept vital and nourishing throughout the year?

Waving good-by to Rennie, the carolers turned and started down the walk, singing all the way, "How silently, how silently ——"

It made Rennie think of Kendal.

4.

Austin Young surprised Rennie and Peter by meeting their bus. "Thought I'd save Oliver coming in," he explained. He looked glad to see Peter again. "How're the books?"

The question, merely good-natured banter, revealed the secret regret of a man who hadn't had a college education.

Peter pointed to his suitcase. "See that? It's full of them. We've got a lot of studying to do, next couple of weeks."

All the way to Firbank, Austin talked about Periwinkle Farm and the potato crop. When they were nearing the house, he turned to Peter. "You know my little blue pickup? I don't need it this time of year. Come home with me and drive it back. It'll give you two something to run around in while you're here."

How nice of Austin!

Firbank glistened under a blanket of snow. The late afternoon sun turned the icicles that hung from the roof into crystal pendants. Enveloped in silence, framed by bare branches, the house looked almost forsaken.

But indoors, all was warmth and that hearty affection with which Oliver invariably welcomed Rennie and Peter. When they walked into the living room, Daphne leaned forward and reached out.

"I have so much to tell you! Next term, I'm going to be in a seminar — Italian Renaissance. Isn't that terrific? Ever since I saw your Botticelli prints, I've been in love with the Renaissance."

Austin was waiting in the doorway, smiling shyly. Promising to come right back, Peter left with him.

Standing in the middle of the room, looking around, Rennie suddenly felt lost. One thing she'd thought she could count on was that Firbank wouldn't ever change. But the walls were completely different. Except for those charcoal drawings of the war prisoners, none of the pictures were the same. Serenity's portrait, which had always hung in Oliver's study, was over the mantel. It looked marvelous there, but out of place. That gave Rennie a strange uneasiness.

Oliver sensed this. "It's our preview of the exhibition," he explained. "Miss Chase, the director of the museum, came to see us before Christmas and selected these pictures out of the lot thee starred last summer. They're the ones that are going to New York. I thought Daphne'd get a better idea of how they harmonize if they were hung. Unfortunately, we don't have enough wall space. The pictures are too close together. In the museum, they'll show to better advantage." Taking Rennie's arm, Oliver drew her to the fireplace. "Thee sees, this is where one walks into the gallery. The first thing one encounters is Grandmother's portrait. On the left are some early seascapes."

"Oh!" Rennie exclaimed, startled. She averted her eyes. There was the dune where Peter told her about Charlemagne and the Milky Way! "I didn't know you were putting that one in."

"It does belong to Daphne's unfolding period," Oliver conceded, as if he thought Rennie were objecting because this painting wasn't one of the best, "but she insisted on its being included." He drew Rennie to the wall beside the couch. "Thee remembers these — *The Repatriates*. They're going, too." Oliver commented on each picture as he steered Rennie around the room. Suddenly remembering his domestic duties, he let go. "Look in the dining room. I'll join thee in a minute, soon as I've basted the chicken."

On the threshold of the dining room, Rennie stopped short and retreated a step. She was face to face with her portrait. The light wasn't the same here as in Oliver's study. It came from the north rather than the east. Was that why the portrait made a fresh impact on her? Rennie felt as if she'd caught an unexpected glimpse of herself as she passed a mirror.

Oliver came in from the kitchen.

"It looks more like me," Rennie blurted out.

"No," he said gently, "*thee* looks more like *it*. What a lovely work to have the exhibition end with! Wait and see — I believe it will elicit the approval of the critics more than anything else there. Miss Chase agrees."

Rennie stared at her portrait, puzzled, wondering what anyone saw in it.

"We're expecting the proof of the catalogue any day," Oliver told her as they went back to the living room. "It's illustrated!" He turned to Daphne, shaking his head incredulously. "The Museum of Contemporary Art. What an honor!"

He must believe she'll make it to New York, Rennie thought, or he wouldn't go on about it like this.

"Heather and Stephen are coming over for the opening."

"May Peter and I come?"

If, instead of simply looking at Rennie, Daphne could have shouted, her delight wouldn't have been more convincing.

"Will Heather and Stephen stay for our wedding? I hope so."

But Daphne and Oliver looked doubtful about that.

Apart from the preview of the exhibition, nothing at Firbank seemed changed. Rennie ran up to her room in the ell, impatient to see the pond. It was too dark. Tomorrow!

Peter was given the room in the main wing that Heather used last summer. When they sat down to supper in the warm kitchen, with the familiar blue-and-white plates, the pewter teapot, the loving silence, it was as if they'd never been away.

After she'd finished washing up, Rennie peeped into the woodshed, curious to see what Daphne was working on, knowing she wouldn't mind. As Rennie opened the door, intense cold hit her. No one could stay in there very long. The potbellied stove didn't seem to be lit and there was no sign of any painting in progress. Rennie shut the door quickly.

"It's awfully cold in the woodshed," she told Oliver when she went back. "I should think Daphne'd freeze."

"That stove heats it up good and fast," he replied. "Any time she wants it, I can make a roaring fire. But she hasn't been inclined to paint lately. Thee's right — it's cold tonight. Going to be a hard freeze. I'm worried about my little plants down in the Forest."

So he was still struggling with his antidefoliation project.

"I can't bear to think he might fail," Rennie confided to Peter later, "after all the effort he's put into that thing. It really is quixotic."

In the morning, Rennie jumped out of bed and ran to the window.

"Hi," she called to the ice-covered pond, "I'm back!"

A flock of gulls was sitting on it.

When Rennie came into the kitchen, Peter was already there, standing by the window. He was trying to learn about the birds. Oliver, obviously enjoying himself, was identifying the ones in the feeders.

"We get at least a dozen tree sparrows and slate-colored juncos each morning, perhaps half as many purple finches and goldfinches — that's their dull, winter plumage — four blue jays, three song sparrows and two white-throated sparrows."

"Is that a bobwhite feeding on the ground?"

"Yes. They're tentative in their approach, scaring easily, but once they start, they gobble a lot of grain. We've had a flock of evening grosbeaks and two or three of the lovely little redpolls. Those appear only about every five years."

In the afternoon, Nancy and Sandy came out with their sleds and took Rennie sliding on the hill across the lane. Peter tried out Oliver's snowshoes. They were tingling when they came back and stood around the fire in their ski socks. Oliver made cocoa. Daphne sat in the armchair, listening eagerly as they told her about the fun they'd had. She seemed to be reliving the days when she could enjoy the winter woods.

It's almost, Rennie thought, as if we're standing in for her.

The days were full. Their friends invited Rennie and Peter over to dinner. They never stayed late because, they explained, they had to be up early to help Oliver before they began to study.

Although they'd brought that suitcase full of books, they missed the college library. There were topics they wanted to look up.

Oliver thought he could help. He telephoned to Professor Anselm, the Chairman of the Forestry Department at the university. "Everything's arranged," he announced, when the conversation ended. "You're to go to his office at ten o'clock tomorrow morning. Room Three Twenty-four in the Earth Sciences Building. He's going to take you over and introduce you to the librarian. She'll supply you with the books you need."

It was a good thing Rennie and Peter left early the next morning because Oliver'd lent them his field glasses and, as they drove along the edge of the pond in the blue pickup, Peter kept stopping to look at the birds.

"That's a great blue heron," he told Rennie, proud of his new knowledge. "Spending the winter here." He handed her the glasses. "See the meadowlarks flying over the marsh grass? And those are some kind of warbler in the bayberries." He was getting to be a pro! "Oliver says there are flocks of horned larks on the sand and in the dune grass. Sometimes — very rarely — a snow bunting is with them. I didn't see any; did you?"

"I wouldn't know," Rennie said, laughing.

When they reached the university, they were overwhelmed by its size. So many lecture halls and dormitories! Compared to little Tilbury College —— They went round and round, looking for the Earth Sciences Building.

Professor Anselm was a short, wiry, bald man with a kind, intelligent face. The way he treated Peter and Rennie — as friends and equals — took them by surprise. Because no professor had ever done that before, Peter felt he ought to explain that they hadn't graduated yet.

Professor Anselm nodded. "So Mr. Otis said. What a wonderful man," he added, "to be doing all that at his age!"

"I remember when you came over to Firbank last summer," Rennie told him. Then, emboldened by his friendliness, she asked, "Professor Anselm, do you think it's ever going to be a success — his Vietnamese Forest? We've been so afraid ——"

"That experiment of his for restoring contaminated soil? Is it going to be a success? It is! If you mean, has he found a formula that

254

will do the trick, I don't know. Most likely not. But that is imma-terial. Plenty of us who are trained for that kind of research, with labs and staff and money could come up with a formula if we put our minds to it. But who has? Until Mr. Otis pricked our con-sciences, not by staging a protest, but simply by putting his own very limited resources and physical strength into his concern, work-ing quietly on his own land, few of us American scientists ever thought it was our duty to do something about the contaminated soil in Vietnam. But it was our government that destroyed the land, wasn't it? Shouldn't more of us feel an obligation to restore it? Mr. Otis started something. It's his intention that's been significant, not his results. The rest of us will take it from there."

"Wait till we tell Austin that the Vietnamese Forest isn't a flop," Rennie whispered as they stood in the corridor, while the Professor locked his office.

He was taking them to the library himself, as if they were im-portant!

When they were crossing the campus, he asked Peter, "Where are you going to graduate school?"

"I'm not applying yet. We're getting married the end of May. So going to grad school will have to wait."

"People have been known to do both," the Professor observed.

On the way home, Peter said suddenly, "Someday, you'll go to grad school, too, Rennie. Get a Ph.D."

"*Me?*"

"Of course! How do you think you can become an art historian if you don't? Who knows? Could be, if I get a good job for a few years, you'll become the first Doctor Holland."

"You're kidding."

"I'm not. If I find the kind of job I'm hoping for, you won't need one. What's to stop you from starting right in on your master's?"

If! With unemployment at its peak, what chance did this year's graduating class have? The likelihood of Rennie's starting work for a master's was pretty slim.

"We don't know where we'll be — whether it's near a university.

And not every grad school has a decent art history program." Then, already seeing herself enrolled, Rennie exclaimed, "I'll write a doctoral dissertation about Daphne's paintings and drawings! She can supervise it: the first scholarly evaluation of her work."

What a beautiful prospect!

Contemplating the possibility Peter had just held out — that she might have not just a job, but a lifework — Rennie realized how close this came to being part of her central wish.

"I hope," she said, still dreaming about it, "our kids won't feel gypped, like Heather. I must never let that happen, Peter."

She'd play with the kids. But she couldn't do everything. What she'd let go would be the housekeeping. It was fun in Neville, cooking that Christmas dinner, helping her mother, showing off. And she loved doing things for Oliver and Daphne. But in her own home, it would be different. They didn't have to keep it as neat as Firbank. They'd eat peanut butter and jelly sandwiches.

A doctoral dissertation! That would take a lot longer than a term paper — years. Could she do it? Convey the incredible beauty of Daphne's work, explain her technique to others, as Daphne had explained it to her, step by step?

Yes, Rennie thought, feeling a surge of confidence she'd never known before. With Daphne looking over my shoulder, advising, inspiring, loving me, maybe I can.

5.

It was too cold for Rennie and Peter to ride to Monthly Meeting in the back of Oliver's truck, so they took Austin's, dashing ahead in order to get there before Sam and Jorim. They wanted to be the ones to carry Daphne into the meetinghouse tonight because early tomorrow they were leaving for college.

"It'll be our way of saying thank you for the beautiful vacation," Rennie told Peter.

They stood in the drive, by the syringa bush, waiting for Oliver's truck to appear.

"Remember that Chocomarsh you got me in the air terminal the first time I came here — the one you put in my book bag? It ended up an awful mess. I'd meant to give it to Daphne. That was all I had to give her. But I forgot."

"You've given Daphne something better, something very special."

"Me? What?"

Before Peter could explain, Oliver stopped his truck beside them. Rennie watched Peter lift Daphne out and lower her into the wicker chair with awkward gentleness. Triumphantly, they carried her in. When she was installed on the bench she always occupied, Rennie joined her. Peter sat down next to Rennie and Oliver, coming in last, took the place beside him.

Oliver had explained that Kendal Meeting had a new Clerk — Edith Ellis — adding, "The Clerk presides, but there's no special status or authority attached to the office."

Rennie looked swiftly at Peter, wondering how he would react to the news that the presiding officer was a woman. But he showed no surprise.

A table had been brought in from the vestibule and placed in front of the lowest facing bench. Edith Ellis and the Assistant Clerk, a man Rennie didn't know, were sitting behind the table, going through a pile of papers.

Suddenly the room grew quiet. Edith Ellis was standing up. "At Kendal Monthly Meeting of Friends, convened for business on First Month twentieth," she announced. Then she sat down again.

Rennie thought that if they had to work through all those papers, Friends had better get going fast, but instead they bowed their heads and settled into silence.

"This is the Eleventh Query," the Clerk said, rising again after what seemed a very long time. She read: *"Do you respect the dignity and worth of every human being as a child of God? Do you, as* voters, workers, and employers, as consumers and investors, endeavor to create political, social and economic institutions that will sustain and enrich the life of all? Do you strive to overcome national, racial or religious prejudice and discrimination?"

The Clerk sat down again and Friends bowed their heads. They were supposed to be giving silent answers to these questions. There was something both upsetting and glorious, Rennie thought, about being asked what you're doing instead of being told what to do. She glanced surreptitiously at Peter, knowing this Query would appeal to him. But she herself couldn't concentrate on it very long. She was thinking of what Oliver had told them — that they'd be asked tonight to choose the four Friends who would have oversight of their wedding.

Of course they wanted Oliver and Daphne. As for the other two —— Peter suggested the Youngs.

"They've been awfully good to me, not at all like bosses with their hired help. Is that okay with you?"

Rennie agreed. She liked Austin and Judy, though she'd never quite forgiven Austin for saying that Oliver ought to sell Firbank.

She and Peter had also been told that they were entitled to ask the overseer whom they held in particular affection to read the certificate aloud after they'd signed it. Naturally, they both wanted Oliver.

A faithful overseer, he had explained, was one who not only gave the wedding careful oversight, but who had a continuing concern for the couple. This, he said, wasn't always easy to do without seeming to be inquisitive or intrusive. But, should problems ever arise, he was prepared — if wanted — to join with Peter and Rennie in seeking a solution.

Remembering how she'd rejected a Quaker wedding the first time she came here just because she didn't want anyone to know about her affairs, Rennie was amused at herself — the person she'd been. How little she'd understood about friendship, or caring for others or faith! She'd been unable to distinguish between intrusion and support.

258

She remembered, too, that funny slip she'd made during her first meeting here — only inside her mind, fortunately — when she'd misquoted the marriage promise, substituting what the kids said at college, "as long as nobody gets hurt," for the Quaker "as long as we both shall live." It really wasn't funny at all. It had betrayed the extent of her confusion and anxiety.

There was indeed a lot of business — the reading of the minutes of the previous session, the report of the Finance Committee, news from Quaker relief workers overseas, efforts to secure better conditions for Blacks and Indians. The agenda went on and on. Rennie wondered how such a small group could undertake so much.

They never voted. Something mysterious happened: the Clerk "took the sense of the Meeting," as if she might be taking its temperature without a thermometer. Then she framed a minute. Rennie was surprised to find that Friends were far from being of one mind. They disagreed on almost every item, for not everyone perceived truth the same way. Their search for unity was a religious aspiration. It didn't always succeed. Oliver once remarked that the very steadfastness that made Friends endure persecution for their belief could become downright stubbornness in the face of lesser issues. Quaker history was full of inexcusable quarrels.

It almost looked as though one might be shaping up right now. Sensing the prospect of drama, Rennie felt a little excited.

Under consideration was an ancient meetinghouse back in the hills. Henry Klein, the Clerk of the Finance Committee, explained that in the Eighteenth Century, there was a large community of Friends in that area, but later they moved away, laying down their Meeting and transferring the ownership of the property to Kendal Meeting. Over the years, the building had been rented for various purposes and the proceeds put into a special fund. At the present time, it was vacant and in bad repair. Something had to be done. The Committee asked for authorization to pay for the repairs out of the rent fund.

This seemed a very legitimate request, but Judy Young was of the opinion that in these days, when so many people were in need, it was wrong to spend money on salvaging a useless building. The place should be sold and the proceeds given to the poor. Several people agreed with Judy. Someone else felt equally strongly that the meetinghouse ought to be preserved. There weren't many buildings of that vintage still in existence around here, he said. Though plain, like any Quaker meetinghouse, it had good lines. If it were repaired, it could become a little museum.

Rennie glanced past Peter at Oliver, wondering where he stood in this controversy. With his love of old houses —— But he was careful not to let his feelings show.

One after another, Friends popped up to express their views, some in favor of preserving the property, others determined to sell. The discussion became so heated that Edith Ellis asked Friends to stop and seek guidance together. They drifted off into silence.

Suddenly, Ben Ashaway, little Simeon's father, rose and said he'd been wondering why Friends couldn't repair the building and turn it into a day care center. There were many working mothers in the neighborhood who would benefit from having a place where they could leave their children in good hands.

The suggestion met with instant enthusiasm. A day care center, Friends agreed, was really badly needed in that area. So, for that matter, was a clubhouse for teen-agers and older people. There was no limit to the use such a building could be put to. It would once more become a vital force in the community, as well as being a tie with the past. Several people offered to draw up plans and raise additional funds for running expenses. Others volunteered to meet with the residents of the area and ask them to join Friends in setting up the programs they wished to have. The young Friends wanted to help. There was so much sentiment in favor of restoring the building and putting it into use that the Clerk had no difficulty determining the sense of the Meeting.

This wasn't a compromise, but a fresh approach, one in which both sides could unite. Out of the patient waiting, a creative solution had emerged. No one felt vanquished, bypassed or overridden.

There was something really magnificent, Rennie thought, in this performance. She had seen the distance between polarities diminish to the vanishing point. Only thoroughly mature people could have achieved this.

"Now," Edith Ellis was saying, "may we have a report from the committee appointed to look into the clearness for marriage of Peter Hallburt Holland and Serenity Millburn Ross?"

John stood up and said simply, "The committee met with them last summer. We found them clear for marriage."

"Thank thee, John Ludlow. Do Friends feel comfortable about taking responsibility for the accomplishment of this marriage?"

Suppose there was a difference of opinion on this matter, too! Suppose someone should raise an objection! But there was immediate unity.

"Then we're ready to appoint a committee of oversight. Peter Holland and Serenity Ross, are there Friends you would like to have as overseers?"

Peter stood up and answered gravely, "Yes. The Otises and the Youngs."

When these four had agreed to serve, they were appointed. For a second, after he sat down, Peter turned and put his arm around Rennie's shoulder, looking joyfully into her eyes. Then he let go and became sedate again.

"There being no further business," the Clerk said, "we adjourn, purposing, if consistent with the divine will, to meet again on the twentieth of Second Month."

The session was over. Yet, instead of getting up and going home, Friends bowed their heads and sank into a profound silence again.

Rennie wriggled. Another silence! She was impatient to telephone her parents and let them know that they were free at last to issue the invitations. Well, it really was too early, but they could be thinking about the list, anyhow. Picturing them as they went over the names together, Rennie asked herself what fun her parents would have, working on that list, when there was no room at the wedding for their friends. The Dixwells, the Goffes, the Whalleys

— these weren't business associates. They were her parents' lifelong friends, who meant as much to them as the Kendal people did to Peter and her. Looking around, she wondered whether one couldn't possibly squeeze in an extra person on each bench. No, it would be tight.

Neil and Alice were sitting directly across the aisle. Rennie imagined herself walking down this aisle with Peter, heading for that two-seater in the middle of the gallery, which was used only at weddings. When she started to make the promise in the presence of all those people, she hoped she'd remember the right words and not say "as long as nobody gets hurt." That would be a real boo-boo! But she didn't think it would happen, because she and Peter were trying so hard now not to let anyone get hurt.

New Year's Day he'd told her father that he felt the custom of the bride entering the meetinghouse with the groom put as much responsibility on the groom as when the father of the bride gave her away.

"At least," Peter had said, "I take it as seriously. I promise you, Mr. Ross, even if you don't give Rennie to me in the meetinghouse, I'll take the best care I can of her as long as I live."

Listening to Peter make this solemn declaration, Rennie'd hoped her parents didn't remember that childish outburst of hers last summer, when she told her father he couldn't give her away because he didn't own her. She'd seen with horror how close she was to losing her parents. No argument of hers, however logical, no defense of her lifestyle, however legitimate, would convince them. She was really losing her parents.

Like if they died suddenly, she'd said to herself then.

Died? The possibility had shaken her. It had never crossed her mind that her parents might die until they were very old. Peter's father was likely to, any time. But Rennie's parents!

They'll die for me right now, she'd said to herself on New Year's Day, if I don't do something quick to hold them.

After that outburst last summer, she'd read about Woolman's visiting the Indians, walking through the wilderness in the dead of winter, simply to make friends with them. Face to face with those alien, hostile people, even tomahawks, he had tried to understand, to learn from, to help by following the leadings of truth. In terror, Rennie wondered how *she* could follow those leadings, when she didn't even know what they were.

Love was the first motion.

What she actually said then must have sounded strange, coming from her — perhaps phony — but Rennie'd meant it when she told her father, "I don't want you to give me away. I want to stay yours and Mother's, even after I'm married. How can I ever not be? I'll walk through life with Peter the way we'll walk into the meeting-house, but I'll be yours, too." Almost as if she'd been somebody else — but she meant this, too — she'd gone over and kissed her father.

He looked flustered. Still, he didn't protest.

Acting on another impulse, Rennie had sat down on the couch next to her mother. "You used to sew a lot when I was young — those cute smocked dresses I never liked because I just wanted to wear jeans. Remember? Mother ——" Rennie had hesitated, afraid of being rebuffed. "Would you —— Wait!" She ran up to her room and returned with Daphne's sketches. "Look, this is the wedding dress I want. It's very simple. Don't you think you could make it for me, maybe out of organza? I'd be so proud, getting married in the gown you made, instead of bought, for me."

That was the first time Rennie's mother showed any enthusiasm. Her face lit up. She had a part in the wedding! But then, as Rennie had added, "I'm not wearing a veil, or stuff like that," she looked disappointed.

"Not even a cap?"

Rennie shook her head.

Now, sitting in the quiet meetinghouse between Peter and Daphne, Rennie thought that, when it came to the veil, she'd handled matters with her mother in the same old way. She sighed. For the first time, she grasped how Daphne saw her in the portrait, almost like two people — the person she wanted to be projecting from the person she still naturally was.

Just as if this were a meeting on First Day, Neil stood up, looking very serious, and began to speak.

"At our wedding, Philip Ludlow told about Thomas Ellwood, an English Friend who lived back in the Sixteen Hundreds. As an old man, Ellwood still remembered the 'weighty frame of spirit' he and his wife were in at their wedding, feeling that the Lord was joining them. Recalling this feeling later, he said, proved to be of good service on all occasions. Philip observed with a chuckle that by 'all occasions' Ellwood probably meant those times when he and his wife had a spat! The recollection of that feeling at their wedding brought them back together. I've remembered this story because, as a matter of fact ——" Neil hesitated, looking down at the floor for a second, then forcing himself to reveal what was too personal, "the feeling Alice and I had at our wedding pulled us through once or twice. What I want to say is, I hope Rennie and Peter will have the same feeling when they're married and that it will be of good service to them on all occasions."

When Neil sat down, Friends bowed their heads and entered another silence.

Speaking to the whole Meeting, Neil had actually given a message to Rennie and Peter. Not altogether, though. He'd been speaking about love generally — love put to the test — and the need for drawing on divine assistance.

It seemed to Rennie that this double way of looking at the same thing — the personal and the universal — applied to her portrait, too. Not until yesterday did she understand why the portrait seemed so important to Oliver and that Miss Chase. Rennie'd thought of it merely as having to do with herself, forgetting what Oliver had told her when she posed — that it was more than the likeness of an individual; that it was the dawn of that day he and Daphne hoped her whole generation would wake to. Looked at like that, the portrait was significant, no matter who sat for it.

Caught up in the silence, thinking that the wedding itself couldn't be more solemn, Rennie became aware of a strange jerking beside her. Daphne'd never twisted and pushed like this before. She was extending her good arm, trying to grab the back of the bench in front, struggling to get to her feet. Wondering what she should do, Rennie instinctively reached up and put her hand under Daphne's elbow to steady her till she was standing upright.

Daphne felt moved to speak! She had a message for Rennie and Peter, too. Judging by her expression, it was a beautiful message. She stood there, looking as though she were envisioning the loveliest scene she ever painted. Not frustrated, as she usually was when she opened her mouth this way, but perfectly serene, Daphne stood there a minute in the awesomely quiet meetinghouse. Then she let go of the bench and Rennie supported her till she was seated again.

I heard thee, Rennie told her just as silently, bowing her head, fighting back the tears. I understood every word. Thank thee!

6.

The last day of March, when Rennie woke up in that college room that she was beginning to get attached to, she told herself happily that in just two months, she and Peter would both be bachelors (of art) and both married! This term was passing so quickly that it wasn't hard to wait. If only Peter had a job, if only they knew where they were going after the wedding —— Anxiety about the future was getting to him again. It was depressing.

Why wouldn't he feel rejected? He'd worked very hard to become qualified for a job and now that he was ready, there wasn't any. In another few weeks, he'd have fulfilled all the requirements for independence and the right to become a self-respecting husband, yet independence and self-respect were being denied him. He was willing to do almost anything, go anywhere, but the job placement bureau at Tilbury held out very little hope.

It isn't fair! Rennie thought rebelliously. This year, we've tried to do all the right things and still we're not being given a chance.

She was lying there, turning off the alarm, when the telephone rang. The moment she heard the anguish in Oliver's voice, she knew.

"Serenity."

That was all he said, but she knew.

No, Rennie thought. No! It's not that bad. She's had a stroke, but she'll recover, just like last time.

"Daphne's left us."

"Oh, Oliver!"

"Yesterday afternoon around four o'clock. Must have been almost instantaneous. She was still holding her brush. Thee knows, the past six months, she wasn't up to working. But yesterday she said she wanted to paint. I thought she was feeling stronger. So I lit a fire in the woodshed and took her in there. Then I went to the kitchen to make tea, looking back from the doorway to be sure she was comfortable, and she gave me the most radiant smile! Maybe she knew it was our farewell. It couldn't have been more beautiful."

"Oh, Oliver." That was all Rennie was able to say.

"Heather's flying over as soon as she can arrange things — tomorrow or next day. We're having a meeting of thanksgiving in Kendal Friday afternoon at two. Even if thee and Peter can't be there, I wanted you to know."

"I'll come. Peter can't. His senior project's due next week. But I'll come for sure. I'll come tonight."

"*Will* thee?"

That Oliver hoped she'd come surprised Rennie. She wanted to be with him. But the tone of those two small words told her how glad and grateful he was, how much he needed her.

"Thee will come? Oh, and Serenity, will thee notify thy father?"

She called him right way. He said of course he'd go.

"Won't Mother come, too?"

"I doubt it. She doesn't like funerals and it's a terribly long ride. But I'll pick you up in New York."

"No, Daddy. I don't want to wait till Friday. Heather won't arrive for a day or two. It's so awful — Oliver's there alone. I want to be with him."

"At a time like this? That's an imposition. You'll just be in the way. Besides, how can you miss a week of school, so close to finals? Be sensible, Rennie. It could spoil everything. You might not graduate."

She'd managed to control herself for Oliver, but now Rennie lost her grip and started to cry. "Daddy, please don't keep saying those things. I have to go to Firbank."

As soon as she could get her father to stop talking, Rennie pulled on her clothes and ran to Peter's room. This was the first time she'd been there all year. It looked familiar and strange.

"I have to go," she sobbed, as Peter took her in his arms.

"Of course you do. We'll leave right after breakfast."

"Can you go? What about your project?"

Peter stroked Rennie's hair. "I'm not letting you go alone. I want to be with Oliver, too. There's a lot I can take off his hands the next few days. After the service, we'll drive to Neville with your father and get back here Saturday noon. It'll give us the rest of the weekend to work. I don't have that much left to do on my project. Anyway, what good is it, if there are no jobs?"

"The exhibition," Rennie sobbed, suddenly realizing. "It's only three weeks away, but Daphne'll never see it. And the wedding! She won't be our overseer, Peter."

He wiped her eyes with the palms of his hands. "Go get your stuff together. We'd better fly. I'll call Austin, see if he'll meet us."

It was raining in Tilbury, but when the plane came down in Rhode Island, the sun was out and spring was deliciously in the air. Austin, usually so talkative, said almost nothing till they reached Firbank. Then he asked Peter whether he'd help him fix up the meetinghouse Friday morning.

"We think there'll be more people than we have seats for. Those folks from out of town — the art crowd and all their other friends. Oliver and Daphne used to be very active in civic affairs, too, not just in Kendal, but throughout the state. Those reporters — couldn't tell you how many have been here, bothering Oliver, just when he has so much on his mind."

Reporters! Rennie thought. Was Daphne *that* well known?

"So if you'll go in with me Friday morning," Austin was saying to Peter, "we can bring up six benches from the basement. There used to be a lot more Quakers living around here and those benches stood under the windows. In recent years, with so few people, we stored them. They'll give us forty-eight more seats."

"Oh," Rennie cried. "I didn't know you could do that."

Her parents' friends! There'd be room for all of them at the wedding! She'd tell her father on Friday.

When Rennie and Peter walked into the house, the dogs greeted them with such a clamor that Oliver came to the front hall. For the first time, he really looked like an old man. The vitality had gone out of his face. Nevertheless, Rennie and Peter saw at once that nothing could have pleased him more than their coming.

Not that he was alone — far from it. Jorim was bringing a sling full of firewood into the living room. Clara stood by the bay window, opening a long florist's box, and Judy came in with a platter of sandwiches and the silver coffeepot.

"You two must be starved," she said. "Sit down on the couch."

Oliver set a little table in front of them and Judy poured the coffee. As soon as Peter had eaten, he went out to help Jorim and Austin.

With characteristic grace, Clara was arranging chrysanthemums that had been sent by the museum, sticking them into an antique vase on the candle stand in the bay window.

The arrangement looked familiar. Rennie was sure she'd seen it somewhere else. This double image — the cream-colored, feathery flowers bunched in a sea green vase; their reflection on the polished mahogany table. Where had she seen these mauve-tipped petals gleaming on an almost crimson wood surface?

Monet! That's what this reminds me of — his oil painting in the Metropolitan. Claude Monet painted chrysanthemums that very same color, reflected in the high polish of a table.

The preview of the exhibition was still up. Over the mantel, Serenity smiled at the dog or child, but, as usual, she ignored her great-granddaughter. Rennie wondered whether Oliver hadn't really hung the pictures for Daphne because he knew all along that she'd never get to New York.

Next week, he told her, noticing her gaze, the museum was sending a truck for the pictures.

Lion and Duffy dragged themselves around Daphne's armchair, whimpering, unable to find peace. As she watched them, Rennie felt something inside her snap.

About to remove the little table he'd placed in front of her for lunch, Oliver saw it happen. He put the table down again and bent over to rest his fingertips on Rennie's shoulders, looking at her for a moment with deep tenderness. Then he straightened up and sat down beside her.

"After her stroke, Serenity," he said slowly, gazing at the fire, "Daphne kept asking why her life had been prolonged, what it was good for, the condition she was in. When thee came, she discovered there was something she was still called to do. Thy coming gave the remainder of her life meaning."

Suddenly overcome with emotion, Oliver got up and left the room.

Clara took Rennie's hand, pulled her up and led her into the kitchen. "Let me show you what there is for supper. You just have to warm it."

When Oliver and Peter and Rennie sat down at the round table and held hands, it seemed unbearable. But out of the silence, Oliver said something that made Rennie feel quite different.

"Strange how a thought that's been in the back of one's mind for years comes forward as needed," he murmured, letting their hands go. "When Grandmother died, Daphne and I found solace in words someone quoted during the meeting. They're William Penn's. I've been reminded of them all day." He stopped because his voice was faltering. Then, calm again, he quoted, *"We think not a friend lost because he is gone into another room, nor because he is gone into another Land; and into another world no man is gone, for that Heaven which God created and this world are all one."* Reaching for his fork, Oliver looked from Rennie to Peter. "Thank you for coming. I hope you'll be able to make up the time."

Early the next morning, Oliver went to Kendal to take care of business. Rennie was still washing the breakfast dishes when a car drove in. A strange man got out. Rennie hoped it wasn't another reporter, because she wouldn't know what to say. How could anyone describe Daphne, convey the magnanimity of her spirit?

The man came to the back door. Professor Anselm! As soon as he heard about Daphne, he rushed over!

But when he came in, manifestly happy to see Rennie again, jovially asking for Oliver, she realized that he couldn't have heard. Breaking the news was almost too much for her.

Professor Anselm looked terribly embarrassed. "I didn't know," he said. "Forgive me. Never would have barged in at a time like this, if I'd known. I just happened to be over this way and I thought I'd say hello to Mr. Otis, see how those plants of his are doing in the decontaminated soil, now that spring's here." He backed toward the door. "Do give him my sympathy. I'll drop in another time."

"Wait! Don't go away. Peter's outside, feeding the hens. He'd love to go down to the Forest with you. I know Oliver'll be sorry he wasn't here."

"How's he taking it?"

"Bravely."

As Professor Anselm started to shut the door behind him, he shook his head. "Poor Mr. Otis. What's going to become of him here, alone?"

That's what Rennie wondered, too, as she scrubbed the sink and glanced out through the window above. Touched by the rays of the sun, the breasts of the mourning doves turned a beautiful iridescent rose, but the birds' lament sounded sadly in the trees. The bluebirds, looking over their nesting holes, called gently, What's going to become of Oliver?

He's not helpless, Rennie insisted. It's not as if he'd lost the person who was taking care of him. He was doing the taking care of. He'll manage.

270

When Oliver returned, he had a stream of callers. He was composed, inquiring after everyone's family, overlooking no one else's trouble because of preoccupation with his own. One by one, the callers took Rennie aside and asked, "What's going to become of Oliver?"

"I don't know," she answered.

What she thought was, If one more person asks me that ——

7.

Stephen's grad school roommate met Heather's plane and drove her to Firbank, coming in only long enough to offer his condolences before rushing back to Boston.

Rennie'd expected Heather to take command of the house, the way she did last time, but Heather didn't even try. She was too upset. She let Rennie prepare supper, pretending to help, picking up a dish and then standing there, holding it, unable to recall what she'd intended to do. Finally, she gave up and went to her room.

"It isn't just the shock," Rennie told Peter, when he came in. "It's those guilt feelings. She keeps wishing she'd appreciated her mother more. Why didn't she think of that sooner?" Looking at Peter, Rennie thought, He's different — relaxed, more like his old self. "Has something happened? I haven't had a chance to speak to you all day."

"Professor Anselm wants to see me when I've finished my project."

"What about? Tell me quick, before Heather gets back."

"I don't know. He just asked, would I come. It's funny — he hardly knows me and he seems more interested in what I'm going to do next year than anyone at Tilbury."

"Maybe it's a job!"

"I don't think so. I'm not in his field."

"He wouldn't ask you to come all that way," Rennie said hopefully, "if he weren't serious."

After supper, Oliver and Peter went out to finish the chores. Heather helped Rennie wash up. She talked incessantly, really leaning on Rennie now. This had never happened — that an older person looked to her for support. But Heather suddenly had developed an admiration for Rennie.

"You're so serene," she exclaimed.

Rennie turned to her swiftly. "I *am?*"

"Yes. Last summer, you seemed to be all agog."

"I was. Remember how your mother was kissing me when you arrived?"

"That struck me as rather odd."

"I knew it! You see, I was uptight. That's why she kissed me — to make me feel better. Before I came here, I was mixed up, with the girls at college telling me the kind of person I had to be. What's liberating about becoming the person others decide you've got to turn into? But your mother gave me a new self-image, something so much larger than I'd ever dreamed of, it was staggering. My own mother can't see how much I want her to understand this. She isn't even coming Friday."

"I thought your parents always came when someone died."

"Just Daddy. He'll arrive in Kendal at two. Right after the meeting, he'll take Peter and me back with him. There won't be time for him to see Firbank." Suddenly Rennie had an idea. "Heather, do you think your father'd mind — would it be an imposition if my parents came Thursday night? It's a long ride for one day. I don't know whether they'd do it, but could I ask them?"

"I'm sure Father wouldn't mind. He's always regretted not being in touch. There's no one else of that generation left. And now that Father's alone —— Stephen and I want him to come back to London with me, but he says he belongs at Firbank. What do you think will become of him here, alone?"

Not that again! Rennie wanted to cry.

Instead she said, "Of course he belongs here! How could he leave the house and the dogs and the garden and the Vietnamese

Forest, just when it's beginning to succeed? Professor Anselm told Peter this morning, whatever happens, that must go on. And Kendal Friends couldn't get along without Oliver Otis. Besides, if he left, what would he do with the pictures?"

"They're a problem. I'll try to complete the inventory, if there's time. I'm going back to England in three weeks, right after the opening."

Rennie hung up the dishcloth. "England! I'd love to go there sometime. It'll be years before Peter and I can do anything like that. The museums! That one — isn't it called the Tate? — where they have the Turner landscapes. My prof showed us the slides. Your mother told me Turner painted like the Impressionists fifty years before they came on the scene."

"There's more to England than just the Tate," Heather told Rennie, smiling for the first time since she arrived. Becoming sad again, she murmured, "I wish we didn't live so far away."

"Don't worry about your father, Heather. He can take care of himself."

Heather put her arm around Rennie, as if to thank her for her hopefulness. But, in her heart, Rennie knew that sooner or later Oliver would have to leave Firbank.

When she asked him whether he'd mind having her parents come Thursday night — if she could persuade them — his face lit up. "That would be first-rate," he exclaimed.

Rennie rushed to the phone.

"No," her father said flatly. "Mother says funerals depress her."

"It's not a funeral, Daddy. Daphne left her body to the Harvard Medical School so other stroke victims might be helped. This is just going to be a meeting of thanksgiving for her life, a memorial service, I guess you'd call it. Oliver will be so pleased if you spend the night. Friday morning we'll row across the pond and look at the ocean. I'll show you the house in Kendal where your grandmother was born and the place downriver where her father had his boat-yard before he worried about getting rich. Please bring Mother. Tell her I want her very much, Daddy."

"Well, I'll speak to her."

Thursday afternoon, Carol Carr breezed in. Rennie was impressed. A couple of years ago, Carr Collages were all the rage. Half the kids at college had posters of them in their rooms. Now those were definitely out, but it was still exciting to meet the artist. She was a warm-hearted, eccentric type, who never should have discarded her bra or else she should have worn a larger cardigan, one that wouldn't gap so between the buttons.

What did this popular, abstract, crazy artist have to do with someone like Daphne?

Heather told Rennie that ever since Carol studied with her mother, years and years ago, she'd been devoted to her.

"The minute I read about it in the paper," Carol declared in a chain-smoker's voice, "I simply had to pop over."

It sounded as if she lived down the road. She'd actually come all the way from Provincetown. Heather and Oliver seemed touched.

Carol walked around the living room like a judge at an exhibition. "What are you going to do with all these, Oliver? Soon as the show opens, you'll be overrun by dealers trying to make a buck. Don't sell *anything* till you've had it appraised. Wait and see. Daphne's work is going to be worth a fortune someday."

Rennie looked at Oliver anxiously. He wouldn't sell his grandmother's portrait, would he? Or *The Repatriates,* or any of the others that had meant so much to Daphne? The seascape with the dune where Peter told Rennie about Charlemagne and the Milky Way ——

"Who's going to handle all that business for you?" Carol asked.

Oliver didn't answer. The idea of making money out of what Daphne produced for the pure joy of creating obviously revolted him.

"What a marvelous woman!" Carol jabbered on. "Somebody ought to write a biography."

Rennie thought of that doctoral dissertation she'd dreamed of doing, supervised by Daphne herself. Without Daphne, nothing would ever be the same.

When Carol reached the dining room and saw Rennie's portrait, she pretended to faint. "That," she declared loudly, "that's going to steal the show! What a likeness, what a more than likeness!"

Rennie felt the blood rush to her face. She ran outdoors and looked for Peter. He laughed.

"Is she going to spend the night? Suppose your folks come?"

"Wowee! That'll be a disaster!"

But by the time Rennie ventured back to the house, Carol had left. Nevertheless, Rennie was becoming more and more apprehensive about her parents' visit. Would they come? And if they did, would it be a success? She simply couldn't see her mother at Firbank. Her father'd been jealous of Oliver all his life. Could he put aside these childish emotions now and reach out in sympathy to the poor man?

Rennie desperately wanted her father to find Firbank all that he'd mooned about for over fifty years. She wondered suddenly whether that was why he never came back — because he was afraid the reality wouldn't live up to his dream. He couldn't risk having it shattered. So he stayed away, except for those rare occasions when he felt it his duty to put in a quick appearance.

I must make his dream real, Rennie told herself, willing this with all her might. I must make him happy again at Firbank. Oh, I hope I can! If only Daphne were still here.

Around nine o'clock in the evening, when Rennie'd just about given up hope, her parents arrived. It was twenty years since her father'd last been to Firbank and the old farmhouse at the corner of the road, that used to signal the turning into the Firbank lane, was no longer there. So they'd wandered in the dark from one end of Salt Pond to the other. They looked tired and unsure of themselves as Oliver welcomed them with his usual cordiality. His pleasure in seeing his cousin glowed in his face.

But Rennie's father was stiff, out of his element. Her mother looked impressed by the spaciousness, the distinguished simplicity of the house she'd heard so much about, its genuine antiquity. Yet, as she mumbled those inane phrases she believed etiquette required of her on entering a house of mourning, she was pathetically ill at ease. Rennie noticed her startled expression when Oliver answered, "Thank thee."

Surprisingly, it was Heather who kept the situation from becoming sticky. After letting her hair down with Rennie ever since she arrived, she suddenly turned around and became a poised hostess, sensing, perhaps, how badly her father and Rennie needed help. With the charm of a cultivated British matron, reserved, yet gracious, she absolutely wowed her long-lost Yankee cousins.

While Rennie was taking her parents up the curving stairs to the large, front bedroom, Heather made tea and got out the cookies Edith Ellis had brought. By the time the Rosses came down again, Heather was sitting in the living room behind the little table with the tea tray. She'd even thought of using Daphne's lovely Spode china and the cozy, which delighted Rennie's mother who, apparently, had never seen one in actual use.

And Peter — dear Peter! Unaffectedly, merely because he'd been nicely reared, he jumped up to take the teacups from Heather and carry them (without spilling) to his future in-laws. He had never before met them anywhere but on their own ground. Here he felt at home, while they were strangers. He still had that nice, relaxed expression.

All at once, it was as if a hurricane had hit the house. Rennie's father jumped out of the chair, rattling the teacup in its saucer, almost dropping them both in his excitement.

"That," he exclaimed, rushing to the fireplace, "that's Grandmother!" He stood looking up above the mantel with the loveliest expression — the way he used to look at Rennie when she was small, before she began that painful struggle to become self-reliant.

"Hasn't thee ever seen this, Ed?" Oliver asked, surprised. "Daphne painted it shortly before Grandmother died. Well, thee only came here on those sad occasions, when thee wouldn't have gone into my study. It used to hang in there. Nice, isn't it?"

Rennie's father nodded, smiling. "That little pink parasol! I remember it. She used to look down on me just this way, when I was a little guy. Joan, come here! See? That's what I've been trying

276

to tell you about all these years — her warmth, her gaiety, her courage ——"

As Rennie's mother joined him, he grabbed her arm, turning to her with shining eyes. "See what I mean?"

Peter quietly took away the threatened cup and saucer, putting them down on the tray.

"That woman really had serenity," Rennie's father exclaimed, shaking his head incredulously as he looked at the portrait again. "When I was a bad boy, she'd just take me on her lap and look at me the way she's looking at me now, and she'd tell me about the animals on the farm or the creatures down around the pond."

Peter went back to the fireplace. "Let me show you something else," he said. "It's even better." His eyes were shining, too. "Come into the dining room."

He led the way and they followed him like lambs!

Rennie stayed with Heather and Oliver.

"William Penn was right," he said, turning from one to the other. *"They that love beyond the world cannot be separated by it. Death cannot kill what never dies."*

8.

When Rennie came down on Friday morning, Oliver was standing by the kitchen window, watching the birds gobble the food he'd just put out.

"Daphne loved the chickadees," he murmured. "I never could figure out why. The way she adored color, I'd have thought the cardinals or the blue jays ——" He smiled as the little, black-white-and-gray creatures devoured his sunflower seeds.

Rennie started to cook breakfast. He'd eaten hours ago, Oliver said. She wondered whether he'd slept.

"Thoreau thought that's how Quaker women looked, with those

dark dresses and bonnets they wore in his day, set off by snowy fichus — like so many chickadees! Lucky Daphne didn't live then. She'd have hated somber clothes. I remember how the gray uniforms we wore in the Mish irked her. By the way, Serenity, thee'll have to choose another woman to act as thy overseer."

Rennie shook her head. "Daphne's the one I wanted."

"I know."

Suddenly noticing the clock, Rennie said, "Peter'd better come in. Austin's picking him up in half an hour. They're going to the meetinghouse to bring up those benches."

Oh, she thought, I haven't told Mother and Daddy yet that they can invite their friends to the wedding.

They'd been so overwhelmed last night, when Peter showed them Rennie's portrait, that they never returned to the living room. Rennie's father had simply mumbled something about the long ride and they'd better go straight up to bed.

It was just as well. Those words of Penn's had brought tears to Oliver's eyes, though Rennie thought they were quite possibly tears of joy. This was something she'd noticed during the past few days — the veritable joy that seemed to surmount his grief. He and Daphne had created a perfect relationship. It was gloriously completed. If there'd been those bad moments Neil spoke of — no couple lived happily ever after — if there'd been such moments, Oliver had forgotten. He had nothing to regret. He simply rejoiced in the perfectness he'd shared with Daphne.

Now, seeing Peter cross the dooryard with a basket of eggs, Oliver exclaimed, "It's like having a son late in life! Thank you both for coming. You've helped Heather and me more than you can guess." He went to the back door to open it in welcome, though Peter was still yards from the house. "A perfect April day! One can almost hear the trees putting out their leaves."

"Clapping their hands," Rennie added, recalling the words Mary Lancashire read when Simeon died.

Oliver looked at her gratefully. *"For ye shall go out with joy and be led forth with peace* — yes, that's just how it was for Daphne. Exactly!"

He spoke a few appreciative words to Peter and went into his study.

Peter was having his cereal and Rennie was standing at the stove, frying his eggs, when Heather came down, looking unrefreshed by sleep.

Remembering how magnificently she'd risen to the occasion last night, Rennie felt a motion of love that surprised her. She rested the spatula against the frying pan and, reaching up, put her arms around Heather. Grief and regret and bewilderment agitated the tense body.

As Rennie let go, Heather gave her an appreciative little smile. Then she went to look for Oliver.

"Peter, I'm going to make you a sandwich. You won't have time to come home for lunch."

"Never mind. Alice Hill's feeding Austin and me. Sam and Jorim, too. Have a good time on the beach." He kissed Rennie good-by.

Left alone, she followed him in thought to the meetinghouse, recalling how he and she had triumphantly carried Daphne in the last time they were there. She didn't think she could stand looking at the wicker chair this afternoon.

While she was scrubbing the sticky frying pan, her parents came down in their country clothes, apologizing for sleeping so late.

"That's okay. We have all morning."

"Honey," her mother said, as she saw what Rennie was doing, "you know I love antiques, but not in the kitchen! Oliver really ought to have a Teflon pan. I'll send him one."

It was ten-thirty by the time they left the house and walked down to the pond. Only three and a half hours to recapture her father's childhood dream, come back, fix lunch, get changed and drive to Kendal!

In the rocky field, the oaks still had their brown, last-year's leaves. The cedars and junipers were dull gray green and, at the water's edge, the bulrushes were broken. Another week or two and life would be returning, but Firbank looked bleak now. This seemed to get to Rennie's parents.

"Death is so depressing," her mother complained.

Rennie wondered why she took it so hard. She hadn't even known Daphne. Her hairdo worried her. The scarf she'd brought so the wind wouldn't ruffle her hair flattened it.

Rennie's father brightened when he saw the old boathouse. But he shook his head as Rennie, pulling in the painter, asked him to row.

"Out of practice," he said.

Dreamily, Rennie turned to him. "Remember, Daddy, how you used to read to me from *The Wind in the Willows?* Remember Rat, the joyous oarsman?"

He nodded. The recollection seemed to please him.

Getting the two of them into the boat was *something*. When they reached the mud flat below the dunes and Rennie was trying to figure out how she was ever going to put her parents ashore, they told her they'd rather not go. It wasn't worth the trouble.

"Ocean looks the same everywhere," her mother said, laughing. "We can see it any time from the Goffes' porch or the Whalleys'."

Not *Daddy's* ocean, Rennie wanted to retort.

"By the way," she announced instead. "There'll be room for them at the wedding. For the Dixwells, too, and anyone else you'd like to invite. There are forty-eight more seats than I thought."

She expected this news to delight her parents, but it didn't have much effect. "Doubt if they'll come," her father muttered. "If it had been in Neville, we could have counted on quite a crowd. But way off here —— Still, we'll give it a try."

Disembarking was even worse than Rennie'd feared. Hanging on to the dock, she watched anxiously as her father hoisted himself out. He puffed when he bent to give a hand to her mother, who was afraid to make the leap.

By the time they got back to the house, Oliver and Heather had left.

Rennie put some food on the round table, thinking, as the three of them sat down, that probably this was the first time anyone ever ate here without pausing for grace. But she couldn't suggest this to her parents, though she felt pretty sure Oliver would have, if he'd been home. Suddenly tired, she longed for that breather, the comforting silence that would have eased her tension, maybe even restored her sense of the wedding's spirituality, which seemed to retreat whenever her parents discussed arrangements.

While they were eating, her father mentioned the portrait for the first time.

"We're absolutely wild about it," her mother said. "It's a beautiful thing."

"Wonderful likeness! Why didn't you tell us when you posed for it?" Rennie's father sounded hurt.

"I did."

"Hm. Well, I don't remember. But it's a gem. We've talked it over and we intend to own it. Do you think, if I speak to Oliver, he'll give it to us? After all, it's our daughter."

"We ought to offer to pay for it, Ed."

"Do you think we should, Rennie? How's Oliver fixed? That picture must be worth something, but we want it. We think it'll look lovely in the living room."

Rennie didn't want her portrait hanging in Neville. "It has to stay here," she blurted out. "With your grandmother's. *The Two Serenitys* — they belong together."

"Shouldn't mind owning Grandmother's, either," her father murmured with more than a hint of envy, as if to say, Why Oliver? "You should have told us a lot of things, Rennie. I never knew Daphne was a painter — an important one. Never knew till I read the write-up in the *Times*, day before yesterday. Big write-up. She was about to have a show at the Contemporary Art," he added, impressed. "Did you know that?"

"Yes," Rennie answered wearily. "I should have told you."

Although it was late when they reached Kendal, Rennie made her father stop the car so that she could point out the place where Josiah had his boatyard, and the yellow house with the veranda, flanked by stone urns, where Serenity was born. But her father didn't seem to care.

Only, when they got out at the meetinghouse, he looked across the street and that lovely expression of last night returned to his face. "Joan," he cried, "see that tree? The huge one with its leaves just coming out, like a cloud of monarch butterflies? It's a copper beech. Someone in my family planted it. Grandfather Edmund, I think. He's the one I was named for. Tree must be close to a century old."

Rennie felt better the moment she caught sight of Peter. He was helping Sam and Jorim with the parking. So many cars! Rhode Island, Connecticut, Massachusetts, New York. Who were all those people?

That she'd known only one small segment of Daphne's long life hadn't occurred to Rennie before. Now she saw that the rest of it had touched hundreds of others, who felt this impulse to stop whatever they were doing today and travel great distances, simply to give thanks for her life.

"Come on," she said, as her father still stood looking across at the tree. "We're late."

The vestibule was jammed. Someone — was it Peter? — had removed the wicker chair.

9.

The hushed room was already packed. On the facing benches, the kids who cleaned Firbank sat in solemn rows. Nancy and Sandy looked about to cry. Billy Green was sitting up there, too, though Rennie didn't think he'd ever done much work at Firbank or anywhere else. Too busy, ripping off. She wondered how he was getting along.

The only three seats left together were on one of the benches Peter had placed under the windows.

"Isn't there any organ?" Rennie's mother whispered as they sat down.

Rennie shook her head.

"What about the wedding march? How will you keep step when you walk down the aisle?"

Rennie glared, wishing to goodness her mother'd shut up.

Heather had placed the flowers that were sent from out of town on the sills of the tall windows. Ordinarily, there weren't any flowers in the meetinghouse. In accordance with ancient custom, Kendal Friends renounced everything that might distract them from worship. Rennie thought the flowers made the meetinghouse look nice, but unnatural. They gave it an exotic smell.

Sitting between her parents, wondering whether Peter would find a seat when he came in, Rennie couldn't seem to center down, to be herself. She kept imagining how her mother was feeling in this homely place with no music to soothe her, nothing to look at, no one to tell her when or how to pray. This was so different from anything her mother had ever experienced, from the imposing setting she'd visualized for her only daughter's big moment, that she must be feeling even more depressed about the wedding than about death.

What can I do? Rennie asked herself miserably. How can I make what's right for me right for her, too?

Some stranger had taken Daphne's usual place. Friends no doubt avoided it. Rennie couldn't get herself to look in that direction again. With relief, she saw that Peter, Sam and Jorim had sneaked in. They were standing at the back.

Down front, near where Oliver and Heather were sitting, John Ludlow was getting up to speak. Rennie recalled the night he told Peter and her about Simeon's death — how defeated he looked. Now his face expressed some of Oliver's surmounting joy.

"We're meeting to give thanks for the life of our friend Daphne Otis," he said in a steady voice, "as well as for the love through which her husband and daughter made her last years victorious. And they were victorious in every sense — professionally, but even more in the impact they had on other people's lives. No one could visit Daphne without feeling uplifted."

Rennie wondered what else John was going to say about Daphne. There was so much one might mention and he wouldn't want to talk long. Which of her many outstanding attributes would he choose?

"At the beginning of their life together," John went on, "Daphne and Oliver resolved to turn all the treasures they possessed into the channel of universal love. And that was what they did. It was the business of their lives. Their home became this channel."

As John sat down, Rennie bowed her head and thought of Daphne and Oliver picnicking by the lighthouse all those years ago, reading Woolman, suddenly deciding to throw over that jewelry job and live at Firbank. Oliver had speeded at twenty-nine miles an hour because he couldn't wait to break the news to Serenity!

Hadn't been for that, Rennie thought, I'd still be a mess.

Her father bumped against her arm. He was fidgeting, the way he used to do when he came here with his grandmother. Now he was an old man, too heavy and puffy for boats. Rennie's effort to recreate the delights of his childhood had fallen absolutely flat. He didn't even climb the dune to look at the ocean. But Serenity's portrait — that had stirred him.

Overtaken by it, he'd recalled her love in all its fullness. He'd remembered how, when he was in disgrace with his parents, she'd looked at him in a way that communicated unqualified acceptance — not of his naughtiness, but of himself. Young as he was at the time, he'd understood this and when he saw her portrait last night he relived that experience with elation.

Serenity's love, Rennie thought. It's the one lasting thing for him. All these years — he's never forgotten.

His grandmother's serenity, which he remembered wistfully and Rennie craved, wasn't, she realized now, a virtue in itself. It was only the state of mind that seemed to come naturally to those who looked for the divine spark in everyone — a spark one could usually appeal to — knowing also that it didn't always get the upper hand.

One of the strangers — he looked as if he might belong to what Austin called "the art crowd" — got up and apologized for speaking. Not being a Friend, he said, he didn't know whether it was proper to say this, but ever since he had come in here he'd been thinking about Saint Augustine — something the saint said that applied particularly to Mrs. Otis. He hoped the Friends wouldn't mind if he mentioned it. He'd known her for years and he'd always thought that the one special thing about her was her great beauty — the beauty of her person, of her character — maybe one should call it her spirit — and of her art. Saint Augustine had called beauty "the radiance of truth" and truth was what he'd seen shining in Mrs. Otis.

Rennie liked that, but she was still thinking of love and what a dope she'd been to believe that Oliver could get along better because he'd *given* care the past few years instead of *receiving* it. Maybe, she thought, it's easier for a dependent person suddenly to shift for himself than for one who's ministered devotedly to be left with no one to minister to. Maybe it's easier for Oliver having no one to love him than having no one to love.

Living alone, on whom would he pour out that boundless *giving*, other than on his birds and his land? Wouldn't he just shrivel, like the defoliated trees?

I guess that's what people were trying to tell me when they kept asking, What's going to become of Oliver? But being Oliver, *being* Oliver, he'll find a way to give again.

Now Mary Young was getting to her feet, hoisting herself up by gripping the bench in front, just as Daphne did the last time Rennie was here. Rennie never saw Mary without thinking of the disappointment she'd felt the day she first came to Firbank, when Mary was standing at the door in welcome. Not knowing about Daphne's stroke, Rennie'd assumed it was she who had come to the door. That gave Rennie a shock because her father had talked so much about Daphne's beauty. Mary was a homely old woman, the wife and mother of potato farmers, whose knobby hands and thin body seemed to proclaim how hard she'd worked all her life.

I couldn't be a farmer's wife, Rennie thought, looking at her. It's okay helping out at Firbank, but to work like that all the time —— I'm glad Peter didn't have another identity crisis and decide to grow potatoes.

Mary turned to pick up a book that lay on the seat beside her purse. "When my husband died," she said in a barely audible voice, "Daphne Otis brought me this book." She glanced down at the title. "*Some Fruits of Solitude*. Daphne said the reflections in it meant a great deal to her. I'd like to read a few of them now.

They that love beyond the world cannot be separated by it.

Death cannot kill what never dies.

Nor can spirits ever be divided that love and live in the same divine principle, the root and record of their friendship.

If absence be not death, neither is theirs.

Death is but crossing the world as friends do the seas. They live in one another still."

Looking as though the message she had felt moved to bring drained her last ounce of strength, Mary shut the book and slowly let herself down onto the bench.

Did Daphne live in Rennie still? Wasn't that exactly what Rennie'd kept trying to have happen with Serenity? Because she was her descendant, her namesake, a throwback, she'd believed she might become the kind of person Serenity was, that somehow she could incorporate her spirit. But when she looked at the portrait, her great-grandmother refused to speak to her.

She spoke to Daddy, though. Right away!

He'd known her. Was that what made the difference?

Did Daphne live in Rennie still?

The silence overtook her, that infinity that couldn't be contained in words. It reached beyond the world, loosening Rennie with the assurance that she could let go because she wouldn't drift away forever. She'd come back.

What Daphne'd given her she could pass on to others someday, when she had training and experience, when she could make art live for other young people the way Daphne made it live for her, not as pigment spread on flat canvas, but as the projection of a spirit.

Someday ——

Only, right now, it's Heather who needs Daphne — what Daphne gave me. Why can't I pass that on to her? How?

Rennie didn't know. Still, floating on the silence, she sensed the comfort of promise. In its own time, way would open.

When this meeting's over, she said to herself, I'll speak to her. I don't know what I'll say, maybe nothing, but I'll bring her this thing of Daphne's that's in me. I'll give it to her — the root and record of our friendship.

After the meeting —— But there wouldn't be time. Rennie's father would be in a tear, impatient to hit the road. He wouldn't let her stop and speak to anyone. He was always in such a hurry to get home.

Suddenly the silence evaporated. All around the room, people were shaking hands and murmuring. Rennie didn't know which way to turn first — toward her father or her mother. How funny it would seem to shake hands with them, like strangers! She'd never done that. She couldn't do it now. Turning from one to the other, smiling at them, she reached out in both directions at once and placed a hand on theirs.

Her mother was heaving a sigh, as if she'd been holding her breath. "They made it seem so beautiful," she murmured. "I always thought that dying ——" She looked relieved, as if a fear she'd carried with her all her life was fading away. Then she said, looking around the room. "That dress she designed will look perfect in here. And the little old-fashioned bouquet ——"

Rennie gave her mother's hand a squeeze.

"I'm going to hunt for the material tomorrow. It has to be just right — ethereal."

The crowd they were caught in moved slowly toward the door. Peter was waiting there. He put his arm around Rennie's waist as they went down the steps, out into the sunshine. She could see he had something to tell her — something nice.

"Guess what! I saw Billy Green before the meeting. Oliver's giving him a job in the Forest this summer. Invited him to live at Firbank. What it'll do for Billy to be with Oliver!"

"I knew he'd find a way."

Mary Lancashire was standing on the lawn, looking up at them. Happy expectancy shone in her wrinkled face. "Edmund!" she called, before he reached the bottom step. "Edmund! I knew thee when thee was so high."

Rennie's father walked toward her, beaming.

"I remember, thee used to come to meeting with Serenity Otis."

"Right. Couldn't sit still. Can't now." He laughed, turning to look at Rennie's mother a second, then back to Mary Lancashire. "To think you've remembered me all these years!"

He was in no hurry to leave.

Nancy and Sandy were running across the lawn.

"Rennie! Peter! We're coming to your wedding!"

"So are my sisters," Peter told them. "They're sort of shy. Will you be nice to them?"

"Sure. And you know the little table? Can we carry it?"

"What little table?"

"The one with the certificate — that long thing. It's always rolled out on the little table that usually stands in the vestibule and after the boy and girl promise to love each other forever, two people carry the table over to their bench so they can sign their names. Haven't you ever been to a wedding?"

"Not one like that. And we didn't know about the little table, but you're the only two people we'd let carry it for us. Will you? See you then!"

As the girls took off across the lawn again, Rennie glanced at her father anxiously, certain he was impatient, maybe even angry with her for keeping him waiting. But he was still listening raptly to Mary Lancashire, turning to Rennie's mother from time to time to make sure she was taking in every word.

"Peter, let's ask Mary Lancashire to be the other overseer. She knew Daphne for over fifty years. Is that okay with you?"

288

By way of answer, Peter drew Rennie nearer to her parents and the old woman, whose recollections still made her wrinkled face glow.

How happy she looked when Rennie asked her! "Thee reminds me of thy great-grandmother," she said.

"You think so? You really do?"

Rennie's father beamed. He was in no hurry to go away. He'd come home.

Oliver and Heather were standing by the syringa bush, surrounded by a host of friends.

Rennie let go of Peter's hand. "Be right back," she said. "I'm just going over to see Heather."

10.

Ten days later, Professor Anselm returned.

He was afraid Oliver might leave Firbank and he wanted to impress on him how important it was to keep the Vietnamese Forest going. The National Academy of Sciences, he explained, had made a study of the ecological damage caused by defoliation chemicals. The study showed that nature alone couldn't heal those scars in a hundred years. But, the professor believed, American scientists might succeed, if they only understood the need to tackle the job. Oliver must persuade them.

Rennie wouldn't have known all this if Professor Anselm hadn't told Peter when he went to see him. The professor repeated what he'd said to Oliver: he absolutely must publish an account of his experiment — not only the techniques he developed and the results, but particularly the moral obligation that drove him to undertake it. Professor Anselm realized that Oliver couldn't write and work outdoors at the same time. So, if this was agreeable to Oliver, he was going to offer Peter a fellowship, though not in astronomy — that wasn't his to give. But if Peter wished to switch later, he'd have a master's degree in forestry to his credit. Since Firbank was within commuting distance of the university, Peter could take the experiment off Oliver's hands.

Oliver had thanked the Professor. Nothing, he said, would make him so happy as having Peter and Serenity living with him. Firbank belonged to Serenity, too. And if anyone would nurse his seedlings faithfully, it was Peter. Nevertheless, Oliver wasn't ready to give up his experiment yet. With Serenity taking over the housekeeping, he thought he could manage to keep going outdoors and write in the evenings.

"You mean," Rennie cried, when Peter got back to college and told her, "we're going to live at Firbank? Oh, Peter!"

"I never thought I'd have the chance to go to grad school so soon! Only, Rennie, this isn't going to be much fun for you — just keeping house."

"At Firbank? I'd love it. But you want to be an astronomer."

"Well, I am coming down to earth," Peter quipped. He was jubilant, though. The world was recognizing his manhood. "I can help Oliver with the chores. If he'd only let me take over the experiment, too —— I'm almost as interested as he is."

"All that hard work. Oliver shouldn't be doing it."

Hard work — the minute Rennie said the words, it dawned on her what hard work she was letting herself in for, keeping house on a farm. In the excitement of that first moment, she'd made light of it, but now that she pictured all there was to do, she wasn't so sure. Cooking, cleaning, preserving — was this what she'd had in mind for next year and the year after? If she and Peter lived at Firbank, the women of the Meeting wouldn't feel they had to keep bringing in food. The children of the First Day school couldn't be expected to clean. It would all fall on Rennie. Still, to be living there, to take care of Oliver, to make it possible for Peter to start grad school ——

"You know," he was saying, "going into another field may be the best thing that could happen to me. Some of the most original research is being done nowadays by scholars who've cut across disciplines. They're breaking out of the old compartments, creating new fields. I may want to do something I haven't even thought of yet. Remember Monthly Meeting, when Friends started with opposite views and ended up with a third way that was better than either of the other two? Things might work out like that for me."

The following week, when Daphne's exhibition opened, Rennie and Peter were in the middle of exams. Peter couldn't possibly leave college, but Rennie rushed to New York for the afternoon.

At the door of the museum, Heather was waiting for her. She looked different — much more relaxed and self-possessed than when Rennie saw her last, after the meeting of thanksgiving. In fact, Heather looked happy.

"I couldn't wait for you inside any longer," she said, hugging Rennie. "I'm so impatient to tell you what's just happened."

Before the opening, the trustees of the museum and Miss Chase, the director, had given a luncheon in honor of her father and herself. "Of Mother really," Heather murmured sadly. But then the happiness returned to her face. She told Rennie that, over coffee, the chairman of the board of trustees announced that they intended to publish a monograph — a biography and comprehensive study of Daphne Otis and her art!

At that point, Miss Chase had turned to Oliver and assured him that he was the only person who could do justice to the book. Would he undertake it? They knew he had other commitments, but the trustees were anxious to get this out. Naturally, Oliver would have to engage someone to assist him. The museum's Publications Fund was prepared to underwrite the expense.

"When Miss Chase mentioned an assistant," Heather told Rennie, "Father turned to me and exclaimed, 'Who but Serenity? She'll be living at Firbank. Next to thee, she's the only one who could really help me.'"

Rennie thought she was going to collapse from joy, right there on the sidewalk.

"You're the only one I'd want to have interpreting Mother's life-work, anyway," Heather was saying. "You understood her. Besides, you can't think what a comfort it is to me to know that you'll be taking care of Father. When he suggested you, I said to him, 'That's right. Rennie's the only one. But first, she and Peter have to have a holiday. They've worked much too hard and will do again, come September. Stephen and I would like them to visit us — fly to London right after the wedding.' "

"Heather!"

"I'm serious."

"But who'll help Oliver, if we go away?"

"Stephen and the children and I are coming in July. I'll plan the monograph with him then. Stephen and Olly will do his work outdoors. Meanwhile, you and Peter can stay in our flat. Or you can drive our car to Yorkshire, where Mother spent her childhood. Seeing the wildness of those moors and the beauty of the dales will tell you a great deal about her."

A pilgrimage, Rennie said to herself. We'll be making a pilgrimage and ending up at Firbank, like Oliver and Daphne. England! The museums, the cathedrals, the countryside!

But Rennie shook her head. "It would be wonderful. Only, we don't have the money. Even if we stayed with you, the trip —— Maybe someday."

The museum was jammed. All those people with notebooks must be critics or art historians. Oliver was standing in the lobby, talking to some men and women. When he saw Rennie, he broke away and came over to greet her.

"It's marvelous! The way the pictures are hung, the lighting! I'll take thee up to the gallery." He handed her a book.

How happy he looks, Rennie thought. He's being the two of them — experiencing the pleasure Daphne would have had, as well as his own. *They live in one another still.*

Heather was already surrounded by some people who wanted her to tell them about her mother.

"First come and meet the trustees," Oliver was saying to Rennie. Taking her arm, he drew her toward the group he'd just left and introduced her.

It hadn't occurred to Rennie that anyone but Oliver and Heather would notice her here. So she wasn't prepared for the reception. Gradually she realized that these people had been looking forward to meeting her. They wanted to see how her real-life face compared with Daphne's drawing. Rennie's cheeks got hot. She managed to smile, though. She didn't run away. They were nice, understanding people. No one needled her about the portrait.

Then, Oliver led Rennie up a long, marble staircase. In the gallery, there was such a mob that it was impossible to see the pictures. Rennie's portrait was completely hidden.

"Thee and Peter will have to come after exams," Oliver said. "By then the crowds may have thinned out."

"Won't they be even worse, when it's open to the public?"

"Maybe." Oliver's face was shining. "Heather told thee about the monograph? I thought thee'd be pleased. We'll have a lovely time, working together! That's if Peter's willing to take over the Forest. Does thee think he might?"

"He's dying to."

Giving Rennie a grateful look, Oliver said, "Professor Anselm dropped in the other day and told me he hopes Peter will stay in his department. He likes him."

Some artists buttonholed Oliver. They were curious about Daphne's technique.

While he talked to them, full of enthusiasm, expressing interest in their work, Rennie stood in the middle of the gallery, awed. The grandeur of the place, the intensity of the crowd, Daphne's art, which drew everyone together —— Looking down, Rennie noticed the book Oliver had given her when she arrived. She'd been so overwhelmed that she'd just held it without even realizing it was the catalogue. *The Two Serenitys,* the title read. There was Rennie's great-grandmother on the front cover! And on the back one, Rennie!

Peter, she cried inside herself. Peter, I need you! This is too much joy and sadness and beauty to bear alone.

If only he were here ——

Someone had stepped out of the crowd and was standing in front of her, waiting for her to look up.

"Serenity! I'm so happy to meet you. I'm Aquila Chase. Mr. Otis said you were coming."

Dazed, Rennie saw kind, reassuring eyes, a quiet dignity. She took the outstretched hand. Her strength came back. "How did you know?" The moment she said it, Rennie realized the question was silly.

Miss Chase laughed — a low-pitched, resonant laugh. She nodded toward Rennie's portrait.

Although she'd only just met this woman, Rennie heard herself blurting out, "If Daphne were here, she'd know how I feel."

"A lot of us are thinking that," Miss Chase said softly.

Heather caught up with them and led Rennie off to a quiet corner. She wanted to tell her how relieved she was that her father wouldn't be doing the heavy work any more. "You and Peter are an absolute blessing," she said. Then she began referring to conversations she'd been having with Rennie's mother.

Rennie looked at her in amazement. "What about? What would you and Mother ——?"

"The wedding festivities. Father's looking forward so eagerly to having your family at Firbank — yours parents and brothers, their wives and children — getting reunited. All these years, he never understood why Edmund didn't want to come. It grieved him."

"I don't think Daddy understood what was behind it, himself. He's sweet, but awfully unperceptive. That's just the way he is. Mother isn't any better."

"Well, it's past. Father wants this to be a memorable occasion. Before flying home on Wednesday, I'm going to try to get everything arranged. Your parents and the Hollands will stay at Firbank. The Ludlows and Hills and Youngs have offered to put up your brothers and their families. Father's planning a dinner the evening before the wedding for all of you, including the overseers and the committee on clearness. When I told your mother that, she said she'd like to provide the food. Your sisters-in-law are anxious to help. As a matter of fact, everyone's terribly pleased. It's going to be just lovely!"

"Oh, Heather, I wish you were going to be there."

"So do I. But now that you'll be living at Firbank, there'll be lots and lots of time for us to spend together."

When Rennie got back to college, *she* had something to tell *Peter!* "A monograph! Just think! It will be the basis for my doctoral dissertation. And you're going to take over the Vietnamese Forest. Oliver's really got his hands full now."

Peter was so excited, Rennie didn't have the heart to tell him about Heather's invitation. She knew he'd be as disappointed as she was.

She didn't tell her parents either, when she called them to announce that she had a job, the best job anyone could possibly imagine. She was being employed by the Museum of Contemporary Art!

"Wait till you go to the exhibition," she cried. "Wait till you see the catalogue!"

11.

Carol Carr's prediction was accurate — Rennie's portrait stole the show.

If she had become a cover girl or had been chosen Miss Universe, Neville couldn't have been more impressed. Whole car pools formed to visit the museum and see the portrait. Suddenly, Rennie's parents were the most talked-of people in town. It was as if they'd won the sweepstakes.

Rennie hardly dared go home. But on their last free weekend before Graduation, she and Peter braved it.

When Rennie went to her room, she found the wedding dress hanging in the closet. Her hand trembled as she took it out and held the hanger at arm's length. Filled with apprehension, she decided to try it on now, while she was alone. The material was lovely — "ethereal," as her mother had put it.

But I mustn't expect it to look anything like that sketch Daphne made, Rennie warned herself. How could Mother ——? No one could, really, and she didn't even know Daphne.

Stretching for the zipper, adjusting the skirt, smoothing it, Rennie finally faced herself in the long mirror. She was overwhelmed. That dreamlike aura Daphne had envisioned was reflected! Rennie had been certain that no material, however gossamer, could translate Daphne's sketch into an actual garment. Yet, here she was, standing in her room, clothed in that mysterious beauty.

Running down the hall, she burst into her mother's room and threw her arms around her. "How did you manage it? This is heavenly — far more beautiful than I ever believed it could be!"

Her mother looked gratified.

"How did you do it?"

"I almost didn't. You'll never know how close I came to giving up."

Rennie's mother surveyed her, looking, Rennie thought, satisfied with her daughter's appearance for the first time in years.

"What happened?"

"That sketch of Daphne's told me a lot I never knew about you. I began to realize that when I picked out those models at the Bridal Boutique, I was just interested in the gowns — their style, the way they compared with ones I'd seen in magazines. Daphne's sketch made me visualize how she saw you. That changed everything. But I wasn't able to transfer the idea to a pattern. As I hadn't bought the material yet, I decided to give up the whole thing."

"I'm glad you didn't."

"Well, I was just about to ring you and explain that we'd have to order a gown, when Daphne passed away. I simply couldn't bring myself to tell you then. Maybe it was seeing you at Firbank or seeing the portrait — I don't know — but in the meetinghouse, I seemed to be saying to myself, It's not how Rennie's going to look in that dress that's important. It's how she'll feel. That was like a relevation. Suddenly, I knew I could do it."

Rennie hugged her mother again. "I'm so happy with it."

"You know," her mother murmured, "the way I was brought up, being in style was what mattered. Fashion and durability. Nobody considered how the person wearing the clothes felt in them. In fact, nobody cared much how we four girls felt about anything, just so we behaved nicely."

"How ghastly!"

"Oh, I don't know. We got along. But then all those modern child-rearing notions came in. Maybe by the time I had you I was a bit too old."

"You're okay," Rennie assured her. Who'd have thought the day would ever dawn when she'd tell her mother that?

After dinner that evening, while they were still sitting at the table, Rennie's father made a little speech. He was in a festive mood, but, watching his Adam's apple work, Rennie knew that he was having to control his emotions.

There was a time, he said, when the generation gap between them had seemed insurmountable. Luckily, that was over. "I don't know," he observed with a touch of humor Rennie didn't think he had in him, "whether it's because you've grown older or Mother and I have grown younger. At any rate, we're very pleased with the way things have worked out and we want to say this, not just in words, but with a little gift for your Graduation." He fished in his pocket and handed Peter an envelope. "It's for you both."

Rennie could see by the way Peter fumbled with the metal clasp on the envelope that he was having trouble controlling his emotions, too. When he finally produced the contents and Rennie took in what he was holding, she gasped. She couldn't believe her eyes. Roundtrip tickets on the *Queen Elizabeth!* And a check with the memo: "For travel in England."

"Daddy! Mother! That's no *little* gift!"

Peter was baffled.

"I didn't tell you," Rennie cried, wishing now that she had. "Heather and Stephen invited us to spend the summer. Reason I didn't tell you — I didn't think we could go. Mother and Daddy must have found out somehow." She turned to her parents. "Thank you so much!"

They're not so unperceptive, after all, she said to herself, realizing that, in one of those conversations with her cousin Joan, Heather must have let on how much she hoped way would open.

Peter got up from the table and shook hands with his future in-laws, politely thanking them, though he obviously was still puzzled and reluctant to accept such a generous gift.

All evening, Rennie repeated the invitation Heather had extended the day of the opening, trying to convince Peter that it was all right to accept.

"Oliver won't need us while Heather and her family are at Firbank. We'd just be fifth wheels. I know what that's like."

"England! I never thought we'd get there for years and years."

"I should have told you that night, when I got back to college," Rennie reflected, "even if I thought it would disappoint you. From now on, I'll tell you everything — for better, for worse. And you'll tell me, won't you? Promise?"

"With divine assistance."

12.

Passports, luggage, the marriage license, thank-you notes, Class Night, Graduation — it was all beautiful, but enough to make one dizzy.

Then, at last, the peace of Firbank! The moment Rennie got there with her parents, she relaxed. Now, she could begin to live.

All the windows were open. Daphne's flower bed was in bloom. Oliver, in his shirt sleeves, was polishing the antique brass handle on the front door. How his face crinkled with pleasure when the car drew up!

The living- and dining-room walls looked bare without the pictures that had gone to the exhibition. Otherwise, everything was shining, reflecting the enthusiasm with which Oliver and Heather had washed the windows and polished the furniture in anticipation of this weekend.

Rennie's father brought in the ice chests that her mother had stocked so carefully in Neville. Puffing and perspiring, he carried the suitcases up the curving stairs.

A blue air letter, addressed to Rennie, lay on the table in the entrance hall. It was from Heather, saying how much she wished that she could have stayed for the wedding. But, Heather wrote, she'd be present in spirit.

> At the precise moment — eight o'clock in the evening here — Stephen and I will be centering down in the sitting room, joining Kendal Friends as they celebrate your marriage. A fortnight later, we'll be driving to Southampton to meet your ship!

Rennie didn't see how she could wait twenty-four hours to show Peter the letter.

She ran up to the ell. This was the last time she'd have Heather's room. On the bureau, in the blue-and-white jar, there was a little bunch of flowers. Dear Oliver! It made Rennie think of that afternoon on the back porch, when Daphne painted the wildflowers and they both had that moment of panic, fearing Rennie's family wouldn't come to the wedding.

And are they ever coming! she said to herself. Going to the window, she announced to the pond, We're here for good! Any time we leave now, you'd better believe it's just temporary. This is home for Peter and me.

He arrived the next day, bringing his parents and sisters, Beth and Evey. Rennie's mother was bustling around the kitchen. Her father was helping Oliver extend the dining room table. The way he welcomed the Hollands, one would have thought it was his house.

It is, Rennie insisted to herself. Serenity left it to all of us, didn't she?

So that Peter's mother — Rennie was trying hard to get used to saying "Mom"— would know she appreciated the gift, Rennie was wearing the amethyst ring. Peter noticed it the moment he came in. He gave Rennie a look of thanks. That made her think of the afternoon on the back porch again — how Oliver and Daphne had shared their secret hope that the wedding would be postponed until the spring flowers were out. She and Peter could also tell each other their thoughts without saying a word!

After the greetings and introductions were over, he took his parents up to the front bedroom. Heather had prepared it with the best linens.

The only arrangement she had slipped up on was a room for Beth and Evey. Apparently, she'd forgotten all about them. When Rennie had discovered this the day before, she telephoned Nancy and Sandy, who said it would be great to have the girls sleep over.

"Will you come to our dinner tomorrow night?" Rennie asked.

Would they!

The Hollands had barely arrived when Rennie's young friends appeared and took Peter's terribly shy sisters to the beach.

Then Jane and Eddy drove up with their brats. What brats! They exploded out of the car, making a beeline for Daphne's flower beds, exciting the dogs. How was Oliver going to stand them?

But Rennie's father had been looking forward to this moment. "All aboard!" he shouted. "We're going over to the dunes. You'd better come along, Eddy, just in case someone has to be fished out. And," he added firmly, "to row."

Mom came downstairs a little later, explaining that Dad was taking a rest. She was a person, Rennie'd always thought, who felt comfortable with herself. But how would she hit it off with Rennie's mother, who was stiff with strangers? Rennie needn't have worried. Mom acted as if they were old friends. Shyly at first, then with increasing trust, Rennie's mother responded.

Firbank had hardly recovered from the first incursion when Larry and Victoria arrived with their brood. Rennie ran out to greet them as they came streaming across the lawn, Larry carrying the baby. He dumped him in Rennie's arms.

"Boy, you weigh a ton," she told the confused-looking child. "Am I glad you weren't twins!"

He was the cutest of the lot. Rennie wondered why she'd always resented it when she was elected to baby-sit. Maybe it was because she hadn't been quite grown up herself. She carried the baby into the kitchen and showed him off to Mom. "The youngest Ross," she said proudly. "Lawrence Ballantine. Don't ask me why Ballantine. I don't know."

Rennie put him on the floor and let him crawl. That was a mistake. He was getting under everybody's feet till he settled down under the round table and fell asleep.

"He's as well off there as anyplace," Victoria decided.

Her two other children thought the house was just made for hide-and-seek. It was a relief when Peter offered to take them out and show them the hens.

Oliver invited Larry to go down to the Vietnamese Forest. This was what Rennie'd always wished for — that Larry could have a chance to be with Oliver.

It was almost dinner time when they returned. Jonathan and his family were just driving in. They'd stopped on the way to visit the Mystic Seaport and they all looked beat. Jocelyn had been car-sick. Matty declared that she was too exhausted to cope.

Taking Jocelyn by the hand, Oliver escorted her up to his bathroom, regaling her on the stairs with stories of Heather's mishaps when she was a young traveler.

Rennie wandered through the house, talking to everybody, enjoying the scene. In the kitchen, four Ross women ran around, unwrapping their confections, hunting for serving dishes in the strange cupboards, bumping into each other. At the front door, the Ludlows and the Youngs, Mary Lancashire and the Hills were arriving. They looked cool and calm. Jocelyn came downstairs, smelling of eau de cologne, blissfully sucking a lemon drop, wearing nothing but her underpants. She was followed by Oliver and Dad, who were deep in conversation.

Rennie said to herself, They have a lot in common — a certain rare quality and that nice dash of humor. It's like seasoning.

Peter and Austin were bringing in a picnic table and placing it under the dining room window for the children. Judy followed them with china and silver. In the living room, the Hills and the Ludlows introduced themselves, quickly making friends with everyone. Mary Lancashire only had eyes for her old friend Edmund. He was tickled!

Jane had made the most impressive hors d'oeuvres — her specialty. But, Rennie thought, this was surely the first time they'd been served with grape juice. Pretty wonderful grape juice it was, having come from the arbor that covered the back porch.

At last dinner was ready. The grownups sat down at the huge dining room table. The children had their own place under the window.

Oliver, seated at the head of the table with Rennie's and Peter's parents on either side, looked around the room joyfully. He thanked everyone for coming. Heather wished them to know how sorry she and Stephen were that they couldn't be present. Then he asked his guests to join in giving silent thanks for the meal, for the beautiful occasion that brought them together, for the love that bound them one to another.

At the foot of the table, Rennie, sitting with Peter and the four girls, thought her heart would burst with happiness as hands were held all around. She couldn't eat much. Telling Beth and Evey how glad she was that they'd made friends with Nancy and Sandy, now that they'd be coming to Firbank often, she tried without success to make them talk.

"I suppose all these Rosses are a bit overwhelming," she said, laughing. "The Hollands are outnumbered."

Beth surprised her. "You'll be a Holland yourself, tomorrow," she said.

"Right!"

When everyone had finished the meat course, Nancy and Sandy jumped up to clear. Matty withdrew to the kitchen to dish up the dessert, waking Lawrence Ballantine. He howled. Victoria rushed out of the dining room.

Meanwhile, little Edmund decided it was more fun on the pond and he took off. The sun was going down, but he was a brave little boy and that didn't deter him. Neither did his parents. Eddy, sitting across the table from Neil, made the most of this wonderful opportunity to discuss boats. Jane had found a brand-new listener in Judy and she was airing her views on the victimization of mothers.

Jocelyn, wearing the dress Matty had hoped to preserve for the wedding, slid down from her chair. She climbed up on Oliver's to inform him that she was now ready for another story and another lemon drop, treating him to a free, introductory sample of how her lungs performed when her requests weren't instantly honored.

This was all but drowned out by competing decibels that suddenly resounded in the entrance hall. Vigorously protesting, little Edmund was hauled in by Peter's father.

Eddy and Jane were surprised. "How did you know? We never even missed him."

"Teachers have eyes in the back of their heads."

He made a joke of it, but Rennie worried. With his heart condition, running down to the pond ——

Even Matty's crème brûlée didn't lure the children back to the table. They never settled down again. Not long after the meal was officially over, the Hills, Ludlows and Youngs announced that, since tomorrow was going to be a big day, they thought they'd better take their guests home. Austin and Judy offered to drop Nancy and Sandy and Peter's sisters off on their way.

As he was about to leave, Larry put his arm around Rennie's shoulders and drew her aside. "You've brought us back to our inheritance," he said, looking at her with a depth of feeling his eyes rarely revealed. "We missed out on a lot, never coming here. I hope my kids will have it. See you tomorrow!"

The sudden hush was unbelievable.

Dad announced that he felt so refreshed after his nap, he hoped he would be accorded the privilege of washing the dishes. This reassured Rennie, who was still wondering whether the sprint after Edmund had been too much for his heart.

"Son," Mom said to Peter, "it's a beautiful night. Take Joan and Edmund and Oliver out and show them the stars."

Dad washed up, Mom dried, and Rennie put the dishes away.

"It was so wonderful," she kept repeating, overflowing with happiness.

Carrying a stack of plates to the cupboard, she looked down at the indigo design, remembering how beautiful these dishes had seemed the first time she came here. She still loved them, but she suddenly saw that they were tyrants, too. The realization made her stand still a moment, holding the plates against her stomach, staring at them.

Meal after meal in the years ahead, they'd demand washing, rinsing, setting up to drain, stacking in the cupboard. Rennie might get away with feeding Peter peanut butter and jelly sandwiches, but Oliver was used to those good meals the women of the Meeting prepared so lovingly. And if Rennie let the house go —— Oliver was too sweet to complain, but it would hurt him.

After all, she said to herself, putting the dishes away, he's a pernickety old man.

Dust collected in the cracks between these beautiful, wide floorboards, which Oliver had spent a good part of his life cleaning and waxing. Polishing the antique brass handle on the front door — everything he did to preserve the fabric of the house that had been handed down to him was a source of pleasure.

Nowadays, Rennie argued with herself, people don't bother. Why should I? And yet, if Firbank isn't kept up ——

Her feet, which had almost flown from the sink to the cupboard and back to the sink, where Dad was still washing up and Mom was presenting Rennie with a new stack of plates, dragged now, already aching with fatigue as she warned them of the endless trips they'd have to make in the years ahead.

Dad had just finished scrubbing the sink and Mom was hanging up the towels when Oliver brought Rennie's parents indoors. They all went to the living room, except Rennie, who was disposing of the last lot of dishes, and Peter, who came out to get her.

"It's just dawned on me," she whispered, throwing her arms around his neck. *"Keep your heart with all diligence* — I think I know now what it means. I hope —— Oh, Peter, I hope I will."

He held her tightly a second. Then, taking her hand, he led her in to join the others.

Mom and Dad had evidently been saving up questions for Oliver.

Without a minister, what made a Quaker wedding legal?

The state, he said. It recognized marriages performed after the manner of Friends.

How could silence mean anything?

"It isn't empty," Oliver assured them. "We're waiting to experience the presence of God together, hoping to understand His purpose for us as individuals and as a people. That's why silence generally leads to action."

This was language with which Peter's parents were familiar. They nodded. Rennie's said nothing, but they were listening to every word.

"In the truly gathered silence, there's no need for anyone to speak," Oliver continued. "Hearts communicate without speech. Then, again, under the leading of the Spirit, someone may feel moved to express what the group is feeling — its needs and aspirations."

"Do you mean anyone is free to speak, *anyone at all?*" Dad asked.

"It's no small thing to break the silence. A speaker must first ask himself if he feels truly led. If he does, he has an obligation to share his insight."

"Anyone?" Mom repeated incredulously.

"Even women," Peter put in, glancing wickedly at Rennie.

He was his old, fun-loving self!

"Even children," she added. "Oliver says that would be in right ordering, but I just hope Jocelyn and Edmund won't feel led tomorrow!"

"It's going to be a big day," Mom observed. "We'd better get to bed."

In the entrance hall, they said good night. On the second step, her father stopped and turned, looking down from Rennie to Peter. His Adam's apple quivered.

"I think," he murmured, "it's going to be a very nice wedding." Tears sprang to his eyes. "Pete — I mean, Peter, take care of our little girl." Before Peter could answer, he rushed upstairs.

"I'll do my best," Peter called after him, putting his arm around Rennie. "I promise."

As he drew Rennie to him, she wheeled around, pressing her forehead against his cheek.

Oliver was in the living room, standing beside Daphne's chair. He stooped stiffly to pat the dogs when Rennie and Peter came in.

They wanted to thank him and say how much they looked forward to living at Firbank.

"I'm the one who's thankful," he assured them. "Wait here a moment." He went to the woodshed and returned with a picture. "Our wedding present."

It was the little water color of the maple leaves outside the window, which Daphne made the first morning Rennie was at Firbank, when she wanted to express how Rennie looked to her — full of promise. Oliver had framed it.

"There is more day to dawn," he quoted happily. "The sun is but a morning star."

Now, Rennie and Peter couldn't find words with which to thank Oliver.

"I left these walls bare," he said, seeing their emotion, "because since you'll be living here, I wanted to consult you. What I thought was — it would be nice to put the exhibition pictures up here again when they come back from New York. Then we'll be seeing them the way they last looked to Daphne. Would you be in accord with that?"

Imagine his asking them how to arrange things at Firbank!

But my portrait, Rennie thought. I don't want that in the dining room, where everyone who comes in —— How can I say this to him?

306

Peter read her thought. "There's just one thing. Rennie'd be happier if you put her portrait back in your study. It's been embarrassing for her ———"

"Afraid not," Oliver said, shaking his head. "It's not going to hang in my study again."

A second ago, he'd been so anxious to please them. Now ——— This was so unlike him.

A smile began playing around his mouth, mischievous at first, then radiant. "Miss Chase telephoned this morning. I thought I'd wait to tell you till we had this quiet time together. It's about thy portrait, Serenity. The museum wishes to acquire it."

13.

During her wedding, Rennie got to thinking about the hamster — how it cocked its ears and scampered over the bedclothes. That seemed as incongruous as what she'd told Peter when they were going into the meetinghouse: "I wish Lion and Duffy were here."

Peter had nodded. "Yes, the dogs should have been at our wedding."

Walking in from the vestibule with her hand in Peter's, entering the gathered silence their friends and relations had prepared, Rennie felt it was just like coming here on First Day, expectant and quiet. This was no different, except that their parents and the overseers were in the gallery, waiting for them. Rennie's mother and father sat next to her side of the narrow marriage bench. Peter's parents were on his side. Oliver, Mary Lancashire and the Youngs sat behind them on the upper benches.

Looking down at the bouquet she was clutching, Rennie thought that if she and Peter had been married last fall, Daphne would have been sitting up there. But Daphne wouldn't have been happy. She wanted them to wait.

Early this morning, the last day of May, Peter went out into the Firbank woods and picked every one of those wildflowers Daphne had envisaged, all but the robin's plantain, which he couldn't find. So he brought Rennie a fistful of tiny bluets instead. Their bright yellow eyes winked at her from the centers of the pale petals. "Quaker-ladies," Oliver'd called them.

Rennie was approaching her parents. They looked spellbound. Whether it was the dress — with the afternoon sun shining through the tall windows, it actually did have that mysterious shimmer Daphne envisioned — or whether they were asking God's blessing, they seemed entranced.

Mom and Dad looked as if they'd been centering down all their lives, though when they'd asked Oliver about the silence they'd been baffled. Now they were experiencing it.

As Rennie glanced up at Oliver, he gave her that affectionate nod she loved.

Turning and sitting down with Peter, Rennie faced all the rest of the company. Awed, she thought, I've become the girl on the third-floor landing — the one I used to talk to when I was small!

Her brothers, their wives and wiggling kids, the Hills and the Ludlows, Billy Green — was everyone here? It was when Rennie picked out John Ludlow that she thought of the hamster — how Simeon had loved it, how John had loved Simeon.

Row after row, clear back to the door, the benches were occupied. Not only had Kendal people come, but those friends of Rennie's parents traveled all the way from Neville — a whole slew of them.

Not now, Rennie admonished herself. Later, out on the lawn, I'll see everyone.

Now she must turn inward, focus on the solemnity of the moment. All that came to her, though, was the rush of joy she had felt, standing at the kitchen door very early this morning, watching Peter go off into the woods to pick the wildflowers.

After Peter disappeared in the dark woods, Rennie stood there a little longer, feeling the smooth floorboards under her bare feet, smelling the spring freshness. The tulips were still tightly shut, asleep. So, apparently, was everyone in the house. Only she and

Peter were awake, seeing the rosy dawn. With a rush of joy, she recalled those words Daphne loved so much that Oliver often read them after breakfast on First Day. *All things were new and all the creation gave another smell unto me than before, beyond what words can utter.*

Yes, Rennie thought now, cushioned on the silence the way she'd been cushioned on a cloud in the plane, *beyond what words* ——

She felt Peter looking at her. When she turned to him, she saw that he was giving the signal. It was time. She rested the bouquet on the bench. They stood up and he reached for her right hand.

Looking at her with his whole self in his eyes, Peter said distinctly, "In the presence of God and these friends, I take thee, Serenity Ross, to be my wife, promising, with divine assistance ——" For a fraction of a second, he paused, searching her eyes, as if to make sure she believed it. Then he went on, "to be unto thee a loving and faithful husband as long as we both shall live."

Longing to communicate to him that her heart stood in perfect sincerity, Rennie looked at Peter and said softly, "In the presence of God and these friends, I take thee, Peter Holland, to be my husband, promising, with divine assistance, to be unto thee a loving and faithful wife as long as we both shall live."

Peter slid the ring on Rennie's finger. Then he bent and kissed her.

They sat down again.

Bowing her head, Rennie stared at her hand. While she was trying to take in the full significance of the wedding ring, there was a rustle near the door and she glanced up. Nancy and Sandy were carrying in the little table.

They placed it in front of Peter. The long certificate was rolled out on the table with a weight laid over each edge to keep it from curling up. The weights were skinny, maroon cushions, stuffed with sand, used only at weddings. They'd been in the Otis family for generations.

As Peter took up the pen that lay beside the right weight and signed his name, Rennie noticed how beautifully the certificate was engrossed in large italic letters. *Whereas Peter Hallburt Holland . . .* He put the pen down. Nancy and Sandy moved the table a few inches nearer to Rennie. They glowed with admiration as she wrote carefully under Peter's name, *Serenity Ross Holland.* How strange it looked!

Nancy pushed the weights aside and picked up the certificate, holding it at arm's length, top and bottom. Mounting the steps to the gallery with great dignity, she handed the long scroll to Oliver. When she came down again, she and Sandy carried the table back to the vestibule.

Watching them lug it up the aisle — those nice kids in their pretty summer dresses — Rennie thought, If they ever ask me whether sex is okay before marriage, what will I say? What *will* I?

There was no time to consider this because Oliver was standing and holding the certificate up before him. *"Whereas,"* he read, *"Peter Hallburt Holland, of Charlesbury, State of Ohio, son of Hallburt Holland and Ann, his wife, and Serenity Millburn Ross, of Neville, State of New York, daughter of Edmund Ross and Joan, his wife, having declared their intentions of marriage with each other to Kendal Meeting of the Religious Society of Friends, held at Kendal, Rhode Island, according to the good order used among them, their proposed marriage was allowed by that Meeting.*

"Now these are to certify that for the accomplishment of their marriage ——"

Rennie knew the words. But Oliver's voice invested them with more than their inherent meaning. It bespoke his simplicity of heart. All those First Days that Rennie had heard this young-sounding voice read from the Bible in the sunny kitchen! Oliver would pause at a cadence and glance toward the dooryard, enjoying the sonority of a passage. Now he paused between phrases in the same way. When he came to the promises, Rennie told herself they would resound in her soul forever.

"And Peter Hallburt Holland, taking Serenity Millburn Ross by the hand, did on this solemn occasion declare that he took her to be his wife, promising, with divine assistance ——"

Tears sprang to Rennie's eyes, tears of joy.

"And in further confirmation thereof, they, the said Peter Hall-burt Holland and Serenity Millburn Ross (she, according to the custom of marriage, adopting the surname of her husband) did then and there to these presents set their hands."

We're married!

"And we," Oliver concluded, "having been present at the solemnization of the said marriage, have, as witnesses thereto, set our hands." Rolling up the certificate, Oliver asked everyone present, including the children, to sign it at the rise of the meeting. Every guest, he explained, was a witness.

There'll be over a hundred names on it! Rennie thought, already seeing the certificate hanging on the wall at Firbank beside her great-grandparents'.

Friends were bowing their heads, settling into silence.

We're married! Rennie exulted again. We don't have to stay apart any more! Sinking into the quiet, she thought, Still, the last nine months were the best. We felt free. Instead of egging each other on, we were helping each other. We were staying apart *together*. But it was hard — too hard, sometimes. And we slipped, though mostly in fantasy. That was bad, too. Just the same, for us it was the right thing. And if we have to be separated sometime or face something hard, we've had experience. Have we ever!

She wondered again what she would say, if the girls asked her ——

Is it okay? I don't know. It wasn't for us. Too many people got hurt. And it made us want to be alone when we needed the friendship of mature people. We were old enough to have sex, but too young to understand what it's all about.

That's what she would tell the girls.

As long as I believed that, any time we wanted to, we could just say good-by, nice knowing you, I wasn't really loving. If breaking up could be that easy, what was there to break? Actually, I'd have hurt terribly. Even after we broke up, part of me would have gone on being loving and faithful to Peter as long as I lived. How can what one's shared ever be unshared?

Across her thought Rennie became aware of someone talking.

311

Looking up, she saw it was Ben Ashaway, standing in the far corner of the room. He must have been talking for some time, because he said he was concluding with the words of George Fox: *"And the Lord answered that it was needful I should have a sense of all conditions. How else should I speak to all conditions? And in this I saw the infinite love of God. I saw also that there was an ocean of darkness and death, but an infinite ocean of light and love, which flowed over the ocean of darkness. And in that also I saw the infinite love of God."*

Oliver! Rennie thought. Over the ocean of darkness and death, light and love are flowing for him!

In his late seventies, he was being asked, not by one institution but by *two,* to realize the dream of his youth and write.

Turning toward Peter, Rennie saw to her surprise that his mother was standing up. Could *she* be about to speak?

Mom looked out over the room in a shy but friendly way. Then, in her musical voice, she said, "Last night, my husband and I were told that anyone who feels led to speak here is welcome to do so. There's something we want very much to say and we decided I should be the spokes*woman.*" Her expression became downright mischievous. She reminded Rennie of Peter that day at the airport, when he stuffed the whole Chocomarsh into her mouth. "This is an opportunity I'll never have in my church," Mom put in.

Rennie peeked at Peter. How was he taking this? Just trying hard not to laugh!

"As a matter of fact," Mom went on, turning serious, "we have only to recall the women in the Bible — Ruth, Esther, the ones who knew Jesus — to realize that women have played an active part in transmitting God's infinite love through the ages. The daughters of Jerusalem wept for Jesus. Women followed Him from Galilee. They had the courage to stand by the cross. From there, they led the early church into the world. Why shouldn't they speak?

"My husband and I are teachers. We're deeply concerned about young people — not just our own, but those entrusted to us at school. That has made us appreciate the care Kendal Friends gave our son and our new daughter, helping them to grow into an understanding of the commitment they've just made. May God bless these children and all the folks who gave them a spiritual home."

Mom said this beautifully, Rennie thought. But it gave her a shock. Never, absolutely never had she thought of herself as a woman in the way Mom spoke of. She'd thought plenty about being a female. But to be a woman who transmitted the infinite love of God — that this was her function had never occurred to her. And yet, wasn't that precisely what made Serenity great? Wasn't that what Daphne did?

And now *me*. I'm going to be the woman of the house at Firbank! Can I really make it a place of friendliness, refreshment and peace, where God becomes more real to those who dwell there and those who visit? It's my central wish.

Looking at the opposite benches, where her brothers sat with their wives and the kids, who were beginning to get out of hand, Rennie said to herself, I want them all to come, not just Larry. All of them. Summer vacations, Thanksgiving, Christmas, all through the year. A lot of work, but that's what it takes — diligence in love.

Lawrence Ballantine, sprawled on Victoria's lap, was waking up. Would he howl, the way he did last night? But this wasn't like waking under a strange table with dishes being banged overhead. He was still snuggling against his mother, safe and contented. And like anyone who was led of the Spirit, he felt an obligation to share his joy with those who were in the silence with him.

Listening to him, Rennie thought happily, Now we're part of the ongoing creation, Peter and I. Tonight we'll be starting a home, a place inside our encircling arms for our children to come to someday.

Lawrence Ballantine's babbling was so beautiful, Rennie glanced sideways to catch her parents' eyes. They were undoubtedly moved by it, too. But, no. They weren't noticing. They must be centering down. Rennie felt like shouting her gratitude to them for sticking with her while she fumbled. She was a little sorry for them, too. Now they'd never own her portrait. Still, this morning, when she told them where it was going to hang, they seemed very proud.

From the first, they'd seen in it what Daphne intended to communicate: Rennie's promise — what Oliver called the dawn of that day her whole generation would wake to — though they couldn't have put this into words.

It's all because of Peter, because he loved me. Hadn't been for that, I never would have come to Firbank.

Rennie longed to reach for his hand.

Oliver was touching his shoulder, indicating that the meeting was about to end. The two of them should walk out while their friends were still supporting them in silence.

Getting up, Rennie turned toward her parents. They were looking at her now. She'd see them again in a few minutes, outside, at that nice reception on the lawn in back. But, right now, she wanted them to know how deeply she loved them, too. Her eyes sent them the message.

I hope, she thought fervently, turning back to Peter, that from our encircling arms serenity will spill over onto everyone.

Hand in hand, Rennie and Peter walked toward the door, past the bench where she'd sat with Oliver and Daphne the first time she ever came here. In the row behind, a man had said ——

That's what I'll tell Nancy and Sandy! *There is that near you which will guide you. O wait for it and be sure ye keep to it.* You don't have to ask me. There is that near you. But wait for it — really wait — and be *sure* ——

Peter was drawing Rennie forward so fast, they were almost running. Skimming over the gray carpet, they dashed through the vestibule, out into the sunshine. There wasn't a soul around.

Peter took Rennie in his arms.

"Wasn't it beautiful?" she gasped, as he squeezed the breath out of her. "I thought I was going to be scared, but it felt just like any First Day. It is *our* first day."

Agreeing joyously, Peter let her go. "What were you thinking about during the silence?"

"Oh, Peter, to tell thee that is going to take as long as we both shall live!"

314